LAWLESS

DIANA PALMER

LAWLESS

MIRA®

MIRA®

ISBN 1-55166-708-8

LAWLESS

Copyright © 2003 by Diana Palmer.

All rights reserved. Except for use in any review, the reproduction or
utilization of this work in whole or in part in any form by any electronic,
mechanical or other means, now known or hereafter invented, including
xerography, photocopying and recording, or in any information storage or
retrieval system, is forbidden without the written permission of the publisher,
MIRA Books, 225 Duncan Mill Road, Don Mills, Ontario, Canada M3B 3K9.

All characters in this book have no existence outside the imagination of the
author and have no relation whatsoever to anyone bearing the same name
or names. They are not even distantly inspired by any individual known or
unknown to the author, and all incidents are pure invention.

MIRA and the Star Colophon are trademarks used under license and registered
in Australia, New Zealand, Philippines, United States Patent and Trademark
Office and in other countries.

Visit us at www.mirabooks.com

Printed in U.S.A.

First Printing: July 2003
10 9 8 7 6 5 4 3 2 1

To the men and women of the Texas Rangers

CHAPTER ONE

CHAPTER ONE

It was a blistering hot day in south Texas, even for early September. Christabel Gaines was wearing a low-cut white top with faded blue jeans, a book bag slung casually over one shoulder. The top outlined her small, firm breasts and the jeans clung lovingly to every softly rounded line of her young body. The faint breeze caught her long blond hair in her pretty bow-shaped mouth, against her wide forehead and high cheekbones. She moved the strands away, her big, warm brown eyes amused at something one of the students with her was saying about a classmate. It was a long, dull Monday morning.

Debbie, a girl in her computer class, was suddenly staring past Christabel toward the parking lot. She whistled softly. "Well! I know what I want for Christmas," she said in a loud whisper.

Teresa, another classmate, was also staring. "Hubba, hubba," she said with a wicked grin, wiggling her eyebrows. "Anybody know who he is?"

Curious, Christabel turned around to see a tall, darkly handsome man walk gracefully across the lawn toward them. He was wearing a cream-colored Stetson, jerked down over his eyes. His neat long-sleeved white cotton shirt was fastened with a turquoise bola tie. His long, powerful legs were encased in gray slacks, his feet in gray hand-tooled boots. On his shirt pocket, a silver star in a circle glittered in the sunlight. Across his lean hips, a brown leather holster and gunbelt were fastened. In the gunbelt was a .45 caliber Ruger Vaquero pistol. He usually carried an automatic pistol, a .45 Colt ACP, but it was having a new custom handle and the Texas Ranger star added. Today also happened to be match day at the Jacobsville Gun Club's Single Action Shooting Society, which he belonged to. The quick-draw-and-shoot group wore Western garb to meets. So it was convenient for him to wear the wheel gun to work just this once.

"What have you girls done?" one of the boys asked with mock surprise. "The Texas Rangers are after somebody!"

Christabel didn't say a word. She just stared with the others, but her dark eyes twinkled as she watched him stride toward her with that single-minded determination that made him so good at his job. He was the sexiest, most wonderful man in the world. She owed him everything she had, everything she was. Sometimes she wished with all her heart that she'd been born beautiful, and maybe then he'd notice her the way she wanted him to. She smiled secretly, wondering what the other girls would say if they knew her true relationship with that dynamo Texas Ranger.

Judd Dunn was thirty-four. He'd spent most of his life in law enforcement, and he was good at it. He'd been with Company D of the Texas Rangers for five years. He'd been up for promotion to lieutenant, but he'd turned it down because that was more of an administrative job and he liked field work better. He kept that long, lean body fit by working on the ranch, ownership of which he shared with Christabel.

He'd been made responsible for Christabel when she was only sixteen. The D bar G Ranch had been run-down, flat-busted, and ready to crash and burn. Judd had pulled it out of the red and made it show a profit. Over the years, he'd put his own money into enlarging the crossbreed beef cattle herd they oversaw. With his canny business sense, and Christabel's knowledge of computers, they'd been just beginning to show a small profit. It had allowed Christabel to work on her diploma in computer programming, and Judd even had an occasional spending spree. His last, a year ago, involved that cream-colored Stetson slanted over his dark brow. It was made of compressed beaver fur and it had cost him a paycheck. It did suit him, she had to admit. He looked rakishly handsome. Sadly, there hadn't been any spending sprees this year. There had been a drought and cattle prices had dropped. Times were hard again, just when they'd been looking up.

Any other man would have noticed with amusement the rapt stares of Christabel's two pretty companions. Judd paid them the same attention he'd have given pine straw. He had something on his mind, and nothing would divert him until he'd resolved it.

He walked right up to Christabel, towering over her, to the astonishment of her classmates.

"We've had an offer," he said, taking her by the upper arm as impersonally as he'd have an apprehended felon. "I need to talk to you."

"Judd, I'm only between classes," she protested.

"This won't take a minute," he muttered, narrowing his black eyes as he searched for a secluded spot. He found one under a big live oak tree. "Come on."

She was escorted forcibly to the tree while her companions watched with wide-eyed curiosity. Later, she knew, she was going to be the focus of some probing questions.

"Not that I'm not glad to see you," she pointed out when he released her abruptly, away from prying ears, "but I only have five minutes...!"

"Then don't waste them talking," he cut her off abruptly. His voice was deep, dark velvet, even when he didn't mean it to be. It sent delicious shivers down Christabel's spine.

"Okay," she conceded with a sigh. She held out her hand, palm-up.

He noted the signet ring—his signet ring—that she always

wore on her ring finger. Although she'd had it resized, it was still too big for her slender hand. But she insisted on wearing it.

She followed his gaze and flexed her hand. "Nobody knows," she said. "I don't gossip."

"That would be the day," he agreed, and for just an instant, affectionate humor made those deep-set black eyes twinkle.

"So, what's the problem?"

"It's not a problem, exactly," he said, resting his right hand lazily on the butt of the pistol. The Texas Ranger emblem was carved into the maple wood handle. The new grip for his automatic would have the same wood and custom emblem. The holster and gunbelt that held it were hand-tooled tan leather. "We've had an offer from a film crew. They've been surveying the land around here, with a representative from the state film commission, looking for a likely spot to site a fictitious ranch. They like ours."

"A film crew." She bit her full lower lip. "Judd, I don't like a lot of people around," she began.

"I know that. But we want to buy another purebred herd sire, don't we," he continued, "and if we get the right kind, he's going to be expensive. They've offered us thirty-five thousand dollars for the use of the ranch for a few weeks' filming. That would put us over the top. We could even enlarge our electric fencing and replace the tractor."

She whistled. That amount of money seemed like a fortune. It was always something on a ranch, equipment breakdown or cowboys who wanted more money, or the electric pump went and there was no water. In between, the vet had to be called out to look at sick cattle, there were ear tags and butane for branding, and fencing materials... She wondered what it would be like to be rich and have anything she wanted. The ranch that had belonged jointly to his uncle and her father was still a long way from being prosperous.

"Stop daydreaming," he said curtly. "I need an answer. I've got a case waiting."

Her eyes widened. "A case? Which case?"

His eyes narrowed. "Not now."

"It's the homicide, isn't it?" she asked excitedly. "The young woman in Victoria who was found with her throat cut, lying in a ditch with only a blouse on. You've got a lead!"

"I'm not telling you anything."

She moved closer. "Listen, I bought fresh apples this morning. I've got stick cinnamon. Brown sugar." She leaned closer. "Real butter. Pastry flour."

"Stop it," he groaned.

"Can't you just see those apples, bubbling away in that crust, until it gets to be a nice, soft, beautiful, flaky..."

"All right!" he ground out, glancing around quickly to make sure nobody was close enough to hear. "She was the wife of a local rancher," he told her. "Her husband's story checks out and she didn't have an enemy in the world. We think it was random."

"No suspects at all?"

"Not yet. Not much trace evidence, either, except for one hair and a few fibers of highly colored cloth that didn't match the blouse she was wearing," he said. He glared at her. "And that's all you're getting, apple pie or no apple pie!"

"Okay," she said, giving in with good grace. She searched his lean, handsome face. "You want us to let the movie company move in," she added with keen perception.

He nodded. "We're going to be short about a thousand dollars after we pay estimated taxes next week," he told her quietly. "We're going to have to buy more feed. The flooding wiped out most of our hay and corn crops, not to mention the alfalfa. I got the silo fixed, but not in time to help us out any this season. We're also going to need more vitamin and mineral supplements to mix with the feed."

"And we'll have to buy supplemental feed or sell off stock we need," she said, drawing in a long, wistful breath. "Wouldn't it be lovely if we had millions, you know, like that television show they used to have that was set up around Dallas? We could buy combines and new tractors and hay balers..."

He pursed his lips and smiled at her enthusiasm. His dark eyes slid over her pretty figure, lingering involuntarily on her breasts. They looked like little apples under that clinging fabric and he got an unexpected and rather shocking ache from looking at them. He dragged his eyes back up to meet hers. "Wouldn't you like some new jeans instead?" he asked, nodding toward the holes in hers.

She shrugged. "Nobody around here wears nice stuff. Well, Debbie does," she amended, glancing back toward her classmate, who was dressed in a designer skirt set. "But her folks have millions."

"What's she doing in a vocational school?" he wanted to know.

She lifted her face. "Trying to land Henry Tesler's son!"

He grinned. "He's a student, I gather."

She shook her head. "He teaches algebra."

"One of those," he agreed with twinkling eyes.

"He's real brainy." She nodded. "Real rich, too. Henry's dad owns racehorses, but Henry doesn't like animals, so he teaches." She checked the wide, unfeminine watch on her wrist. "Oh, my gosh, I'll miss my class! I have to go!"

"I'll tell the film company they can come on down," he said.

She turned to sprint back after her classmates, who were wandering toward the side entrance of the main building. She stopped and looked over her shoulder apprehensively. "When are they coming?"

"Two weeks from Saturday, to take some still photos and discuss the modifications they'll need to make to set up their cameras."

She groaned. "Well, tell them they can't rev up their engines near the barn! Bessie's in foal!"

"I'll tell them everything."

She studied him with admiration. "You do look really sexy, you know," she said. "My classmate Debbie wants you for Christmas," she added mischievously.

He glowered at her.

Her eyes sparkled. "It's only three months away. Tell you what, if you buy me a see-through red nightie with lace, I'll wear it for you," she teased.

He refused to let himself picture her that way. "I'm 14 years older than you," he pointed out.

She wiggled her ring finger at him.

He took four long steps and towered over her. "If you dare tell anybody...!" he threatened darkly.

"I don't gossip," she reminded him. "But there's no legal or moral reason in the world why you can't look at me in flimsy lingerie," she pointed out, "whether or not people know we're married."

"I told you five years ago, and I'm telling you now," he said firmly, "nothing of that sort is ever going to happen between you and me. In two months you'll be twenty-one. You'll sign a paper, and so will I, and we'll be business partners—nothing more."

She searched his black eyes with the familiar excitement almost choking her. "Tell me you've never wondered what I look like without my clothes," she whispered. "I dare you!"

He gave her a look that would have fried bread. It was a look that was famous in south Texas. He could back down lawbreakers with it. In fact, he'd backed her own father down with it, just before he went for him with both big fists.

She glowered up at him with a wistful sigh. "What a waste," she murmured thoughtfully. "You know more about women than I'll ever know about men. I'll bet you're just sensational in bed."

His lips became a thin line. The look was taking on heat-seeking attributes.

"All right," she conceded finally. "I'll find some nice young boy to teach me what to do with all these inconvenient aches I get from time to time, and I'll tell you every sordid detail, I swear I will."

"One," he said.

She lifted both eyebrows. "Excuse me?"

"Two."

Her hand tightened on the book bag. "Listen here, I can't be intimidated by a man who's known me since I wore frilly dresses and patent leather shoes..."

"Three!"

"...and furthermore, I don't care if you are a..."

"Four!"

She turned on her heel without finishing the sentence and made a beeline for the side entrance. The next number would result in something undignified. She remembered too many past countdowns, to her own detriment. He really was single-minded!

"I'm only humoring you to make you feel in control!" she called back to him. "Don't think I'm running!"

He hid a smile until he was back at the black SUV he drove.

The same week, Jack Clark, a man who worked for them, was caught red-handed with an expensive pair of boots he'd charged to their account. Christabel had found it on the bill and called Judd down to show it to him. They'd fired the man outright. She didn't tell Judd that the man had made blatant advances toward her, or that she'd had to threaten him with Judd to make him stop.

A few days after he was fired, their brand-new young Salers bull was found dead in a pasture. To Christabel, it seemed uncannily like foul play. The bull had been healthy, and she refused to believe Judd's assertion that it was bloat-causing weeds that had killed him and left four other bulls in the same pasture alive. After all, Jack Clark had vowed revenge. But Judd brushed off her suspicions, and even told Maude he thought she was trying to get attention, because he'd ignored her while he was dickering with the film people. That had made her furious. She'd told their foreman Nick Bates what she thought, though, and told him to keep an eye on the cattle. Sometimes Judd treated her like a child. It hadn't bothered her so much before, but lately it was disturbing.

* * *

Judd turned up early Saturday morning two weeks later in his big black sport utility vehicle, accompanied by a second burgundy SUV which was full of odd people. There was a representative from the Texas film commission and a director whom Christabel recognized immediately. She hadn't realized it was going to be a famous one. There was also an assistant director, and four other men who were introduced as part of the crew, including a photographer and a sound man.

She learned that the star of the film was an A-list actor, a handsome young man who'd sadly never been on a horse.

"That's going to limit our scenes with your livestock," the director told Judd with a chuckle. "Of course, Tippy Moore has never been around livestock, either. You might have seen her on magazine covers. They call her the Georgia Firefly. This will be her first motion picture, but she was a hit at the audition. A real natural."

Judd pursed his lips and his black eyes lit up. "I've seen her on the cover of the sports magazine's swimsuit issue," he confessed. "Every red-blooded man in America knows who she is."

Christabel felt uncomfortable. She glanced at Judd, all too aware of his interest, and could have wailed. They were married, but he took no notice of her at all. He was fond of her, he indulged her, but that was as far as it went. He hadn't even kissed her when they were married. It was sobering to realize that in two months, it would all be over. She'd tried everything to make him notice her, even teasing him about a boy at school who wanted to marry her. That had been a lie, and he'd caught her in it. Now he didn't believe anything she said. She studied his tall, sexy physique and wondered what he'd say if she walked into the study one night while he was going over the books and took off all her clothes.

Then she remembered the terrible scars on her smooth back, the ones her drunken father had put there with a short quirt when she was sixteen. She'd tried to save her poor horse, but her father had turned on her. She could still remember the pain. Her back had been in shreds. Judd had come to see her father on business that Saturday morning, when he was working at the Texas Ranger post in San Antonio. So much of the memory was hazy, but she recalled clearly how Judd had come over the corral fence after her father, with such silent menace that her father had actually dropped the quirt and started backing away. It hadn't saved him. Judd had gone for him with those big fists, and seconds later, the drunken man was lying in the dirt, half insensible. He'd been locked in the tack shed seconds later.

Judd had picked her up in his arms, so tenderly, murmuring endearments, yelling hoarsely for Maude, their housekeeper, to call the police and the ambulance service. He'd put her in the ambulance himself and ridden into the hospital with her, while her invalid mother wept bitterly on the porch as her husband was taken away. Judd had pressed charges, and her father had gone to jail.

Never again, Judd had said coldly, was that man going to raise his hand to Christabel.

But the damage had been done. It took weeks for the wounds to heal completely. There was no money for plastic surgery. There still wasn't. So Christabel had white scars across her back in parallel lines, from her shoulders to her waist. She was so self-conscious about them that despite her teasing, she'd never have had the nerve to take off her clothes in front of Judd, or any other man. He only wanted to get rid of her, anyway. He didn't want to get married. He loved his job, and his freedom. He said so constantly.

But he knew who Tippy Moore was. Most men did. She had the face of an angel, and a body that begged for caresses. Unlike poor Christabel, whose face was passable, but not really pretty, and whose body was like the poor beast's in the story of Dr. Frankenstein's monster.

Judd and the director, Joel Harper, were talking about using one of the saddle-broken horses for a scene, and the advisability of having their foreman, Nick Bates, around during shooting.

"We're going to need set security, too," Harper said thought-fully. "I like to use local police, when I can, but you're out of the city limits here, aren't you?"

"You could get one of our Jacobsville policemen to work here when he's off duty," Judd suggested. "Our chief of police, Chet Blake, is out of town. But Cash Grier is assistant chief, and he'd be glad to help you out. We worked together for a few months out of the San Antonio Ranger office."

"Friend of yours?" Harper asked.

Judd made a rough sound in his throat. "Grier doesn't have friends, he has sparring partners."

Christabel had heard a lot about Cash Grier, but she'd never met him. She'd seen him around. He was an enigma, wearing a conservative police uniform with his long thick black hair in a ponytail. He had a mustache and a little goatee just under his lower lip these days, and he looked...menacing. Crime had dropped sharply in Jacobsville since his arrival. There were some nasty rumors about his past, including one that he'd been a covert assassin in his younger days.

"He knocked Terry Barnett through a window," Christabel re-called aloud.

Harper's eyes opened wide.

Christabel realized that they were staring at her and she flushed. "Terry was breaking dishes in the local waffle place be-cause his wife, who worked there, was seeing another man. He caught them together and started terrorizing the place. They say he ran at Grier with a waffle iron, and Grier just shifted his weight and Terry went through the glass." She whistled. "Took thirty stitches, they said, and he got probation for assault on a police officer. That's a felony," she added helpfully.

Judd was glaring at her.

She shrugged. "When you spend time around them, it rubs off," she explained to Harper with a sheepish grin. "I've known Judd a long time. He and my father were...business partners."

"My uncle and her father were business partners," Judd corrected easily. "I inherited my uncle's half of the ranch, she inherited her father's."

"I see," Harper said, nodding, but his thoughts were on the film he was going to make, and he was already setting up scenes in his mind for a storyboard. He was considering logistics. "We'll need someone to cater food while we're working," he murmured. "We'll need to set up meetings with city officials as well, because some of the location work will be done in Jacobsville."

"Some of it?" Christabel asked, curious.

Harper smiled at her. "We're shooting some of the movie in Hollywood," he explained. "But we'd rather locate a ranch setting on a working ranch. The town is part of the atmosphere."

"What's the movie going to be about?" Christabel wanted to know. "Can you tell me?"

He grinned at her interest. He had two daughters about her age. "It's a romantic comedy about a model who comes out West to shoot a commercial on a real ranch and falls in love with a rancher. He hates models," he added helpfully.

She chuckled. "I'll buy a ticket."

"I hope several million other people will, too." He turned back to Judd. "I'll need weather information—it's going to cost us a fortune if we start shooting at the wrong time and have to hole up for three or four weeks while the weather clears."

Judd nodded. "I think I can find what you need."

"And we'll want to rent rooms at the best hotel you have, for the duration."

"No problem there, either," Judd said dryly. "It isn't exactly a tourist trap."

Harper was fanning himself with a sheaf of papers and sweating. "Not in this heat," he agreed.

"Heat?" Christabel asked innocently. "You think it's *warm* here? My goodness!"

"Cut it out," Judd muttered darkly, because the director was beginning to turn pale.

She wrinkled her nose at him. "I was only kidding. Law enforcement types have no sense of humor, Mr. Harper," she told him. "Their faces are painted on and they can't smile..."

"One," Judd said through his teeth.

"See?" she asked pertly.

"Two...!"

She threw up her hands and walked into the house.

Christabel was just taking an apple pie out of the oven when she heard doors slam and an engine rev up. Judd walked into the kitchen past Maude, who grinned at him as she went toward the back of the house to put the clothes in the dryer.

"I made you an apple pie," Christabel told Judd, waving it under his nose. "Penance."

He sighed as he poured himself a cup of black coffee, pulled out a chair and sat down at the small kitchen table. "When are you going to grow up, tomboy?" he asked.

She looked down at her dusty boots and stained jeans. She could imagine that her braided hair was standing out in wisps around her flushed face, and she knew without looking down that her short-sleeved yellow cotton blouse was wrinkled beyond repair. In contrast, Judd's jeans were well-fitting and clean. His boots were so polished they reflected the tablecloth. His white shirt with the silver sergeant's Texas Ranger star on the pocket was creaseless, his dark blue patterned tie in perfect order. His leather gunbelt creaked when he crossed his long, powerful legs, and the .45 Colt ACP pistol shifted ominously in its holster.

She recalled that his great-grandfather had been a gunfighter—not to mention a Texas Ranger—before he went to Harvard and became a famous trial lawyer in San Antonio. Judd held the record for the fastest quick-draw in northern Texas, as his friend and fellow Ranger Marc Brannon of Jacobsville held it for southern Texas in the Single Action Shooting Society. They often practiced at the local gun club as guests of their mutual friend Ted Regan. A membership at the club was hundreds of dollars that law enforcement people couldn't usually afford. But former mercenary Eb Scott had his antiterrorism training school in Jacobsville, and he had one of the finest gun ranges around. He made it available at no cost to any law enforcement people who wanted to use it. Between Ted and Eb, they got lots of practice.

"Do you still do that quick-draw?" she asked Judd as she sliced the pie.

"Yes, and don't mention it to Harper," he added flatly.

She glanced at him over her shoulder. "Don't you want to be in pictures?" she drawled.

"About as much as you do, cupcake," he mused, absently appreciating the fit of those tight jeans and the curve of her breasts in the blouse.

She shrugged. "That would be funny. Me, in pictures." She studied the pie, her hands stilled. "Maybe I could star in a horror movie if they put me in a bathing suit and filmed me from behind."

There was a shocked silence behind her.

She put a slice of pie on a saucer and added a fork, sliding it in front of Judd.

He caught her hand and pulled her down onto his lap. "Listen to me," he said in that deep, tender tone he used when little things were hurt, "everybody's got scars. Maybe they don't show, but they're there. A man who loves you won't care about a few little white lines."

She cocked her head, trying not to let him see how it affected her to be so close to him. She liked the spicy aftershave he wore, the clean smell of his clothes, the faint whiff of leather that came up from the gunbelt.

"How do you know they're white?" she asked.

He gave her a worldly look and loosened the tie at his collar, unbuttoning the top buttons of the shirt to disclose a darkly tanned chest with a pelt of curling black hair. She'd seen him without his shirt, but it always unsettled her.

He pulled the shirt and the spotless white undershirt under it to one side and indicated a puckered place in his shoulder, from which white lines radiated. "Twenty-two caliber handgun," he said, drawing her hand to it. "Feel."

Her hand was icy cold. It trembled on that warm, muscular flesh. "It's raised," she said, her voice sounding breathless.

"Unsightly?" he persisted.

She smiled. "Not really."

"I don't imagine any of yours are that bad," he added. "Button me up."

It was intimate, exciting, to do that simple little chore. She smiled stupidly. "This is new."

"What is?"

"You never let me sit in your lap before," she reminded him.

He was looking at her with an odd expression. "I don't let anybody sit in my lap."

She pursed her lips as she got to his collarbone. "Afraid I might try to undress you?"

His chest rippled, but when she looked up, his face was impassive. His eyes were glittery with suppressed humor.

"That wouldn't do you much good," he commented.

"Why not?"

One black eyebrow arched. "You wouldn't know what to do with me when you got my clothes off."

There was a clatter of falling potatoes on the floor.

Judd and Christabel stared toward the door where Maude was standing with both hands on the edges of her apron and potatoes still spilling out around her feet.

"What the hell is your problem?" Judd asked darkly.

Maude's eyes were like saucers.

"Oh, I get it," Christabel said, grinning. She had one hand on Judd's shoulder and the other on his tie. "She thinks I'm undressing you. It's okay, Maude," she added, holding up her ring finger. "We're married."

Judd gave her a royal glare and gently dumped her out of his lap and onto the floor. She grinned at him from the linoleum. He leaned back in the chair and finished adjusting his shirt. "I was showing her one of my scars," he told Maude.

Maude had picked up the potatoes and she was trying very hard not to say anything stupid. But that innocent remark produced a swell of helpless laughter.

"Now don't do that," Christabel groaned, getting up. "Maude, it was very innocent, and he really was showing me his scar."

Maude nodded enthusiastically and went back to her potatoes. She cast a quick, amused look at Judd, who had a forkful of apple pie suspended in midair and was glaring at her.

"Sure he was," Maude agreed.

Judd's eyes narrowed. "I'm armed," he pointed out.

Maude put down her knife and potato and spread out her arms. "Me, too," she said, wiggling her eyebrows.

Judd glowered at her, and at Christabel, who was grinning from ear to ear. "Now I know where she gets it from," he told Maude.

"He's just jealous because he can't make jokes," Christabel said wickedly.

Judd gave her a measuring glance and went back to his pie.

CHAPTER TWO
CHAPTER TWO

That night, after Judd had gone back to his apartment in Victoria where he was stationed, Christabel lay awake for hours worrying about Tippy Moore and Judd's odd reaction to the news that she was going to be in the movie. He seemed fascinated by the woman, just from her photographs, and it was obvious enough to be painful. He might hold Christabel on his lap and reassure her about her scars, but it was impersonal. He'd never even touched her in an inappropriate way, despite her efforts.

Her mind went back to that Saturday long ago when her life had changed so drastically. She could smell the scents of blood and leather, feel the whip on her back...

Through waves of pain, she heard a deep, gravelly voice cursing steadily. It was the only sound audible, although five other cowboys were standing around her with grim faces and stiff posture where she lay. The corral was dusty, because it hadn't rained, and there were traces of hay in her disheveled blond hair. She was lying on her stomach and her blouse was in ribbons. Blood seeped from the deep cuts in her back. There had been hard thuds and groans from somewhere nearby, followed by sounds of a door slamming. A minute later, she felt someone kneel beside her.

"Christabel, can you hear me?" Judd's voice asked harshly at her ear.

Her dark eyes opened, just a slit. It was hard to focus, but she remembered that Judd Dunn was the only person who ever called her by her full name. Everybody else called her "Crissy."

"Yes?" Was that her voice? It sounded weak and strained. The sun was so bright that she couldn't get her eyes open.

"I'm going to have to pick you up, honey, and it's going to hurt," he said curtly. "Grit your teeth."

She swallowed hard. Her back felt raw. Her blouse was sticking to the lacerated skin and she could feel the hot, wet blood cooling as it soaked the fabric. It had a funny smell, like metal.

Judd's strong arms slid under her legs and around her rib cage as carefully as he could. He swung her up, trying to avoid gripping the torn flesh. Her small breasts were pressed hard against the warm muscle of his chest and she sobbed, trying to stifle the sound as pain lanced through her viciously.

"What about...Daddy?" she choked.

His black eyes flashed so violently in that lean, tanned face that two of the cowboys climbed the corral fence to avoid him. "He's in the tack room," he said shortly. "He'll stay there until the sheriff's deputies get here."

"No," she cried. "Judd, no! You can't have him...arrested! Mama's sick and she can't run the ranch. I can't, either...!"

"He's already under arrest," he bit off. "I'm a Texas Ranger," he reminded her. "But I had your foreman radio the sheriff's office from my car. They're already on the way."

"Who'll run our part of the ranch?" she repeated, still mostly in shock from what had happened so unexpectedly. Her father had a history of violent behavior when he drank. In fact, Ellie, her mother, was now an invalid because Tom Gaines had knocked her off a ladder in a drunken rage and broken her pelvis.

Emergency surgery hadn't completely healed it, and she had weak lungs to boot.

"I'll run the ranch, your part and my own," he said shortly, and kept walking. "Be still, honey."

Tears ran down her pale cheeks. Her eyes closed and she shivered. He looked down at her with his lips in a thin line. Her long blond hair had come loose from its ponytail and it was matted with her own drying blood. He cursed under his breath, only stopping when the ambulance came careening up in the driveway.

Maude, the heavyset, buxom housekeeper, was wringing her hands on the porch. She ran forward, her hair disheveled. "My poor baby," she sobbed. "Judd, is she going to be all right?"

"She will be. I can't say the same for Tom. If she won't press charges, by God, I will!"

A small thin woman with gray-streaked fair hair came hobbling onto the front porch in a tattered old chenille robe, tears running down her cheeks as she saw her daughter.

"She'll be all right. Go back to bed, Ellie," Judd called, and for her his voice was gentle. "I'll take care of her."

"Where's Tom?" she asked shakily.

His voice changed. "Locked up in the tack room."

Her eyes closed and she leaned against the post. "Thank God...!"

"Maude, get her the hell back to bed before she passes out on the floor!" Judd yelled and kept walking straight toward the EMTs who were just getting out of the ambulance. Behind them, a sheriff's patrol car arrived with lights flashing and a deputy got out of it to approach Judd.

"What happened?" Deputy Sheriff Hayes Carson asked, his eyes on Christabel's back.

"Tom happened," he replied tersely, waiting for the EMTs to get the gurney ready for Christabel. "He was beating her filly with a quirt. She tried to pull him off."

Hayes winced. He'd been a deputy for five years and he'd seen plenty of battery cases. But this... Christabel was barely sixteen, thin and fragile, and most people around Jacobsville, Texas, loved her. She was forever baking cakes for bazaars and taking flowers to elderly shut-ins, and helping to deliver warm meals to invalids after school. She had a heart as big as Texas and to think of Tom Gaines's big arm bringing a quirt down on her back with all his might was enough to make even a veteran law enforcement officer nauseous.

"Where is he?" Hayes asked coldly.

Judd pointed in the direction of the tack room, his eyes never leaving Christabel's tear-drenched face. The tears were all the more poignant for the lack of even a sob. "Key's by the door." He met Hayes's eyes. "You keep that son of a bitch locked up, no matter what it takes. I swear before God, if you let him loose, I'll kill him!" he said in a tone that sent chills down even Hayes's back.

"I'll see that bail's set as high as possible," he assured the other man grimly. "I'll go get him. Is he drunk?"

"He was," Judd said shortly. "Now he's crying. He's sorry, of course. He's always sorry...!"

He eased Christabel down onto the gurney. "I'm going with her," he told the EMT's.

They weren't inclined to argue. Judd Dunn was intimidating enough when he wasn't in a temper.

He glanced back at Hayes. "How about calling the Ranger office in San Antonio and tell them I'll probably be late in the morning, and to get someone to fill in for me."

"Will do," Hayes said. "I hope she'll be all right."

"She will," he said somberly. He climbed into the ambulance and sat down across from Christabel, catching her soft little hand tightly in his own. "Can you give her something for pain?" he asked as the tears continued to pour from her eyes.

"I'll ask for orders." The EMT got the hospital on the radio and explained the patient's condition. He was questioned briefly by Dr. Jebediah Coltrain, the physician on call.

"Give me that," Judd said shortly, holding out his hand for the mike. The EMT didn't argue with him. "Copper?" he asked abruptly. "Judd Dunn. Christabel's back looks like raw meat. She's in agony. Have them give her something. I'll take full responsibility for her."

"When haven't you?" Copper murmured dryly. "Give me back to Dan."

"Sure." He handed the mike to the EMT, who listened, nodded, and proceeded to fill a hypodermic from a small vial.

Judd pulled off his hat and wiped off the thick sweat from his straight black hair that was dripping onto his broad forehead. He tossed the hat aside and stared at Christabel with glittery eyes.

"Judd," she whispered hoarsely as the needle went in. "Look after Mama."

"Of course," he returned. His fingers tightened around hers. His face was like stone, but the deep-set black eyes in it were still blazing with fury.

She searched his eyes. "I'll have scars."

"They won't matter," he said through his teeth.

Her eyes closed wearily. It would be all right. Judd would take care of everything...

And he had. Five years later, he was still taking care of everything. Christabel had never felt guilty about that before, but suddenly she did. He had the responsibility for everything here, including herself. Her father had died of a heart attack soon after his arrest. Christabel's mother had died the year Christabel graduated from high school, leaving just Maude in the house with her. Judd came to stay during the Thanksgiving and Christmas holidays, and the three of them had good times together. But Judd had never wanted a physical relationship with his young wife, and went to extreme lengths to make sure they didn't have one.

This year he'd transferred to the Victoria Texas Ranger post, when an elderly ranger working it had retired. It hadn't been long after his friend, fellow Texas Ranger Marc Brannon and Josette Langley had married, and Cash Grier had come down here from San Antonio to become Jacobsville's assistant police chief. Marc had worked out of the Victoria office, too, briefly, but he'd left the Rangers to become a full-time rancher when Josette had become pregnant. Judd visited them and their son Christopher often.

So he'd let her sit in his lap tonight. But it hadn't meant anything, and it never would. His pulse hadn't even raced, she recalled miserably. But when the director had mentioned Tippy Moore, he'd smiled, and there had been a purely masculine look in his eyes.

She knew Judd was no virgin, even if she was. He had a worldly air about him, and women seemed to sense it, as her friend Debbie had at school. Later she'd remarked that he was probably great in bed and had broken women's hearts everywhere.

Christabel had brooded after that, because she recalled some odd remarks from her mother long ago about Judd and the company he kept in San Antonio. Apparently he was no stranger to permissive women, but he never brought any of them to the ranch. Her mother had smiled knowingly about that. He wouldn't want to parade any of his lovers in front of Christabel, she'd remarked. Not when they were secretly married.

It had devastated her to think that Judd didn't honor his wedding vows, even if it was a paper marriage. Realistically, he couldn't have gone without a woman for several years, she knew that. But she hated picturing him in bed with some gorgeous companion. She'd cried for two days, hiding her tears in the henhouse while she gathered eggs, or while riding fence line with the boys.

Her tomboyish nature had disturbed her invalid mother, who said that Christabel should be learning how to dress and set proper place settings instead of throwing calves for branding and grooming the horses in the rickety stable. Christabel paid her no attention, and went right on with her chores. She felt that she had to hold up her part of the responsibility for the ranch somehow, and helping with the daily chores before and after school and on weekends was her way of doing it. Judd noticed, at first with amazement, and then with affectionate indulgence.

He did care about her, in his way. But it wasn't the way Christabel wanted him to care. She had a terrible premonition about the change the movie company's arrival the following month was going to make in her dreary life. Judd had already stated his intention of getting an annulment in November. What if he fell head-over-heels for the internationally famous model that most adult men drooled over? She couldn't help thinking that the model might find him equally attractive. Judd was a dish.

She started to roll over and put the pillow over her head. Plenty of time for those worries after she got through the computer class exam at school on Monday. The exam! How could she have forgotten! She reached for her alarm clock and set it for an hour earlier than usual. A little last-minute cramming never hurt anybody.

She got through the exam and her other classes and went home to do chores. She'd just finished grooming her mare—the same one she'd managed to save from her father's brutality when it was just a filly—when she heard a car drive up.

Maude had gone to the store, so she went to see who it was. She was surprised to find a black and brown Jacobsville police car sitting there. A tall, well-built man in uniform with his thick black hair in a ponytail turned at her approach and came down the steps with a hand on the butt of his .45 automatic in the holster on his well-laden duty belt, sharing space with a leather ammunition clip holder, along with leather baton, aerosol, flashlight and knife holders.

It was Cash Grier, the assistant chief. Crissy had seen him just once, but she'd heard a lot about him. He was like Judd, she supposed, all business and stone-faced.

On a wicked impulse, she put both hands high over her head. "I confess. I did it!" she called. "I robbed Jacobsville Savings and Loan, and the money's in the barn. Go ahead, get a rope!"

He stopped and his eyebrows rose. His chiseled, very disciplined mouth in between the full mustache and the small goatee turned up at both sides and his dark eyes twinkled in a swarthy, scarred face.

"Suit yourself. Lead me to a tree," he replied.

She grinned. It changed her face, made it radiant. She rubbed her dirty right hand on her equally dirty jeans and extended it. "Hi! I'm Christabel Gaines. Everybody calls me Crissy except Judd."

He shook the hand. "What does Judd call you?" he asked.

"Christabel," she said on a sigh. "No imagination, and he hasn't got a sense of humor. If you don't want to arrest me, why are you here? We're not even in your jurisdiction. The city limits sign is four miles thataway." She pointed.

He chuckled. "Actually, I'm looking for Judd. He left a message for me. I understand there's a movie company coming out here to film and they need on-site security from some of my off-duty officers. I'd volunteer," he added, "but they'd worry me to death trying to get me to play the lead in their movie. I'm good-looking, in case you haven't noticed," he added with a wicked grin.

It took her a minute to get it, then she burst out laughing.

"Are you going to be in it?" he persisted with a grin.

She nodded. "I'm going to play a lilac bush next to the porch steps. I understand the makeup will take all day."

He chuckled. She was a real charmer, and pretty to boot. He liked her personality. It had been a long time since a woman had appealed to him so much at a first meeting.

"I'm Cash Grier, the assistant police chief," he introduced himself. "I guess you figured that out already. What gave me away—the patrol car?"

"It does stand out," she remarked. "Very nice."

"We like to think we have the sexiest patrol cars in Texas," he agreed. "I look good in a police car," he added.

Her dark eyes gazed up into his. "Let's see."

"Oh, no," he replied. "It's too much for some women. We'll have to work up to letting you see me in the car." He lifted both eyebrows and his eyes twinkled. "I look pretty good over a cup of coffee, too."

It was a hint, and she took it. "Okay. Let's see."

Before they got into the house, the ranch truck pulled up with Maude in it. She got out and pulled a sack of groceries out from beside her. Her green eyes went from the patrol car to the tall uniformed man. She turned to Christabel and glared. "Well, what have you done now?"

"This is Cash Grier, our new assistant police chief. He says he looks good over a cup of coffee," she told Maude. "I'm going to let him prove it."

She gave Grier a speaking look. "I've heard about you. They say you play with rattlesnakes and send wolves running."

"Oh, I do," Grier assured her genially. "I like a spoon to stick up in my coffee," he added.

"Then you'll be right at home, here. That's how Crissy makes it."

"Here," he said, taking the burden out of her arms with a flair. "Women's lib be damned, no dainty little woman should have to carry heavy packages up steps."

Maude caught her breath and put a hand to her heart. "Chivalry lives!" she exclaimed.

He leaned down. "Chivalry is my middle name," he informed her. "And I will do almost anything for a slice of pie. I have no pride."

Maude chuckled, along with Crissy. "We have a nice pie left over from yesterday, if Judd didn't eat it all. He's a fanatic on the subject of apple pie."

"There's some left, because I made two," Crissy told Maude. "Come along, Mr. Assistant Police Chief, and I'll feed you."

Grier stood aside to let Maude go first. "Beauty before titles," he said with a grin. "And please don't tell my superior that I'm susceptible to bribes."

"Chet Blake is, too," Maude informed him. "I hear he's your cousin."

He sighed as he followed the women into the house. "Nepotism rears its ugly head," he agreed. "But he was desperate, and so was I."

"Why?" Crissy asked curiously.

"Don't be rude," Maude chided. "He's barely got in the house. Give him some coffee and pie. Then grill him!" she added with a chuckle.

Grier had two slices of pie, actually, and two cups of coffee. "You're a good cook," he told Crissy while he sipped at his second cup.

"I learned early," she replied, twirling her cup around under her hands. "My mother was an invalid until her death. I learned to cook when I was ten."

He sensed a history there, and he wondered about her relationship with Judd Dunn. He'd heard rumors of all sorts about the odd couple who shared the D bar G Ranch.

She looked up, noting the curious look in his dark eyes. "You're curious about us, aren't you?" she asked. "Judd's uncle and my father were partners in this ranch for ten years. Circumstances," she said, boiling down the tragedy of her life into one word, "left us with a half interest each. I'm good with computers and math, so I do most of the bookkeeping. Judd is good with livestock, so he takes care of buying and selling and logistics."

"What happens if one of you gets married?"

"Oh, but we already..." She stopped dead. Her eyes held apprehension and self-condemnation in equal parts.

He glanced at her left hand with the man's signet ring cut down to fit her finger. His eyes lifted back to hers. There was keen intelligence in them. "I never tell what I know," he told her. "Governments would topple." He grinned.

She smiled back at him. "You don't know anything," she informed him deliberately.

His gaze was speculative. "Is it real, or just on paper?"

"I was sixteen at the time," she replied. "It's just on paper. He...doesn't feel like that."

His eyebrows lifted. "But, you do?"

She averted her gaze. "What I feel doesn't matter. He saved more than the ranch. He saved me. And that's all I'm going to tell you," she added when he stared at her. "In November I turn twenty-one and I'm a free woman."

He pursed his lips and studied her face. "I'm thirty-eight. Years too old for you..." His voice trailed off, like a question.

It had never occurred to her that a man would find her attractive. Judd treated her like a sore foot. Maude ordered her around. Boys at school were interested in the pretty, feminine girls who flirted. Crissy was friendly but she didn't flirt or dress suggestively. In fact, she was much more at home around horses and cattle and the cowboys she'd known most of her life. She was shy with most men.

She flushed. "I...I...don't interest men," she blurted out.

He put his coffee cup down slowly. "Excuse me?"

"Do you want some more coffee?" she asked, flustered.

He was fascinated. The women who filed through his life had been sophisticated, as worldly as he was, chic and urbane and sensuous. They thought nothing of coming on to him with all sorts of physical and verbal sensuality. This woman was untouched, uncorrupted. She had a freshness, a vibrancy, that made him wish he was young again, that he'd never had the experiences that had turned him bitter and cold inside. She was like a jonquil blooming in the snow, a stubborn flash of optimism in a cynical cold landscape.

He frowned, studying her.

The flush grew worse. "You're intimidating when you scowl. Just like Judd," she said uneasily.

"Blame it on a jaded past," he said, biting off the words. He pushed his chair back, still frowning. "Tell Judd I've put a note on our bulletin board about the site security job. So far we've got over a hundred applications. We only have twenty cops," he added on a sigh. "My own secretary signed up."

"Your secretary?"

He nodded, pushing the chair back under the table slowly. "She says if they hire her to do security, they'll have to give her a badge and a gun, and she can arrest me anytime she feels like it if I make her work late."

She laughed in spite of herself. He'd gone far away for a minute there, and she'd felt uncomfortable.

"Are you a bad boss?"

"I'm temperamental."

It showed, but she wasn't going to say so.

"Thanks for the coffee and pie," he said quietly.

"You're very welcome."

He turned and went down the hall. His back, she noted, was arrow-straight. He walked with a peculiar gait, a softness of step that was vaguely disquieting. He walked like a man who hunted.

He got to the front steps and turned so suddenly that she went off balance and had to catch one of the porch posts to save herself.

"Do you like pizza?" he asked abruptly.

She was still reeling from his sudden stop. "Uh, yes."

"Friday night," he persisted, dark eyes narrowed. "There's a band. Do you dance?"

"I do," she said.

"What will Judd do, if you go out with another man?"

She was uneasy. "I...well, I don't really know. I don't think he'd mind," she added. "It isn't that sort of relationship."

"He may mind having you go out with me," he said flatly. "He knows more about me than most people do around here."

She was shocked and intrigued. "Are you a bad man?"

Something terrible flashed in his dark eyes. "I have been," he said. "Not anymore."

Her face softened as she looked at him. She wondered if he realized how much his eyes gave away. There were nightmares in them.

She let go of the post and moved a step closer to him. "We all have scars," she said, understanding what Judd had been saying to her that day in the kitchen. "Some show, some don't, but we all have them."

His eyes narrowed. "Mine are deep."

She began to smile. "Mine, too. But all of a sudden, I don't mind them so much. They seem less conspicuous."

His broad chest rose and fell. He felt light. "Funny. So do mine." He smiled.

"The only place that serves pizza and beer and has a dance band is Shea's Roadhouse and Bar, out on the Victoria road," she told him. "Judd never goes there. I'm afraid he won't like me going there."

"I'll take care of you," he told her.

She sighed. "People have been taking care of me all my life, and I'll be a grown woman in less than two months." She studied his face. "I have to learn how to take care of myself."

"Funny you should mention it," he said, and his eyes softened. "I wrote the book on self-defense for women."

"Not that kind of taking care," she muttered.

"I'll teach you, just the same. Ever shot a gun?"

"Judd taught me to shoot skeet," she told him. "I'm hell on wheels with a .28 gauge. I have my own, a Browning." She didn't add that he hadn't taken her shooting in years.

He smiled, surprised. Many women were afraid of shotguns. "Imagine that!"

"Do you shoot?"

He gave her a look that reduced her height by three inches.

"You're a police officer. Of course, you shoot," she muttered.

"Eb Scott's got a nice firing range. He lets us use it for practice. I'll teach you how to shoot a pistol FBI style."

"Can you ride?" she asked.

He hesitated. "I can. I don't like to."

He was probably a city man, she guessed, and hadn't had much to do with horses or ranching.

"I don't like pistols," she confessed.

He shrugged. "We can't like everything." He looked down at her with mingled emotions. "I suppose I really am too old for you."

Cash, who was four years older than Judd, thought she was too young. Maybe Judd did, too. That would explain, as nothing else did, the hesitation he showed in getting involved with her. It hurt.

"On the other hand," he murmured, misreading her look of disappointment, "what the hell. That movie star who's a grandmother just married a man twenty-five."

Her eyes brightened and she grinned. "Are you proposing? After only two slices of apple pie? Gosh, imagine if I cooked you supper!"

He burst out laughing. He hadn't laughed like this in a long time. He felt as if all the cold, dead places inside him were warming.

"Imagine," he agreed, nodding. "Pizza, Friday night," he added.

"Pizza and beer," she corrected.

"Beer for me, soft drinks for you," he said. "You're not legal yet. You have to be twenty-one to drink beer in Texas."

"Okay, I'm easy—I'll drink bourbon whisky instead," she agreed.

He gave her a sardonic look and went down the steps. He hesitated and looked up at her. "How many people know you're married?"

"A handful," she said. "They also know that it's a business arrangement. It won't damage your reputation."

"I don't have a reputation to damage anymore," he replied. "I was thinking of yours."

Her face broke into a smile. "How nice of you!"

"Nice." He shook his head as he opened the door of the patrol car. Static was coming from the radio. "I can think of at least a dozen people who would roll on the floor laughing if they heard me called that."

Her dark eyes twinkled. "Hand over their numbers. I'll phone them!"

He grinned at her. "See you Friday. About five?"

She nodded. "About five."

He drove off with a wave of his hand and Crissy went back into the kitchen, where Maude was standing by the sink looking worried.

"What's your problem?" Crissy asked her.

"I overheard what he said. You just agreed to go out on a date."

"Yes. And your point is?"

"You're married, darlin'," Maude reminded her. "Judd is not going to like this."

"Why should he mind?" she asked reasonably. "He's said often enough that he doesn't want me for keeps. It's just a business arrangement."

Maude didn't say a word. She was remembering the look on Judd's face when she'd walked into the kitchen unexpectedly and found Crissy sitting on his lap. Crissy hadn't noticed anything different, but she had. She turned back to her chores. Judd wasn't going to like this.

CHAPTER THREE

CHAPTER THREE

Judd drove up in the yard Friday afternoon in his big black SUV, just an hour before Christabel was expecting Grier to pick her up. She was nervous. Worse, she was dressed to the teeth, and Judd noticed.

She'd left her blond hair undone, and it flowed like golden silk down to her waist in back. She didn't wear a lot of makeup, just powder and a light lipstick, but her eyes looked larger, a liquid brown that dominated her face and soft little chin. She was wearing a slinky black skirt with black high heels fastened around the ankle, displaying the sexy arch of her little feet. The black vee-necked blouse she had on was unusually tight, emphasizing her small, firm, rounded breasts in a way that made Judd ache in all the wrong places. A wide fringed black Spanish mantilla completed the outfit. It wasn't expensive, and it was old, but it was sexy. He wasn't used to seeing Christabel dressed like that. And suddenly he wondered why she was, and why she wouldn't look him in the eye. He knew from long experience that she was hiding something.

He propped a big booted foot on the bottom step of the porch and his narrow eyes fixed on her face.

"All right, spill it," he said tersely. "Why are you dressed like that, and why did you come running out the minute you heard me drive up? Are we going on a date, and you forgot to tell me?" he added.

She lifted her eyes and glared at him. The sarcasm hurt. "Wouldn't that be the day?" she asked with equal sarcasm. "As it happens, I'm going out dancing."

He didn't react for several seconds. Then sudden anger hardened his lean face. "Dancing? With a man?"

She straightened. "Yes. With a man." Her smile was provoking in the extreme. "Go ahead, Judd, tell me you haven't touched another woman since we married. Tell me you don't date."

The expression on his face was impossible to read. He moved up the steps, towering over her. "Who is he? Some boy from school?"

She realized with a start that what had seemed harmless and fun was becoming shameful and embarrassing. Her face colored.

"Not a boy from school," he guessed. His eyes narrowed again. "Are we going to play twenty questions? Tell me!" he said abruptly.

"It's Cash Grier," she blurted out, disconcerted by the authority in his tone.

Now he looked menacing as well as angry. "Grier is even older than I am, and he's got a past I wouldn't wish on my worst enemy's sister, much less you! You're not leaving the house with a man like that!"

Her self-confidence was wilting. She clutched her small purse to her chest. "I'm not running away with him," she began, trying to recapture lost ground. "We're going out for pizza and beer..."

"You're underage."

"I know that! I'm not drinking the beer, he is," she muttered. "We're going to dance and eat pizza."

His eyes slid over her very slowly. She felt as if he were stroking her bare skin and she felt wobbly on the unaccustomed high heels.

"Where did you meet Grier?" he persisted.

She threw up her hands and walked back into the house, leaving him to follow. Obviously, he wasn't going to stop until he knew everything. She wondered what he meant about Cash's past. Cash himself had hinted at something unpleasant.

She tossed her purse and mantilla onto the big easy chair and perched herself on its wide arm, crossing her legs at the ankles. Odd, how intent his eyes were on them for a few seconds.

"He came out here to talk to you about providing on-site security for the movie people," she said. "You weren't here, so I gave him coffee and pie and he asked me out."

He leaned against the doorjamb and stared at her from under the low-angled brim of his creamy Stetson. He looked elegant like that, and so sexy that she ached just looking at him. He had powerful long legs in nice-fitting jeans that did nothing to disguise the muscles in them. The .45 automatic he usually carried was in its new holster, replacing the revolver he'd used in the cowboy club shooting match. It sported the new maple handle and the Texas Ranger logo. His white shirt was taut against a muscular chest, a dark shadow under it giving hints about the thick curling dark hair that covered those hard muscles. The Texas Ranger star was on the pocket of that spotless white shirt. Usually he wore a jacket with it this time of year, but it was hot for early October. There was a faint line of perspiration on his top lip.

"He isn't taking you to Shea's," he said tautly.

Her eyebrows arched. "Why not? Judd, I'm almost twenty-one," she reminded him. "Most of my friends have been going there on Friday nights for years. It's not a bad place. They just sell beer."

"They have fistfights. Once, there was a shooting out there."

"They've had two bouncers since Calhoun Ballenger almost wrecked the place protecting his wife, Abby, before they were married. That was *years* ago, Judd!"

"The shooting was last year," he pointed out.

She sighed. "Cash is a police officer. He carries a gun. If anybody tries to shoot me, I'm sure he'll shoot back."

He knew that. He also knew things about Grier that he wasn't comfortable disclosing. The man would take care of her, certainly, but Judd didn't like the idea of Christabel going out with another man. It bothered him that it did. "It doesn't look right."

Her eyes met his, and she felt the years of loneliness making a heavy place inside her. "I go to school, I do the books, I check up on the boys while they're working, I ride fence lines and help dip and brand cattle and doctor sick ones," she said. "I haven't been to a dance since my sophomore year of high school, and I don't guess I've had a real date yet. I'm lonely, Judd. What can it hurt to let me go out dancing? We're only married on paper, anyway. You don't want me. You said so."

He knew that. It didn't help.

She got up from the sofa and went to him. Even in high heels, he towered over her. She looked up into his turbulent dark eyes. "I'm only going out for one evening," she pointed out. "Don't make me feel like I'm committing adultery. You know me better than that."

He drew in a long breath. Involuntarily, his lean hand went to her loosened hair and he gathered a thick strand of it in his fingers, testing its silky softness. "I've never seen you dressed like this."

"I can't go out with a man like Grier wearing jeans and a sweatshirt," she said with a gamine smile.

He frowned. "What do you mean, a man like Grier?"

She lifted one shoulder, uneasy at the contact of his fingers that was making her whole body tingle, and trying to hide it. She could even feel the heat of his body this close, and smell the spicy oriental aftershave he liked to wear. "He's a very mature, sophisticated sort of person. I didn't want to embarrass him by showing up in my working gear."

He frowned. "I've never taken you anywhere," he recalled.

She blinked, disconcerted. "You saved my life," she pointed

out. "Saved the ranch. Kept us all going, looked out for me and Mama while she was alive. You're still shouldering the bulk of the responsibility for running things around here. You didn't need to start taking on responsibility for my entertainment as well, for heaven's sake!"

He frowned at the way she put it, as if everything he did for her was a chore, an obligation. She almost glowed when she smiled. She had a pert, sexy little figure, even if she didn't know it. She had such warmth inside her that he always felt good when he was with her. Was Grier, with his cold, dark past, reacting similarly to the brightness in Christabel? Was he looking for a place to warm his cold heart?

She'd agreed to go out with the man. Was she attracted to him? He, of all men, knew how very innocent she was. She'd considered her paper wedding vows binding. He doubted if she'd ever really kissed anyone, or been kissed, unless you could call that cool peck on the cheek he gave her in the probate judge's office a kiss. He thought about Grier, a ladies' man if there ever was one, kissing her passionately.

"No," he said involuntarily. "Hell, no!"

"What?" she queried, puzzled by the look on his face.

He moved, one of those lightning-fast motions that could even intimidate their cowboys. His lean hands framed her rounded face and tugged it up so that her dark eyes were meeting his at a proximity they'd never shared.

"Not Grier," he said huskily, his eyes falling to her parted, full lips. "Not the first time..."

While she was trying to get enough breath to ask him what he was talking about, he bent his head. She felt the slow, easy brush of his hard mouth on her lips with real intent for the first time in their turbulent relationship.

She gasped and stiffened.

He lifted his head just enough to see the shock and puzzlement in her eyes. "Just so you don't go overboard with the first man who kisses you, Christabel," he whispered with unusual roughness in his voice. "I'm your husband. The first time...it should be me."

She opened her mouth to speak but he bent his head again before she could. His lips crushed down over hers with a pressure that grew more intense, more demanding, by the second. She clutched at his arms to save herself from falling as sensation piled on sensation. She felt a surge of heat in her lower body, along with a sudden heavy throb that made her shiver. She wondered if he could feel it, while she could still think.

His hands went to her waist and slid up and down, his thumbs brushing just under the soft underside of her breasts, in a lazy, arousing pattern that made her want to lift up toward them. She went up on tiptoe, pushing her mouth against his, opening her lips to his hungry demand. She felt a vibration against her lips, something like a muffled groan, just before his arms suddenly swallowed her and lifted her into the hard curve of his body.

Her arms were around his neck now, holding on for dear life, while his mouth probed at hers and she felt his tongue suddenly go right inside it. She'd heard and read about deep kisses. None of that prepared her for the sensations she felt. She was trembling. She didn't know why, and she couldn't stop it. He was going to feel it any minute. She moaned in frustration at her own inability to control her reactions. Inexplicably, the moan made him stiffen. One lean hand went to her hips and gathered them in fiercely to the thrust of his body. There was something alien about the feel of him, something vaguely threatening. He pushed her closer and she gasped as she realized what was happening.

He realized it at the same time and jerked away from her. He didn't let her go at once. His eyes were blacker than usual as they pierced her own.

Her mouth was swollen. Her eyes were shocked, stunned, dazed, delighted. She was shivering just slightly. Her breath came in husky little jerks. He looked down, at the bodice of her blouse, and saw hard little points.

His eyes met hers again. His hands were almost bruising on

her upper arms as he held her there. "That's how easy it is," he said tersely.

"How...easy?" she parroted breathlessly.

"For an experienced man to knock you off balance and make you give in to him," he continued. "Grier knows even more than I do. Don't let him get too close. He's not a marrying man. In any case, you're not free to experiment, paper marriage or not."

She wasn't getting any of it. She just looked at him, completely disoriented. She'd never dreamed that he'd kiss her like that. He'd sworn in the past that he was never going to touch her. She felt hot and shaky all over. She wanted to lie down with him. She wanted to touch his skin. She wanted him to kiss her breasts, the way men kissed women in those shameful late-night satellite movies that she watched secretly when Maude had gone to bed on the weekends.

"Are you listening to me?" he asked impatiently.

Her head fell back against his shoulder. She pressed one cold hand to his chest and moved it back and forth involuntarily.

"I'm listening. This dress is really hot. Could you help me take it off...?" she whispered wickedly.

He glared down at her. "Stop that," he said curtly. "I'm trying to talk to you."

Her eyes were half-closed, her body completely yielding. She felt as if she'd melted into him, become part of him. She wondered what it would feel like to lie under him on a bed. She reddened at the images that had flashed unexpectedly into her mind. Judd, in bed with her, stark naked and hungry for her. Heavens, she'd have died for it!

Her hunger for him was in her face. It amazed him that she was so immediately receptive to him, so hungry. He hadn't meant to touch her in the first place. It was Grier, damn him. He was uneasy about having her go out with Grier. He didn't trust the man. It disturbed him that this sudden relationship of hers had happened under his nose and without his knowledge. In his wildest dreams, he'd never expected that Grier could be drawn to a woman Christabel's age. He didn't trust Grier's motives, and he didn't want Christabel seduced. He was going to have to talk to Grier.

He watched her while his mind worked. She was still shivering faintly. He knew how she felt. He felt the same way. His body ached. He'd never expected such an explosive passion to flare up between them. He should never have touched her. He'd been stupid to let jealousy provoke him into it. He hoped she didn't know enough to see how susceptible he was to her. He moved back a step, just in case.

She took a step forward. "I can rush right to town and buy a red negligee," she said breathlessly. "I'll borrow one. Steal one. There's a bed only ten feet away...!"

"I told you that we were never going to have any sort of physical relationship," he said with ice dripping from every syllable.

"You started it," she reminded him glibly.

"I did it deliberately. I know Grier. You haven't dated," he said through his teeth. "You know nothing about men, and that's my fault. You can't go out with a man like Grier without knowing the dangers. It was a lesson, Christabel. Just a lesson!"

She was staring at him. Just staring, as all her dreams of belonging and being loved in return went up in smoke. She'd always thought of Judd as being very fastidious about women. But innocence could recognize experience, and she knew at once that she was completely out of his league. She didn't do a thing for him. He'd only been showing her what a trap passion could be. But it felt different now when she looked at him.

"Have you heard a word I've said?" he asked, exasperated.

"A few, here and there," she said, but she was looking at his mouth. "I'm not sure I understand the lesson completely. Could you do that again...?"

He took an angry breath and his lips flattened. He could taste her on them. That irritated him even more.

"No, I couldn't do it again!" he raged, furious. "Listen to me, damn it! We are getting an annulment in November, period! I

don't want marriage and a family. I love my job, and my freedom, and I'm not giving up either one. Is that clear?"

Breaking out of her trance, she moved away from him. Yes,
it was painfully clear. But she smiled deliberately, anyway. Her
voice, like her breathing, was jerky. "Okay. It's a great loss to
my education, but if you feel that way, just don't expect me to
offer to take my clothes off for you ever again. I'll fix some coffee if you'd like some," she added. "Cash isn't due for thirty minutes."

"Fine."

She went to the kitchen and made coffee. It calmed her. By
the time she put a cup and saucer on the table, along with the
condiments, her hands had stopped shaking.

"Do you want it in the study?" she called.

"No. I'll drink it in here." He moved into the room and sat
down at the small kitchen table. He'd removed his hat and rolled
up his sleeves. His hair was still mussed from her restless, hungry fingers, and his mouth, like hers, had a slight swell from the
urgency of the kisses they'd shared.

Grier was going to notice that, he mused. Perhaps it would
make him hesitate. He wondered why he felt so arrogant when
he looked at her now. It felt almost like possession. He clamped
down hard on those thoughts. He didn't want to be married. He
wasn't ready for family life. Infrequent liaisons were enough for
him. Love was dangerous, and he wanted no part of it. He'd seen
it destroy his father, and he knew that women had no staying
power. His mother had left his father. Judd's one serious love
interest had walked out on him ten years ago when he refused
to give up his hazardous job for her. It was just as well to avoid
tangles. Christabel was very young...

"You're very solemn," she pointed out.

"I don't want you to get the wrong idea about what just happened," he said, pinning her with his eyes.

"I'm not dim," she told him. She avoided looking directly at
him. She was too shaken to hide her emotions. "You said it was

only a lesson. I hadn't planned to jump into the back seat with Grier and have my way with him, you know."

He cleared his throat. "He drives a pickup. There is no back seat."

She glared at him. "You know what I mean!"

"And it's not you jumping on him that worries me."

She lifted both eyebrows. "Why not? Do you think I wouldn't know how? I do know what goes on between men and women, even if I'm not the voice of experience!"

"I know," he murmured dryly.

"Excuse me?"

He cleared his throat again. "I pay the satellite bill."

She was very still. That had never occurred to her before.

He cocked his head. "The titles are self-explanatory. *Passionate Partners, Lust in the Sand, The Curious Virgin*...shall I go on?"

She groaned and put her face in her hands.

"Just remember that what you're watching is staged and pure fantasy," he pointed out. "It's not like that in real life."

She moved two of her fingers and looked at him through them, curiously.

He leaned back, feeling his experience keenly as he met that glance. "Two kisses and a pat, and they go at it endlessly with accompanying groans and tormented expressions, in positions that even the Kama Sutra hasn't listed," he explained.

She was still watching, listening, waiting.

He let out a long sigh. "Christabel, a woman doesn't accept a man's body that quickly, or that easily, without a lot of foreplay. And most men can't last long enough to go through the whole catalog of outrageous positions. One usually suffices."

She was fiery red, but paying complete attention while trying not to look as if she was. And he was aching to show her, rather than tell her, how satisfying a physical coming-together could be. All at once, he felt things he didn't want to feel. And for the one woman on earth who was off limits to him, even if she was the only wife he'd ever had.

He finished his coffee and glared at her. "I don't mind if you go out with Grier, as long as you're discreet," he said, hating the words even as he spoke them with deliberate carelessness. His black eyes pinned hers. "But you don't cross the line with him."

She knew exactly what he meant and she was insulted. "As if I would, Judd!"

"Until it's annulled, it's still a marriage," he continued. "And a few people around town know about it."

"I understand why you're so worried about gossip..." she began, and then bit her tongue, because it was a subject he hated.

His chin lifted and his eyes narrowed dangerously. "My father was a minister," he said roughly. "Can you imagine how it was for him, and for me, to have all of Jacobsville talking about my mother and her blatant affair with the vice president of the local manufacturing company? They didn't even try to hide it. She moved in with him and lived with him openly while she was still married to my father. Everybody knew. His whole congregation knew, and he had to preach every Sunday. When her lover dropped her for someone younger, after he'd had his fill of the affair, she begged to come home again and pretend that it never happened. My father even tried to let her."

He averted his eyes to the table, cold with the memory of how those days had been for him. He'd loved his mother. But his father, despite his faith, had been unable to forget what she'd done. In his world, as in Judd's, vows were sacred. "In the end, it was the gossip that made it impossible for him to forget. It didn't stop, even after she left her lover. Some of his congregation refused to speak to her. It affected him, even though he tried not to let it. In the end, he asked her to leave, and she went, without an argument."

"You were only twelve when that happened, weren't you?" she asked gently, trying to get him to talk about it. He never had.

He nodded. "I loved her. He did, too, but he couldn't get over what she did. It was too public for either of them to get past it, in a small town."

Her hand itched to slide across the table to his, but she knew he'd sling it off. He was unapproachable when he talked about the past.

"Did she write to you?"

He shook his head. "He told her that she could, but she moved to Kansas where she had a cousin, and apparently never looked back." He toyed with the handle of his coffee cup. "We heard that she married again and had a child before she died. All we had was a card announcing the funeral and a dog-eared photograph of Dad and me that she kept in her wallet." His voice became tight and he sat up straighter.

"Was the child a boy or a girl?" she asked.

He was staring into space with blank eyes. "A girl. She died of spinal meningitis when she was six, and my mother died in a car crash a few months later." His teeth clenched. "She was a good mother," he added absently. "Even if she was a lousy wife."

She studied him quietly. "Sometimes people fall in love with the wrong people," she began. "I don't think they can help it."

His black eyes bore into hers. "In my book, if you make a vow before God, you keep it. Period."

She sighed, thinking that it was highly unlikely that he'd kept the wedding vow he made to her when she was sixteen, but she didn't say it. "I expect she was sorry for what she did to your father."

His broad shoulders moved restlessly. "He said she wrote him a letter. He never told me what was in it, but he admitted that his own pride had killed any hope of them getting back together. He couldn't bear having everybody know what she did to him." He smiled sadly. "She was his first woman," he added, with a glance at Christabel's wide-eyed stare. "And his last. I don't suppose some people today even think it's possible for a man to be faithful to one woman his whole life, but it's not so rare a thing in small towns, even in the modern world."

"I guess you've thought about how it would have been, if he could have forgiven her."

"Yes." He turned the coffee cup in his big, lean hands. "It was a lonely life after she left. I could never talk to him the way I could to her, about things that bothered me. I guess I drew inside myself afterward."

He'd never talked to her this way before, as if she were an adult, an equal. She studied his hard face and ached to have his mouth on hers again. She knew she'd never be able to forget how it felt.

He pushed back from the table and got to his feet. "I need to get back to Victoria."

She got up, too, eyeing him curiously. "What did you come down here for?"

"Leo Hart phoned me about some Salers bulls that have died mysteriously. He said he'd heard that our young one was poisoned. I wanted to talk to you about it."

"Yes, I tried to tell you when it happened that I thought Jack Clark was responsible, and you wouldn't listen..." she began.

He held up a hand. "You know you didn't have the boys check that pasture for bloat-causing weeds," he pointed out. "I told Leo so. I warned you about that, Christabel. You can't accuse people of crimes without solid proof."

"I wasn't! Judd," she said, exasperated, "there were four other young bulls in that pasture with him. They didn't die."

"I know that. They were lucky."

She grimaced. "They were Herefords," she said impatiently. "The only bull we lost was a Salers, and he was one of the same group that Fred Brewster bought calves from. He thinks Mr. Brewster's bull was poisoned, and I still think ours was, too."

He picked up his Stetson and slanted it across his brow. "Prove it," he said.

She threw up her hands. "I don't save dead bulls!" she exclaimed. "You wouldn't believe me and I couldn't afford an autopsy! We buried him with the backhoe!"

"Dig him up."

She gave him a speaking glare. "Even if I did, where am I going to get the money to have an autopsy done?"

"Good point." He sighed. "I'm skint. I used the last of my savings to repair that used tractor we had to have for haying."

"I know," she said, feeling guilty. "Listen, as soon as I graduate next year, I'll get a job in town at one of the businesses. Computer programming pays good wages."

"Then who'll do the books?" he asked. "I don't mind writing checks to pay bills, but I'm not burying myself in ten columns of figures and justifying bank statements. That's your department."

"I'll justify the statements and do the printouts at night or on the weekends."

"Poor Grier," he said sarcastically.

"I only just met the man," she pointed out.

"Stay out of parked cars with him," he said with rare malice.

"He drives a truck," she reminded him pertly, throwing his own earlier statement back at him.

"You know what I mean." He turned and started out the front door.

She followed him, seething inside. He didn't want her, but he didn't want any other man around her, either.

"I'll do what I please, Judd," she said haughtily.

He whirled at the front porch. "You put your name on a marriage license," he reminded her curtly.

"So did you, but that's not stopping you from doing what you want to!"

He lifted an eyebrow and went on down the steps to his truck. "The film people are coming back Saturday to set up their equipment," he added. "The director's bringing Tippy Moore with him, and the guy who's playing the cowboy—Rance Wayne."

She couldn't have cared less about the movie people. She hated the way Judd's eyes twinkled when he mentioned Tippy Moore. The woman was internationally famous for her beauty. Christabel was going to look like a cactus plant by comparison, and she didn't like it.

"I can hardly wait," she muttered. "Do they like pet snakes?

I'm thinking of adopting a black one and keeping it in the living room..."

"You be nice," he said firmly. "We need the money. There's no way we can fix the barn or buy new electric fencing without that grubstake."

"Okay," she sighed. "I'll be nice."

"That'll be a change," he remarked deliberately.

"And that's just sour grapes because I didn't dress up and look sexy for you," she said, striking a pose. "You can go home and dream about me in that red negligee, because that's the only way you'll ever see it," she added.

He made a rough sound in his throat, something like laughter, and kept walking.

She stared after him with flashing dark eyes, wishing that Cash would drive up before he left so that she could flaunt her date in front of him.

Daydreams so rarely come true, she thought wistfully as Judd climbed in behind the wheel, started the SUV, and drove off with a perfunctory wave of his hand.

It was a full ten minutes later that Cash Grier drove up in his black pickup truck. It was a huge, new vehicle with a spotlessly clean bed.

"Well, I can see that you don't haul cattle," she remarked as she went out to meet him at the bottom of the steps.

"Maybe I just keep an immaculate truck," he chuckled.

He looked really good. He was wearing a black turtleneck sweater with a casual jacket and dress slacks. His shoes were polished to a perfect shine. His dark hair was in a neat ponytail. He was easy on the eyes.

"You look nice, even out of uniform," she pointed out.

He was doing some looking of his own, with eyes at least as experienced as Judd's. She thought about the way Judd had kissed her and she flushed.

"You look a little uptight," he remarked. "Second thoughts about tonight?"

"Not a single one," she said firmly.

"Not worried about what Judd will say?" he persisted as he helped her into the truck.

"Judd said he didn't care," she replied. "He was here earlier."

Which explained her flustered look and the deep swell of her lower lip, Cash thought privately and with some amusement. Apparently Judd was more jealous of his paper wife than Christabel realized, and had made sure that she had a yardstick to measure men by. He had a feeling he'd never measure up to the hero-worship she felt for her husband. But she made him feel good inside, young inside, and he wasn't going to fall at the first fence because of a little competition.

She fastened her seat belt while he got in and fastened his own, his eyes smiling as he approved the action.

"I have to tell most people to put their belts on," he pointed out.

"Not me," she said. "Judd taught me early that I would not ride with him if I didn't wear it."

"You've known him for a long time."

"Most of my life," she agreed. She sighed. "He's taken care of me for five years. It isn't that he's possessive," she said defensively. "He just wants to make sure that I'm safe."

He gave her a rakish grin. "You're as safe as you want to be," he said.

She chuckled. "Now that's encouragement, if I ever heard it!"

CHAPTER FOUR

CHAPTER FOUR

Shea's Roadhouse and Bar was about a mile out of Jacobsville on the road that went to Victoria. It was big and rowdy on the weekends, and despite the fact that beer and wine were served at the bar, it wasn't the den of iniquity that Judd called it. There were two bouncers usually. One had broken an arm in a fall, so that just left Tiny to keep things orderly. It wasn't hard. Tiny was the opposite of his name, a huge, hulking man with a sweet nature and a caring personality. But he could be insistent when people got out of hand, and nobody lasted long in an altercation with him.

She said as much to Cash when they were seated at one of the small wooden tables waiting to be served.

"Altercation," he repeated with a slow smile. "You sound like a cop."

"Blame Judd," she said on a sigh. "It really does rub off when you hang out with law enforcement types."

He chuckled, toying with his napkin. "Are you sure he didn't mind that you came out with me?"

She pursed her lips. "I think he did, a little. He's very conventional."

His eyebrows arched. "Are we talking about the same Judd Dunn?" he asked pleasantly. "The one who handcuffed a prostitute to the former mayor of Jacobsville when he caught them together in a brothel, and had someone tip off the newspaper?"

She cleared her throat. "He was a policeman here at the time..."

"...and chased a speeder all the way to Houston to give him a ticket?"

She moved one hand uneasily.

"...and then padlocked the local pool parlor until the owner promised to stop serving beer to minors?"

She sighed. "Yes. I suppose he used to be more unconventional than he is now. He feels that he shouldn't embarrass the Texas Rangers. The exact figure changes from time to time, but this year, there are only 103 of them in the world."

He gave her an amused glance. "I know. I used to be one."

Her dark eyes widened. "You did?"

He nodded. "In fact, I worked with Judd for a while. I taught him those martial arts moves he uses so eloquently these days."

"You know martial arts?" She was hanging on every word.

He chuckled. "There's a movie cowboy up the road near Fort Worth who also runs a martial arts studio. He taught me."

She named the actor.

He nodded.

"Wow!" she exclaimed, obviously impressed.

"Now don't look like that," he muttered. "You'll embarrass me."

She cocked her head, recalling something she'd heard about him earlier. "You're one to talk about Judd being unconventional," she added with a wicked grin. "We heard that you used the movie camera in your police car to film a couple in the back seat of a parked car up in San Antonio...?"

He chuckled. "Not the police camera—my own. And it was two local police officers I knew that I captured on tape. I made them promise to behave with more decorum before I gave them the only copy of the tape."

"You make a bad enemy," she pointed out.

He nodded, and he didn't smile.

Around them, the band was just tuning up. It consisted of two men playing guitars, one with a fiddle and one with a keyboard. They broke into "San Antonio Rose," and couples began to move onto the big dance floor.

"They're pretty good," she said.

"They're missing their bass player," he noted.

"I wonder why?"

"Oh, he's in jail," he said, smiling as the waitress approached.

"Why?" she asked.

"Some other guy was dating his girl. He chased them to her house in his car and made a scene. She called us." He shrugged. "Fortunes of war. Some women are harder to keep than others, I guess."

"Poor guy."

"He'll be out Monday, wiser and more prudent."

"Hi! What can I get you?" the waitress, an older woman, asked.

"Pizza and beer," Grier told her.

"Pizza and coffee," Crissy said when it was her turn.

"No beer?" she asked.

"I'm not twenty-one yet," Crissy replied easily. "And my... guardian," she chose her words carefully, "is a Texas Ranger."

"You're Crissy," the girl said immediately, chuckling. "I had a crush on Judd when we were younger, but he was going with that Taft girl from Victoria. They broke up over his job, didn't they?"

Crissy nodded. "Some women can't live with the danger."

"Doesn't seem to bother you," the waitress said, tongue-in-cheek, as she glanced pointedly at Grier before she went away to fill the order.

Crissy chuckled as Grier gave her a meaningful look. "No, I'm not chickenhearted," she agreed. "I worry sometimes, but not to excess. Judd can take care of himself. So can you, I imagine."

"Well enough," he said, nodding.

The crowd was growing as Crissy and Grier finished their pizza and drained their respective beverages. The music was nice, she thought, watching the couples try to do Western line dances on the dance floor.

"They give courses on that at the civic center," Crissy told Grier. "But I could never get into it. I like Latin dances, but I've never found anybody who could do them around here, except Matt Caldwell. He's married now."

Grier was grinning from ear to ear. "Modesty prevents me from telling you that I won an award in a tango contest once, down in Argentina."

She was staring at him breathlessly. "You can do Latin dances? Then why are you just sitting there? Come on!"

She grabbed him by the hand and tugged him onto the dance floor and up to the band leader.

"Sammy, can you play Latin music of any kind at all?" she asked the young man, one of her former schoolmates.

He chuckled. "Can I!" He and the band stopped playing, conferred, and the keyboard player grinned broadly as he adjusted his instrument and a bouncing Latin rhythm began to take shape.

The floor cleared as the spectators, expecting something unusual, moved to the edges of the dance floor.

"You'd better be good," Crissy told Grier with a grin. "This crowd is hard to please and they don't mind booing people who only think they can dance. Matt Caldwell and his Leslie are legendary at Latin dances here."

"They won't boo me," he promised, taking her by the right hand and the waist with a professional sort of expertise. He nodded to mark the rhythm, and then proceeded to whirl her around with devastating ease.

She kept up with an effort. She'd learned from a boy at school, a transfer student from New York with a Latino background. He'd said she was good. But Grier was totally out of her class. She watched his feet and followed with a natural flair. By the time they were halfway into the song, she was keeping up and adding steps and movements of her own. As the band slowly wound down, the audience was actually clapping to the beat.

Grier whirled her against him and looped her over one arm for a finish. Everybody applauded. He pulled her back up, whirled her beside him, and they both took a bow. She was breathless. He wasn't even breathing hard.

He led her back to their seats, chuckling. "Let Caldwell top that," he muttered.

She laughed, almost panting from the exertion. "I'm out of shape," she murmured. "I'll have to get out of the house more."

"Gosh, you guys were great!" the waitress said as she paused briefly at their table. "Refills?"

"Thanks. You bet," Grier said, handing her his empty bottle.

"Me, too," Christabel added, pushing her cup to the edge of the table.

"Back in a jiffy," the girl said with a grin.

"Does Judd dance?" Grier asked her.

"Only if somebody shoots at his feet," she returned, tongue-in-cheek.

"That'll be the day."

"That reminds me," she said, and leaned forward. "I need your advice. I'm almost positive that somebody poisoned one of our young bulls. Judd won't believe me, but I'm sure I'm right."

He was all business. "Tell me about it."

"We bought a young Salers bull in early September. The Harts have a two-year-old Salers bull, and Leo Hart was going to buy Fred Brewster's young Salers bull, that came from the same batch ours did up in Victoria. But they found Fred's bull dead in a pasture just recently, because Leo Hart called Judd about ours. Ours died before Fred's, so we dragged ours out to the pasture behind the tractor and buried him with a borrowed backhoe."

"You didn't have him autopsied?" he asked.

She grimaced. "Cash, we were sitting pretty last year. But we had a drought in the spring and summer and cattle prices fell. Right now, it takes all Judd can make to keep me in school and pay his rent on his apartment in Victoria. We sell off cattle to pay for incidentals, and buy feed for the cattle when we don't have enough grass for graze. He even works extra jobs just so we can make ends meet." Her eyes were cloudy. "We're having hard times. Once I graduate, I'm going straight to work to help out. I was a computer whiz already and I didn't want to go on to vo-tech school in the first place. But Judd said I needed expertise in spreadsheet programs so that we could keep better records. He was right. It's just hard to manage, that's all. I imagine you know how that is."

He didn't. Nobody knew how much money he had in foreign banks from the early days in his profession, when he was doing highly skilled black ops jobs for various governments. He didn't advertise it. But he could have retired any time he felt like it. Holding a conventional job kept his skills honed and people in the dark about his true financial situation. And his true skills.

"Anyway," she continued, "he says that I didn't check the pasture before I put the bulls in it, and they binged on clover and got bloat. Since we don't use antibiotics as a preventative—and we certainly can't afford to use vegetable oils for that, either—Judd said the tannins in the clover caused the bloat." She sighed impatiently. "Listen, I know pasture management as well as he does, and I'm not stupid enough to stick susceptible young bulls in a pasture without feeding them hay or grass first. And the Hereford bulls were in there at the same time, all four of them. *They* didn't get bloat!"

"Didn't you tell Judd that?"

She nodded. "I guess he thinks there's a special Salers gene that attracts bloat," she muttered irritably.

He tried not to laugh and failed.

"Anyway, it happened right after we fired that Clark man," she added. "Jack Clark. He's got a brother, John. They're unsavory characters and they get fired a lot, I hear. We fired Jack for stealing on purchase orders. I suppose he didn't realize we check purchase orders to make sure they're not being abused. He bought himself a two-hundred-dollar pair of boots at the Western Shop and charged it to us with a photocopied purchase order. He gave back the boots, and we returned them, so we didn't press charges. But we fired him, just the same."

"He's working for Duke Wright now," he told her. "Driving a cattle truck."

"Duke had better watch him" was all she said. "One of our new cowboys said that the Clark boys had been suspected of poisoning cattle someplace that one of them was fired from a couple of years ago. Our guy was working with them at the time."

Grier was watching her closely. "This is serious. Are you sure Judd didn't believe you?"

"I didn't tell him all I've just told you, because I didn't find out about the Clarks being suspected of poisoning cattle until a few days ago," she said. "I didn't tell him that we found a cut in the fence there, either."

"You should tell him about that, and the other information. A man who'll poison helpless bulls will poison people, given a chance."

She nodded with a sigh. "I've told the boys to keep a close eye on our other stock, and I ride the fence lines myself when I get home from school."

"Alone?"

She stared at him blankly. "Of course, alone," she said shortly. "I'm a grown woman. I don't need a baby-sitter."

"That's not what I meant," he replied. "I don't like the idea of anybody going out to distant pastures alone and unarmed. You don't pack a gun, do you?"

She grimaced. "I guess I should, shouldn't I?" She laughed self-consciously. "I have this crazy nightmare sometimes, that I've been shot and I'm trying to get to Judd and tell him, but he can't hear me."

"Take somebody with you next time you ride fence," he coaxed. "Don't take chances."

"I won't," she promised, but without agreeing to take along an escort. She did have that .28 gauge shotgun that Judd have given her. She could take that with her when she rode fence, she supposed. Cash made sense. If a man wouldn't hesitate to poison a helpless bull, he might not stop at trying to kill a young woman. Fortunately, the waitress came back with coffee and beer in time to divert him, and they waited until she left before they resumed their conversation.

"Do you want me to talk to Judd about the bull?" he asked.

She shook her head. "It won't do any good. He makes up his mind, and that's it." She touched her cup and noticed that it was blazing hot. She pulled her fingers back. "He's distracted lately, anyway. Those film people are coming this weekend, including the stars." She glanced at him. "I guess everybody's heard of Tippy Moore."

"The Georgia Firefly," he agreed. His face grew hard and his eyes were cold.

"Do you know her?" she asked, puzzled.

"I don't like models," he said, tossing back a swallow of beer.

She waited, not liking to pry, but his expression was disturbing.

He put the bottle down, saw the way she was looking at him, and chuckled. "You never push, do you? You just wait, and let people talk if they want to."

She smiled self-consciously. "I guess so."

He leaned back. "My mother died when I was about nine," he mused. "I stayed with her in the hospital as long as they let me. My brothers were too young, and my father..." He hesitated. "My father," he began again with loathing in his tone, "was absolutely smitten with another woman and couldn't stay away from her. He used to taunt my mother with how young and beautiful his mistress was, how he was going to marry her the minute my mother was out of the way.

"She was ill for a long time, but after he began the affair, my mother gave up. When she died, he was too busy with his mistress to care. He only came to the hospital one time, to make arrangements for her body to be taken to the funeral home. His new woman was a minor-league model, twenty years his junior, and he was crazy for her. Three days after the funeral, he married her and brought her home with him." He picked up the beer and took another long swallow. His eyes stared into space. "I've never hated a human being so much in my life, before or since."

"It was too soon," she guessed.

"It would always have been too soon," he said flatly. "My stepmother threw out my mother's things the minute she set foot in the house, all the photographs, all the handwork—she even sold my mother's jewelry and laughed about it." His eyes narrowed. "That same year, my father sent me off to military school. I never went back home, not even when he finally wised up, eight years too late, and tried to get me to come home again."

Some men hated physical contact when they recounted painful episodes. But she slid her hand over Cash's anyway, something she'd never have done with Judd. Grier glanced at her hand with a start, but after a few seconds, his fingers curled around it. They were strong fingers, short and blunt, with a grip that would have been painful if they'd contracted a centimeter more. She noticed that he wore no jewelry except for a complicated-looking silver metal watch on his left wrist. No rings.

"I lost my mother the year I graduated from high school," she recalled. "I was older than you were, but it hurt just as much. But I had Judd, and Maude," she added with a smile. "She came when I was just a baby, to help Mother, because she was so frail. Maude's been like a second mama to me."

"She's a card," he mused, turning her hand over to examine the tiny scars. "What do you do with your hands?" he asked curiously, noting short nails and cuts.

"Fix broken fences, mend tack, use calf pulls, get bitten by horses, climb trees..." she enumerated.

He chuckled. "Tomboy."

"I'm not made for a mansion or a boardroom," she said with

a grin. "If women are really liberated, then I'm free to do anything I like. I like livestock and planting gardens and working around the ranch. I hate the idea of an office and a nine-to-five lifestyle. I'm a country girl. I wouldn't mind being a cattle baroness, of course."

"There's nothing wrong with that."

"Of course, I'm a full partner in the ranch," she said thoughtfully. "And I keep the books and make decisions about breeding and diet and upgrades of equipment. When I get through this computer course, I'll be able to rewrite spreadsheet programs and keep up with my breeding program better."

"And Judd doesn't mind giving you that authority?" he asked, puzzled.

She smiled curiously. "Why would he? I'm good at what I do, better than he is, and he knows it. Besides, I don't have a clue about marketing. That's his department. Oh, and he pays bills." She grimaced. "I don't mind keeping bank statements reconciled and doing projection figures, but I draw the line at writing checks."

"I don't like that, myself," he had to admit. He chuckled. "I had you pictured as a nice little kid who went to school and let Judd do all the hard work."

"Fat chance," she scoffed. "No man's supporting me while I sit back and read magazines and paint my fingernails. I'm a hands-on partner."

"Judd never seemed like the sort of man who'd tolerate a female partner," he murmured dryly.

"You don't know him well, do you?" she asked, smiling. "He fought really hard to get women into the Jacobsville police force, and he won't put up with men who denigrate the worth of women in business or law enforcement. Besides, he can cook and clean house better than I can. If he ever gets married for real and has kids, his wife will be lucky. He loves kids," she added absently, hating the thought that he was determined to get an annulment the second she turned twenty-one, next month, and just about the time that Tippy Moore would be on hand.

"You look worried."

She shrugged. "Tippy Moore is world-famous and beautiful," she said without thinking. "Judd really perked up when they mentioned she was starring in this movie. He's never been around women like that. He's a minister's son and rather unworldly and conventional in some ways."

"You think she'll captivate him."

She met his gaze evenly. "I'm no beauty," she said flatly. "I'm backwoodsy and I know computers and cattle, but I can't compete with an internationally famous model who knows how to act seductive. She'll draw men like flies, you watch."

"Not me," he said easily. "I'm immune."

"Judd won't be," she said worriedly.

"Judd's a grown man. He can take care of himself." He was remembering, and not wanting to disillusion her by admitting, that Judd had very little trouble attracting beautiful women in the old days. The man was no Romeo, but he was handsome and confident and aggressively seductive with women he wanted. He was also successful. He didn't mention that to Crissy. It would have crushed her. He wondered if she knew how much her feelings for Judd showed when she talked about him.

"I suppose he can," she murmured. She picked up her cup and sipped her hot coffee. "I wish we didn't have to have film people climbing all over the ranch," she added impatiently. "But they're offering us a small fortune to use it for location shooting, and we need the money so badly that we can't refuse." She sighed. "That old saying's right, isn't it, that everybody has a price. I didn't think I did, but I do want to replace that Salers bull." She smiled doggedly. "We don't insure against cattle losses, but at least he'll be a tax deduction as a business loss." She shook her head. "I paid five thousand dollars for that bull. If Clark did poison him, and I can find a way to prove it, I'm going to take him all the way to the Supreme Court. I might not get my five thousand back, but I'll take it out in trade."

He chuckled. "I like your style, Crissy Gaines."

She smiled at him over her coffee cup. "If I can get proof, will you arrest him for me?"

"Of course." He sobered. "But don't go looking for trouble alone."

"Not me. I'm the cautious type."

He doubted that, but he wasn't going to argue about it. "Are you game to get back on the dance floor?"

"You bet!"

He grinned and took her hand, leading her back out. The band leader, noticing them, immediately stopped the slow country tune they were playing and broke out with a cha-cha. Everybody laughed, including the couple of the evening out on the dance floor.

Saturday morning, bright and early, the director, the assistant director, the cameraman, the cinematographer, the sound man, two technicians and the stars of the movie came tooling up the dirt driveway to the ranch in a huge Ford Expedition.

Judd had just driven up in the yard a minute ahead of them. Christabel and Maude came out on the porch to meet them. Maude was in an old housedress, with her hair every which way. Christabel was wearing jeans and a cotton shirt, her hair in a neat braid. But when she saw the redheaded woman getting out of the big vehicle, her heart fell to her boots.

It didn't help that Judd went straight toward the woman, without a single glance back at Christabel, to help her down out of the high back seat with his hands around her tiny waist.

She laughed, and it was the sound of silver bells. She had a perfect smile—white teeth and a red bow mouth. Her figure was perfect, too. She was wearing a long swirly green dress that clung to the long, elegant lines of her body. Judd was looking at her with intent appreciation, a way he'd never looked at plain little Christabel. Worse, the model looked back at him with abject fascination, flirting for all she was worth.

"She's an actress," Maude said with a comforting hand on her arm. "She'd never fit in here, or want to, so stop looking like death on a marble slab."

Christabel laughed self-consciously. "You're a treasure," she whispered.

"And I'm cute, too," Maude said with a wide grin. "I'll go make a pot of coffee and slice some pound cake. They can come in and get it when they're ready."

"Christabel!" Judd called sharply.

She glanced ruefully at Maude and hopped down the steps with her usual uninhibited stride and stopped beside Judd as he made introductions.

"This is Christabel Gaines. She's part owner of the ranch. Christabel, I'm sure you remember Joel Harper, the director," he said, introducing the short man in glasses and a baseball cap, who smiled and nodded. "This is Rance Wayne, the leading man." He nodded toward a handsome tall man with blond hair and a mustache.

"This is Guy Mays, the assistant director," he continued, introducing a younger man who was openly leering at the model. "And this is Tippy Moore," he added in a different tone, his eyes riveted to the green-eyed redhead, who gave Christabel a fleeting glance that dismissed her as no competition, and then proceeded to smile brilliantly up at Judd.

"I'm very glad to meet you," Christabel said politely.

"Likewise. We're ready to start shooting Monday," Harper told Judd. "We just need to discuss a few technical details..."

"If you want to know anything about the livestock," Christabel began.

"We'll ask Judd," the model said in a haughty, husky voice. "He'd surely know more than you would," she added with deliberate rudeness.

Christabel's dark eyes flashed. "I grew up here..." she began belligerently.

"Judd, I'd love to see that big bull you told us about," the model cooed, taking Judd's arm in her slender hands and tugging him along.

Christabel was left standing while Judd walked obediently toward the big barn with Tippy and Joel Harper and his entourage. She wanted to chew nails. She was, after all, a full partner in the ranch. But apparently they considered her too young to make big decisions, and Judd was too fixated on the redhead to care that she'd been dismissed as a nobody on her own place.

She glared after them until the sound of a horse approaching caught her attention. Nick Bates, their livestock foreman and ranch manager, came riding up, his tall, lithe figure slumped in the saddle.

"What's your problem?" she asked him.

"I've been chasing cows," he muttered darkly. "Some damned fool cut the fence, and five cows got out. We ran them into another pasture and I came back for the truck and some wire to fix the break."

"Not the pregnant cows," she said worriedly.

He nodded. "But they seem all right. I had the boys herd them into the pasture down from the barn, just in case."

"Who left the gate open?" she wanted to know.

"None of my men," Nick assured her, his dark eyes flashing in his lean, rugged face. "I rode up to Hob Downey's place and talked to him. He spends his life in that rocking chair on the front porch most of the year. I figured he might have seen who cut the wire."

"Did he?" she prodded.

"He said there was a strange pickup truck down there early this morning, one with homemade sides, like a cattle truck would have," Nick told her. "An older truck, black with a red stripe. Two men got out and one acted like he was fixing the fence, then Hob went out on his porch and yelled at them. They hesitated, but a sheriff's patrol car came up the road and they jumped in the truck and went away real fast. It was a small opening, just wide enough to get a cow through, and not visible except up close."

She moved closer to the horse, worried and thoughtful. "I want you to call Duke Wright and ask him if he's got a black truck with a red stripe, and ask who was driving it this morning."

Nick leaned over the pommel, meeting her eyes. "You've got some idea who it is," he said.

She nodded. "But I'm not mentioning names, and what I know, I'm keeping to myself. Get down from there."

He lifted both eyebrows. "Why?"

"I don't want to have to go to the barn to saddle Mick," she admitted. "The film crew's down there. They make me nervous."

Nick swung down gracefully. "Where are you going?"

"Just out to see how that fence was cut," she told him.

"I already told you..."

"You don't understand," she said, moving closer. "The fence where the bull died had been cut, too, remember? I never mentioned it to Judd, and we fixed it, but I noticed how it was cut. No two people do the same thing exactly alike. I can tell if it was Maude or Judd who opened a cola can, just by the way they leave the tab. I know what the first wire cuts looked like."

"I've got to find Denny. He picked up some new salt licks. We'll take those out when we fix the fence."

"Good enough." She swung gracefully into the saddle and patted the gelding's red neck gently, smiling. "I'll take good care of Tobe, okay?"

He shrugged. "I never doubted it. Want me and Denny to get the truck and follow you over there?"

She shook her head. "I'm no daisy." She noted the rifle that protruded from the long scabbard beside the saddle horn. "Mind if I take this along?" she added.

"Not at all. I'd feel better if you did. Remember the safety's on. Is Judd down there?" he asked abruptly, nodding toward the barn.

"Yes, so you'd better go straight to the equipment shed. What he doesn't know won't get me dressed down."

He started to argue, but she was already trotting away.

She didn't really need to look at the cuts to guess that Jack Clark had been around, making mischief. He might have just wanted to let the cows out, or he might have planned to steal some. But she wanted to get away from Judd and the others. If she were lucky, they'd be long gone by the time she got back. Besides, it wouldn't hurt to make sure her theory was correct. If she could get any sort of evidence to give Cash, he could take care of Jack Clark for her.

She remembered the look in Judd's black eyes when he'd helped Tippy Moore down from the SUV, and the way he'd let her lead him away after insulting Christabel. He hadn't even seemed to notice that she'd *been* insulted, either. Her heart ached. Just as she'd dreaded, the model's arrival marked a turning point in her life. She wished she could turn the clock back. Nothing was ever going to be the same again.

CHAPTER FIVE

As Crissy suspected, the fence was cut in the same place that the other one had been, very close to the vertical brackets of the hog wire. She swung down from the saddle and examined the cuts carefully. The wire cutters that had been used both times weren't sharp and the cuts weren't neat and clean.

She turned, leading Tobe by the reins, and sighed angrily as she looked toward the flat horizon. Jack Clark had stolen from them, and they'd fired him with justification. But Clark had a vindictive streak a mile wide, and he wanted vengeance. Crissy was afraid that it wasn't going to end with poisoned bulls and cut fences. She hoped that Duke Wright would have some news for Nick about the Clark brothers when he phoned him.

She spotted Hob Downey on his porch and walked up to greet the older man.

Hob was in his seventies. He'd been a cowboy all his life, until he was forcibly retired by his boss. He knew more about horses than most anybody, and he was lonely. He sat on his front porch most every day, hoping that somebody would stop and talk to him. He was a gold mine of information on everything from World War II to the early days of ranching. Crissy visited him when time permitted, but, like most young people, time was in short supply in her life.

"Hi, Hob!" she called.

"Come sit a spell, Miss Crissy," he invited with a grin.

"Wish I had time, Hob. Nick says you saw some fellows in a pickup truck down by our fence this morning."

He nodded. "Shore did. Skulking around like. I don't have a telephone, or I'd have called you."

"Was one a tall man with a bald head?" she asked carefully.

He grimaced. "One was wearing a hat pulled down low on his forehead, so I can't say if he was bald. Couldn't say how tall he was, either. The other fellow was wearing a shirt that could have drove a colorblind man crazy. Kept on the other side of the truck, mostly, couldn't see him well."

She sighed. "How about the truck?"

"Had a big rust spot on the left front fender," he offered. "Rest of it was black with a thin red stripe. Had homemade gates, unpainted. Looked to me like they were about to collect a cow or two, Miss Crissy."

She'd have to find out if the Clark brothers had a pickup truck, or drove one of Wright's fitting that description, and what color it was.

"Cut that fence, didn't they?" he persisted.

She nodded. "But don't let that get around, okay?" she asked. "They might be dangerous, and you're all alone out here."

He chuckled. "I got a shotgun."

"You can't stay awake twenty-four hours a day," she pointed out.

"They might come back and try again."

She couldn't be sure of that. "You just keep your eyes open and watch your back," she told him.

"Somebody mad at you, is that it?" he wanted to know.

"Something like that. Thanks, Hob. You take care of yourself, and lock your doors at night."

"You, too, Miss Crissy. Sure you won't sit a spell?"

She smiled. "I'll come back when I can. But I'm up to my ears in movie people right now. I have to get back home."

"We heard they was going to make a movie at your ranch. You going to be in it?"

She laughed. "Not me! See you, Hob."

"See you."

She got back on Tobe and turned him toward the dirt road that led back to the ranch. It was disconcerting to think that Jack Clark and his brother John might have been responsible for two attempts on their livestock. They might try again, and they couldn't afford many losses right now, not even with the added revenue the movie shoot would bring in. They needed a new direction or they were going to go under.

Specialization, she thought, was the only answer to their problem. They could do what Cy Parks did and raise purebred livestock—but that required a hefty bankroll up front that they didn't have. They could do what a few other producers had done and try marketing their own brand of organic beef. But that would entail upgrading their production methods and finding a buyer who wanted quality organic beef...maybe an overseas buyer, because those profits were really high, according to Leo Hart, who sold organic beef to Japan.

If only horses could fly, she thought, and laughed at her own whimsy. Judd had tried that angle already, and failed. They were told that their cattle weren't lean enough for the high priced markets, that they were fed too much corn and too little grass. That was why Christabel had been nudging their cattle into pastures to fatten them on grass—and had lost their prize Salers bull in the process.

But it wasn't the grass—rather, the clover—that had killed that bull. And that cut fence was no accident, either. It was the Clark brothers. She knew it, even if Judd wouldn't listen. Cash would. And somehow, she was going to prove it!

* * *

She walked Tobe down to the barn, noting that the big SUV was gone, and so was Judd's truck. What a relief. At least she didn't have to worry with company today.

But the relief was short-lived. After she'd unsaddled and brushed Tobe, and taken the rifle back to Nick, there was unwelcome news.

"Duke Wright doesn't own a black pickup with a red stripe," Nick told her with a sigh, pushing back the hat from his sweaty blond hair. "And he doesn't have any cowboys who do."

She grimaced. "I was so sure...!"

"Maybe he borrowed it," he said.

Her eyebrows lifted. "You think?"

"Anything's possible." He gave her a long look. "Judd wanted to know where you were. I told him you rode over to check on the cows that got out of the pasture." He held up a hand. "I didn't tell him the fence was cut. I figured you'd tell him when you wanted to."

She smiled. "Thanks, Nick. I owe you one."

He shrugged. "No problem. I've already told the boys to keep their eyes open for any suspicious vehicles around here."

"Good idea. And keep that pasture where you moved the cattle under twenty-four hour guard, even if you have to pay somebody overtime," she added firmly, inwardly grimacing at another expense they could ill afford. "Make sure he's carrying a rifle, too."

He nodded gravely. "I'll do that."

She hesitated. "And take pictures of the way the fence is right now, and save that wire where the cuts are," she added as an afterthought. "If anything ever comes of this, we'll need evidence."

"You bet! I'll put it in the equipment shed."

"Thanks, Nick." She wandered back up to the house. Maude was wrapping untouched slices of cake and grumbling.

"'Can't eat cake,' she said. It's got calories." She glared at Crissy, who was smothering a grin. "And doesn't drink coffee, because caffeine's bad for you. They didn't have time for it, anyway, and she gave our house a look that I'd have liked to push her off the steps for!"

"They won't be here long," she said comfortingly.

"That's what you think! I heard that director tell Judd that it would take a couple of months for them to shoot the movie, and even then, that they'd probably have to come back to reshoot some scenes after they finished."

That meant they'd be here until Christmas. She thought about Judd being around that model all the time, and her heart sank. It was worse than she'd ever dreamed it might be.

"That model was really playing up to him," Maude was muttering. "Hung on him like a chain the whole time, smiling up at him, laughing with him. She's stuck on him already."

"And he's stuck on her, isn't he, Maude?" she asked quietly.

Maude reddened. "He's married, honey."

"He isn't, to hear him tell it." She sat down in the nearest chair. "Be a dear and hand me a cup of coffee. I'm whacked."

She related her suspicion about the cut fence to a concerned Maude.

"You tell Judd?"

She hesitated. "No."

Maude glowered at her. "That's reckless. When I go to my sister's on the weekends, you're here all alone. The bunkhouse isn't close enough for the men to hear you scream. You should tell Judd."

"He didn't believe me about the bull being poisoned, Maude," she said, accepting a cup of black coffee with thanks. "And he isn't going to believe the fence was cut deliberately, either."

"Show him."

"Even if I show him the evidence he still won't believe me. He thinks I'm just trying to get his attention."

Maude smiled. "You are."

She shrugged. "That's no secret. But I don't tell lies." She sipped coffee. "When are the film people going to start?"

"Tomorrow, bright and early."

She choked on her coffee. "So soon?" she groaned.

"They want to get a start while the weather's good. They've

already moved into the Jacobsville Commercial Hotel, where they'll sleep. They hired caterers to bring the crew breakfast and lunch out here, and the electricians have been talking in Martian to Judd about what they want to do with portable generators," she added facetiously. She shook her head. "That director fella says they're bringing in huge trucks to carry all their equipment, and trailers for the stars to use for dressing rooms and makeup. They hired Bailey's Tour Service to bus the cast and crew out and back every day."

"Are they bringing portable rest rooms?" Crissy asked hopefully.

"Judd told them they could use the ones in the bunkhouse. Won't be any cowboys in there during working hours, except for the nighthawks, and nothing short of a tornado would wake Billy and Ted when they get to sleep."

"Good point," she mused, sipping coffee.

"The mayor is going to be in the film, along with the chief of police," she added.

"Nice move, politically speaking," she agreed.

"They're going to do some of the shots in town. It doesn't hurt to impress people before you start tearing up highways and causing traffic jams."

Crissy grinned. "Maybe they'll cause gout and get kicked out of town!"

"Not a hope. Too many people around here think they were born to be movie stars." Maude shook her head. "It's going to be a nightmare, darlin'," she said heavily. "And that model...!" She wrinkled her nose. "She'd kill an asthmatic with the perfume she bathes in."

Crissy's dark eyes lowered. "And she's beautiful."

"She's that."

"No way I could compete with somebody like her," Crissy said wistfully.

Maude turned around. "Judd's known you most of your life," she said. "You're good, and kind, and you have a way of making a man feel special and tender. Besides that, there isn't much that you can't handle here, from cattle management to ranch improvements. You've got a good brain. Most men are attracted by beauty, but only if there's something behind it to keep them interested. She's a pretty face and figure with bad manners. Judd will see through her."

"Think so?" she finished her coffee. "I'm glad I'm in school," she said when she'd put the cup in the sink. "I won't have to be around them much."

"They'll be shooting on the weekends, too," Maude said hesitantly.

She turned in the doorway, frowning. "You said something about generators?"

Maude nodded. "To run all the lights they'll be using in the house and the barn..."

Her face froze into a caricature of its normal self. "In the house? In my house!"

Maude grimaced. "Didn't Judd mention it?"

"No!"

"Just the living room and the kitchen," she said gently. "They're going to need to change a few little things here and there...they're paying extra for it!" she interrupted herself to say quickly when Crissy started turning red in the face.

"Judd said they could do that?" she groaned.

"We need the money, he told me," she said softly. "It's only for a little while, Crissy. Just a little while. It's a lot of money."

"And we're going under without it, I know that" came the miserable reply. "It's just that I didn't expect anything like this. It's...like an invasion! We won't have any privacy!"

Maude nodded. "I know, but we'll get through it somehow. Just get out of the way and let it roll over us," she advised. "In other words, darlin', take the money and run. It'll be over before you know it! Honest!"

It wasn't. Crissy came home from classes the next day to find the driveway completely blocked, to keep curiosity seekers out.

There were five or six cars parked on the side of the dirt road that led up to the ranch, and people had spread blankets on the buffalo grass, using binoculars to watch the movie crew while they ate snacks. There were half a dozen trailers, two flatbed trucks, at least two tractor-trailer rigs, and what looked like a small army of people carrying equipment.

Crissy couldn't forcibly move the tractor-trailer rig that had the driveway blocked, so she had to leave the pickup truck there and walk the half mile to the ranch house. Arriving at the steps, dusty and sweaty and tired, she was stopped at the steps by one of Cash Grier's men working security.

"Sorry, Miss Gaines," the officer said apologetically, "but they're shooting a scene in the living room right now. You can't go in this way."

She turned without a word and went toward the back of the house. On the way, she tripped over a huge bundle of extension cords and almost went headfirst into a camera setup just outside the kitchen window. If Judd had been anywhere on the place, she'd have tossed her books straight at his head.

Inside, a soundman was working with a boom while two total strangers, a man and a woman, sat at her kitchen table with empty cups while lighting men hovered with meters and tapes and portable lighting equipment.

Maude motioned her to the back hall and dragged her into her own bedroom. "We have to be very quiet," she whispered. "They're shooting one scene in the living room today."

"When will they be through?" Crissy asked.

"Well, they started just after you left this morning. They've already shot it ten times," she began.

Crissy groaned audibly.

"The boom showed up in one scene. Then somebody coughed in the next one. The model flubbed her lines three times because she didn't sleep last night on account of the train running so close to the hotel. Then the leading man tripped over that old Persian rug you won't throw away because your mother loved it, and after that a light went out..."

"I want to move to Alaska today," Crissy said in a pitiful tone, putting her books aside to sit down heavily on her bed.

"But the director thinks they can finish it by suppertime," Maude concluded.

"And this is just one scene," Crissy thought aloud. "My gosh!"

"It's bound to get easier as they go along," Maude assured her. "Things are always hard at the beginning." She frowned. "I don't know about the fights, though."

"Fights?"

"It seems the lead actor doesn't like the assistant director. They worked together before and had a bad fight over a woman. The actor lost. So now the actor is giving the man fits and refusing to do scenes his way. Miss Moore doesn't like the assistant director, either, and he hounds her unless Judd is around. The writer is having to come down here, too, because the actor says he's not doing the scene in the barn the way it's written. He says his part is stupid and Tippy Moore gets the best lines. He says his contract guarantees him as many lines as she gets."

Crissy shook her head. "What sort of changes are they making to my house?" she asked.

"Just a little new furniture and rugs and curtains and stuff, on account of, in the movie, the heroine redecorates the hero's house for him." She brightened. "They're redoing the kitchen, too, and we get to keep all the stuff they use for props!"

"What if we don't like it?" Crissy wanted to know.

"We'll like it," Maude assured her. "The director told Judd they'd get all new appliances for the kitchen, too. Tippy Moore's going with him and the prop man and some assistant cameraman to pick them out. She said it needed a woman's touch."

That was disheartening. It was Crissy's house, not Tippy Moore's. She should have had some input into purchases. But nobody cared for her opinion. She felt as if she'd landed in hell.

It couldn't get any worse. It just couldn't. She had to try to think of the money. They needed it so badly.

Maude patted the younger woman on the back. "Buck up, now. It's only for a little while. She'll go away and he'll get his mind back where it belongs."

By the end of the week, Christabel had figured a way to get breakfast eaten before the tour bus rolled down toward the barn with the actors—by getting up before daylight. She groaned at the number and size of the trucks and trailers scattered around, and the number of support people that it apparently took to make a movie. There was sound equipment, cameras, rails to support moving cameras, huge reflectors and fans and booms. It looked like an invasion of technicians, and Christabel couldn't wait to leave.

She gathered up her books and darted out the side door to the old pickup truck she drove to school. It had belonged to her father, and was one of the few things she owned free and clear. It was old, and it needed a new paint job, but it ran very well, thanks to Nick.

Just as she opened the truck door, she saw Judd drive up at the front steps. Her heart raced and she hesitated. But just then, he got out of his SUV and went around the hood to open the passenger door. The redheaded model climbed down beside him, laughing up at him with that smile that had graced half a dozen magazine covers. Christabel smiled wistfully, and climbed into her truck.

As she drove away, she saw Judd's arm slide around Tippy Moore's thin shoulders as they walked toward the barn where the film crew was waiting for her. So much, she thought, for her pitiful dreams.

The days dragged while the film crew worked. Fortunately school took up most of Crissy's time. When she was home, she was out with the men, supervising the various seasonal projects that had to be completed before winter set in. She didn't bother trying to dress up or wear more makeup or change her hairstyle from its customary bun on top of her head. It was impossible to compete with a beautiful woman like Tippy Moore. She wasn't going to get caught trying.

Not that Judd noticed her very much. He was busy at work because of the ongoing investigation into the murder in Victoria. Cash had been keeping her informed about the investigation. Most Texas peace officers knew about it, because of the way the victim had been killed and abandoned. Cash thought it had the ritual look of a personal vengeance killing because of the mutilation and the way the victim's body was displayed after death.

"They're not making much headway on the case," he told Crissy while they talked one Saturday afternoon beside his patrol car next to the front door of her house. "They haven't even got a suspect."

Inside the house, the kitchen was occupied by lights and cameras and a hundred thick electrical cords hooked up to a portable generator that looked as if it could power every light in Jacobsville.

"Maybe it's one of the Clark brothers," she said, only half facetiously.

He didn't smile, as she'd expected him to.

"I was kidding!"

He still didn't smile, but it wasn't because of the subject at hand. He was looking over Crissy's shoulder and glaring as if all the hounds of hell had suddenly been loosed in the yard.

"Did you come to arrest Miss Gaines?" came a honey-sweet voice from behind Crissy. "It can't be for speeding, not in that deathtrap of an old truck she drives!"

Crissy turned and glanced at the model. Tippy Moore was dressed to the hilt in a sweeping white circle skirt with a tiny blue bodice and a wide blue belt. She was wearing extremely high heels, and her long, wavy reddish-blond hair was in a lovely tangle around her beautiful face. She smiled up at Cash with that stunning radiance that made her face leap off magazine covers with such vitality. She propped her hands on her hips and tossed her hair, obviously right at home with any man who came near her.

But Cash didn't seem to be impressed. In fact, he became instantly, actively hostile. He glared at the woman with pure malice.

Taken aback at his response, Tippy laughed, a sound like the tinkle of silver bells, and tossed her hair again. "Cat got your tongue, Mr. Policeman?" she teased.

Cash's dark eyes narrowed. He gave the woman an appraisal that would have done justice to a cattle auction and his attention went right back to Crissy.

"How about a burger and fries?" he asked her with a tender smile. "You can ride in my car and I'll let you play with the siren."

Crissy chuckled, unspeakably delighted that he preferred her to an international model. "I'd love to. Can I come as I am?" she added, indicating her faded, stained jeans, and the old T-shirt she wore with dirty boots. She'd been helping the men move cattle to a new pasture.

He shrugged easily. "You look fine to me." He gave Tippy a speaking glance. "I appreciate a real woman who doesn't look like a painted dress-up doll."

Tippy flushed red, whirled on her heel, almost unbalancing herself, and started back toward the house.

"Why the hell would a woman wear heels that high when she can't even walk in the damned things?" Cash asked loudly.

Tippy walked faster.

Crissy took Cash's arm and pulled him toward his patrol car.

"Let's go before she gets into the gun cabinet," she said in a stage whisper.

Grier flashed her a grin. "Spoilsport."

They sat in a booth at the local café and Cash told her more about the investigation.

"They don't have a clue who committed the murder," he said. "Or why. She was raped, and murdered brutally with a knife, in a way I won't even tell you about. But she had no enemies and no associations with any criminals."

"They're sure it wasn't her husband?"

"They're sure," he said. "He was so shaken when they found the body that he had to be hospitalized," he added quietly. "I've never seen a man like that in my life. It gets worse," he added through his teeth. "She was three months pregnant. It was their first child."

"God almighty!" she whispered. "How horrible."

"Her husband doesn't even know if he wants to keep the ranch," he added. "A rancher named Handley was leasing land from him to raise bulls on, but all his bulls got poisoned."

Her eyebrows went up. "That's where Fred Brewster's bull came from," she murmured thoughtfully. "His and ours were from the same sire." She frowned. "Fred's bull died, I heard."

"Could have been coincidence," Cash said, but he was making mental notes.

She was frowning. "Our fence was cut, where our young bull died, and one was cut where we had some cows get out. I examined the cuts in both fences myself and had them photographed," she told him. "They were the same. I'm convinced that Jack Clark did it, but when Nick checked with Duke Wright, he doesn't have a black truck with a rust spot and a thin black stripe..."

"What was that?" Cash asked carefully.

She hesitated. "Hob Downey lives on the border of our north pastures," she told him. "He saw a black pickup truck with a rust spot on a fender, a thin red stripe and homemade cattle gates sitting next to my fence. He said two men got out of it and were looking at the fence. Hob couldn't tell if they cut it."

Cash had whipped out a pad and pen. "Hob Downey," he said, checking the spelling. "Has he got a phone?"

"No. Poor old thing, he can't even afford heat. He has a wood stove. He's living on his Social Security, and it isn't much." She gave him directions to Hob's house. "Why are you so interested?"

He studied her and grimaced. "I can't tell you," he said finally. "I'm sorry. This is something I'm not at liberty to talk about."

She grinned. "Have I helped you crack a case without know-ing it?"

He put the pad away. "I'll let you know, the minute I can, if you have," he promised.

She sipped her coffee. "You were very rude to Miss Moore," she said. "You don't like her at all, do you?"

"She reminds me of my stepmother."

"She reminds me of a redheaded serpent," she murmured without looking at Cash. "I feel like I don't even live there any-more. I can't go in my own house without tripping over an actor or a piece of equipment."

"Seen Judd lately?"

Her face tightened. "He drives down from Victoria every af-ternoon when he gets off work to pick up Miss Moore and take her to her hotel. She doesn't like riding in the bus with the lesser people," she added with a wicked grin.

He studied her curiously over his coffee cup, seeing through the humor to the hurt. "Judd isn't naive. She's a novelty. She'll wear off."

She laughed without humor. "Think so? I've never seen him so animated."

"Any man appreciates a pretty woman."

"Not you," she blurted out. Her eyes searched his intently. "She couldn't believe you weren't head over heels with her at first glance."

"I've seen a hundred like her over the years," he said coldly. "Selfish, vain, unaware of anything that goes on around them. She must be twenty-six or twenty-seven, and her days as a model are numbered. If she doesn't make it in films, she's going to be unemployable in a few years."

"Don't sound so happy about it," she chided.

"Brains last. Beauty doesn't."

"Funny, that's just what Maude said," she recalled as she fin-ished her coffee. "Maybe it's like in school, where the popular girls are always the prettiest ones. But they don't like the really nice boys, who aren't quite as handsome and well-known as the sports heroes."

"Hero and sports are two words we can do without combining," he said, waving a finger at her.

She grinned. "I know who the real heroes are," she assured him. "The whole country does, now."

He nodded grimly. "Hell of a way to have to learn it."

"Stop being so grim," she murmured, placing a gentle hand on his forearm. "You'll scare people."

He slid his own hand over hers and smiled at her. "You're a novelty in my life, did you know? I can't remember ever having a woman for a friend."

Her dark eyes sparkled. "We all need someone to talk to," she said. "Think of me as a man with earrings and dress sense."

He cocked an eyebrow. "I know men who wear earrings. In fact," he added, "I used to wear one."

"How exciting! Why did you stop?"

He glowered. "My cousin Chet didn't think it was dignified for an assistant chief to encourage younger officers to break his dress code in the Jacobsville department," he said disgustedly.

She slid her free hand over his. "You'll do, as you are. Thanks for rescuing me from the film maniacs, by the way. Sometimes I wish I could move to a quieter house."

"They'll leave by Christmas."

"Think so?" She sighed. "I hope you're right. If I have to play Santa Claus, I know a redheaded model who's getting her own five foot live rattlesnake under the tree."

He chuckled, and so did she. From a distance, they looked more intimately involved than friends would. Judd Dunn saw that as he hesitated in the doorway with mixed emotions, the foremost of which was a sudden, inexplicable urge to knock Cash Grier through the front window of the restaurant.

CHAPTER SIX

CHAPTER SIX

Cristabel and Grier were so involved that they didn't notice Judd until he pulled out a chair noisily and straddled it beside them. They both glanced at him with surprise.

Her heart jumped, but she tried to hide it. He was angry. Very angry.

"What have I done now?" Christabel asked with studied carelessness.

He glared at her. "What did you say to Tippy? She was in tears when I left."

She was too unsettled by the bold question to answer it.

Cash wasn't. His dark eyes flashed. "Crissy didn't say anything to her. She came up and started flirting with me, and I snubbed her," he told Judd. "I don't like models. If she was upset, it was my fault, so don't blame Crissy."

Judd's eyebrows rose. "What have you got against her?"

"Nothing, personally."

He stared at Cash with open curiosity. "I had to bring her back to the hotel in town. She couldn't work. The assistant director is furious."

"Damn, I really hate it for him," Cash said without inflection.

His face tautened. "You can tell him for me that I don't pander to the egos of spoiled brats of any age." He got up. "Crissy, I'll run you back to the ranch. I want to follow up on this lead."

She stood up, caught between Cash's anger and Judd's agitation, without a way to turn. She'd wished that she'd brought her own truck with her.

"You can ride back with me," Judd said, "and save Cash a trip."

Great, she thought, I won't have any lungs left by the time we get there, I'll be pickled in that expensive perfume Tippy wears. Probably Judd's vehicle was saturated in it.

"I don't mind driving her," Cash said pointedly.

Judd moved closer to the older man. He didn't blink. His wide-brimmed hat was cocked low over one eyebrow, and there was aggression in every taut line of his powerful body. He was spoiling for a fight.

Cash knew it, and had sense enough not to let it escalate. "Okay," he said easily. "Crissy, I'll phone you next week and we'll take in a movie on my day off."

"Great," she said, grinning at him. "Thanks for lunch."

He shrugged. "I enjoyed it. See you, Judd."

Judd nodded and Cash moved around him nonchalantly, as if he didn't perceive the visible threat of Judd's stance.

Crissy knew he was upset. She supposed it was because of what Cash had said to his model. She picked up her small shoulder bag and slung it over her arm.

He turned and looked down at her disapprovingly. "You could have changed clothes before you came into town looking like that."

Her eyebrows lifted. "If you don't like the way I look, then *you* go out and move cattle and ride fence lines and check water holes, and put out feed and muck out the stalls and...!"

He held up a hand and sighed angrily. "I know we need more men. I don't like you having to be one of them."

"I'm a rancher's daughter," she reminded him. "I'm not doing anything I haven't done since Dad first put me on a horse."

He searched her big, dark eyes, and noted the circles under them, the new lines of strain in her face. "They're getting on your nerves, aren't they?" he asked.

She didn't have to ask who he meant. "I couldn't change clothes because they had my bedroom blocked," she said flatly. "I'd already made the assistant director mad by leaving my books on the kitchen table. I had to put them back in the truck until he got his scene filmed. He didn't say anything, but steam was coming out his ears. It's my house and I have to have permission to use the bathroom. Of course they're getting on my nerves!" She took a slow breath. "But we need the money. So everything's okay."

He turned and went out. She followed him to his big black SUV. He waited until they were both inside, strapped into their seat belts, before he started the engine and spoke again.

"Yes. We need the money," he agreed quietly. "I hate to keep stressing that, but it's true. I want you to graduate before you start taking on more work." His glance at her was eloquent. "You should be going to parties and dancing and having fun, like other women your age, instead of doing the dirtiest jobs on the ranch."

"I see," she nodded. "You're encouraging me to commit adultery so that you can hit me for alimony when you divorce me."

He hesitated and then burst out laughing. "Damn it!"

She grinned, glancing out over the fields as he drove. "I'll make up for lost time when it's all legal. Meanwhile, I'll kick around with Cash and keep it all low-key."

"Is it?"

She turned her head toward him. "Is it what?"

"Low-key."

"Cash is my friend, Judd," she said. "I know you think I'm disgustingly old-fashioned, but I took a vow and I'm keeping it until I don't have to anymore."

His eyebrow jerked. He hated the pleasure the statement gave him. He shouldn't care if she dated. He wanted his freedom.

Even Tippy didn't threaten that. But Christabel did. She made him light up inside. When he was in the darkest moods, she could bring him out of them with a quip, with a grin, with that outlandish humor of hers. He'd never known anyone else who made him feel...whole. The idea of losing all that to some other man made him uneasy. He kept dreaming about her in a red negligee...

He shrugged off the idea. He wasn't opening that can of worms. He was recalling something Cash had said, just before he left.

"What lead was Cash going to follow up on?"

"Beats me," she said with determined carelessness. "He jerked out a pad, jotted something down, and said he had to track down a lead."

"Oh."

"You still don't believe our bull was poisoned?"

He shook his head and then glanced at her. "Get Nick to work on that clover in the pasture that caused the bloat. If we're going to feed grass to cattle, it needs to be just grass."

"I will." She sat beside him without speaking, wishing that she could talk to him the way she talked to Cash, that he'd listen to her ideas and not brush them off as if they were so much dust.

"Why do you think it was poisoned?" he asked suddenly.

She wanted to pour it all out—the cut fences, the pregnant heifers that almost got loose, what Hob had told her, what she'd told Cash. Fred Brewster's dead bull. But she had no real evidence, and she didn't want to find herself watched like a hawk every time she rode out alone from now on. She could investigate this. It wasn't a big deal. Besides, she rationalized, Judd had enough on his mind lately with that brutal, senseless murder he was investigating. She knew that he must have seen the victim. It was probably wearing on him heavily.

"Just something I heard," she said after a minute. "It was probably just talk, connected with the Clark brothers. They aren't well liked around here."

"Tell me about it," he agreed, diverted. He turned onto the ranch road, whipping up dust. "They've been fired from half a dozen jobs in the past year. They don't stay anywhere long."

"Where are they from?" she asked curiously.

"Haven't a clue."

That was something she might check on herself. She toyed with the window button. "Do you still have that old mock .45 that shoots .22 caliber ammunition?"

"Yes. Why?"

"How about cleaning it up and getting me some bullets for it? I've got a yen to take up target shooting."

"Why?"

"You're full of questions today."

"You're lacking in answers."

"Cash said he'd teach me to target shoot," she said, and hoped he wouldn't get her in trouble by asking Cash to confirm that lie.

"I could teach you," he said, bristling. "I'm a better shot than he is."

"I know that, but you're so busy lately...." She almost bit her tongue for saying that. He was touchy about the investigation of the killing. He hated to talk shop with her, with anyone, because what he had to see was so gory. He didn't like having his sensitivities exposed.

There was a very long pause.

"I'm not trying to invade your privacy," she said at once. "I know what you're having to help investigate, and that you hate talking about it. I wasn't prying. I read an article about how hard it is for law enforcement people to handle homicides. I know it bothers you, deep inside where it doesn't show."

He looked at her intently as he slowed for a turn. His eyes went back to the road. "You know too much about me," he said inexplicably.

She shrugged. "I've lived most of my life around you."

He laughed hollowly. "I have to look at things that no human being should ever have to see. I'm a lawman. It shouldn't upset me. I should be able to handle anything that comes along."

She nodded. "That's in the article I read," she said unexpectedly. "That's why it's so hard for law enforcement people to admit they need counseling, or even talk to someone about things that bother them. You're all tough guys and gals. It shouldn't even dent you, because you're made of steel." She turned in her seat, as far as the seat belt would allow, and met his curious eyes. "But you're not. Part of you is very human, and it hurts to look at people when they've been killed. That only means you feel compassion, not that you're weak."

He seemed less strained. He stared out the dusty windshield as they approached the ranch house.

She smiled. "Of course, we both know that you can chew up ten penny nails," she added with a wicked grin.

He let out a chuckle as he braked behind the big truck that was permanently blocking the driveway and went around it on the grass.

"I can't do that," she remarked, wincing as she saw the ditch barely two inches from the passenger-side tires. "I just know I'll run off into that gully if I try."

"With that attitude, you would." He pulled up at the front porch. It was strangely deserted. "Why does Cash hate models?" he asked her bluntly.

She hesitated. But her loyalty to Judd was stronger than her loyalty to Cash. "His stepmother was one," she told him. "She split up his family."

"Tough."

She nodded. "He can chew up ten penny nails, too," she offered.

He didn't smile. His hand reached out and tugged at a long wisp of blond hair that had escaped from her bun. "You should be wearing pretty clothes and hanging out at the mall."

She made an insulting noise. "Don't stereotype me."

His eyebrows arched. "Was I? I thought young women your age liked those things."

"I like bulls," she said. "Beautiful Salers bulls and young Hereford bulls, and crossbreed calves that other ranchers would envy, raised organically."

He shook his head.

"So do you," she pointed out.

He chuckled. "Maybe I do." He twisted the soft hair around his thumb and studied it. His whole face clenched. He hesitated, but only until he saw the quiet compassion in her expression. "This victim was just twenty-five," he said abruptly. "She was pregnant. She was lying in the dirt, off the highway in tall grass. She looked so alone, so vulnerable, so helpless, lying there nude except for a ripped blouse. She'd been stabbed repeatedly and mutilated as if the person who did it hated her femininity. I wouldn't have told her husband how bad it was, but the media reported every gory detail. He ended up being sedated in the hospital."

Ignoring the certainty that she shouldn't touch him, involuntarily her fingers touched the strong hand holding her hair. "You'll catch the guy who did it," she said firmly.

He cocked an eyebrow. "Guy?"

"She was found in a ditch, and the crime scene was ritualistic. Her hair was haloed around her head, she was lying with her face up and her eyes open in a spread-eagled position. There was a handful of dirt in her mouth. Everyone in law enforcement said that it had all the earmarks of a vengeance killing, as if the killer hated her. Could it be a serial murder? Most serial killers are white men between the ages of twenty and thirty-five, loners, they..."

"Good Lord!" he muttered. "How do you know that?"

"Cash has been keeping me posted and I've read all about the crime scene. I like to read about profiling, too," she said. "And there are lots of these real-life detective shows on TV about how murders are solved. Since I know somebody in the business of catching crooks, it doesn't hurt to know a little."

He laughed. "Not scared I'll come home in a box one night?"

Her fingers caressed his strong hand. "You can take care of yourself," she said softly. "You're quick-witted, and you don't trust people." She sighed. "But I do say a lot of prayers when you're working on a case like this."

He smiled tenderly at her. "That's nice."

She wrinkled her nose. "Just don't get shot, okay? Or if you do, get shot just a little."

"I'll do my best," he promised.

She searched his black eyes slowly. "My quality of life would diminish without you. Even if you marry some hotshot international model."

Both eyebrows went up. "Marry?"

"Right. Dirty word." She removed her fingers. "God forbid you should ever put on a ring that isn't attached to a grenade or something." She reached for the door handle.

He caught her by the nape of the neck and pulled her face firmly but gently under his. "I'm already married," he whispered, just as his hard mouth covered hers fiercely for a brief moment. He let her go and moved out of the truck while she was still recovering from the shock.

He opened her door and lifted her down by the waist, holding her in front of him for a few smoldering seconds. "Don't get too involved with Grier. We're not going to be married for much longer, but I'm still going to feel responsible for you. Grier is a real hard case. He's got a history I can't tell you about. You'd have a better chance of domesticating a wolf."

The part about not being married much longer was disturbing. She tried not to react. What was he saying, something about Grier...

"Cash is my friend," she said.

He drew in a long breath. "He's my friend, too. Sort of. Just...don't get too close to him. He's not quite what he seems."

She smiled up at him. "Okay."

His eyes searched hers hesitantly. They fell to her mouth and averted. He shook her, very gently, before he let go. "I worry about you, too, out here with just Maude and the boys. Maybe it wouldn't hurt to let Cash teach you how to target shoot. Nobody knows more about guns than he does." His chin lifted. "Well, except me," he added in that deep, honied tone that rippled down her backbone like velvet. His powerful body tensed just faintly. "Christabel, are you sure you don't want me to teach you to shoot a pistol?" he added suddenly.

"I don't want to impose on your free time, Judd," she said without making a point of it. "You work hard enough to deserve a little relaxation."

"Are you trying to tell me something?" he asked curiously.

"Not a thing, actually. Except that I know you like to spend your free time with Miss Moore."

His eyes narrowed on her face. "Are you jealous?" he asked in a slow, soft tone, as if he'd only just thought of it as a possibility.

She caught her breath. Her heart was running away, and she couldn't risk betraying how she felt. She didn't want to trap him by making him feel sorry for her.

"It's a paper marriage, Judd, you said so yourself. You can do whatever you like," she added bluntly. She didn't dare add that she was investigating cut fences and poisoned cattle, and that Cash was the only person she could talk to about it. "Let Cash teach me to shoot the pistol. He likes spending time with me."

Now the pause was long and heated. He didn't say another word. But he breathed with such control that she knew he was furious. She didn't know why. It was obvious that he was smitten with Tippy Moore, so why should he care if she got shooting lessons from Cash? Maybe it was a male thing. There were so many male rituals that women never quite understood...

"I won't come in," he said curtly. "I'll see you next week."

"Sure. Thanks for the ride."

She didn't look back as she mounted the porch. She went straight in the front door and tripped over a power cord, falling headfirst into a chair and ruining a scene she didn't realize they'd been shooting.

"Oh, that's just perfect, after the sixteenth take!" the assistant director, Gary Mays, bit off furiously, while the star, Rance Wayne, and two minor actors in the scene gaped at him. "You stupid, clumsy woman...!"

Christabel pulled herself up with the help of the cameraman and righted herself quickly. She stomped right up to the assistant director and glared up at him. "You listen to me you half-assed, bad-tempered, would-be tyrant, this is my damned living room you're standing in! I've been walking around here on eggshells for days, trying to keep out of the way, and it's not my fault that this place is wired like a minefield with electrical cords! There wasn't even a sign up that said you were working in here! If you want privacy, you make a sign and you use it when you're shooting! And keep a civil tongue in your thick head when you talk to me, do you understand me?"

The assistant director gasped and stumbled over words as the actors, the sound man, the cameraman, and the support crew chuckled audibly.

There was another laugh behind her, deep and slow and appreciative.

"She's got a temper, Gary," Judd told the assistant director. "It doesn't pay to make her lose it."

"So I see." Gary laughed, but without any real humor. "Sorry, Miss Gaines," he murmured reluctantly.

She nodded curtly. "That'll do." She gave Judd a curious glance, because she hadn't expected him to come into the house. She didn't know that he'd seen her fall and had rushed back in the door to make sure she wasn't hurt. Now, he just looked at her, with an oddly shimmering look in his black eyes.

"We'll put up a sign next time," Gary said, turning away.

"You okay?" Judd asked quietly, moving closer to study her.

She nodded, flattered by his concern. "Just unsettled. I hit light."

He nodded, too. But the way he looked at her was different. New. Unfamiliar.

She puzzled over that look all night long, and never did figure it out.

Tippy Moore was furious, and she didn't pull any punches. She was waiting for Crissy the next morning before the big generators were turned on.

"You tell that...that...small-town excuse for a policeman that I'll wear whatever shoes I like!" she gritted, her green eyes blazing.

Crissy's eyes popped. "Excuse me?"

"I can so walk in them," Tippy continued, unabated. "And he can just not talk to me from now on, forever! I was only being friendly, God knows why!"

She was too surprised to answer. The other woman was fuming.

"I wasn't flirting with him!" Tippy Moore continued. "I was trying to be civil. He made me feel like a case of measles! Well, I'm not interested in some small-town hick cop, not when I can have any man I like! You tell him that!"

Crissy found the woman's response to Cash's attitude curious, to say the least. "Cash doesn't like women," she said, trying to soften the blow. She couldn't tell the model why Cash reacted that way to her, it wasn't her business.

"He likes you" came the sharp reply, followed by a look that plainly shouted "God knows why."

"I'm just a rancher," Crissy said gently. "I don't dress up or flirt or threaten him in any way. We're friends."

The other woman was still angry. "I'll bet you were spoiled rotten as a kid," she muttered absently. "Pampered and fussed over and given anything you ever wanted. Daddy's little treasure," she added sarcastically.

Crissy's face tightened. "You don't get spoiled on a ranch, Miss Moore," she replied coolly. "There isn't time. Everybody pulls his or her weight, or the whole outfit goes on the skids."

"Why does Judd spend so much time here?" she asked.

Crissy's eyebrows arched. "He owns half the ranch. It takes both of us to keep it running, and the only money coming in is what Judd makes—and what we're getting to let you film the movie here."

"So that's why..." Tippy murmured slowly, and actually flushed. "I thought Texas Rangers made a lot of money. They're special."

"More special than you know," Crissy told her, feeling resentful and more than a little protective of her husband. "But they don't make princely salaries, and it takes a lot to run a cattle ranch."

"Why doesn't he sell out?"

"Because I can't afford to buy him out," she said flatly. "This may not look like much to you, but it's been in my family, and Judd's, for over a hundred years. Neither of us would sell it unless we were starving."

"It's just a piece of dirt with a little grass on it."

Crissy's brown eyes narrowed coldly. "Family matters. Tradition matters. Duty and honor and responsibility matter. Money does not," she added flatly, and with an edge in her voice that was unmistakeable as she gave the model a long and insulting scrutiny.

Tippy lifted her chin haughtily. "Do you love Judd?"

"Judd is my business partner," Crissy began shortly.

"Good. See that you don't get any ideas about him," Tippy added. "I have plans for him."

"As what, your valet?" Crissy asked, too angry to choose her words. "Or do you just collect men as you go along and add them up by the presents you get? One man would never be enough for a woman like you, anyway, I imagine."

Tippy's face froze, her hands clenching at her sides. "You know nothing about me!"

"And you know nothing about me!" came the reply. "Don't ever warn me off Judd again. He and I have known each other since I was in patent leather shoes. Don't think you'll cut me out of his life on an acquaintance of a few weeks, Miss Moore. Judd may be diverted by a pretty face and figure, but he's not stupid. He can see right through the gloss to the ugliness."

Tippy's breath caught. Then she smiled coldly. "If this is a contest, you've already lost," Tippy drawled softly, green eyes flashing. "Judd will do anything I want him to. Money's tight, is it? Then how could he afford to buy me this?"

The model held up her hand and flashed an emerald ring that would have cost in the hundreds, if not thousands. Crissy felt sick at her stomach. Judd wasn't one to buy presents for women, except at Christmas, and that was always something useful rather than frivolous. He'd given Crissy a leather jacket last year. For him to buy something as expensive as that ring, he had to be head over heels in love with the woman.

Crissy didn't say another word. Her heart felt as if it had been shattered. She lowered her eyes and turned away, walking back to the house with her back as straight as an arrow.

Behind her, the redheaded woman grimaced and set her beautiful lips together hard. Tippy actually winced as she watched the young woman walk away with that steely pride visible in her very carriage.

Filming on the ranch ended after a few days, while the crew moved into town for a week to do some shooting there. Christabel had the house to herself temporarily—except for the equipment left in place that had to be walked around and the big trucks it belonged in.

Judd didn't come until the next Wednesday, and when he did, he had Tippy with him. Crissy had just saddled her horse and was leading him out of the barn when they drove up at the steps. She was packing a borrowed rifle in the scabbard slung from the pommel and wearing boots and denim jeans and jacket, with a weatherbeaten black Stetson pushed firmly on top of her blond hair.

"Where are you going?" Judd asked as he helped Tippy out

of the vehicle. The model was wearing a green silk dress that looked simple and probably cost the earth. Compared to Christabel, she was dressed in a queenly manner. The dress matched the emerald and diamond ring Judd had bought her. Its sparkle in the sunlight hit Crissy right in the heart.

"I'm riding fence lines," Christabel told him without inflection. She didn't add that another fence had been cut. Nick had just phoned the house on his cell phone to tell her about it. He and the two part-time boys were still out there, waiting for her.

"In the middle of the day?" Judd asked, scowling as he checked the watch on his wrist. "We came to have lunch with you."

"You can have it with Maude," she told him, moving to swing gracefully into the saddle. "I've got work to do."

"Why aren't you in school today?" he persisted, bothered by her lack of animation.

"My math teacher had a sick child, and my English teacher canceled classes to go to a funeral."

He noted the rifle and scowled. "Why are you packing a gun?"

She gathered the reins close in her gloved hands and glared down at him. Tippy was standing close at his side. Too close.

"I always carry a rifle," she said. "The men spotted a wolf," she lied.

"You can't shoot it," Judd said shortly. "It's against the law."

"I do know that," she replied tersely, "but I can shoot at its heels and frighten it off if it threatens the cattle." Her face was flushed with bad temper.

"Have you eaten?"

Heavens, he was persistent. "I had breakfast," she told him. "I don't usually eat lunch anyway. I've got to go."

She turned the horse, without acknowledging or even looking at Tippy, and rode off before he had time for another word.

"I don't like this," he muttered. "Something's up. She's not herself."

The model clutched his arm and forced a smile. "I really could eat something, Judd," she said. "Come on. Teenagers have these mood swings. I did, when I was her age."

"She's twenty years old. Almost twenty-one."

That was a shock. Tippy had thought the woman was a lot younger. It altered her perceptions of her rival. The ring she was wearing had hurt Crissy. She shouldn't care, of course...

"That's still not very old," Tippy added. "She's at the age where she can get over things easily," she said, more for her own benefit than his. "Come on. Feed me."

He was watching Christabel ride away, and he felt empty. She hadn't met his eyes. She hadn't smiled at him. And why would she need a rifle? In fact, why was she riding fence alone?

He wanted answers. The minute he got Tippy back to the location set in town he was going to get them out of Christabel.

Crissy found their foreman Nick, and Brad, one of their three part-time men, kneeling beside a bull in the pasture where the new fence had been cut.

Fearing the worst, she swung out of the saddle and knelt beside the bull. It was a Hereford bull, but the best one she had. It was dead.

"Damn it!" she cursed.

"I'm sorry," Nick told her. "I thought these bulls would be safe. I should have known better."

"It's not your fault, Nick. But this time, I'm getting answers. I want a vet out here, right now, and a blood sample taken. If this bull was poisoned like the others, I want proof. I'll quit school and get a job to pay him if I have to."

"I'll phone the vet right now," Nick assured her.

She patted the young bull's head and could have cried. She'd had such hopes for him in their new crossbreed program. He looked so helpless, so vulnerable, like that. Involuntarily, she remembered what Judd had told her about the human murder victim.

She got up and went to the fence, checking where it was cut. The method was the same on the two previous cut fences. The same person. She sighed with helpless fury. Someone was trying to put them out of business. It had to be Jack Clark. But how in the world was she going to prove it?

Nick got off the phone and came back to her. "The vet said he'll be over about five. He'll phone me when he's on the way. We should get photos of the cut fence," he added. "I saved the other wire, just like you asked. That should be photographed, too. And you should tell Judd, or at least the sheriff's department," he said firmly. "It isn't safe for you to be riding out here alone, now, even with a rifle."

She knew he was right, but it hurt to admit it. Not that she was going to do what he said. "I'll get one of the men to ride fence with me from now on," she lied convincingly.

"Good." Nick walked with her to her horse. "I'll get some film and use the bunkhouse camera to get photos of the carcass."

"Judd has enough on his plate right now with the investigation he's got going up in Victoria. I don't want him worried about us as well."

"He owns part of the ranch," she was reminded firmly. "He has every right to know what's going on."

"I told him what was going on weeks ago, and he wouldn't listen," she replied shortly. "He thinks I'm making it up, that it's a bid for attention. Besides, he's so wrapped up with that red-headed model that he doesn't even hear me..." She swallowed. "Sorry. He's got a lot on his mind. So have I."

Nick studied her with compassion, but he was worried, and it showed. "If he asks me, Crissy, I've got to tell him."

She shrugged. "Do what you have to, Nick. But not unless he asks. Deal?"

He smiled. "Deal."

"And I want to know what the vet finds."

"Sure thing."

She turned the horse and rode back toward the ranch. But

halfway there, she dismounted under a spreading pecan tree and sat down under it. No way was she going back home until Judd and his girlfriend finished lunch and went away. It had started out to be a bad day, and it just kept getting worse, she thought miserably.

CHAPTER SEVEN

By the time Crissy got home, unsaddled her mount and gave the rifle back to the cowboy she'd borrowed it from, Judd and Tippy were gone.

Maude was in the kitchen, muttering about the clutter of equipment she was having to work around.

She turned around from the sink when Crissy walked in. "Hiding out, were you? I wish you'd had the kindness to take me with you, instead of leaving me here."

"Was it bad?"

"Bad!" The older woman put a dirty pan in the dishwasher. "She ran you down like a runaway tanker. She's got Judd convinced that you're pouting because he's paying her a lot of attention. She thinks you're totally immature."

"I think she's a pain in the butt," Crissy said curtly, tossing her hat aside before she sprawled on a chair at the kitchen table. "He bought her an emerald ring. From the look of it, it had several diamonds, too."

Maude scowled. "He bought it for her? With what?" she exclaimed. "He doesn't have that kind of money."

"He probably bought it out of his savings," she said miserably. "And what could I say, even if I knew for sure? It isn't fair that he has to spend every penny he makes to keep this place going!"

"Oh, baby," Maude said, grimacing. "I'm sorry. I saw the ring, but I had no idea... Are you *sure* he bought it for her?"

"She said he did. I'm not about to go ask him, if that's what you mean. I'm already in his bad book because I wanted Cash to teach me how to shoot a pistol."

She hesitated. "He doesn't like Cash."

"He says there are things in Cash's past that he can't tell me," she agreed. "But I'm not planning to marry him. He's my friend."

"I think he'd like to be more."

Crissy smiled sadly. "I'm married. Not that it matters to anybody else."

Maude grimaced and started the dishwasher. It made a pleasant churning sound in the silence of the kitchen. "She doesn't know that."

"What difference would it make if she did?" Crissy asked philosophically. "Women like her don't recognize obstacles. She can have any man she likes. She told me so herself," she added with a wicked smile.

"Not Cash Grier," Maude countered.

Crissy laughed, but not wholeheartedly. "At least one man isn't taken in by that poisonous smile."

Maude looked at the younger woman worriedly. "Men will always look at something beautiful. But how many men would want to marry a face that every other man covets? How could he be sure that she'd be faithful to him?"

"If she loved him, she might."

Maude huffed. "She loves baubles, and she can't get past her own assets to notice anybody else's. You watch her," she added firmly. "She'll cut you out with Judd any way she can, and she's vindictive."

"Judd doesn't want me to begin with," Crissy said on a sigh.

"He never did." She discounted that long, lingering kiss. It had been, after all, only a point of comparison for her. It wasn't as if he'd followed it up. Then she remembered the strange, quick kiss in the SUV when he'd brought her home from lunch in town with Cash. She still didn't understand it. But then, Judd wasn't himself lately.

"Where did you go this afternoon?"

"To see my dead young Hereford bull," came the sad reply. "I'm pretty sure he was poisoned, like our young Salers bull. The fence was cut, just like the other two."

"And you haven't told Judd?" Maude exclaimed.

"You know he'd think I was making it up," Crissy said simply. "Tippy Moore would help him think it was just another plea for attention."

"Not if Nick backed you up."

"He'd say I put Nick up to it. No. I have to have proof this time."

Maude bit her lower lip. "Child, this is getting very dangerous. You shouldn't be riding out alone, even with a gun."

"You and Nick!" Crissy exclaimed irritably.

"We're both right, and you know it!"

She exhaled slowly. "I'll tell Cash Grier," she said finally. "He's the one person who'll believe me without reservation."

Maude hesitated. "Judd owns half the ranch."

"I know that, Maude," she replied. "But this is just a dead bull. He's investigating a murdered pregnant woman, and it's hard for him."

"It would be, for a minister's son," Maude agreed. "He was a sensitive boy. He's learned how to hide all that since he grew up, but it's there just the same. Maybe the model keeps his mind off the ugliness he has to see."

"Maybe she does," Crissy said noncommittally. "Could you feed me something?" she added wistfully. "I didn't even get breakfast."

"Of course I can. What do you want?"

"Soup."

"I'll get a jar out of that canned beef soup I made last summer out of the pantry, and make you some corn bread to go with it," Maude said, smiling.

Crissy sighed and leaned back in her chair. "Comfort food," she murmured to herself, and then laughed at her own whimsy.

Before Judd got back to the ranch to question Crissy about why she was avoiding him, Leo Hart phoned her with some information about the herd sire of her Salers bull. He told her that the man from Victoria who bred them, Jack Handley, had fired the Clark brothers and lost his prize Salers bull and all four young bulls it had sired to mysterious causes. When he heard about Christabel's bull dying, he had one of his dead bulls autopsied, and poison was found. He checked and found a pattern of cattle theft and retribution with the Clarks that went back two years. At least four employers had talked of similar problems with them. The Clark brothers were suspects in the death of Handley's bulls, but they had alibis. John had been in Jacobsville visiting his brother, and they had a witness, a man named Gould, who swore they were with him at a rodeo during the time of the poisonings. In fact, Gould worked for Handley and had a reputation as a hard worker who never made trouble.

She told Cash about it, on one of their fishing afternoons in the pay-and-fish trout pond outside town. It was a hobby they both shared—and good eating, when they caught anything. The pond stayed open until the end of October, which it almost was. The afternoons were cool and sunny and pleasant this time of year.

"Leo said he tried to tell Judd about it, but he was in a hurry and didn't have time to listen," she said as they sat with their feet dangling from the dock and watched their corks float.

He glanced at her, straightening his line. "Have you had any more trouble?"

She shook her head. "I know the Clarks are guilty. I just wish I could prove it."

"We had a tip about a black pickup truck with a red stripe, one like Hob Downey saw parked near your fence, in connection with the murder in Victoria. But we checked every ranch in Jacobsville and we didn't find a single one that matched it. If it was the Clarks, maybe they ditched it after Downey saw it."

The vet had confirmed that poison had been used on her Hereford bull. Crissy had told Cash, but she still hadn't told Judd.

He searched her eyes for a long time, and then looked back toward the lake. "If they did poison your livestock, we'll catch them sooner or later."

"We ought to ask Hob if he's seen that black pickup truck anywhere since then," she commented. "He might have remembered something more, too."

"Have you talked to him about the latest bull that was poisoned?"

"No," she confided. "The Hereford bull wasn't kept in a pasture near his place. He couldn't have seen anything."

"Suppose we stop by there on the way back to the ranch and talk to him anyway?"

She smiled. "If we catch two more fish, we can share with him. He does love a nice pan of trout. He and my dad used to fish together."

"You don't talk about your father much."

She drew in a long breath. "When he was sober, he was a wonderful man. But the scars are deep—physically as well as emotionally. It hurts to remember sometimes."

He only nodded, but his face was expressive.

Half an hour later, they packed up their six fish in an ice-filled chest and drove down the highway to Hob Downey's little cabin.

His old beat-up truck was still parked where it had been the day Crissy had ridden up to talk to him. She frowned. He usually drove into town to get groceries at least once a week. Odd that he'd have parked in exactly the same spot. Either that, or the truck hadn't been moved. And something else was odd. The front door was closed, but the screen door was standing ajar. Hob always kept it closed, so that he could open the wooden door without having one of his cats rush in by him.

"That's strange," she murmured as they got out of the truck. "He never leaves the screen door open like that..."

Before she finished the sentence Cash, who was several feet in front of her, tried the wooden door, found it unlocked, and opened it. He stopped abruptly and his whole body stiffened.

"What's wrong?" she asked.

"I think you'd better wait here."

She scoffed at that. "I'm no lily," she murmured, following right along behind him to the open door.

There was a smell, a very sickening, sweet smell. Crissy had never smelled it before, and she gave it only a passing thought as she went into the living room where Cash was standing.

The sight that met her eyes was so horrible that she gagged. She turned and ran back onto the porch and lost her breakfast and her lunch, hanging over the porch railing like a limp rag while tears of shock and outrage and grief poured down her white face.

Absently, she heard Cash calling for an ambulance, the coroner, and a crime scene technician from the Department of Public Safety. She also heard him add a call to the Texas Ranger station in Victoria, temporarily located in the sheriff's office there.

Cash got her off the porch and to his truck. He opened the passenger door and seated her on the running board. Seconds later, he handed her a silver flask.

"Don't smell it, don't think about what it is. Just drink it," he said firmly, holding it to her mouth.

She took a long swallow, choked, and cried some more. Cash drew her head to his chest and held it there, smoothing her hair, uttering words she didn't really hear.

The ambulance came, followed by a sheriff's deputy. The coroner arrived five minutes later. Yellow police tape was stretched all around the front yard and the house.

"Why are they doing that?" Crissy asked Cash.

"Because until they can perform an autopsy, any suspicious death is open for classification," he said quietly. "He might have had a heart attack or a stroke, but it could just as easily be a homicide. There was a crowbar next to the body, and the hyeloid bone in the throat was broken," he added professionally. "They'll go over the house with fingerprint tape and document every single clue they can collect, right down to fingerprints and footprints and trace evidence on his clothing."

She gaped at him. "Who'd want to kill poor old Hob?" she exclaimed.

He held her hand in his. "He saw a pickup truck and two suspicious men at your fence," he reminded her.

"Oh, for heaven's, sake, it was only a cut fence, they didn't even steal anything," she exclaimed. "Nobody could prove who it was, and even then, it's not murder or anything!"

He didn't say anything. His eyes were narrowed in on the house where all the activity was located. After a minute, he left her and went to talk to the medical examiner.

A while later, Judd arrived in his SUV, along with the crime scene technicians in their van.

Cash went to meet them. Judd glanced toward the truck where Christabel was sitting and hesitated, but Cash motioned him up onto the porch. They went into the house with the other law enforcement and medical people, and it was several minutes before they came back out.

Christabel had taken three large gulps of brandy from Cash's flask. It had steadied her, but she didn't think she could ever close her eyes again without seeing what was left of poor old Hob Downey. He'd obviously been dead some time, considering the condition of the body. She barely recognized him now.

"Christabel."

She heard Judd's deep voice as if through a fog. He turned her white face up to his concerned eyes and studied it.

"Shock," he told Cash grimly. "She's never seen anything like this. I'm going to run her to the hospital and have the resident check her out."

"You are not," she said huskily. "I'm all right."

Judd actually winced. "That isn't a sight you should ever have been exposed to," he said harshly, and glared at Cash.

"He tried to stop me," she defended the older man. "I wouldn't listen." She got to her feet, a little unsteadily, and handed Cash the flask. She took a wobbly breath.

"What's in that?" Judd asked Cash, indicating the flask.

"Orange juice," she told Judd firmly. "It can't be brandy, because I'm underage, and Cash wouldn't break the law on my account."

Judd knew Cash had, but the circumstances were extreme. It was no time to split hairs. "All right. Cash, drive her home. I can't leave until the guys from the state crime lab finish." He looked as if it was killing him that he had to let her go with Cash.

Christabel stared at him. "It's a homicide, isn't it?" she asked in a hushed tone. "You think somebody killed him!"

His eyes narrowed. "I'm having all the angles checked." He exchanged a long look with Cash. "Once evidence is lost, it can't ever be regained. Get her out of here, Cash."

She started to argue and Cash hesitated. Judd walked right around Cash, picked her up gently, and put her back into the pickup truck, strapping her in. She could feel the heat from his body at the proximity. She felt safe. She wanted to climb into his arms and hold on tight. Then she remembered the ring he'd given Tippy. He'd never given her anything so personal. He never would. Her sigh was audible.

He saw that expression on her face and frowned curiously. His big hands held her arms firmly. "You stay with Maude until I get there, baby," he said in a tone so tender it made her want to cry. "Don't leave the house, and try not to think about what you've seen."

She felt the pain all the way to her soul. "You have to look at things like that all the time, don't you?" she asked.

He nodded slowly.

Her hand went to his hard mouth and pressed there, gently. "I'm so sorry," she whispered. Her voice broke and she bit her lower lip to steady herself.

His chest rose and fell heavily. "So am I." He pulled the palm of her hand to his mouth and kissed it hungrily. "I'd have cut off my arm to keep you from having to see that!" he ground out.

"It's all right," she said huskily, and managed a smile. "I can handle it. You just go out there and get the guy who did it, okay?"

He took a deep breath. She had grit. He smiled back. "You're one tough customer, Christabel Gaines," he murmured. "Okay, tiger. I'll catch the perp. You go home!"

She grinned, despite her pallor. "Okay, boss!"

He smiled grimly. "I'll see you later."

He turned without another word and went back up onto the porch of the house.

Cash climbed in beside her and buckled his own seat belt, with a quick glance at her face. "You're game, Crissy Gaines," he said with pride. "Most other women would have screamed or fainted. You just threw up."

She managed a wan smile. "I'll bet you never have."

"You'd lose." He started the engine and pulled out into the road. "The first homicide I worked as a rookie cop was in a locked house in the summer. There were three victims—a double homicide and a suicide, and the victims had been in there for a week. I actually passed out." He gave her an affectionate grin. "You can't imagine what it was like to have to go to work the next day."

"I can, too. I learned from Judd that cops have really quirky senses of humor on the job."

He laughed. "They do. I found a dead squirrel in my locker, a dead squirrel in my patrol car's trunk, a dead squirrel hanging from my apartment doorknob when I got home—needless to say, I never let them see weakness again."

"Neither will I," she replied firmly, wrapping her arms around her chest. "The first time is always the hardest, isn't it, with anything?"

"Yes." He glanced at her. "But you can live with it. You can live with a lot. It's just getting used to it."

She leaned her head back against the seat. "You think Hob was killed, don't you, Cash?"

He was quiet for a minute. "I don't think anything right now. Like Judd said, we want to do a thorough job of investigation, just in case." He glanced at her. "But for the time being, you don't go riding fence alone, even if you do carry a gun along."

She nodded. She didn't meet his eyes. Judd would have made her promise. Cash didn't know her well enough.

"Feeling better?" he asked.

"Yes. I was thinking about medical examiners," she lied. "Judd's best friend, Marc Brannon, is always joking about one of the medical examiner's assistants up in San Antonio, a crime scene technician named Alice Jones who has a rather quirky sense of humor."

"Dear old jab-him-in-the-liver Alice," Cash chuckled. "Everybody knows her. She's a local legend."

"How do you look at things like that, day after day, year after year?" she wanted to know.

"It goes with the job description. You try to think about the victim, not about how you react to looking at him or her. You think about finding the perpetrator and putting him away, so that he can't do it again. If you're lucky, you don't have to see things like that too often." He sighed. "But some guys can't handle it, especially the ones who are the most affected and refuse to admit that it bothers them. They think they should be above squeamishness over anything connected to the job. Officers like that—and officers who are involved in fatal shootings—sometimes just can't deal with it. A lot of them quit the job afterward. A few others become alcoholics or suicides."

She nodded. Judd had told her all that, too. She glanced up at Cash. "You don't drink."

He shrugged. "Occasionally. Never enough to lose control."

"Neither does Judd."

He smiled slowly. "Judd's one of those hard cases who can't admit weakness. He's never killed a man. In fact, I don't think he's ever had to shoot anybody."

"He shot a man in the leg who was trying to knife another officer, when he was on the Jacobsville police force. The man lived and didn't even limp afterward."

"Lucky Judd."

She studied the hard face across from her. "You've killed men."

His whole body stiffened. He didn't look at her.

She wanted to say something else, something comforting. But he looked like stone. She moved restlessly, embarrassed at having said something so blatantly personal.

Her eyes turned to the landscape passing by. "Hob doesn't have any family."

"The county will take care of the funeral expense, I'm sure," he said after a minute. "He'll get a decent burial, at least."

"Poor old man. He didn't have anything much. Do you really think somebody would kill him just because he saw them cut a fence?"

"I don't know. But no matter what, at least he died quick. He didn't linger."

She sighed. "I hope so. I really do."

Judd stopped by the house on his way back to Victoria. Christabel was in the kitchen with Maude, smiling and helping with bread and pie-making.

"I'm fine," she assured him. "No need to worry about me."

He hesitated, his black eyes narrowed on her face. She was still a little pale. "When did you last see Hob?"

"About a week ago," she said, and then remembered why she couldn't tell him what was discussed on Hob's front porch.

"Was he well?"

"Just like always," she said, glaring at Maude, who was about to say something. "I even told Maude that he looked better than ever, didn't I, Maude?" she added pointedly.

Maude grimaced. "Yes, you did. Poor old fellow. He was a kind soul."

"If you're okay, I'll get back to work," he told Christabel. "You still look shaken."

She managed a smile for him. "That would shake anybody."

"Probably so. Stay close to the house for a while. Let Nick and the boys do the outriding."

"Whatever you say, Judd," she agreed pleasantly.

He gave her a long stare. "I mean it." His eyes narrowed thoughtfully. "Promise me," he added deliberately.

She thought for a minute. "I promise I'll stay close to the house."

"All right."

He gave her a last look, nodded to Maude, and went out the back door.

"Liar," Maude grumbled at her.

"Some of the fence lines *are* close to the house," she replied. "Besides, I'll have to help Nick and the boys check for other breaks. We're shorthanded since Larry quit and Bobby went back to school part time. I'll tell Cash," she promised.

"If Judd finds out..." Maude groaned.

Two days later, Crissy rode to the pasture where they'd put one of four remaining young Hereford bulls. They'd split them up, hoping it would deter any more poisoning. She carried the borrowed rifle again, and Cash's cell phone in a holder on her belt. He'd made her take it, and told Nick to stay close to her around the ranch. Nick couldn't do any more with her than Cash did. And this time, she almost paid the price.

Just as she rode past a huge oak tree near the fence, a man stepped out into her path.

She had good reaction speeds. By the time he was in position, she had the rifle out of the sheath and cocked. She didn't point it at him, but it lay across her blue-jeaned legs and her eyes told him that she'd shoot, given the least provocation.

"You gonna shoot me, boss lady?" Jack Clark drawled, eyes narrow as he stared up at her from the dirt path.

"The second you make a move toward me," she nodded, and she didn't blink.

"I saw you coming this way from the road," he said, nodding toward the highway which was only a few hundred feet away. "I want you to stop spreading rumors about me in Jacobsville," he added in a cold tone. "I didn't steal anything from you. I bought a pair of boots because I tore one of mine up when I was haying with that old tractor you use. You owed me those boots!"

"And if you'd come to us and asked, we'd have replaced them," she replied, feeling scared and sick but determined not to let it show. Her hand tightened on the rifle. "You didn't. You bought the most expensive pair you could find and had them charged to the ranch."

"No cause to fire a man without giving him a hearing." He was giving her a look that chilled her blood. It was the same look he'd given her when he'd worked, briefly, for her and Judd until he was let go in early September. He liked women, but none of them would give him the time of day. He had bad teeth, and an ugly attitude—not to mention a vulgar way of talking to women. He was a homely man, with sharp features and thinning hair, lean and mean-looking. His clothes were always rumpled, and his hair looked as if it was never washed. He was the most repulsive person she'd ever seen. He was wearing a flannel shirt in putrid shades of black and green and yellow that looked almost as repulsive as he did.

"You had your say," she said flatly. She shifted the gun, pressed Cash's prekeyed number into the cell phone and stared down at him with cold deliberation. "You're trespassing. I want you off my land. Now. I've just put the assistant police chief's number into this phone. I only have to press a button and he'll know where I am and why I called."

He hesitated, measuring the distance between them. Even if she could send that number, response wouldn't come at once. At his sides, his fists clenched and he began to smile speculatively. He took a quick step forward.

In that split second, Crissy had the rifle shouldered and was looking down the barrel. "Safety's off," she said calmly. "Your move."

He'd stopped short when she put the rifle up. Now he hesitated again, as if measuring that distance a second time and weighing how quickly she could fire. But one look at her eyes told him what she'd do if he moved again.

His threatening stance shifted. "No call to try and shoot a man for asking a civil question!" he said angrily.

"My arm's getting tired," she said pointedly.

He cursed, a sharp vulgar word that was accompanied by the most disgusting leer she'd ever seen. "It wouldn't be worth it, at that. You're more boy than girl, even if you are blond. I'd rather have something pretty!"

"You'd be lucky!" she muttered.

"I had me a pretty, blond woman once!" he shot back, and then flushed. He turned on his heel and stomped back through the wooded area toward the highway.

"You'll pay, you little bitch!" he yelled back at her. "You'll pay good! I'll make you sorry you ever opened your mouth!"

Her hands were shaking as she put the safety on the rifle. She heard an engine rev up and she caught a glimpse of a battered old tan pickup truck as Clark drove past the path she was riding, laying down on his horn belligerently as he sped away. Definitely not a black truck with a red stripe, either, she noted.

She let out the breath she'd been holding. She put the rifle away and rode quickly back to the house. She wasn't surprised to find her heart beating in her throat like a drum.

She wanted to ask Maude for advice. It had been a scary few minutes, and she wasn't sure what to do next.

But Maude wasn't home when she got there. She made herself a cup of coffee and decided that this time she couldn't handle things alone. She unfastened Cash's cell phone from her belt. She pressed in the number of Cash's office and when it didn't ring, realized that she'd forgotten to push the send button. She pressed it, angrily, and waited for someone to answer.

Cash picked it up himself.

"Cash, could you come out here for a few minutes?" she asked in a ghostly tone.

"Are you all right?" he asked at once.

"Yes. Jack Clark was here. I had to threaten to shoot him."

There was a hesitation. "I know," he said after a minute. "He's here in my office, filing a complaint. He says you pulled a gun on him with no provocation. He wants you arrested."

CHAPTER EIGHT
CHAPTER EIGHT

Crissy didn't know what to say, what to do. She had visions of being arrested and locked up. Wouldn't that make Jack Clark's day, she mused unhappily.

She drew in a steadying breath. "Do you want me to drive into town and turn myself in?" she asked, only half joking.

Cash's voice was cold. "I do not. I'll handle this. See you in a few minutes."

He hung up. Crissy looked around her at the mess of equipment the film crew had left in place for their return, and she felt hopeless. Judd was going to be absorbed by the famous model. The ranch was going to go under from lack of operating capital and breeding bulls. She was going to prison. She laughed almost hysterically and wondered if she could sell her own story to the producer. It would make a much more exciting movie than his romantic comedy.

Cash looked smug when he walked into the living room. He was in uniform, handsome and completely unaffected by Clark's visit.

Crissy, on the other hand, was worried and pale. "Do you want to handcuff me?" she asked.

He chuckled. "No, I want coffee."

She went into the kitchen, leaving him to follow. "I'm not under arrest?"

"No." He sat down, waiting for her to pour coffee into two mugs. "Have you forgotten? You're four miles out of town. I don't have jurisdiction here. Clark knows it, too. He only wanted to shake you up, and he knew that you and I were friends."

"He won't let it drop," she said worriedly as she sat down beside him.

He caught her cold fingers in his. "I told him that any woman alone, faced with a threatening man, had the right to defend herself. Besides that, he was trespassing on private land, without permission. He was in the wrong. He didn't push his luck."

She sighed her relief. "I'll bet he didn't like that."

He studied her face quietly. "You're really frightened of him."

She nodded. "He's vulgar and offensive. He made blatant passes at me when he was working here."

"Did you tell Judd?"

She turned her mug in her hands. "It was too much like carrying tales," she said. "I thought I could handle it. I told Clark I didn't like suggestive remarks, and that he'd lose his job if he kept it up."

"Did it work?"

"I don't know, because that was just before he charged those expensive boots and we fired him."

"He has a record."

She stared at him. "What sort?"

"Sexual assault and battery on a very young teenage girl, when he was in his early twenties," he replied. "The girl almost died of her injuries. She reported him to the police and testified against him. He served six years."

"What happened to the girl?" she asked curiously.

"Her family changed their name and moved away. Nobody knows where they went."

"What about his brother, John?" she wanted to know.

"John never did anything that got him convicted. He was accused of poisoning livestock a time or two, but there's no record that he ever hurt a human being. Since Jack got out of prison, there have been accusations but no arrests, for either of them."

Crissy felt chills go down her spine. Her hands were icy around the hot mug.

"Did Judd ever get you that handgun?"

She blinked. Her mind was elsewhere. "He brought it down and left it with Maude."

"Get it. A pistol is a much better close-range weapon than a rifle."

She took the case it was in from under the kitchen sink and put it on the table.

His eyebrows lifted.

"Well, it isn't exactly the first place a thief would look for a gun," she defended herself.

He chuckled. He opened the case and took out the revolver. It was shaped like an old-time .45 colt, but it shot .22 caliber long rifle bullets. There was a box of shells in the case with the pistol.

"Okay, let's go."

"Where?" she asked, standing up.

"To the firing range. By the end of the day, you'll know how to handle this pistol, and I'll feel better about having you and Maude out here alone."

"I'll go, but we won't be very much alone after Sunday. The movie people are coming back," she said on a sigh.

"I'll be glad to have them here," he replied solemnly. "Clark's not likely to come after you with a crowd of people on hand."

"I hope not." She followed him out to the front porch. "Are you going to tell Judd?"

"I have to," he said curtly.

"But..."

He turned, his dark eyes quiet and worried. "The state crime lab had a preliminary report on Hob Downey. He was hit in the throat with a hard object, probably the tire tool we found near him."

She felt the blood draining out of her face. "I can't believe Hob was killed just because of what he saw when my fence was cut."

He helped her into the passenger side of the truck. "It's more complicated than that."

"How about Jack Clark?" she pressed. "He's the most likely suspect, isn't he?"

"He is. But he has an ironclad alibi for Downey's approximate time of death. In fact, he has an iron-clad alibi for the entire day."

She waited.

He got in and fastened his seat belt. "He was with a well-known local resident of Victoria, a city councilwoman."

"Is she a reliable witness?"

"She is, unfortunately. She told investigators that Clark came by her office and invited her to lunch. He said he wanted to talk to her about buying some land—she's in real estate. She took him to two different properties. It's curious, but it isn't illegal. So Jack Clark's not a suspect," he said heavily. "But don't worry. We'll find whoever killed old Hob."

"How about his brother, John?" she asked. "Does he have an alibi?"

"He was with a co-worker on that Victoria ranch where he works."

"I can't believe Clark tried to have me arrested," she said, rubbing her arms.

"You need a sweater," he pointed out, noting her long-sleeved chambray shirt over a T-shirt.

"I'm not cold. It's thinking of what might have happened if I hadn't had the rifle."

"I'm going to teach you to shoot a pistol today," he said, turning onto the highway. "It will be easier to use on a potential attacker than something as long as a rifle, that he could grab away from you. That takes care of the short term. But we still have to tell Judd about what's been going on."

"Why?" she asked worriedly. "The film crew will be here. You said yourself that nothing will happen with so many people around."

He glanced at her. "Judd has a right to know."

"I'm not telling him," she said stubbornly. "And that's that."

He didn't answer her. They went to the police firing range and she spent two hours pulling a trigger. She seemed to be a natural with a pistol. She was able to put all her shots within the approximate size of a man's torso. But the thought of actually shooting a human being made her sick at her stomach.

"That's why you're learning to shoot properly," Cash told her. "Then you can place your shots."

"What if I miss?"

He turned to her. "What if you don't shoot at all?"

She thought of Clark and the way he'd looked at her, the things he'd said to her. She swallowed her pride. "Okay. Let's try that again."

Her hands were sore when they finished, but she felt more confident. Cash promised to take her out at least once a week to the range and keep up her practice. She forgot that he hadn't promised not to tell Judd what was going on.

The film crew came back and chaos became normal again. Judd walked up behind her just as she was getting out of her truck after class one afternoon. He wasn't smiling, and his black eyes were homicidal.

She stared at him with resignation. "Cash told you."

"He told me. Something you should have done, long ago!" he gritted. "This ranch is half mine. I have a right to know if it's in danger—if *you're* in danger!"

"I'm not. I can shoot a gun..."

"Clark was right here on the property and you didn't know it until he stepped out in front of you," he interrupted furiously. "What if he'd had a gun, too?"

"He didn't."

"That's beside the point. You should have told me!"

"You wouldn't have believed me!" she raged back. Her dark eyes were blazing now, too, her blond hair in disarray from the wind. "You wouldn't believe me when I told you the bull had been poisoned. You said I was jealous of the attention you were giving the film crew! And you'd really have a reason to accuse me of lying now, you could say I was jealous of your fancy model!"

He drew in a slow breath. "I'd have believed a blood analysis done by a veterinarian," he said.

"Sure, as long as you weren't expected to believe anything I told you!"

"Cash knew everything." He made it sound like an accusation.

"Yes, he did. He isn't panting over Tippy Moore, and he'd take my word any day, for anything!" she added with pure venom.

His eyes narrowed dangerously and he stiffened. "Tippy is not your business. She has nothing to do with the ranch."

She wanted to ask him if he was sure about that, when he was spending money he didn't have to buy her expensive jewelry. But she didn't.

She gave him a hard glare before she turned away. "Clark won't sneak up on me again."

"That isn't good enough. Maude isn't always here, and you'll be away from the ranch for a time every day going to school."

"Cash gave me his cell phone," she added, producing it from her pocket to show it to him. "I can call him any time and he'll come."

The look on his face was difficult to assess. He wiped it clean of expression while she was trying to understand it.

"Make sure you've got one of the men along from now on when you ride fence, and carry the gun he's teaching you to shoot."

She stopped and turned. "Which man should I take along? Except for Nick, we only have three left, all part-timers," she said flatly. "Economy is becoming a religion around here. When I finish this semester," she added, "I'm going to quit school and get a job. I'm tired of wearing the same jeans for three years and not having enough cash to buy a single new dress!"

His high cheekbones went ruddy. He didn't say a word, but she knew he understood what she was saying. He didn't think she knew about the ring. But he knew that she economized everywhere, while he was spending his savings to buy expensive rings for his new girl.

"An education is..." he began.

"A luxury, under the circumstances," she returned, moving away. "The way I feel right now, we could put the ranch on the market and forget trying to make ends meet forever! I'm sick of struggling all the time!"

She went into the house in a blue fury. Tippy Moore had opened her mouth to speak and shut it instantly when she saw Christabel's furious dark eyes. She'd heard what was said outside, and she wanted to know more. But Christabel went to her room and closed the door. Judd got into his SUV and sped away without coming inside. Maude, caught between them, just sighed and made more coffee. They didn't need it, but she had to have something to do.

Of course, Crissy couldn't stay in her room forever. She came out for supper. Surprisingly, the film crew was still there, but about to leave.

Tippy Moore gave her a strange look, one that took in the age and wear of the jeans and blouse she was wearing, and the peeling paint on the door facings, and the yellow spots on the ceiling of the hall that indicated a leak.

"Did you want something, Miss Moore?" Crissy asked curtly.

Tippy sighed. "I didn't realize how hard things were for you here," she began.

"My ranch is not your business," Crissy replied tersely.

"It soon might be, though," came the slow reply. For good measure, Tippy turned the emerald and diamond ring. She was wearing it on her engagement finger.

Crissy felt sick all over. So Judd was considering marriage. Well, he'd better get the annulment first, she thought with black humor.

"Your crew is leaving," Crissy pointed out to the model.

"Oh, Judd usually takes me back to town," she returned, her voice almost a purr.

Even as she spoke, Crissy heard the familiar sound of the engine in Judd's SUV. She didn't say another word. She went into the kitchen and busied herself helping Maude fix potatoes, so that she wouldn't have to see Judd again.

Tippy went out to greet Judd, gathering his arm into both perfectly manicured hands. "I wondered if you were coming back. Miss Gaines has been in her room all afternoon pouting, after the argument you had," she added lightly. "My, my, she is frightfully immature, isn't she?"

He hesitated, but only for a second. He went out with Tippy, got in the vehicle with her and drove away.

Judd's visits after that coincided with Crissy's hours at school, and he knew her schedule quite well. It was the second week of November. Her birthday was Friday. In all the years she and Judd had been married, he'd made a point of taking her out to eat on her birthday and presenting her with some small present—usually something practical, like a program for her computer or an audio CD that she wanted.

They'd argued, but she didn't expect that he'd forget, even under the circumstances. She had just a little money put back for an emergency, but now she took it out and went to the local department store. If Judd could buy diamond and emerald rings for his girlfriend, Crissy was entitled to one new dress in two years. She bought a soft blue one that fell in graceful folds to her ankles from a tight waist and low-cut bodice. It had puffy sleeves and there was a big wispy scarf that matched it. She would wear her hair down, she thought, and put it up in curlers so that it would look perfect for her one night out a year with Judd.

But by Friday, she hadn't heard a word from him. In fact, she made a point of skipping class that day at lunch, so she'd have a chance to remind him that it was her birthday—just in case he'd forgotten. But he didn't come Friday. In fact, Tippy Moore didn't show up for work, either.

It was too much of a coincidence for Crissy. With a worried Maude standing nearby, she went right up to Gary Mays, the assistant director, and asked him point-blank where Tippy was.

"She's up in Victoria today, with Judd," he told her with thinly veiled sarcasm. "They were having a retirement party for one of the local law enforcement people, and Tippy volunteered to go with Judd. Bachelors in the department were doing cartwheels, last I heard," he added. "Tippy said Judd was delighted that she wanted to go with him."

"Thanks," Crissy said with a wan smile.

"He didn't say anything about Crissy?" Maude asked.

Gary was looking at the script with the continuity assistant. He scowled. "Why should he have?" he asked absently.

Crissy turned away. "There's no reason at all."

"Crissy," Maude began, full of quiet sympathy.

"I'm okay, Maude," she said and forced a smile. "He'll send me a card or something."

She went down the hall to her room without another word. She was furious and on the verge of tears. That model was ruining her life, her future, all her hopes. She could have thrown things. But what good would it do now? If Judd cared so much for Tippy that he'd forgotten Crissy's twenty-first birthday, there was just no hope left.

And it didn't take long to sink in that Judd didn't mean to take her out at all. He didn't even phone her to ask her plans for her birthday, or to wish her a happy one.

Grier drove up in his big pickup truck just before sundown on Friday, an hour after the film crew had packed up for the weekend and gone. He looked preoccupied, and he grimaced when Crissy came out to meet him on the long front porch.

She could see bad news in his face. Her own fell. "Okay, spill it," she said with a half-hearted smile. "I can see it's not something you're dying to tell me."

"Got any coffee?" he asked.

"Stalling won't help, but yes, I have some coffee. Come on in." She led him inside, and down the hall to the kitchen. "Maude's spending the night with her sister, so I'm cooking supper. Nothing fancy, just an omelette. Want to share?"

"I haven't eaten since eleven this morning," he murmured, pulling out a chair to straddle. "If you don't mind the company, I'd love to."

She smiled, and this time it wasn't half-hearted. "I'll make cinnamon toast to go with it."

He smiled back, although it looked more like a grimace. He didn't have much practice smiling in recent years. It was still difficult, even with Crissy.

He waited until they finished the short meal before he spoke. Crissy had just poured them both second cups of coffee and he'd put cream in his, stirring it far too long with the spoon, when she propped her chin on her hands and stared at him pointedly.

He frowned. "Okay, here it is, straight from the shoulder. Judd's taking Tippy to the retirement party in Victoria tonight. I thought you should hear it from me before somebody else let it slip."

"Oh, I already knew, Cash," she replied. "The assistant director told me."

He sighed heavily. "I'm sorry, kid," he said gruffly.

"It's the first time in five years that he's forgotten my birthday. I bought a new dress, just to wear out tonight. I'm twenty-one today," she said slowly.

"You are?" he asked, surprised. "And Judd went off with Tippy?"

She laughed. "I suppose he forgot. He's spent so much time with her lately...you'd never guess he was a married man, would you? Of course he wouldn't want to take me to any retirement party," she rationalized. "I'm just a kid, like you said. He'd want someone pretty and sophisticated and famous to show off to his friends, not a country hick of a tomboy who has trouble knowing which utensil to use."

"You're no country hick," Grier said forcibly. "Listen here, don't you take this personally. I imagine he thinks he's keeping it from you, that you won't find out." He crossed his long legs and leaned back in the chair with his coffee. "Maybe I shouldn't have told you. Maybe you wouldn't have known otherwise."

"You don't think Tippy wouldn't enjoy rubbing it in when she comes back with the film crew next week?" she mused. "At least now, she won't hit me with it when I'm not expecting it."

"If you'd like to go, I'll take you," he told her with a wicked smile. "I used to work with the guy who's retiring, and I was invited, too."

She smiled back. It was tempting. But even if he played fast and loose with her heart, Crissy couldn't embarrass Judd that way, not after all he'd done for her over the years.

"No," she said, shaking her head. "I don't play that sort of game. I'm not really a vindictive person."

"I know that," he said curtly. "It makes it hard to hurt you."

She searched his handsome face with a grin. "You're a nice man, Cash Grier," she said softly.

He lifted both eyebrows and his dark eyes twinkled. "That's a new one. I guess I've been called everything else at least once."

"Well, anyway, since I'm twenty-one now Judd and I can get a quiet annulment next week, and nobody will ever know we were married in the first place. I get my half of the ranch," she continued doggedly, "he keeps his half, and he gets his freedom, so that he can marry his redheaded ideal woman."

Grier studied her surreptitiously and thought that, in Judd's place, his freedom would be the last thing he'd want. This little morsel had a heart as big as all outdoors and she didn't put on airs or play mind games. She was honest and brave and thoughtful. He was sorry there was such an age difference between them.

"Why do you look so morose?" she teased.

He studied her under narrowed eyelids. "I was wishing I was younger."

She smiled without guile. "Were you? Why?"

He laughed. She didn't have a clue about her own attractions. "Nothing. Just a passing thought." He checked the complicated watch he wore on his left wrist. "I've got a few things to do before quitting time at five." He frowned. "You said Maude had gone to her sister's. Who's staying in the house with you?"

"Nobody, of course. But Maude will be back first thing tomorrow."

He didn't like that. It was careless of Judd, especially after the threats made by Jack Clark.

"You're worried," she said. "Why?"

He was reluctant to tell her, and it showed. "Jack Clark has sworn in front of at least one witness that he intends to make you pay for pulling a gun on him."

"Wasn't trying to have me arrested enough?" she asked facetiously.

"It isn't funny, Crissy," he replied.

"No, it isn't, but right now, it's just another drop in the misery pool," she told him. "My life isn't coming up roses, lately."

"I want you to be paranoid about locking doors and windows at night, even when Maude's here. If any strange vehicle comes up in the yard, make sure you know who's in it before you go rushing out. Keep that pistol handy. The film crew's due out here again next week, right?"

"Right. Bright and early Monday morning. I'm sure Tippy Moore can't wait to rub my nose in her evening out with Judd on *my* birthday," she said with a heavy sigh.

"You do have ranch hands around here, don't you?"

She felt her knees go weak. She'd never had to worry about intruders before. It was an old Victorian house with long, low windows and not much security. She eyed the gun on the table. "Right now, we have three part-time cowboys," she murmured, "and Nick, our foreman. Judd hired him." She looked up. "He worked for the Georgia Bureau of Investigation just out of college, before he moved to Texas, and he's a dead shot."

"Good. That relieves my mind, a little. Will they all be around this weekend?"

She blinked. "Some of them. Nick, definitely. He never goes off much."

Cash didn't look convinced. He finished the last swallow of his coffee and stood up. He took out a card, flipped it over on the table, pulled a pen from his shirt pocket and wrote a number on the back. He slid it across to Crissy.

"That's my other cell phone number. I keep the second phone with me all the time, and it's never turned off," he added solemnly. "If you need me, day or night, you call me. Even if I'm off duty, at the very least, I can have the Jacobsville police out here in three minutes flat, if it takes me a little longer to get here. Okay?"

She felt touched by the gesture. She knew Grier had a reputation as a man who didn't make friends easily. In his new position as assistant police chief in Jacobsville he was already making enemies at city hall with his hard-nosed attitude toward drug offenders. But Crissy adored him. He was like family. He'd already done more for her than anyone except Judd.

She smiled at him warmly. "Thanks, Cash," she said softly. "I really mean that."

He walked to the front door with her trailing his footsteps. He opened the door and turned, silhouetted against the dusk. "Happy birthday, Crissy," he said gently, and bent to touch his hard mouth to her cheek. "I'm sorry it isn't going to be a happier one."

She smiled up at him. "There are a couple of new movies I've wanted to see for a long time. I think I'll treat myself to the show."

"Alone? At night?" He hesitated. "Listen, you can't go out alone. I haven't been to a ballet in years," he said abruptly.

"There's one in Houston. I can get tickets at a minute's notice. Take me along on your birthday outing. I'll buy you supper, too."

Her face brightened. "You're serious? You don't have plans for tonight?"

He burst out laughing. "I don't have plans for any night," he confessed. "I have a hard time...with women, these days. I've got too many rough edges to suit most of them."

Her eyes softened. "No you don't. I love going out with you, even just fishing or having a hamburger in town."

The change in him was surprising. He almost flushed. He cleared his throat. "Well, okay, then. We'll go to the ballet and you can wear your new dress. I'll pick you up at five-thirty."

She smiled from ear to ear. "I'll be ready!"

He stopped on the steps and turned around again. "If you'd rather see a play, I'm game."

"Oh, but I've never been to a ballet!" she protested. "I'd love to see one!"

"Never?" he asked, aghast.

"It never came up," she said weakly, realizing how unworldly she was.

He pursed his lips. "Then the ballet it is. There'll be a symphony orchestra playing for it. Culture is important. It connects us to the past."

Her eyes twinkled. "I thought rodeo was culture," she teased.

He chuckled. "In some circles, it's the only one."

She smiled. "Thanks, Cash!"

He shrugged. "Can't let a nice young woman like you turn twenty-one and not celebrate, can we?" And he was gone.

So, instead of staying home and eating her heart out because Judd didn't want to take her out on her twenty-first birthday, she dressed for Grier instead. When she looked in her mirror, she had to admit that she didn't look too bad. The soft blue dress emphasized her nice figure in a conventional way, and she had the pretty wispy blue scarf to drape over the puffy sleeves that held up the low-cut bodice. The high heels arched her pretty feet at an alluring angle and she liked the cut of the dress, which came to her ankles. It was perfect for the ballet. She wore her hair up in a sophisticated topknot.

What made her saddest was that Judd hadn't even called to wish her a happy birthday. She checked the answering phone's unblinking front every few minutes, to make sure she hadn't missed a call. She thought about picking it up and listening to the dial tone, to make sure it was working, but that would be just too juvenile. If he wanted to ignore her most important birthday, let him. She'd go out with Grier and have a very nice time.

It amused her, and pleased her, that a man like Grier would be willing to spend a boring evening with someone like her. She didn't doubt that he could have gotten any woman he wanted to go on a date with him. He was very attractive, and unless she missed her guess, very experienced with women.

He showed up in exactly one hour, wearing a dark suit with his wavy black hair loose instead of in its usual pigtail and his mustache and the black goatee under his full lower lip perfectly trimmed. His hair came past his collar, neatly trimmed, emphasizing his muscular neck. He looked very European like that, his olive complexion shown to its best advantage above the fine white cotton shirt and subdued blue patterned tie he was wearing. His black dress shoes were polished so well that they reflected the porch ceiling.

"Wow," she said softly, because she'd never seen him dressed up.

He smiled sheepishly. "Thanks. You're not bad yourself." His eyes punctuated the compliment, as they ran over her like an artist's brush. "Ready to go?"

"Just have to lock the door." She did, joining him at the steps.

"How about the windows?" he asked suddenly.

"All secure," she assured him. "I spent the afternoon making sure the locks were in place, and I reinforced them with some broomsticks I had one of the men cut to size for me."

"Smart lady."

She grinned. "Speaking of security, I hope you're packing, because I don't have anyplace to carry a gun."

"I'll second that," he chuckled. "You won't find a cop in the country who doesn't travel armed. Not in these times."

"That's what I thought."

"Judd holds the fastest time for the quick-draw in north Texas," he recalled. "Marc Brannon has it in south Texas. I've always wondered who'd win in a contest."

"I wouldn't want to be on the receiving end from either of them," she said as he helped her into the car. She didn't want to talk about Judd. It was taking all she could do to shut him out as it was.

"Did he call you?"

"No, he didn't," she said flatly. "Not that it matters."

Of course it mattered. She couldn't hide her disappointment. He started the big black truck. "We're going to have a great time," he told her. "They're doing *The Firebird* tonight. I got good seats, even at the late date, too."

"The Firebird?"

"Stavinsky," he said, "one of the modern composers. This is a ballet set to the music. Want me to fill you in on the way to Houston?"

"Would you?" she asked, genuinely curious.

He chuckled. "I'd love to."

The topic took them all the way to the theater where the event was held, and into the parking lot.

There were people dressed in everything from evening gowns to jeans and tank tops, so Crissy felt comfortable in her dress. She and Grier had seats right down front, and the beauty of the production held her breathless, like the sensuous score provided by the orchestra.

She caught Grier watching her once and grinned at him. He grinned back, pleased that she was enjoying the ballet.

She watched the ballerinas in their exquisite costumes flying across the stage to the music, into high lifts and pirouettes on their toes, in the changing colored lights. It was awesome. She'd never seen anything quite so glorious. It was, as she told Grier later, like watching a Degas painting come to life.

CHAPTER NINE

CHAPTER NINE

The lights were all on in the ranch house when they drove up, and Maude came out on the porch to meet them.

"It's your night off!" Crissy exclaimed.

Maude looked worried. "Yes, it was, but you weren't here and the phone wasn't working. When Judd couldn't get in touch with you, he called me and asked if I'd run over and check on you. I only just got here..."

She wondered vaguely why the phone wasn't working. "Cash took me to the ballet in Houston to celebrate my twenty-first birthday," Crissy explained, clinging to his arm with a grin. "We had champagne and supper at a four-star restaurant. I had beef Wellington, Maude!"

Maude chuckled. "Well, well. That was nice of you, Mr. Grier."

"Nice is my middle name. Ask Crissy," he added, teasing.

Maude smiled. "I'll just check the phone again before I go back to my sister's. Crissy, you can leave the porch light on for me when you come in," she added with a wicked grin. "No rush!"

Crissy's heart lifted. At least Judd was worried for her, even if he hadn't been worried enough to come himself. How could he disappoint Tippy, after all, she thought irritably, and leave the gorgeous model standing so that he could rush down to Jacobsville to see about his soon-to-be-ex-wife?

"Don't brood," Grier chided, tapping her on the cheek with his forefinger. "You know he cares about you. If he hadn't, he wouldn't even have bothered to call."

"It's habit. He'll get over it very soon, when we're annulled." She sighed and looked up at him with a speculative smile. "I'll be a free woman in no time. Going to kiss me good-night?"

He pursed his firm lips. "I've been thinking about that. I'm not sure it would be a good idea. I mean, what if I turn out to be addictive?"

Her eyes shone like rain-wet chestnuts in her radiant face. "I love taking chances. Come on. Be daring."

He knew almost certainly that Judd had kissed her. But unless it was the alcohol talking, she seemed to think of kissing as a game. He looked at her mouth and weighed the advantages and disadvantages. But the fact that she was still married to Judd made him hesitate.

He drew her to him, gently, and bent and touched his hard mouth to hers without passion. His heart raced. She tasted like heady wine. But he could feel her lack of response. For her, sparks didn't fly. There was no music. He felt vaguely disappointed as he lifted his head and saw the reality of her response in her smile. She wasn't even shaken.

"Thanks for making my birthday special, Cash," she said softly.

He recovered quickly. "What are friends for?" he teased. "Sleep well. If you need me, you know how to call me, right?"

"Right."

He searched her eyes and smiled. "I had a good time. I'm glad you did. Good night."

"Good night." She stood on the porch and watched him drive away before she went inside and locked the door and turned out the porch light.

Maude came into the dining room, somber and quiet. "Judd should have taken you out, on such a special occasion. Your twenty-first birthday!"

"Judd didn't even phone to wish me a happy birthday, Maude," Crissy told her bluntly.

"He didn't remember that it was your birthday. I didn't have the heart to remind him when he called me. He was very upset when he couldn't reach you on your cell phone. I called and told him you were okay a few minutes ago." She smiled. "He wasn't pleased to hear you'd been out with Grier again," she added with a satisfied look.

"Like I care. At least I had somebody to celebrate my birthday with!" she replied, her eyes clouded with anger. "Like my dress?" she indicated it, twirling around. "I bought it to wear to go out with Judd tonight."

"My poor baby." Maude stared at her with compassion.

Crissy's chin lifted proudly. "I'm no baby. Not now. I'm a grown woman, and I'm going to start acting like it. No more mooning over a man who'll never want me. Especially when there's one who does!"

Maude didn't comment. She only smiled, sadly.

The next morning, Christabel was feeding a foal in the barn when she heard a vehicle pull up outside in the dirt road. She glanced toward the entrance when a door slammed, just in time to see Judd coming toward her.

Her heart jumped into her chest and started racing. He was so good to look at. She couldn't remember a time in years when that long-legged, easy stride of his hadn't triggered excitement. He was wearing his Ranger uniform, including the star and the .45 automatic in its hand-tooled holster. Atop his dark hair, the creamy Stetson was tilted at a rakish angle across his black eyes. All that was immediately visible of his lean face was his straight nose and thin mouth and square jaw.

She was immediately aware that she was wearing ripped

jeans, mucky boots and a faded green checked blouse with a button missing. Her hair was part in and part out of her neat braid and she didn't even have lipstick on. Trust Judd to show up the minute she looked her frumpiest, even if she shouldn't care. The hurt was still fresh that he'd forgotten her birthday and instead had gone on a date with another woman.

Her face closed up when he was near enough to see it. She turned her attention back to the foal.

"Out chasing crooks, Mr. Texas Ranger?" she asked.

He shoved his hat back on his head, his black eyes glittering down at her.

"What's this about you going to Houston with Grier?"

She lifted both eyebrows and stared at him as if he'd gone crazy. "I've been going places with Cash for weeks, didn't you notice?"

"Just around town, not on elegant dates to Houston," he said flatly. He hesitated, uncertain of his ground. "Maude told me about the ballet," he said flatly. His thin lips made a flat line across his tanned face. "Then Grier mentioned it to me when I stopped by his office this morning."

"I like him," she said, dark eyes flashing.

It was a declaration of war, and he took it like one. "Grier's thirty-eight," he pointed out. "He has a mysterious past. He's too worldly for a sprout like you."

"I said, I like him," she repeated calmly. She finished giving the bottle to the foal, patted him, and went out into the aisle, closing the gate behind her.

"You heard me."

She didn't look up at him. It would have been fatal, and she had to keep her resolve. "You've spent five years taking care of me. I appreciate all you've done for me. I know it was a sacrifice, in a lot of ways," she continued, as she cleaned the bottle at the rusty sink and put it on the shelf. "But I'm almost through school and even you have to admit that I know what I'm doing around here. I can keep books as well as you can. I can buy and sell stock. I can hire men." She turned and forced her eyes up. It was an effort. "It's time I took on full responsibility for my half of the outfit. I have to start standing on my own two feet, and you have to let me."

"When you're twenty-one," he began doggedly.

She took off the signet ring he'd put on her finger five years before, caught his big, lean hand in hers, and tucked the ring into his palm, closing his fingers around it. "I won't need this anymore. I turned twenty-one yesterday," she said with as much dignity as she could muster.

His expression was priceless. "What?"

"I was twenty-one yesterday," she repeated, her eyes flashing fire at him. "While you were showing off Miss Supermodel at your party in Victoria, I was being wined and dined by the man who's too worldly for me! He bought me a beautiful supper, with champagne to toast my coming of age, and took me to see *The Firebird* in Houston!"

His face was like stone. He winced. "Christabel..." he said softly. "I'm sorry!"

She shrugged and averted her eyes, pretending that her heart wasn't breaking. "Don't sweat it. I had a wonderful birthday. But you can go ahead and get the annulment anytime you please. Just don't expect me to sit home and wait for it." Her eyes flashed up to his. "If you can date while we're still married, then there's no reason at all that I can't!"

She started out the door of the barn, blond hair straggly, back arrow-straight.

Judd watched her with regret eating him alive. How could he have forgotten such an important date in their lives? He looked down at the signet ring that she'd worn so faithfully for the past five years, and he felt guilty. He'd always taken her someplace on her birthday, given her little presents.

He remembered that ring that Tippy had talked him into buying her, and he felt sick. At least Christabel didn't know about that, he consoled himself.

He slid the signet ring back onto his little finger and stared at it blankly. She'd said that he could go ahead and get the annulment anytime he liked. Was it because her relationship with Cash Grier was heating up? His eyes narrowed angrily. Well, she could wait for that annulment until he was ready. And he wasn't. Not yet.

The guys in Victoria knew he was acquainted with Tippy Moore and they'd asked him as a special favor to bring her to the retirement party. He'd done it, without thinking. Tippy liked him and hung on him all the time. He was flattered that a woman that beautiful, and that famous, found him attractive. But there was a curious thing about her. She touched him, from time to time, but she didn't like being touched. She was ice cold to men who flirted with her, men who showed their enthusiasm for her face and figure. She adored lawmen and always made time to speak to them, whatever the reason. Judd had noticed that she was actually uncomfortable around other men, and she kept close to him when they were together for any length of time— like on location in town, and especially when that assistant director, Gary Mays, came close to her.

She was a puzzle. He found her pleasant company, and she stroked his ego. But he hadn't considered how it would look to Christabel, who was legally his wife, whether or not anyone knew. By taking Tippy around with him, he was encouraging Christabel to do the same thing with Grier.

He'd opened a door that he could no longer close, and it made him uneasy. He hated the thought of Christabel with Cash Grier, whose past was, at best, ten degrees off normal. The man was dangerous, lawman or not, and just by being with him, Christabel was taking chances. He had enemies.

On the other hand, she was in danger herself. Grier had read him the riot act this very morning about leaving Christabel alone at the ranch after her confrontation with Jack Clark, and the threats he'd made. He'd been negligent, on all counts, even by buying Tippy that expensive ring that he couldn't really afford.

She was used to rich men giving her anything she admired. He wasn't one.

He looked at the signet ring with sad eyes. He'd hurt Christabel, who'd spent the whole of their married life looking out for him and taking care of ranch business when he couldn't. He'd repaid that loyalty by making her feel insecure and valueless. Now she wanted an annulment, when he was just beginning to feel...

He clamped down hard on the thought. There was no future for him with her. He had to think ahead, to an annulment. Immediately after came the thought that Cash Grier was trying to settle down and that he was very interested in Christabel. If he was thinking in terms of marriage, he could think again. That annulment could wait. It could wait a long time.

Tippy Moore came back to work the next Monday, and her first words to Crissy were about the great time she had with Judd in Victoria at the party.

"I'm so glad," Crissy returned easily, and with a big smile, "because I went to the ballet in Houston with Cash, and we had dinner and champagne in a five-star restaurant. It was a night to remember."

Tippy's triumph fell flat. That was her sort of routine evening. She hadn't known that Cash Grier was so cultured, or that he had the kind of money that could afford such an expensive outing. Apparently the little country girl there didn't realize how expensive it was, either. Judd's idea of gourmet cuisine was a fast-food hamburger and fries. She was very fond of him, of course, and his job made him a rarity, a collectible, in her world. But she'd learned quickly that he wasn't wealthy. Well, it wasn't his money or lack of it that impressed her, she told herself, it was his profession. She felt safe with him. She was safe with him, safe from other men—men like Cash Grier, who was a real threat.

"I didn't realize a hick policeman would know what a ballet was," Tippy muttered.

"Cash has an interesting background," Crissy said. "He was a Texas Ranger, too, and he worked for the government."

Tippy looked uncomfortable. "Does he know which fork to use?" she asked sarcastically.

"He taught me," Crissy said. "A lot. It was a nice celebration, for my twenty-first birthday," she added deliberately, and coldly. Crissy felt better, even if Judd's rejection did still hurt.

Tippy averted her eyes. She hadn't known that. She felt guilty, God knew why. Certainly the other woman had a crush on Judd and would have wanted to be with him on her most special birthday. But it was no concern of hers! She turned slowly and went back to work.

The annual Cattleman's Ball was held the Saturday before Thanksgiving, and Cash had already invited Christabel to go with him. She was delighted not to have to stay home that night, too, while Judd showed off his fancy model at the ball. She knew Judd wouldn't take her. They were hardly speaking at all now, to Maude's dismay.

Grier, with his hair down below his collar, dark and faintly waving, freshly shaven and wearing a suit, was striking. Christabel was proud to be seen with him. At least, she thought miserably, she still had her pretty blue dress to wear, and nobody in Jacobsville had seen it. She didn't feel as dowdy and out of fashion as she had only the year before.

Judd didn't even look her way. He came in late with the redhead, just in time to watch Christabel and Grier on the dance floor. Good thing most people didn't know she and Judd were still married, Christabel thought, because he would have raised eyebrows everywhere with Tippy Moore on his arm, even if they hadn't been. She kept her eyes on Grier and smiled as if she hadn't a care in the world.

He cocked an eyebrow after the band wound down the slow melody they'd been playing and, after Matt Caldwell had a whispered conference with the bandleader, the band broke into a Latin medley.

"Are you game?" Grier asked her.

Her eyes widened. "You bet!" she laughed, remembering the fun they'd had doing it at Shea's.

He chuckled as he drew her onto the dance floor, where Matt and his wife were the only occupants so far.

"Okay," he murmured, marking the rhythm. "Let's show 'em how!"

He turned her into the rhythm and the rest was magic. Even Matt Caldwell raised his eyebrows as the couple flew across the floor to the throbbing drums and quick melody.

Christabel was laughing with pure joy. She'd never had a partner who could do these dances until Cash came along. She'd wished and wished that Judd would take her to a dance, any dance, just once, and let her show off. Well, she was, now. Even if it wasn't with him, she was having the time of her life. Her breaking heart succumbed to the delicious rhythm of Latin musical fire.

By the time they wound down, she could hardly breathe. She sagged against Grier, who wasn't even breathing hard, and laughed delightedly to the cheers and applause of the other guests—including the Caldwells.

"Remind me to take you up to Houston to a Latin dance club I know," Grier told her as he escorted her off the floor. "We'll shame them out the door!"

She grinned up at him. "You're great!" she exclaimed.

"Takes a good partner," he replied with a shrug, but his eyes twinkled.

Judd Dunn was glaring at the two of them for all he was worth. Beside him, Tippy was glaring, too.

"She likes to show off, doesn't she?" she said cattily. "I guess he does, too."

He wouldn't have mentioned for the world that he'd never seen Grier dance before. He'd never seen him smile much, either. It annoyed him that he was doing both with Christabel.

"Silly to make such a spectacle of herself in front of the whole town," Tippy continued.

Judd looked down at her darkly. "Can you do Latin dances?"

She averted her eyes. "What has that got to do with anything?"

He noticed that Christabel was standing very close to Grier at the punch bowl, and then he got a look at the older man's face as he looked down at her bent head. It caused something to explode inside him. Grier was a good law enforcement officer, he was steady and calm in the face of danger, and he was afraid of nothing on earth. But he was also a man, and Christabel was still an innocent. Judd felt protective of her. Possessive of her. He didn't want Grier hitting on her.

"Excuse me," he told Tippy, and walked over to join Grier and Christabel.

"Aren't you dancing?" Grier asked him dryly, and he was suddenly holding Christabel's hand tightly in his big one.

Judd's black eyes narrowed. He didn't smile. "I thought you had to be in Dallas Monday morning, early."

"I do. I'm flying out tomorrow afternoon." Grier smiled lazily. "Do you have a problem with that?" he added very softly, and with a visible threat in his eyes.

It was a challenge. Judd's eyes narrowed. "Maybe I do," he said in the low, quiet tone that made ranch hands go very still.

Christabel didn't understand what was going on, but she knew it was explosive. She let go of Grier's hand and caught Judd by the sleeve.

"I want to talk to you for a minute," she said firmly, and started toward the side door that led out onto the patio just as a waltz filled the big room and Harley Fowler led Janie Brewster onto the dance floor.

Judd was surprised enough by the unfamiliar assertiveness to go along, oblivious to Tippy's black glare as they went outside.

In the faint light from the long windows, Christabel turned to Judd. "What's the matter with you?" she asked curtly. "We're getting an annulment, Judd. I have every right to go out with Cash. I haven't said a word about you and Tippy Moore, have I?"

No, she hadn't. It had irritated him. For years, she'd been possessive about him, teasing, vamping him, hinting about red negligees. Now she was worlds away, and with Grier, of all the damned men in the world...!

"Grier eats kids like you for breakfast," he said shortly. "He's lived in the shadows most of his adult life, working for secret government agencies..."

"How exciting!" she enthused.

"Listen to me!" he bit off. "He's killed men..."

Her eyebrows arched. "And your point is?"

His lips made a thin line and he exhaled shortly. "He's not a cuddly pet you can keep inside and feed up," he continued doggedly. "He's a renegade, a wild card. He's not housebroken."

She lifted both eyebrows. "And what makes you think I want to keep a man for a pet?" she asked with a pleasant smile. "Now that I am twenty-one, I'm free for the first time since I was sixteen—to date and do what I please." She searched his exasperated face with a curious painful pleasure. "I've never been able to experiment. Before," she said huskily, with her hands deliberately shaping her full hips, her lips parted, her eyes come-hitherish.

The one soft word set him off unexpectedly. He caught her around the waist, dragged her into the shadows, and riveted her soft body to his powerful lean one.

"You damned, irritating little flirt...!" he bit off against her mouth.

The shock of the kiss was electrifying. He'd rarely ever touched her, and if he had, it had been tenderly, with absent affection. The only serious kiss she'd shared with him had been the first time she went out with Grier. This was something else. He was rough with her, as if he wasn't in control at all. One big, lean hand smoothed down to the base of her spine as his mouth devoured hers. He pushed her into the curve of his body and she felt again that hard, insistent pressure against her belly, a pressure she'd felt once before, when he was showing her what a pushover she could be with Cash.

She gasped under his mouth, giving him the opening he wanted. His tongue thrust hard and deep past her open lips. He'd never done that before! Her short nails bit into his upper arms as odd, throbbing pulses shot through her lower body. She'd never felt anything like it. She shivered helplessly as a hot tension pulled her muscles tight and made her feel swollen all over. There was nothing tentative either in his kisses or the hold he had on her body. He meant business. She was too hungry for him to hold anything back. She gave in completely, trembling as she met his experienced passion with fierce enthusiasm.

He dragged his mouth from hers finally and looked down at her with narrow, cold eyes in a face as hard as stone.

She could barely see him. Her eyes were misty. She felt dazed, shocked, dizzy. Her hands let go of his arms and pressed into the white of his cotton shirt, smoothing over it helplessly, feeling his strength.

He was off balance, too, and determined not to let it show. He pushed her away with a faint shove and stared down at her arrogantly. He was almost vibrating with passion, but he kept it carefully hidden. Except for the quick throb of his pulse, nothing showed on the surface.

"Hell, no, you aren't free to experiment," he told her flatly, his voice deeper than usual, but just as harsh. "I haven't even started proceedings on the annulment yet. You keep that in mind. If you 'experiment' with Grier, you're committing adultery!"

She put her fingertips to her swollen mouth. Her mind spun crazily. "You said you were going to file for an annulment the day I turned twenty-one!"

"I haven't yet," he told her icily. "It never occurred to me that you'd be so hot to shack up with one of my friends—especially not a man Grier's age!"

"He's only four years older than you are!" she accused in a choking tone.

"If I'm too old for you, he damned sure is," he returned at once. "When the annulment goes through, I'll tell you. Until then," he added in a tone that was curiously possessive, with eyes that ate her slender figure, "you belong to me."

The way he said it made her knees weak. She hated her inability to think up a snappy reply. She couldn't even pretend to be amused. Her mouth was hot and swollen, like her young body. She was aching for something. She was hungry, empty. Her lips carried the taste of him, masculine and spicy and minty, with an undertaste of whiskey. She could smell his aftershave on her face. She was drowning in unfamiliar longings. She wanted to step close to him and feel his body respond to hers as it had when they kissed. She wanted his mouth hard and hungry on her lips again. She wanted to feel his skin against hers...

"On paper," he added when her lack of response to the statement made him uncomfortable. "After the annulment becomes final, what you do is no concern of mine. Ever again."

He turned on his heel and walked back into the hall, leaving Christabel standing alone in the darkness with her heart on the stone floor.

She'd only started back in when she saw Judd going out the door with Cash. Apparently there was some trouble between Leo Hart and Janie Brewster as well, because they were going out the same side door that Christabel and Judd had just come back in from. She heard later that Janie and Harley Fowler had held the crowd spellbound with an impromptu waltz.

Grier and Judd came back in, and soon afterward, Judd took Tippy Moore home. She argued, from the look of things, but he was determined. Grier wouldn't tell Christabel what was said between the two men. But he was grinning when they left the hall at midnight.

CHAPTER TEN

CHAPTER TEN

Things were peaceful around the ranch after the Cattleman's Ball, because Judd and Christabel weren't speaking. The film crew broke late Tuesday so that everyone could spend Thanksgiving at home. Even the famous model apparently had family somewhere back east, because she went, too. Christabel had expected Tippy to stick close to Judd during the holiday.

Since she and Judd weren't speaking, Christabel assumed that she and Maude would have the house to themselves. Judd did turn up on Thanksgiving morning, though, silent and preoccupied. Missing Tippy, Christabel thought wickedly. She was polite to him, but that was all. Maude glared at both of them while she and Crissy worked in the kitchen.

"Some Thanksgiving this is," she scoffed. "With the two of you like wrestlers squaring off and looking for a better hold."

Judd glared at Christabel. She glared right back.

Maude threw up her hands and started working on her pumpkin pie.

They ate in a companionable silence. Judd had halfheartedly watched the Thanksgiving Day parade, but without any real interest. He was still brooding about the murder case and the lack of suspects. He was worried about Christabel as well, especially since Jack Clark had actually come onto the ranch to confront her. He'd confronted Nick, and the man had told him about the cut fences as well. Too late, he believed her about the poisoned bull. He should have listened, and not dismissed her worries as childish fantasy. Now they had two poisoned bulls to deal with, as well as a murdered neighbor.

He was worried because there weren't enough men around the place to keep a proper eye on things. Their foreman, Nick, was good, but he'd been away from law enforcement for several years and his senses weren't finely honed by day-to-day work situations, as Judd's were. Christabel could shoot a gun, true, but what if Clark invaded the house in the middle of the night, when she and Maude were asleep?

"Could you try a little harder to make my Thanksgiving miserable?" Maude asked both of them after a particularly long silence. "I mean, if you're going to do a job, do it right."

They looked shamefaced.

"The turkey is just right," Christabel offered.

"And the dressing is out of this world," Judd agreed.

Maude looked vaguely placated as she dug into a second helping of mashed potatoes.

"Have you had any luck finding Hob Downey's killer?" Christabel asked abruptly.

Judd glanced at her and shook his head. "Jack Clark was my best suspect. His alibi is ironclad."

"That's what Cash said."

He put down his fork, hard. His black eyes blazed. "If you could just manage five minutes without mentioning Grier to me...!"

She put down her own fork and glared back at him. "He's my friend!"

"Listen..." Maude began.

"He's a black ops survivor with the staying power of a jackrabbit! He'll never be able to settle in a small town!"

"...if we could just get along..." Maude continued.

"What do you know about settling anywhere?" Christabel demanded fiercely. "And just how long do you think your high-society redheaded companion would last here? Or can you really see her pushing a grocery cart around the local supermarket?" she added.

"Stop it!" Maude interrupted. "Stop it, stop it! I am not refereeing a prize fight over my perfectly cooked turkey!"

They stopped in midsentence and stared at her. She was standing now, with her arms folded and her mouth making a straight line.

They glanced at each other and picked up their forks with resignation.

Maude sat down.

"Why should I expect her to settle down here in the first place?" Judd muttered, half under his breath.

Christabel chewed a small piece of turkey. "Because she's wearing that diamond and emerald ring you bought her on her engagement finger, and she says our business is now her business, too," she told Judd through her teeth. "So, when's the wedding?" she added sarcastically.

Judd didn't say anything. Maude was looking at him as if he'd grown horns. Christabel was still chewing. She didn't look up. Pity. His face was a classic study in guilt.

He put his fork down and got up, wiping his mouth on his napkin before he put it gently on the table. "I have to get back up to Victoria. Happy Thanksgiving." His voice was as subdued as the regretful look he sent over Christabel's bowed head. She still didn't look up. Grimacing, he glanced at Maude, who was still glaring, and walked out the door, without dessert.

It wasn't until the SUV was moving away that Crissy sipped coffee and looked at Maude.

"I didn't know about it being an engagement ring," Maude muttered.

"She didn't tell you because it wouldn't hurt you," Crissy said coldly.

"He didn't think you knew about the ring, did he?" Maude guessed.

"Well, he does now," she said coldly. She got up and started arranging empty dishes and aluminum foil on the counter. "Cash refused my invitation to join us for Thanksgiving so I'm taking supper to him later."

Maude wanted to say something, but she wasn't sure what would be appropriate. Crissy was hurting. Probably Judd was, too. She didn't know why he'd bought the model that expensive ring, but she was sure that he regretted it, and that he hadn't wanted Crissy to know. Perhaps he hadn't expected Tippy to tell her. Men were like that, Maude thought wistfully, so blind to the real nature of women when they had a perceived rival.

"If he doesn't file for an annulment soon, I'm going to," Crissy added as she filled a plate. "Let him marry her. He'll find out pretty quick that *she* won't sit around for five years waiting for him to notice her!"

Maude winced. "Baby, Grier is a lobo wolf. He isn't marriage material."

She looked at the older woman curiously. "Marriage material? Cash is my friend. I really like him. But I wouldn't want to marry him or anything."

"Judd thinks you would." She sighed. "And Grier hopes you would."

Crissy's eyes widened. "You're kidding."

Maude shook her head. "You haven't seen the way he looks at you. Judd has. It's why he's suddenly started being hostile to a man he used to consider a friend. He's jealous, Crissy."

She felt her cheeks go hot, but she turned back to her chore. "Sure he is. That's why he bought her an engagement ring and took her out for the evening on *my* birthday and didn't even get me a card, much less a present!"

Maude wished she had a good excuse for that. She didn't.

* * *

Neither did the man driving hell for leather back to Victoria. Judd felt sick at his stomach. He hadn't realized that Tippy would broadcast the fact that he'd raided his meager savings to buy her that expensive bauble. Certainly he hadn't wanted Christabel to know. She'd gone without luxuries for so long, just to keep the ranch working. She'd sacrificed even her youth for it. He'd repaid her by buying expensive presents for a woman he barely knew, and forgetting Christabel's most special of birthdays. She was bitter and hurt, and he couldn't blame her. Looking back, his own actions shocked him. No wonder she was turning to Grier. Damn the man, he had everything going for him when it came to attracting women. He could do intricate Latin dances, and he was cultured. He was in a league of his own as a womanizer, something Christabel didn't know. Or did she?

He hit the steering wheel with the palm of his hand, furious at his own inability to interpret his turbulent feelings. Taking Tippy around flattered his ego. He'd attracted a woman that any bachelor would die to escort. But it was taking a toll on his private life, and his professional one. He knew that she wasn't the sort of woman who could live with his job and his lifestyle, even if she'd been physically attracted to him—which she definitely wasn't. She was used to luxury and life in the fast lane. Funny that she hated Cash Grier, when he was exactly the sort of man she needed.

But Grier wanted Christabel. He could see it every time the older man looked at her. He was smitten. He'd marry her in a heartbeat if she was free. She didn't seem to know, but Judd did. His lips made a thin line as he considered the possibilities once he put his signature on a legal paper. Her conscience wouldn't slow her down when she wasn't committed to their paper marriage.

He could already picture Cash Grier down on his knees brandishing a wedding ring. Well, Christabel could go whistle for her annulment! It wasn't going to happen. Not yet, at least. After the new year, they could reassess their positions, when tempers cooled.

Right now, he still had two murders to solve around the area, and no viable suspects. But he knew the murder of the Victoria woman and the brutal death of Hob Downey were connected. It would make things easier if he wasn't also worried about the poisoning of the cattle he co-owned with Christabel, and her discovery of poor old Hob Downey's body. He knew the Clarks had been linked with cattle poisonings before. So despite their ironclad alibis, he couldn't dismiss the Clarks as his prime suspects. But he knew better than most people how dangerous circumstantial evidence could be. He was angry at Jack Clark for the confrontation with Christabel. At least, that's what any impartial outsider would make of any accusation coming from him. If only there was just one shred of physical evidence that would lead them to either of the brothers. But, to date, there wasn't any.

He thought back to Thanksgiving Dinner and felt miserable that he'd let himself fly at Christabel like that. It was the mention of Grier. She couldn't have a single conversation without dragging the man's name into it. If only there were some way to get Grier out of Jacobsville for good! But he hadn't a clue how to accomplish it. Nor did he realize, then, why he even wanted to do it.

Crissy had Thanksgiving supper with Grier and then went home and phoned the Harts. Leo wasn't home, so she tried Rey Hart. She was curious about the Harts' Japanese connections, and their interest in overseas markets. Rey was marketing vice president, and nobody knew more than he did about opening up new avenues of profit.

"I wondered if you and Judd might be interested in this opportunity," Rey replied when she asked about the visiting dignitaries. "Cy Parks was, too, but he's already contracted his cattle for the next year, and so have the Tremaynes. Your steers would be perfect, if you're interested. You're like us, you raise organic beef. That's just what our contacts want for their restaurant chain in Osaka and Tokyo."

Her heart skipped. "Does the market pay well?"

He chuckled. "It pays very well indeed," he said. "Especially now. Japan suffered some losses in its own beef resources last year. Now it's starting again. They're looking for stud cattle as well as prime organic beef. This is the best time to form alliances." He quoted her a price and she had to sit down.

"Oh, that's just extraordinary," she said heavily. "We've been selling at a loss for so long now...!"

"Tell me about it," Rey replied. "Interested?"

"Yes! So will Judd be, when he hears about it."

"Suppose the two of you come over here tomorrow about one and meet with our guests? They're staying with Corrigan and Dorie."

"Could we possibly do it Saturday? I'm off from school tomorrow for holidays, but Judd has to work."

"Sorry, I forgot. Sure. Saturday at one. That suit you?"

"Yes! Oh, Rey, you don't know how grateful we are," she began.

"Everybody's having a hard time right now," he interposed. "Why do you think we're looking so fondly at overseas markets? We'll all be helping each other out. Which is what cattlemen—and cattlewomen—do, isn't it?"

She smiled. "It is. I wish we could do something for you."

"Well, you could..."

"What?" she asked eagerly.

"Bring Cash Grier with you. He's fluent in Japanese, as we aren't, and I'd like to have someone from our side translate as well as someone from their side, just to make sure we don't misunderstand anything."

She chuckled. "Cash would love it."

"Great! We'll see you Saturday at one, then."

He hung up and she ground her teeth together. She knew Cash would go if she asked him, but it wasn't going to make things easier with Judd. Still, if there was any hope of pulling their operation out of the red, this was it. It was like a gift from heaven.

She dialed Judd's number before she got cold feet. It rang several times, and she was about to hang up when she heard his deep voice on the other end.

"We've got a marketing opportunity," she said quickly.

There was a pause. "What sort?"

She outlined the Harts' deal, and the profit to be made, and then waited for him to answer.

"I don't speak Japanese," he began.

"Neither do I. But they have translators," she added, mentally praying that she wouldn't have to mention Cash and have him blow up in her face again.

He made a rough sound. "Grier speaks it fluently. We might take him along and let him translate. If you can talk him into it," he added with thinly veiled sarcasm.

"The Harts already did," she prevaricated. "They want to make sure they understand all the details."

"Oh." He seemed to relax. There was another pause. "About dinner," he said slowly. "I didn't mean to jump down your throat like that."

He never apologized. This was as close as he was ever likely to come. She smiled to herself. "Me, too," she said stiffly. "Happy Thanksgiving."

"Yeah." There was another pause. "Would you marry Grier?"

Her heart jumped. "Excuse me?"

"If he asked."

She couldn't make her mind work. The question was completely out of left field.

"Forget it," he said abruptly, when she hesitated. "It's none of my business, once the annulment goes through. I'll see you about twelve-thirty Saturday."

"Okay, I'll be..."

He hung up.

She glared at the phone and put it down. He was the most exasperating man she'd ever known. But at least they were speaking again.

* * *

Grier agreed readily to accompany them, but he went in his own vehicle. Judd drove Christabel over to the sprawling Hart ranch in his SUV. He was wearing his work clothes, to her surprise.

"I'm on a case," he told her. "I asked off just long enough to do this, but I have to go right back."

"Another murder?" she asked.

He shook his head. "The same one. We think we may have a lead. There was a witness who saw a suspicious truck hanging around outside the woman's house."

"Did she live in town, in Victoria? "

He shook his head. "She and her husband had a little ranch outside the city limits. We're trying to find out if the Clark brothers ever worked for them."

"I wouldn't be surprised if they were involved somehow," she said.

He scowled intently. "Don't mention this new development to anyone else. Period."

She wanted to tell Grier, but that look was intimidating. "Okay. Nobody else. Right."

He turned his attention back to the road. "Things may be looking up after all."

"If we can make this deal, they certainly will," she replied. "Imagine a price like that for exporting our beef to another country, when we can't even give it away here!"

"It's a minor miracle, and we needed one."

She almost bit her lip through not agreeing with him. The ring he'd bought Tippy was eating into the very marrow of her bones. The lack of operating capital was a real threat, and Judd had compromised the ranch with that sparkly gift. He had to know it, without being told.

"Rey says these gentlemen are very nice, and honorable businessmen," she added before he had time to wonder at her silence.

"He'd know. The Harts are savvy businessmen. They know a good deal when they see one." He glanced at her curiously. "Did Rey call you?"

She shook her head. "I'd heard these businessmen were going to be out at their ranch, hoping to buy organic beef. It seemed the right thing to phone the Harts and ask if we could get in on their deal." She flushed. "I didn't think about how pushy it sounds until just now."

"It sounds like competent business thinking. If I had fewer murders to contend with, I might have thought of it myself." He changed the subject. "Have you heard from Joel Harper about when the film crew's coming back?"

"Yes. He said they'd be back December 4," she replied tersely.

His black eyes met hers before they went back to the road. "Christmas will be here before we know it," he remarked, thinking about the pretty pearl necklace and stud earring set he'd bought her for a combination late birthday and Christmas present. It was pure gold with pink pearls, her favorites. She was going to love it.

She stared out the window. "So it will." She was wondering if the beautiful supermodel had plans for him that would include that holiday. But she couldn't afford to let him know her worries. He didn't want her. She wasn't throwing herself at him.

He pulled up at the Hart ranch office building and cut off the engine. She jumped down from her side just as Cash pulled up next to them in his pickup truck. He was in uniform, obviously working today.

"I hear I'm in demand as a translator," he teased Crissy.

She grinned back at him. "You just translate us a good deal, and I'll recommend you to anybody you like."

He chuckled.

Judd turned away from both of them and went toward the office.

The Japanese corporation executives were charming and highly intelligent. Both of them spoke English, although the nuances of idiom and Texas drawl were formidable opponents of real understanding.

Cash spoke the language with a fluency that brought delighted smiles from the Japanese, even from their two translators. He seemed right at home, down to the custom of bowing instead of shaking hands, and knowing exactly how to phrase questions without offending.

"Mr. Kosugi would like both of you to be his guests in Osaka in January," Cash told Christabel and Judd. "If you agree, he'll assign one of his staff to help you with arrangements, meet you at the airport, and conduct you around Osaka. When you see his facilities, and meet his family and staff, you'll sign a formal agreement."

Judd scowled. "That's an expensive trip, Cash," he began.

"This is our, how do you say it, treat," Mr. Kosugi told them with a smile. "It is the way we do business."

Judd was still scowling. "I work in law enforcement," he began.

"Yes, you are Texas Ranger," the older gentleman said excitedly. "We read about you Rangers, and watch American movies of Texas."

Judd smiled. "Yes. So I can't accept gifts."

"You can make me a gift of two tickets," Christabel said easily. "I will take him with me to Japan."

"Christabel," Judd began.

She drew him to one side and glared up at him. "We're still married, for the moment," she said forcefully. "What I own, you own. If I get two tickets, I can give one to anyone I like, which includes you. Even your boss can't complain if your wife gives you a present. All you have to do is ask for personal time off, to go with me."

He hesitated. He glanced at Grier, who was watching with great interest. It occurred to him that Grier would be an even better travel companion for her, because he also spoke Japanese. His eyes began to burn. He looked down at her. "All right. I don't like it, but I'll do it."

"It isn't as if Mr. Kosugi is going to ask you to rob a bank for him or do personal favors for him, either," she pointed out. "This is ranch business, Judd. And if we don't go, there isn't going to be a ranch for much longer."

He couldn't argue with that. He wanted to, but she was right. He hated the thought of giving up his uncle's legacy and her birthright because he was too stubborn to admit she was right. Neither could he admit that his extravagance had hurt them even more.

"I'll go," he said heavily. "But," he added firmly, "I'm going to tell my boss the circumstances first."

She smiled softly. "I can't imagine you being less than honest with anyone," she replied.

His heavy brows drew together. "I haven't been honest with you," he said slowly.

Her cheeks flushed. She averted her face and all the old bitterness came back. "Your private life isn't my concern anymore, Judd. Let's just concentrate on the ranch."

She turned and went back to the others before he could say another word.

The weekend, and the following week, came and went, and in no time, the film crew was back. Crissy glared at Tippy Moore for all she was worth when she got home from school, especially when Judd showed up at the end of the first day of filming to drive Tippy to her hotel. It was the same old thing, all over again, just when Crissy had hoped that she and Judd were finally starting over, with the Japanese deal. Fat chance, with the Georgia Firefly on the job. She was still wearing the damned ring, too.

Crissy threw herself into her studies and tried to ignore what was going on around her. She began to feel that the movie people were going to live with them forever, and her nerves were wearing thin.

Cash came by early one Monday morning a couple of weeks into filming, and the crew was just breaking for coffee and doughnuts when he pulled up in front of the house.

Cash was in uniform and he looked somber. Crissy's class for that day had been cancelled, and she was at home, trying not to get in the way. She went to meet him. She was in jeans and a sweatshirt, with her hair in a neat braid at her back.

"This is a pleasant surprise," she told him with a smile. "What's up?"

"Nothing earthshaking, but I need to talk to you." He drew her over to one side. "Have you heard what happened Saturday night?"

"No," she said, surprised. "I didn't go to school today because my teacher was sick, so I've been isolated from any news."

"It seems that Jack Clark made a pass at Janie Brewster out at Shea's Bar and Roadhouse, and knocked her around. He threatened her with a knife as well. I've got him in jail."

"Poor Janie," she said, shocked. "But how lucky for her that he's locked up. Lucky for me, too." She sensed there was more. "Who arrested him?"

"I did," he confessed, "after Leo Hart and Harley Fowler both had a go at him. The man is a martial artist, very competent. I used tricks I'd almost forgotten taking him down."

She was still savoring the news. She'd been a little afraid of Jack Clark. Now, she was safe. So was poor Janie.

"His brother John came down late last night to visit him in jail. He promised to get him a good attorney." He sighed. "He's going to have a little trouble with that. It seems he may lose his job in Victoria. God knows where he thinks he'll get the money for a trial lawyer."

"You look very worried," she pointed out. She moved closer, wary of the redheaded supermodel hovering nearby. "What is it, Cash?"

He rested his hand on the handle of his .45 automatic in its holster on his duty belt. "Crissy, John Clark has a friend who drives a black pickup truck with a red stripe."

CHAPTER ELEVEN

It took a minute for the statement to sink in. Her breath sighed out roughly. "That's the truck old Hob saw near my cut fence," she recalled.

He nodded. "I just told Judd. That truck has been the missing link. We knew it had a connection, but we couldn't find it. Apparently it doesn't belong to Clark at all. It belongs to a buddy of his on the ranch he's working at, outside Victoria, a man named Gould."

"Can you arrest him? Can Judd?" she asked.

He grimaced. "It's not that simple. We can't arrest him without proof. The truck is the only lead we have right now."

"I heard Hob say what sort of truck it was," she fired back.

"Yes, but that's only hearsay. It's not enough evidence to arrest a man on suspicion of murder. We have to go slowly, and see if we can find enough evidence to get a search warrant," he told her. "If he suspects a thing, he may take off like a bird, even with his brother in jail."

She frowned and rubbed her arm with a restless hand. "Well, one Clark's off the streets for the foreseeable future. Isn't he?"

"Janie swore out a warrant for aggravated assault," he said.

"Harley Fowler and Leo Hart swore out assault charges as well. I got him on resisting arrest and assault on a police officer. But if his brother can get a good lawyer and he can make bond—well, it's a risk."

"For anyone who saw that truck or knew about it," she guessed worriedly.

"Don't look like that," Cash said huskily. "I'd never let anything happen to you!"

Her eyes met his and she noticed, for the first time, the emotion in them that he couldn't quite hide.

"It's the police, again!" Tippy Moore drawled from nearby, tossing her long red-gold hair for the benefit of any man in view. She smiled sarcastically at Grier. "You almost live here, don't you? Have you come to arrest somebody, or can't Miss Gaines manage a day without you in it?" she added nastily.

Cash's dark eyes slid past Crissy to the beautiful woman just joining them. "I'm gathering information for a homicide investigation. Unless you think you can solve the case, you're superfluous," he said curtly.

Tippy's perfect eyebrows arched. "Who got killed?" She glanced at Crissy, deliberately lifting her left hand so that the light caught the diamonds and sparkled wildly. "Someone Miss Gaines knows?"

"Certainly nobody you know," he replied flatly. "I'm pressed for time."

"Heavens, you don't think I'm trying to detain you?" she scoffed. Her eyes gave him a once-over that was just short of an insult. "I told her to tell you, you're not my type!"

His dark eyes narrowed on her face. Crissy thought she'd never seen eyes that cold. "A compliment, surely," he replied softly. He even smiled. "My taste doesn't run to your sort of woman, Miss Moore. I don't have to pay women to go out with me."

Tippy Moore's face burned red. She glared at him. "I'm no call girl," she managed to get out. "But if I were, buster, there wouldn't be enough money in the world to get you in my bed!"

"You've got that right!" he said icily.

Her small hands clenched at her sides. Her hair seemed to glow. "I've turned down motion picture stars and millionaires and even princes! What makes you think I'd look twice at a hick cop like you? I've already got everything!"

He cocked an eyebrow and gave her a look that would have eaten through rust. "What you've got, lady, is a pretty face and a passable figure. In five or six years, you won't find a fashion magazine that will even want to feature you in the advertisements. Then what will you do, when men who panted after you can't find enough excuses to get away from you?"

Obviously, she'd considered that herself, because she went pale.

"You have no apparent education, no manners, no culture, no consideration for other people. And you think a pretty face makes up for the lack of those attributes?" he asked. "Why don't you take a good look in a mirror? You're a lot less attractive to men than you think you are. And I've got your number, even if Judd Dunn hasn't yet."

"He gave me a ring," she said through her teeth. "He's crazy about me!"

"He's crazy, all right," he shot back. "You'd bankrupt him in two weeks and leave him bleeding on your way to a fatter wallet. You wouldn't even look back to see if he died."

"You know...nothing about me!" she choked.

"I know trash when I see it," he countered with cold eyes.

Her lower lip trembled. She looked devastated. She couldn't even manage a parting shot. She turned and walked shakily back to the set where the director was waiting, her back arrow-straight. But when she got to Joel Harper, she collapsed into his arms and cried like a child.

Cash's lips flattened. "Theatrics," he said harshly. "That woman is a prime manipulator. Judd's out of his mind if he thinks she cares about him."

"I know," she said sadly. But she felt oddly sorry for Tippy.

She'd never seen the poised, sophisticated woman in such a state. She'd been upset before when Cash was rude to her, but this time, she was genuinely devastated. Cash really did seem to hate her. Crissy wondered why his opinion was so disturbing to Tippy, when she seemed to dislike him just as much.

"I've got to get back to the office," Cash told her gently. "Watch your back. I've made sure Nick knows to help. Don't think Clark's less dangerous in jail. I've seen men in worse trouble make bond."

She sighed. "I'll keep my pistol handy. You be careful, too," she said with genuine concern.

He shrugged. "I've survived worse than the Clark boys," he said, and smiled. "See you later."

"Sure."

He walked off without another glance in Tippy's direction. But even with the competition the other woman gave her for Judd's attention, she couldn't help but feel bad for her. Cash had been brutal, and obviously his opinion mattered to the beautiful supermodel. Those tears had been real, even if Cash didn't think so.

While the crew took a break, to give Tippy time for the makeup artist to repair the damage tears had done to her face, Crissy waited outside the trailer until the older woman emerged.

"What do you want, to gloat?" Tippy asked bitingly.

"A model broke up his parents' marriage," Crissy told her quietly. "That doesn't excuse the way he is, but it helps explain it. He was in grammar school, and he loved his mother."

She started to walk away, but a soft hand touched her shoulder lightly, just distinguishable enough to stop her.

"I've been a bitch to you," the model said solemnly. "Why should you care if he cuts me up? In fact, what would you know about the real world, with your sheltered background?" she added bitterly.

Crissy met the beautiful green eyes evenly. "Do you think I live in some fairy-tale world of happy endings and perfect harmony? My father got drunk and almost killed me. My mother died. Judd and Maude are all I have in the world."

She turned away and this time she didn't stop. She probably shouldn't have told Tippy that, but what Cash said was cruel. He'd never apologize, with his history. Funny, she pondered, that she cared about seeing the model in tears. She'd done nothing but give Crissy hell, and taken Judd away to boot. But Judd cared about the dreadful woman, and there was no way Crissy would ever be able to hurt someone Judd loved.

Behind her, the older woman stood frozen, rigid, hating the compassion in that soft voice, the understanding behind it. She'd thought that little Christabel Gaines had the perfect childhood. It was a shock to learn the truth, and it made her feel guilty. She looked at the expensive ring on her finger and measured it against Christabel's ragged jeans and worn old boots. She went back toward the set with her pride around her ankles. She'd never thought of herself as a cruel woman before. It was just that Judd made her feel safe and he was overly protective of his little ranch partner, Miss Gaines. She couldn't give him up. She couldn't! He was all that stood between her and men who were dangerous to her. Men like Gary Mays, the assistant director and—most of all—Cash Grier. Despite Crissy's compassion, they were rivals for the same man. And it was true, that all was fair in love and war.

The last two weeks before Christmas were hectic. Crissy was having final exams at school, and juggling study with ranch chores that seemed to be endless. The chaotic disarray of the film people crowding around her made her life difficult, and she grew more and more impatient. Maude kept out of the way, and Judd never came near the ranch unless it was to take Tippy back to town to her hotel. He was polite to Crissy, but the old easy affection between them seemed to be gone forever. It didn't occur to her that Cash was usually somewhere around whenever Judd came to the ranch, and that Judd noticed.

She and Nick and the part-timers rode fence line, doctored pregnant cows, patched leaky roofs, pitched hay, hauled water, and did the thousand and one other daily chores that kept the ranch up and running. On one free day, she went all the way to Victoria shopping for a particular sort of sterling silver tie tack that Judd had mentioned he'd seen and wanted. It took half the day to locate it, in a small jewelry store. She brought it home triumphantly and wrapped it up. When she and Maude put up their annual Christmas tree in the living room, she tucked it in among the branches where it wouldn't be too obvious. She got Cash a nice new wallet, having noticed how frayed his own was.

Cash's visits had multiplied since Clark's arrest. Crissy noted that Tippy Moore didn't snipe at him anymore. She was oddly subdued when he was around. She kept out of his way and he ignored her completely.

"There's fire in that smoke," Maude commented one afternoon just after Cash had driven away.

"What smoke?" Crissy murmured, her head stuck in her textbook.

"That model and Cash Grier," she replied. "Right now it's smoldering, while they avoid each other. But put them together and it's explosions all the way."

"They hate each other," Crissy said, surprised.

"Maybe. Maybe not." She cocked her head, watching Crissy while she dried plates. "You and Judd both going to Japan?"

"Not until next year sometime, we haven't even decided on a date. But it's the best news we've had in a while." She turned a page. "Judd and I have already decided that we'll use some of the film money to replace that Salers bull. But some of our heifers had already been bred to him, and to that Hereford bull we lost, too. When we knew how many pregnant heifers we had, Nick called a man he knew who does artificial insemination, and we bought seed from a champion Salers bull. We had the remaining heifers serviced. So now we've got a champion calf crop to look forward to in the spring. That's what the Japanese are interested in. No additives, no unnecessary antibiotics, grass-fed with only a minor mix of vitamins and supplements—none from animal parts—and pesticide-free."

"As I recall," Maude grinned, "Judd had to be talked into that organic approach."

"He knew I'd done my homework when I suggested it. Now he's glad, with this overseas deal cooking."

Maude smiled at her warmly. "Child, you are a natural-born cattlewoman."

Crissy grinned at her. "Just like my great-aunt Sarah," she reminded the older woman, "who ran her own ranch long before it became popular for a woman to do it."

"Judd's proud of you," she murmured, averting her eyes to the sink. "He doesn't want you to give up school, no matter how hard finances get here."

"I'll do what I have to," she replied. "Listen, you keep that back door locked when it's just us here," she added. "One of the Clarks is in jail, but the other one isn't."

"I haven't forgotten."

"We can't afford to let our guard down for a minute," she added. "I even carry that pistol in the truck, under my seat." She sighed worriedly. "It was a sad day for east Texas when the Clark brothers moved here."

"Maybe they won't be around too much longer," Maude said.

Those words turned out to be prophetic. Four days after the cast and crew had gone home for the Christmas holidays, John Clark found himself jobless and with no way to afford a lawyer for his brother.

Thinking he'd get money the easy way, he put on a stocking mask and walked into the Victoria Commercial Bank and Trust on Christmas Eve with a shotgun, just before the bank closed early at noon. It was unfortunate for him that the security guard spotted him in time to call for help, and even more unfortunate that help came in the form of the Texas Ranger assigned to that county, Judd Dunn.

Clark fired the shotgun at the uniformed men and nicked the security guard, but not before he and Judd Dunn fired their sidearms. Neither shot missed. Clark went down. He didn't get back up.

Judd drove up in front of the ranch house just about dark. It had been all over the six o'clock news about the attempted robbery and its aftermath. There was extensive footage of Clark lying on the floor in the bank lobby, covered with blood.

Maude had watched it with Christabel, but her sister had called and asked her to come over for the night because she didn't want to be alone on Christmas Eve. Maude felt bad about leaving, under the circumstances, but her sister hadn't been well. Crissy convinced her to go. Then she waited, and hoped that Judd would come to her for comfort.

Incredibly, he did!

Christabel went out to the SUV and waited for him to cut off the engine and get out.

He didn't, for a minute. He stared at her through the dusty side window with eyes that hardly saw her. They were black, dead eyes.

She opened the door and tugged at the long sleeve of his clean white shirt. "I made coffee and fresh bread and a macaroni and cheese casserole. There's apple pie for dessert. Come in."

He cut off the engine and got out of the big vehicle like a sleepwalker. She noticed that his face was unusually pale.

Impulsively, she linked her small hand into his large one and led him into the house and down the hall to the kitchen. It was unusual for him to allow her to touch him. She got drunk on the freedom. It felt right, that big, lean hand so closely tangled in her fingers.

"Sit," she said gently, nudging him into a chair at the small table, which was already set.

"You heard," he murmured, putting his hat in an empty chair.

She nodded. She put nicely cooked vegetables and fresh rolls on the table in containers, along with the macaroni casserole.

She put a plate and napkin and utensils at both places, poured coffee in two cups, handed him one, and sat down. "Say grace, Judd," she said softly.

He did, but with a rasp in his voice. He didn't talk. She didn't expect him to. It was too fresh, too traumatic, for words just yet. She knew that.

By the time they got to the pie, he was calmer and his big frame less rigid.

He smiled faintly. "You know how to handle me, don't you?" he asked, glancing at her.

"I know you," she said simply.

He drew in a long breath and finished his pie. He sipped his second cup of coffee, watching her across the rim. "No questions?"

Her eyes met his and she saw the pain and turmoil in them. "It would be cruel," she replied.

He actually winced. He put down the coffee cup, hard. His mouth made a thin line. He couldn't tell her. He wanted to talk. He needed to talk. But that bristling masculinity that was as much as part of him as his white shirt and silver Ranger badge made it almost impossible. He hated weakness. He couldn't admit to it.

"You're trained not to let things bother you," she began slowly, meeting his eyes. "You have to be strong, so that other people can lean on you when there's an emergency. You can't break down or show emotion on the job, because you have to do the job. That's why it's so hard when things like this happen. You don't want to admit that it hurts when you have to use that gun you wear, or that you're torn up inside." She searched his eyes, noting the surprise there. "But you're very human, Judd, and you were raised in the church, so that makes it worse for you. I'm not going to probe, or pry, or offer platitudes. Work it out however you need to. But if you want to talk, I'll always listen."

His chest rose and fell heavily. "You and Grier," he said dully, staring into his empty cup. "He actually phoned me to say I could talk to him if I needed to."

She studied him with hungry eyes that she veiled with her lashes. "Cash has done a lot of terrible things over the years," she replied. "He's killed people. He knows how it is."

His dark eyes searched hers. "Did he tell you about any of them?"

She shook her head. "He's like you. He doesn't talk about the things that hurt most. But I think he could tell you. I think you could tell him. I know you don't like him, but he's been kind to me."

"Kind when I wasn't," he returned surprisingly. His eyes narrowed on her face. "He's the sort of man who makes other men feel uncomfortable. He's done everything, been everywhere. He's cultured and rich and afraid of nothing on earth."

She wanted to say, "But he isn't you." She didn't dare. He was involved with a woman who made her feel inferior in every way. She wasn't leading with her heart anymore.

She got up and poured more coffee for both of them.

He was watching her, noting the lines of strain in her face, the thinness of her young body, the condition of her faded but clean jeans and shirt and old boots. He grimaced, thinking about that ring on Tippy's finger. He'd also forgotten to bring Christabel's present down with him from Victoria, in the anguish of the day. He'd have to remember to tell her he had it, so that she wouldn't think he'd deliberately not gotten her anything.

She sat down again. "I'm so tired," she murmured. "I've finished exams, and I think I passed everything, but Nick and I have been making running repairs to fences and checking pregnant heifers all afternoon. If this Japanese deal works out, maybe we can hire one more full-time man, so I can get some rest!" she added facetiously.

But he didn't smile. "You're too young to have to shoulder this much responsibility," he said.

Her eyebrows arched. "I'm half owner of this place, and I don't work any harder than you do! In fact, I work less. I'm just a student. You have a demanding job."

His face tautened. "Too demanding, right now," he said through his teeth.

"How's the security guard?" she asked to divert him.

"He's out of danger," he told her. "They're still picking double-ought birdshot out of him, but he'll make a good recovery. He may lose some use of his arm, though. Hell of a thing, he spotted the guy and called for backup, hoping we could take him without bloodshed. I was out on an investigation, not half a block from the bank. I ran all the way and got to the front door just as Clark was threatening a woman with the shotgun. The guard saw me slip into the front door with my sidearm out, and he went for his. Clark whirled. The guard and I fired simultaneously, but too late to avoid return fire. The guard was hit." He looked absolutely haunted. "Clark went down like a sack of sand." He frowned heavily. "People look so helpless when they die, Christabel," he said under his breath. "Like big dolls. They lay there with everybody looking at them, invading their privacy, staring at them...and they can't do anything to protect themselves from all those gaping eyes."

"He tried to kill someone," she reminded him. "Can't you think about what might have happened if you hadn't shown up in time? If John Clark is like his brother, he might not have hesitated to shoot to kill."

"That's what I was afraid he was going to do," he confessed. "The woman told us that she'd antagonized him by speaking up when he held the gun on her. He told her, in fact, that he might as well be hung for a sheep as a lamb. We wondered if he meant that he'd killed already."

She nodded. "Maybe he killed poor old Hob Downey, isn't that what you think?"

"Yes." He toyed with his coffee cup. "The news media jumped on his situation at once. Poor guy, his brother in jail, no money, no job. And the big bad cops shot him when he was only trying to get some money."

She smiled sadly. "We live in bad times, Judd," she said quietly. "The whole world's upside down sometimes."

"I phoned an attorney—the one the department uses—and had him tell me what to do next. Funny, I've been in the Rangers all this time, and I've never been involved in a fatal shooting."

"You were lucky."

He glanced up. "I guess I was. They don't know who fired the fatal shot," he added unexpectedly. "One of us hit low, the other hit high. It will take a ballistics test to determine who fired which shot, but the guard and I both carry .45 caliber weapons. It's Christmas Eve, so the lab is closed. It will be Monday before they can do the examination. Clark's autopsy will have to wait until then, too, I guess. Meanwhile," he sighed, "I have to live with it."

"You don't aim to kill," she reminded him.

"I aimed at his hip, to take him down the quickest way," he said tersely. "But there was a river of blood from that area, bright red, arterial blood." He ran a hand through his thick black hair. "If that was my shot, it went inside and hit the femoral artery."

She wanted to say something comforting, but he was lost in the hell of his own thoughts.

"The other shot was through the heart," he murmured. "Whichever one was mine doesn't matter so much, I guess. He would have died anyway. There'll be a hearing. I gave them a statement and now I'm on administrative leave."

"With too much time to brood on it," she said softly. "You'll need to keep busy. Tomorrow we can dig postholes and put up fence."

His eyebrows arched. "On Christmas Day?"

"If you'd rather watch endless reruns of that old black and white Christmas movie they keep showing around the clock," she began.

His black eyes twinkled, for the first time that day. "We could always watch those satellite movies you like so much," he drawled.

She flushed and grinned. "You stop that. I have to get education where I can find it."

"And I've already told you that those movies aren't like real life."

She cleared her throat. "More coffee?"

He let it drop. "No, I've had enough. Do we still have any beer?"

"About six bottles left over from Thanksgiving, all in the fridge. Want one?"

He nodded. "I'm not a drinker, but I'm making an exception today." He gave her a long, lingering scrutiny. "I'll never have enough to put you in danger. You know that."

She relaxed. She had more reason than most women to be afraid of men who drank, and he knew. She smiled self-consciously. "Isn't it strange how our childhoods affect us years down the road?"

He toyed with the handle of his coffee cup. "I remember how much I missed my mother when Dad wouldn't let her come back," he murmured.

"You loved my mother," she reminded him.

He smiled. "She was a character," he said. "Yes, I loved her. She had a hard life, but she was almost always smiling." He lifted his eyes to her face. "Like you."

She shrugged. "Doesn't cost any more to smile than it does to cry," she said with a grin. "And it uses less muscles!"

He chuckled. "I thought about staying up in Victoria in the apartment overnight. I'm glad I didn't."

She acknowledged the subtle compliment with a smile. "Very wise," she teased. "My apple pie is better than yours," she added, tongue-in-cheek.

"Nothing wrong with black crust and hard apples," he challenged.

"I'll get you that beer," she said, and went to the refrigerator.

* * *

They watched television in the living room next to the tall, brightly lit Christmas tree until late, avoiding the news. Judd sprawled on the sofa in his sock feet and black T-shirt and jeans, and he went through three beers before he stopped. The traumatic experience of the morning had shaken him badly. It was going to be impossible to live with taking a human life, and he knew it. What he didn't know was how he was going to cope with the conscience that was torturing him.

"You're brooding again," Christabel said from her comfortable armchair across from the sofa. "This is a really good movie. You should be paying attention."

He shifted his head on the pillow under it and stared at her openly, from her pert breasts in the low-cut white sweater she was wearing to the subtle curve of her hips as she sat with her legs drawn up under her. Her blond hair was long, draped over her shoulders and down her back. She looked sexy. Very sexy. Usually he tried not to notice that, but he was just slightly tipsy and his control was slipping.

That look was disturbing. He had a way of watching her lately that made her body tingle. He was doing it now. Her eyes went over his lean, fit body in the close-fitting jeans and black T-shirt that showed off the breadth of his chest and the muscles in his upper arms. He was devastating physically. He wasn't bad-looking, either, with that lean face and broad forehead and straight nose. He had a sensuous mouth, very wide and masculine, and a jutting chin that hinted at the stubbornness that was as much a part of him as the thick, straight black hair that dropped onto his broad forehead when he leaned forward, the thick eyebrows over those deep-set black eyes, the high cheekbones of his tanned face....

"You're staring," he accused.

"So are you," she shot back.

His eyes narrowed slowly. They ran over her body like caressing fingers, almost physically touching her. It was like a moment out of time, with the world very far away, just the two of them in the dimly lit living room with the television blaring away, unnoticed.

"Suppose I told you," he said intently, "that a divorce doesn't cost much more than an annulment?"

She colored prettily. She knew what he was saying. He needed oblivion, and she was in a perfect position to provide it. But he'd been keeping company with an international model who probably thought of sex as an appetizer, and she didn't want to have to follow Tippy in his bed. Not that it wasn't tempting. She'd never wanted anything or anyone the way she wanted her husband.

"Suppose I told you," she replied, "that Tippy Moore would be a hard act for even an experienced woman to follow, much less a novice?"

He looked surprised. "You think I'm sleeping with her?"

She averted her eyes. "She doesn't try to make any secret of the fact that she's experienced."

He didn't speak at once. He seemed to be struggling with things he didn't know how to put into words.

"Good God," he said softly, "you're probably not the only person around here who sees it that way, either, are you?"

She shook her head. "It's pretty common gossip."

His jaw tautened. "And a few people know that we're married, too. I didn't think how it might look, that you might have to bear the brunt of it."

She moved one shoulder restlessly and stared sightlessly at the television screen. "I go around with Cash," she said. "I suppose we've both given Jacobsville enough ammunition for gossip."

He swore softly under his breath and his eyes lifted to the ceiling. Christabel was having to live down his behavior, and it had never occurred to him that he was making her the object of gossip. But how could he not have known, he asked himself, when Tippy made headlines wherever she went.

"I wouldn't have to ask if you were sleeping with Grier," he said. "I know you too well."

He actually sounded resentful. She felt herself bristle. She almost lashed out, before she remembered what he'd already been through today. She didn't have the heart to make him more uncomfortable than he already was.

"She's wearing an engagement ring, Judd," she replied in a subdued tone. "I know you plan to marry her. We're only married on paper, anyway, and soon we won't be. I don't blame you for wanting somebody pretty and famous and sophisticated. I never was in the running, that way, and I've always known it."

He scowled as he stared at her, shocked. Did she really have a self-image that low? And was it his fault that she did? He'd been so careful to keep a distance between them all these years, to protect her from becoming intimately involved with him before she'd dated or been around other men. He hadn't wanted to take advantage of their odd relationship, to use her in a way that many other men wouldn't have hesitated, in his position, to do.

But she'd said Tippy was wearing an engagement ring!

"What engagement ring, Christabel?" he said slowly.

Her wise brown eyes slid around to meet his black ones. "That emerald and diamond ring you gave her. Why would a man give a woman a ring that expensive if he wasn't seriously involved with her?" she asked matter-of-factly.

He took a deep breath and settled back onto the pillows. He wanted to say, "Because I let my pride get in the way at a jeweler's when she put it on and refused to take it off. I couldn't bear to tell her I couldn't afford what she considered a bauble." But he couldn't admit that he'd been such an idiot. So now Christabel thought he was engaged to another woman and counting the days until he could get rid of her!

CHAPTER TWELVE

CHAPTER TWELVE

"So I guess we should get the annulment pretty soon," Christabel added, trying to sound matter-of-fact about a painful subject.

He glared at her. "We'll get an annulment when I say so. Besides, right now, we can't afford it."

"We're getting enough from the film deal to pay an attorney," she countered, puzzled.

"Then let's say it's convenient to stay married for a while," he returned, his eyes brooding as they studied her.

"Tippy Moore might not think so," she said with more bitterness than she knew. "It's no secret that she's crazy about you. She doesn't try to hide it."

He didn't say what he knew about Tippy. He liked that faint jealousy in Christabel's soft voice. He liked knowing that she wanted him. She was pretty and sexy and his body began to ache when he stared at those perfect little breasts under her shirt.

"Tippy doesn't know that we're married," he replied. "She thinks we're just business partners."

"She's right," she responded.

The look in his eyes was dark and quiet. "No. You and I are

more than that to each other. We always have been." His gaze
went down her body like hands and narrowed. "Your nipples are
like little stones. You want me. Did you think it didn't show?"
he taunted softly when she actually gasped at the blunt comment.

She got up from the chair. "Maybe you shouldn't have had
all those beers," she said, uncertain of him in this mood. She
didn't want him to do something he was going to regret later,
even if she was dying for it.

"I'm not drunk. You can go to bed with me, if you want to,"
he offered bluntly.

Her raised eyebrows were eloquent and she laughed ner-
vously. "Imagine that, and I'm not even wearing a red negligee!"

"Careful. I'm not kidding." He put both hands under the back
of his head and gave her a scrutiny that could have boiled milk.
"You think I'm a rake," he said gruffly. "You think I've forsaken
my marriage vows, even if they are on paper, for the sake of a
few adventures with other women. My God, you don't know me
at all, Christabel."

She was almost shaking with nerves as she stared down at him
from a distance of a few feet.

"I'm no virgin," he confessed darkly. "But I take my vows as
seriously as you take yours. I haven't had a woman since I married you."

She couldn't manage a single word. Why hadn't it occurred
to her that he was as rigidly conventional as she was, and deeply
religious as well.

"You haven't had a lover? It's been five years!" she choked
finally.

"I know," he replied, and in a tone that almost made her smile.

"But, how...?"

"There are these racy movies on the satellite channel," he
began with a wicked upturn of his lips. "And other means of satisfaction."

She went scarlet. It was such an intimate thing to know about
him. But, then, he knew all her secrets, too—at least, the ones

that mattered. He wasn't having sex with Tippy Moore. That jumped out at her like a spring. It made her exultant.

"Lost for words?" he mused, watching her closely. "Shocked?"

She nodded.

He drew in a long breath. "I've had a hard day. I'm half lit, even on three beers. But I sure as hell am capable, and I want a woman tonight. Considering our situation, the only available woman is you."

She was still standing there, rigid, unmoving, her heart beating her to death.

His eyes fell to her breasts, where two hard little points were thrusting against the white sweater. "You're ripe for a man and you'd die to have me." He caught the flash of her eyes and the smile widened. His eyes went over her like hands. "I want you, Christabel. Right now."

She hesitated, not because she didn't want to, but because she was still afraid that he was teasing, testing her. She didn't think he was serious.

He noticed that. His black eyes began to burn as he held her own gaze until her heart ran wild.

"You know you want it. Your heart is beating you to death. I can see it from here. Turn the television off and come here, baby," he said in a deep, sensuous drawl. "And I'll make all your guilty little dreams come true."

Like a sleepwalker, controlled by a part of her that she didn't recognize, she went to the television and switched it off. Then she went to stand just in front of him, excited, hungry, curious, her heartbeat raging as she looked down at all that hard muscle.

"Don't you dare tease me," she said huskily. "I won't play games with you."

"I'm not playing." He reached out and caught her hand, tugging until she fell heavily against and onto his long, muscular body. It was new, and heady, to be so intimately close to him after all these years of repressed need. He felt alien against her for the first few seconds. His legs were long and powerful. She felt the muscles in them ripple as they moved, intertwining with hers. She felt something else, too, something he'd rarely let her feel. He wanted her. It was exciting to know that, and a little intimidating, because she didn't have a clue what it was going to feel like later on. She'd heard stories...

He felt her tense. He turned her half under him and looked into her eyes from point-blank range. "I know you're a virgin," he said huskily. "I'm excited by it, and you can feel that, can't you? But I'll be careful. Very, very careful. The last thing I want to do is to frighten you or hurt you."

She relaxed and reached up to him, suddenly aware of her own body's faint swelling, of a new and exciting sensation of pleasure in her most secret places. She ached to have him touch her, kiss her. It amazed her that it had happened so unexpectedly.

"You might regret it later," she whispered.

"I won't. Neither will you. I can guarantee it," he added with confidence.

She stared at his hard, disciplined mouth with real hunger. She could hardly get a decent breath. He smelled of faint cologne and aftershave and soap. He felt like sweet heaven this close. His body was warm and hard and she felt enveloped by it.

"Maybe I'm dreaming," she whispered, running her hands over him. "All those repressed years without experimentation have driven me mad!"

He chuckled softly. "Think so? If you want to experiment," he murmured, catching his hand in her hair to hold her face gently under his, "you can do it with your husband. Open your mouth, baby...!"

She opened her mouth to gasp, and his caught it. It was like the dance, except that this time, he was slow and tender with her. His lips toyed with hers gently, in a breathless silence that made her far too aware of the steely body against hers, of the warmth of his hands on her back, the expert sensuality of his hard mouth. The other kisses they'd shared seemed innocent by comparison. This time he meant business, and it showed.

Her arms snaked around his neck and she lifted to his kisses with hungry abandon. She felt him moving her top out of the waistband of her jeans. Seconds later, his hands were against bare skin, against the hateful scars her father had left so many years before.

She jerked.

He stilled her instinctive withdrawal by turning her under him, so that he could look down into her eyes. "I have scars of my own, remember?" he said quietly. "Here."

He pulled up his black undershirt and drew her hand to his rib cage. "Feel it?" he asked. "I took a pump shotgun blast there when I was a rookie cop. Fortunately for me, it was a light load and it didn't go in very far. But it left a ridge, like the one in my shoulder left a depression."

She traced it slowly. "I'd forgotten that."

He smiled lazily. "I hadn't." He smoothed her long hair around her shoulders, soft and fine. "Your hair is one of your best points," he murmured as his lean fingers began feeling for buttons on her blouse. "Next to these..."

"Oh...Judd, listen, you can't take it off!" she protested when she remembered her padded bra.

"Sure, I can." He kept going, until he had it open and her padded bra revealed. Then he realized why she'd fought to keep him from seeing it. He scowled. "What the hell are you wearing this padded bra for?" he asked.

She sighed. "I didn't want you to see it. I thought if I looked bigger, you might be more interested in looking at me," she confessed. "Don't men like big women?"

"Taste is an individual thing, honey," he murmured, searching for the fastening. He lifted her with one arm while his fingers expertly released the catch. "I don't like big women. I never have."

While she was getting used to that idea, he moved her so that he could pull the whole works off, baring her to his eyes from the waist up. It was like lightning striking. All her dreams about him hadn't been this explicit. She was soaring with joy.

He smiled slowly at the way she looked. It was heady to think she hadn't done this with anyone else. He wanted her first time to be with him. He'd never wanted anything so much.

She tried to speak, but his head was already bending. Even as she spoke, he opened his mouth right over her nipple and took most of her soft little breast right into it. His tongue worked on the sensitive nub while his mouth learned her in a silence broken only by her frantic heartbeat and soft sobs of pleasure. Her fingers caught the thick muscles in his upper arms and dug into them with delight as his mouth explored her body.

His hand worked its way down her spine and brought her against him hungrily. He released her breast only to find her mouth, while he eased her under his undershirt so that he could feel her breasts against his bare, hair-roughened chest.

"Judd," she sobbed into his mouth. "I never thought it would feel like this!"

"Neither did I," he whispered roughly. "I want you like hell! Are you still taking the Pill, or do I have to use something?"

Her mind was not working at all. She couldn't think. "How did you...?"

"I saw them on your bedside table, the last time I was here." He lifted his head, and his black eyes pinioned her. "Were you taking them for Grier, just in case?" he demanded suddenly, angrily.

"No!" she gasped. "I would never...!"

"Then, why?" he persisted hotly.

She was almost shaking from the intimate contact with him. He was aroused. He wanted her. She couldn't think. Her young body was on fire with need, hunger, aching thirst. She was going to die if he stopped now. What had he asked? "My...periods were...erratic, and I got sick with them," she said. "The doctor put me on the Pill just...just for a couple of months, until I got regulated." She didn't add that it had been six months ago, and she'd stopped taking them in the second month, without even finishing the prescription. She was a pack rat. She never threw out things until Maude made her. She'd put them on the dresser while she searched for a pen and hadn't put them back. "Don't stop," she pleaded when he hesitated. "Please don't stop, Judd!"

He scowled as she took his hand back to her breast and caressed it tenderly, coaxing it back onto the soft skin.

"Isn't the Pill supposed to be dangerous?" he whispered.

"He said not at my age, since I don't smoke or have headaches regularly." She arched up to his caressing fingers with a soft gasp. Her eyes fell back in her head. "Oh, that's nice! I never realized it would feel like this when I watched those movies!"

His eyes narrowed. He smiled slowly, his black eyes glittery as they went to the soft little mound he was caressing. "If it's safe, I can have you the way I want to," he said huskily, "without anything between us except skin."

"Yes. Any way you want to, Judd, right here, right now..." Her voice broke on a whimper of pleasure. She lifted up to his devouring mouth, clinging, aching for more than this. "Please, please, don't stop!"

"I'm not going to," he bit off against her swollen lips. "I'm starving to death for you. I've got to have you, baby!" he added roughly. "I've got to!"

She barely heard him. She was going under in a veritable flood of sudden passion. His experienced touch sent her mind reeling out of control of her body. She arched up to him, moved restlessly under the slow, sensuous crush of his lean hips, opened her mouth to the devouring kisses that made her young body ache even more.

He caressed her out of her jeans and underwear, and his mouth, his warm, hard mouth, was on her breasts, on her belly. She was gasping, clutching, drowning in new sensations as he worked his way down her tormented body. He touched her in a way she'd never expected a man to touch her, but his mouth covered her small, embarrassed cry. His tongue eased into her mouth in slow, sensuous explorations that augmented the expert caress of his hands.

Somewhere along the way, his undershirt went onto the rug, followed by his jeans, leaving him in the black boxer shorts he favored. They did nothing to camouflage the hungry thrust of his body.

He paused to look down into her face, seeing the lack of comprehension, the lack of sanity that mirrored his own. Her arms were around his neck, her body arched up to his like a sacrifice. Her eyes were slitted. She was moaning softly, moving against him with helpless delight. She made him feel ten feet tall. She made him feel like the greatest lover who ever lived.

The boldness of his eyes managed to get through to her. She noticed his rapt stare and began to feel self-conscious about her nudity.

"Don't be embarrassed," he said roughly. "You belong to me. We're married, Christabel. There's nothing to be ashamed of."

"I'm not, really," she said huskily. "But all the lights are on," she added helplessly and with a shy laugh. "And I've never done this before."

"Do you want the lights off, the first time?" he asked softly. She nodded. "Okay." He didn't add that it was going to be difficult for him, too, in the light. Like her, he had hang-ups that he didn't like admitting.

He got to his feet, lifting her gently into his arms. He searched her dazed eyes for a second before his mouth eased down to cover hers again, tenderly, as he walked past the tall, glittery Christmas tree and down the long hall to his bedroom.

He didn't turn on the light. He put her down long enough to close and lock the door before he carried her to bed. She felt his mouth on her body in the warm darkness of the room, the soft sounds of flesh against flesh barely reaching her ears above her own gasps. It was more intimate than she'd ever imagined it would be, especially when the boxer shorts came off and she felt him, really felt him, in total contact with her.

"Easy," he whispered as she tensed involuntarily. "It's not going to be what you think. We've got all the time in the world. Ease your legs in between mine, honey."

She was puzzled by the soft entreaty, but she did as he asked, and suddenly felt his powerfully muscled body in even closer contact, and a sharp flash of pleasure accompanied the intimate contact.

He felt her sensuous movement and laughed huskily. "Didn't you expect that? Even after all those explicit movies?"

"They aren't quite this explicit," she whispered on a husky laugh, gasping when he moved again. "I didn't realize...it would feel so good! Or be so intimate!"

He laughed, too. His teeth caught her soft upper lip and his tongue played with it while his hands worked a sort of magic on overstimulated nerve endings lower down. She moved again, convulsively this time, arching up to tempt him closer.

She felt his hands slide under her hips to cradle them as his mouth slowly fitted itself to hers and opened it to the slow probe of his tongue.

At the same time, he thrust down, tenderly, and felt her body jerk. He did it again. She gasped softly and he felt her legs move inside his. The third time, she made a sound he'd never heard from her lips and her nails bit into his upper arms before they slid hungrily to the thick hair on his chest.

He lifted his head, breathing roughly. His hips moved faintly from side to side and she sobbed, arching up. Whatever she was feeling, it wasn't pain. Her hands were pulling at him, not pushing.

His lips brushed her eyes, her cheeks, her open mouth as he moved very slowly, very sensuously, into total possession. She wasn't reacting as if it hurt at all. His powerful legs curved closer around hers as he shifted her. She moaned unsteadily and a tiny shiver of pleasure echoed in his own body as she followed the quick, tender movement with one of her own.

"Is it hurting?" he whispered at her mouth.

"No," she choked. "Oh, no, not at all! It's...wonderful!"

He nibbled her lower lip as he moved again. "Can you feel me inside you?" he whispered outrageously.

"Of all the things to ask...!" she gasped.

He bit her upper lip tenderly. "It isn't a ritual of silence, honey," he said huskily. "I like that husky little note in your voice when I move on you. Tell me what you're feeling," he coaxed. "Talk to me."

"Oh, I...can't...talk!"

"Why not?"

Her hands slid around to the powerful muscles of his back and she arched sinuously, shivering. "I'm on fire," she choked, her eyes closed as she sought some lofty, distant goal of pleasure. "I ache everywhere. Such a sweet ache...oh, yes! Do that! It's...so...good, so good, so good...!" Her voice climbed wildly as she began to shiver rhythmically with every slow thrust. "I've never wanted anything as much...as I wanted you. For so long, Judd!" She gasped, lifting up eagerly. "Am I doing it right?"

"Yes. You're doing fine!" Her pleasure enhanced his own. He hadn't expected her to enjoy it this much, especially her first time. He felt proud of his own skill as she moved with him, her tiny gasps of pleasure were like music...

"Oh!" She stilled suddenly, biting her lower lip hard, as pleasure suddenly became stinging pain. She stiffened. "I'm sorry. That hurts, Judd!" she sobbed, disappointed.

"Yes, and I can feel why," he said gently, hesitating. His breath came in rough gasps. He couldn't hold out for much longer, but he didn't want to hurt her any more than he had to. With sudden inspiration, he bent to her shoulder and his teeth clasped on the soft flesh.

"Judd, what are you doing...? Ouch!" she exclaimed, and gasped with pain. But only seconds later, she felt him deep in her body, completely in possession of her. While she'd concentrated on her shoulder, he'd broken the tiny barrier that separated them. She shivered once and then relaxed as he moved firmly and rhythmically against her, pleasure replacing pain with shocking immediacy. She began to move with him, frantically, as the little bites of pleasure increased by the second, lengthening and promising something close to heaven as the urgency grew.

"*That* doesn't hurt," she whispered, and suddenly laughed as the pleasure grew unexpectedly. Her lips found his neck and kissed it hungrily. Her body was leaping like a wild thing as he moved roughly against her. "Yes! It's so sweet!" she choked, lifting to his possession. "Oh, don't...stop!" she wept. "Don't stop, don't...!"

"As if I could!" he bit off at her ear.

The pleasure had him in its mad grip, now, and he was suddenly driving for satisfaction with total disregard for her virginity and his own concern for it. But she didn't seem to mind. She was making little rhythmic whimpering noises that coincided with his sharp, deep, measured thrusts, and her body was begging for his with every downward motion. She whispered to him, explicit, exciting things that would shame her later, in cold daylight. She went with him all the way, lifting, moving, surging, as the pleasure built into waves of urgency that sought a shadowy, distant goal that she couldn't...quite...reach.

Then, when she was mindless and frantic, she was suddenly there, right there, caught up in the grip of madness that brought a sobbing little scream from her tight throat. She wished she could see him. She wished he could see her. She heard the springs going like pistons as he drove for fulfillment. She heard his harsh, desperate gasps, felt the rigor of his body, just before blinding lights exploded behind her closed eyes and she arched convulsively and sobbed out the ecstasy of complete satisfaction at his ear.

It went on and on and on. She couldn't stop moving under him, even as he went rigid and shuddered over her. His skin was damp with sweat. He was breathing harshly, groaning. Her body pulsed with silvery delight, with utter physical joy. She was part of him. She felt him swell, burst, inside her. She cradled him, heavy in her arms, shivering in the sweet, throbbing aftermath of the most explosive pleasure she'd ever known in her young life.

She slid her legs around his, her arms close at his back. She kissed his chest, his throat, his chin with lips that were soft and numb with helpless delight, with love.

He drew in a long, shuddering breath and the pressure of him increased suddenly the length of her body, but only for a few seconds. He rolled away with a rough expulsion of breath and lay there, boneless, suddenly keenly aware of what he'd just done.

It didn't help that he was sated to the very marrow of his bones, or that he knew she'd experienced the same fulfillment that he had. It didn't help that she'd been a virgin, and he'd made her climax the first time he had her. He'd taken advantage of her, and he had no right to, not even under the circumstances.

"Damn!" he ground out.

"And now it's the hair shirt and the flail," she said on an audible sigh. "You're just going to lie there and feel guilty, after you've given me an orgasm my very first time."

He blinked. Surely she hadn't said that? "How do you know what an orgasm is?" he asked bluntly.

"How can I not know, with the subject coming up on every talk show and in every magazine on the newsstand?" She rolled over and pillowed her head on his damp shoulder, curling into his powerful body as naturally as if she'd done it all her life. "Virgins are supposed to have a hard time and bleed a lot, and then cry afterward. I know because two girls in my computer class are living with men, and they said so. They thought I was nuts because I hadn't had sex, at my age."

He smoothed her hair absently, trying not to feel proud of himself. "I don't read magazines."

Her fingers tangled in the thick curling hair that covered the powerful muscles of his chest. He arched involuntarily at the pleasure of the caress. "You do feel guilty, don't you?" she persisted.

He sighed. "Yes. I feel guilty. I had too much to drink and all the walls came down."

"It had to happen sometime," she said softly. "And you said

yourself, we're married. I couldn't very well do it with anybody else."

Especially not with damned Grier, he was thinking, and felt a primitive burst of pleasure that her first time wasn't going to be with the other man.

"I'm glad I waited, Judd," she whispered huskily. "I never dreamed it would be that good my first time. It was incredible! Just incredible!"

He was glad, too, but he didn't know how to admit it.

Her hand curled closer. "I'm so sleepy, and my body throbs every time I breathe, with these fantastic little jolts of pleasure," she whispered. "Is it normal?"

After that earthquake of passion, he thought amusedly, it had to be. He was sleepy himself.

"It's normal," he replied.

"Can I sleep with you?"

His voice was drowsy and amused. "You just did."

She hit his chest gently. "All night," she added.

He drew in a long breath. He didn't want to be alone tonight. He'd only lie awake and brood over the events of the day. Besides that, the deed was done. What difference did it make now if she slept in his arms. He was so relaxed, so fulfilled, that he could barely keep his eyes open. His body throbbed, too, with satiation. He couldn't remember a time when a woman had given him such wild delight.

"You can stay," he said.

She smiled against his shoulder. She might have offered to put on a gown first, but she slid into sleep almost at once, oblivious to the hard, taut, brooding face of the man beside her.

The light fluttered against her heavy eyelids. Christabel moved restlessly and then groaned as unfamiliar twinges of discomfort made themselves felt. She opened her eyes and Judd was standing there in jeans and his black T-shirt, unmoving.

"Hi," she said with faint self-consciousness.

"Hi," he replied. He wasn't smiling.

"What are you doing?"

His heavy brows were drawn together. "Watching you sleep," he said abruptly. "I've got breakfast."

"Coffee, too?" she murmured sleepily.

"Coffee, too. Come on in when you're ready."

He turned, reluctantly it seemed, and went back out again. She moved the sheet aside and noticed that she was nude. There was a noticeable stain on the white sheets. Maude would see that. She grimaced. It was a secret. She didn't want to share it with anyone just yet, not even Maude.

She had a quick shower and then climbed into clean clothes, pausing to strip the bedclothes from the mattress and toss them into the washer before she went down the hall to the kitchen.

The delicious smell of cooked bacon and bread filled the kitchen. She sniffed and smiled. "You're getting better," she re-marked, noting the golden tan of the biscuits as she sat down beside him at the table.

"You burn a batch of biscuits every single damned day for a month and you learn how to cook them eventually," he said carelessly. He watched her pour coffee, his eyes intent on her face. He smiled involuntarily at the way she looked, freshly scrubbed, no makeup, with her hair long and clean and flyaway. She looked older this morning, more mature. More sexy. That made him feel guilty and he turned away.

She glanced at him and caught the intent scrutiny. Her hand went to her hair. "I didn't stop to put on makeup," she said, mis-reading the stare.

"I was thinking how fresh you look," he murmured.

She smiled. "Thanks."

He didn't smile back. He looked more uncomfortable than ever. He drew in a long breath. The look in his black eyes wasn't definable. "Well, there goes your annulment, Mrs. Dunn," he mused, using her married name for the first time in five years.

She looked down at her coffee cup and added sugar to it. "I don't care," she said huskily. "It was worth it."

There was a long pause. Her eyes went to his lean face abruptly as she wished, hoped, he might echo her sentiments. But he didn't. However, he did seem confused. There was an odd, steady warmth in his black eyes that had never been there before. It wasn't affection. It was...something more. Something she couldn't read.

"Is Maude coming back for lunch?" he asked.

"Yes. But she's going to take a plate back over there for her sister to have for supper."

He nodded slowly. His narrowed eyes were all over her face, slow and possessive. "You didn't invite Grier over?" he asked sarcastically. There was a bite in his tone.

She flushed. "No."

"Going to take him dinner?" he persisted.

"Maude said she'd take him a plate by on her way back to her sister's," she replied, flustered by his level look.

His black eyes went back to his plate. He didn't say anything. But he smiled faintly.

She stirred her coffee unnecessarily long. Was he still jealous of Grier even now? Could he want her to himself, and that was why he was asking so many pointed questions? She had to admit, she wanted very much to have him to herself. It promised to be a magical day, if she could get past that sudden cold reserve he was showing her this morning.

He ate without further comment, and so did she. When they finished, she washed dishes and he rinsed and dried them, side by side at the sink overlooking the barn out back.

"If we could afford it, I'd buy you a dishwasher," he commented.

She smiled. "I don't mind doing it like this. Modern conveniences would only ruin me. I'd become a worthless layabout!"

He chuckled, bumping her playfully with his hip. It was the first time he'd ever done that, and she tingled all over with the joy of intimacy.

"Okay. We'll buy you a pair of new boots instead," he added, glancing down at her worn ones with the toes permanently turned up from being soaked and dried several times during rainstorms.

"What? When these are just getting broken in good?" she exclaimed. "Heaven forbid!"

He studied her radiant face with eyes so tender they made her heart ache. "You never ask for a thing," he said softly. "I felt so damned guilty about that ring I bought Tippy. I never meant for you to know about it. Diamonds and emeralds for her, when you don't even own a decent winter coat."

"I'd look terrible in diamonds and emeralds," she commented, trying to defuse a potentially explosive discussion. He might not have slept with Tippy, but he'd given her a ring. He had too many principles to sleep with another woman when he was married. He hadn't even given her a birthday present, and she'd noted the lack of one under the Christmas tree, too. That had hurt. Besides, he was guilty about last night, and it showed.

"You're avoiding the issue. That's not like you."

She looked up at him with her heart in her eyes. "I don't want to argue," she said, trying to put a turbulence of new emotions into words. "Not after last night."

He hesitated, his face growing more grave by the second. "Listen, Christabel," he began slowly. "About what happened..."

She ignored the look, going up on tiptoe. She nibbled at his hard mouth softly and then with deliberate sensuality, opening her lips and fitting them deliberately to his with sudden boldness. His breath caught. She caught her own, expecting to be put firmly away. But his reaction was shocking. He threw down the soapy cloth he was holding and crushed her against the lean length of him, soapy hands and all, wrapped her up tight, and kissed her passionately, hungrily, until she gasped for air.

His powerful body shivered once, faintly, and she knew immediately that he wanted her. He wasn't even trying to hide it. Apparently he was as vulnerable as she was, and it made her wild with pride to realize it. His black eyes splintered with desire as they searched hers.

She reached up to him again. Her mouth opened as his covered it. She moaned huskily under the furious, hard crush of his lips, and his arms enfolded her completely, lifting her half off the floor.

She was dying for him. There was no reserve, no shyness, no coy flirting. Her arms contracted feverishly around his neck.

He lifted his head just enough to see her flushed, submissive face, and his whole face clenched with desire.

"I want you," she whispered huskily, shivering. "Let's go back to bed. I want you so much, Judd! I want to take off my clothes and let you do anything you like to me, right now, in broad daylight!"

He actually groaned. Visions of unspeakable delight danced in his head at just the prospect. But before he could weaken enough to do anything about it, the sound of a car coming up the driveway froze him in her arms.

He frowned. "Maude?" he murmured hoarsely.

"Not this early, surely," she began.

He lifted an eyebrow. "Haven't looked at a clock yet, have you?"

"We just had breakfast," she began.

He nodded toward the clock on the stove. It was ten o'clock in the morning.

She gasped. "Oh, dear. And I haven't even started to heat up the turkey and dressing or put the rolls out to rise...!"

"What a good thing Maude came early," he said abruptly, and put her down firmly. He was smiling, but his whole expression was one of barely contained sensual desire.

"What will she think when she sees us just now eating breakfast?" she exclaimed.

He gave her a long, unsmiling look, and the whole anguish of the day before slid over him like cold molasses. "We can tell her that we were up late talking about what happened in Victoria," he suggested.

She winced. She'd actually forgotten the events of the day before, the loss of control that had sent them careening into each other's arms. How could she have forgotten?

"One day at a time, Judd," she suggested gently. "You'll get through it."

He didn't reply. A car door slammed. By the time Maude came in the back door, they were finishing up the breakfast dishes in a restless silence.

Maude paused in the doorway, feeling like an intruder and not knowing why. She frowned. Judd didn't look upset, but she knew he must be.

"You okay?" she asked him gently.

He smiled faintly. "I'm getting by. We just had breakfast. We were up late."

"Talking, I don't doubt," Maude agreed as she went to the refrigerator, so that she didn't see the guilty looks on their faces. "I'm glad you didn't stay up in Victoria by yourself. You don't need to be alone."

"That's what I thought," he agreed.

She glanced at the two of them and her eyes were speculative, but she didn't say a word. There was so much tension in the air that it was almost palpable. She just nodded and started transferring food out of the refrigerator to the kitchen table.

Four hours later, with dinner eaten, if not with relish by two late-breakfasters, Maude was making up a plate to carry to her sister.

"I'll only be gone long enough to take this to my sister," she said, and wondered why Judd looked relieved and Christabel looked crushed at the announcement.

"Good," he said abruptly. "Christabel doesn't need to be here alone, even with Jack Clark in jail. Both of you remember to keep the doors and windows locked. I'll have a word with Nick before I leave."

"Are you going now?" Christabel asked him, trying not to sound as if her world was shattering. Which it was.

"Right now," he told her without meeting her eyes. "I never should have come!"

"Do you want me to take a plate to Cash Grier?" Maude asked suddenly.

"Don't bother with that," Christabel said miserably. "He can come over for supper."

Judd's eyes flashed furiously, but he set his lips together and didn't say another word. He left the room to get dressed.

"What's going on?" Maude asked, shocked.

Christabel lifted her chin proudly. "Nothing. Nothing at all. He's just upset and not having an easy time dealing with what happened. He has to work it out his own way."

Maude sighed. "If you say so, honey."

Maude waited until he left. Ten minutes later, he was out the door and gone. He gave Christabel one long, last look and actually winced as he met her wounded eyes. But he didn't stop. He wished them both a Merry Christmas and drove away. He was halfway to Victoria before he remembered that he hadn't even told Christabel about the pearl necklace and matching earrings he'd bought her for her combination birthday and Christmas present. But considering the circumstances, that might be just as well. He'd gone nuts and taken her to bed. She'd be expecting happy ever after, and he was more confused about his intentions than he'd ever been in his life. He had to have time, to decide what he wanted to do. At the moment, he was incapable of making decisions.

CHAPTER THIRTEEN

Early on New Year's Eve, with the ballistics test completed and an autopsy performed on John Clark, Judd came by at lunchtime in a quiet and introspective mood.

Christabel was watching the news in the living room when he walked in. Maude had gone to town for groceries. He noticed immediately that the Christmas tree had been taken down. Christabel never liked taking it down until New Year's Day, so this was painful evidence of how uncomfortable she was now with the holiday season. The present he hadn't given her made him uncomfortable. He still had it at his apartment. He was too ashamed at this late date to produce it.

He sat down in his easy chair, tossing his hat aside while Christabel waited quietly for what he had to tell her. The television blared on into the silence.

He shrugged. "I was right. My shot went too far inside and nicked Clark's femoral artery. He could have survived it, but only with immediate medical attention." He smiled broodingly. "I don't feel a lot better. But they said the security guard's bullet was the lethal one, and that's how it'll go on the report."

She was uncomfortable with him after the way they'd parted.

But she cared too much to pretend his condition didn't matter to her. "Intent is everything under the law, Judd, you know that," she reminded him softly. "You didn't mean to kill him. I'm sure the security guard didn't, either."

His eyes were haunted. "No, he didn't. But he's having a hard time. Clark is still dead, and the newspapers blame both of us, despite what the coroner found."

She wanted to climb into his lap and hold him, comfort him. But there was a tremendous distance between them now. He was as unapproachable as if he'd never touched her in the first place.

She was confused, and she felt rejected. She'd never realized what it would be like, to be intimate with a man. It wasn't what she'd once thought. It was agony to be separated from him, even for an hour. But he didn't want her on any permanent basis. He'd had too much to drink, been traumatized, and he'd comforted himself with Christabel in bed. That was all it was, really. For him it was already over. Clark's death wasn't his fault. He'd go back to work, when he'd gone through the administrative procedure and counseling, and, slowly, he'd put everything that had happened right out of his mind, including the night with her. In fact, to look at him, she knew he'd already done it.

"You're very quiet," he remarked.

She lifted her eyes to his. "I'm sorry. You said, they'd finished the autopsy?"

He nodded. "They're burying him day after tomorrow. One of the deputies here is going to take Jack Clark up to Victoria for the funeral. The news media will have a real field day with that."

"We live in strange times," she replied. She studied him sadly. It was hard to talk to him now. "But like you used to tell me, even life is a temporary condition. You'll get through this."

"Sure." His chest rose and fell slowly. He traced her face with slow, dark eyes. "I've been putting this off because I couldn't quite face it. But we have to talk about the future, Christabel," he said finally.

"What future?" she asked with a forced smile.

He drew in a short breath. "I have to see about the divorce."

She didn't react. It was hard, but she managed it. "Yes."

He relaxed. She was taking it much better than he'd expected her to. He still wasn't sure of his feelings, but he had to do something. "I'll get to it as soon as I can. Things are a little hectic right now. They're backed up on investigations, so mine is on hold, probably until after New Year's. I still have questions to answer and a counselor to see. There will be reports, depositions, and all the official aftermath of the shooting."

She studied his hard mouth with growing unease. "You're sorry about what we did, aren't you, Judd?" She had to know.

He didn't answer right away. "Yes," he said finally, biting off the word. "I had too much to drink and you were handy," he said flatly. "I had no right to use you to take my mind off my own problems."

Her heart sank right down to her knees. Talk about being blunt...! "We are married," she began.

"That doesn't excuse it!" He grimaced. "Christabel, I never planned on any intimacy between us. I insisted on it. You know that! You know why!"

He looked very uncomfortable, and all her hopes vanished in the certainty of what he was really saying. It hadn't occurred to her that two people who had been so intimate, so close, could suddenly become strangers in such a short space of time. But he looked remote and trapped. Freedom was as sacred as religion to him. He didn't want her.

"You don't want to stay married to me," she said on a quiet sigh. "I know that."

He wasn't sure what he wanted. He was unsettled, confused. He'd gone in headfirst just after the shooting. He'd needed comforting, he'd needed a woman. He'd used alcohol as an excuse to have Christabel, for whom he'd been slowly dying. But now he was feeling the guilt of having pushed her into a relationship she wasn't ready for. She'd never even dated seriously. He'd taken away her right to choose. Her infatuation with him had played out to its inevitable conclusion and he was thinking about his loss of freedom, his uneasiness with roots and family life. Walls were closing in on him. He had to have personal space, time to get over the trauma of the past few days, the shooting and his radically changed relationship with his young wife. It was killing him, trying to forget how it had been with her in that dark bedroom. He'd never thought her capable of such uninhibited passion. In fact, he'd never thought himself capable of it.

"No. I don't want to stay married," he said doggedly, more for his benefit than hers.

She nodded. "I see."

"You don't," he replied. "But when you've had time to think about it, you'll realize that I'm right," he added coolly, staring her down. "It was a night out of time, Christabel. I crossed the line and you let me. Now we both have to live with it." He leaned forward with his arms crossed over his splayed legs. "At least there won't be any consequences."

He meant the pill that he thought she'd been taking. She didn't dare tell him about that. She stared at the floor.

"And, of course, there's Miss Moore," she added softly.

He scowled, glancing at her.

"Your fiancée," she reminded him, and forced a smile.

She'd said that once before and he hadn't questioned it. He started to deny it now, but it suited him to let her believe it. If she thought he wanted the other woman, she might find it easier to let go of him. It would also make things easier for Tippy who, unbeknownst to Christabel, was having fits keeping Gary, the assistant director, at bay. Her relationship with Judd had accomplished that, at least.

She noted his sudden silence and drew in a slow breath. "So it was an engagement ring, after all, wasn't it?"

He nodded, affirming the lie with a curt jerk of his head that felt like abject betrayal. She looked shattered. He didn't want to hurt her, but his work was his life. He didn't want to settle into family life. It felt like the worst sort of trap. He'd already taken something that he had no right to take from her, because he'd lost control of himself. Thank God she'd been on the pill, or he might have been trapped for good.

The shooting played on his mind, tormented him. He knew he wasn't thinking straight, but he couldn't cope with so many changes at one time. Getting used to the idea that he'd helped kill a human being was bad enough, without the turmoil of an intimate relationship with a young woman who hero-worshiped him. Christabel deserved so much more than a night of passion with him. She deserved a good, strong marriage and children. He thought suddenly about her relationship with Grier and how it might change after the divorce. He felt sick at his stomach and he didn't understand why.

Christabel was trying to deal with this complication and failing miserably. It was hard not to give way to tears, when her throat felt as if she'd swallowed a bowling ball. She blinked fast, to dry the suspicious moisture around her dark eyes.

"Okay," she said huskily. "I won't make any trouble for you, Judd. I hope you'll be happy with her." She clasped her hands together hard in her lap and forced a smile. "I knew you had to be serious to buy her a ring like that, when we can barely pay bills around here. You don't have to worry about that," she added quickly, lifting a hand. "You were right about school. I only lack one semester, and only two classes, to graduate. I can get a job and work in between them, at a convenience store or something," she said, her voice rushed as she made plans. "Then, after I graduate, I'll get a job. With the extra money, we can hire somebody else to work full-time, like we planned."

He winced. "Christabel," he began, hating the pain he could hear in her soft voice.

She swallowed, hard. "You can go to Japan alone to meet with the buyers. You deal with foreign people all the time."

"You're part owner," he interrupted.

She wouldn't look at him. "For now," she said. "When the Japanese deal goes through, we'll make decisions. But I don't want to go on living here and be an unwelcome third wheel after you remarry."

"For God's sake!" he burst out, horrified at the things she was saying. He hadn't realized how drastically things might change with his announcement. He was totally unprepared.

She got to her feet. "It's okay," she said. "Really, it is." She forced another smile. "I may have marriage prospects of my own," she added, thinking of Cash.

So did Judd. He was poleaxed. Somehow, his own muddled thinking had plunged them both into this morass of unthinkable futures.

He stood up, too. "None of this has to be decided today!" he said curtly.

"It's best if it is." She moved toward the doorway. "I hope things work out for you up in Victoria," she added, glancing back at him with eyes that didn't reach past his chin. She kept smiling. Her face was going to be frozen in that position. "Happy New Year, Judd. I hope the next one will be happier—for both of us."

She walked out of the room. He looked after her with a sinking heart and felt as if he'd stepped into a deep hole from which there was no escape. So much pain in those brown eyes, so much torment. She'd run to Grier now, damn him, and he'd marry her in a second, given the chance. But Grier wasn't the sort of man who could make her happy. She'd never understand him, or fit into his world. Any more than Judd himself would fit into Tippy Moore's social set.

He remembered Christabel's clinging arms, her hungry mouth pressed to his, her body moving with aching delight under his on those crisp white sheets in the darkness. She'd been his very dream of perfection. But desire alone wouldn't be enough for her. She'd want him around all the time, she'd want children. He shivered, just thinking about those sort of ties. He'd never even considered having a real marriage. His father's example haunted him. What if Christabel, like his mother, found someone else and ran away? Anyway, he'd only married her on paper so that he could assume responsibility for her and her mother and carry on business while she was underage. He'd kept her at arm's length to ensure there wouldn't be complications. But in the turmoil that followed the shooting, he'd needed someone, so desperately. It had been unthinkable to go to another woman. He'd...used her. Or had he? He remembered her hunger for him with anguish. She'd waited so long, while he'd tried to decide if he could even consider settling down for good. He needed more time...

But she was of legal age now, and she wanted out. Out of business, out of marriage, out of his life. That was what he wanted, too. Or was it? He tried to picture never seeing her alone again, never riding fence lines with her, never sharing coffee late at night with her, never talking to her and having that soft, sweet comfort all for himself. She always knew when he was sad or upset, and just what to say to bring him out of it. At times, she almost read his mind. She made him feel warm inside, just by being near him. And now, remembering the feverish response of her body to him in intimacy, he felt even closer to her. But now, he felt...empty. Alone.

He picked up his hat and slanted it over his brow, frowning. He'd get used to being without her. It wasn't going to be that hard. It was the best thing. She was far too young for him, and she hadn't enough experience of men to settle down yet. His conscience reminded him that Grier would snap her up like a prize trout the minute that marriage license was legally void. Christabel, hurt and rejected, would probably marry him immediately on the rebound.

He started toward the door in a half-blind fog of indecision just as it opened and Maude came ambling in with a bag of groceries.

"Hello, Judd. How are things going?" she asked with a gentle smile.

"Slow, for a change," he replied. He glanced toward the kitchen, where he could hear running water. "Keep an eye on her, will you?" he added. "She's upset."

She gave him a knowing look. "No need to ask why. Don't worry about her," she added with a grin. "I've got news that will cheer her right up. Cash is taking her to the New Year's Eve celebration downtown tonight. He's got tickets and there's going to be a band, too."

Judd scowled. "He's too old for her," he bit off, before he could choose his words.

Maude only smiled at him. "You wouldn't think so, to see them together. She makes him young. And you don't have to look hard to know that he's crazy for her. If she were free, he'd have her in front of a minister so fast...!"

"I have to go," he said coldly. "Happy New Year."

"You, too. That reminds me, you never did get your Christmas presents," she said. "Want me to get them for you? I knitted you some socks. She got you a tie tack—a sterling silver star. Remember, you told her you'd love to have one of those? She went to Victoria and spent a whole day looking for just the right thing...you going right now?" she added when he started out the door blindly.

"Yes." His voice sounded choked. He couldn't bear remembering that he hadn't given Christabel anything. An expensive ring for Tippy, who was only a superficial part of his life, and absolutely nothing for the woman who'd sacrificed so much to keep this run-down ranch going while he worked.

"Well, drive safely, then," Maude called after him. "Not going to tell Crissy goodbye?"

He didn't answer her. He stalked out to the SUV, climbed in behind the wheel, and took off like a rocket.

Maude found Crissy at the sink, with tears running silently down her cheeks. She hesitated in the doorway. "You need me to do anything?"

She smiled through the tears and shook her head.

"Cash said he'd come by about six and take you to the New Year's Eve celebration," she added quickly. "That should cheer you up!"

She closed her eyes. Thank God for Cash. "Yes," she said huskily. "And believe me, I need it. Maude, Judd and I are getting a divorce so he can marry Tippy, isn't that wonderful?"

Maude didn't know what to say.

"I might marry Cash," she continued.

"Don't do that, baby," Maude said gently. "Two wrongs won't make anything right. Besides, you might remember that Judd's going through a traumatic time right now. I wouldn't put too much trust in anything he said while he's this upset. He's not thinking straight. Wait until he gets through counseling and has put the shooting behind him before you make any concrete decisions, okay?"

Maude had no idea what was really going on, and Crissy didn't want to tell her. She drew in a steadying breath and put detergent in the water she was running. "He didn't even get me a computer program or anything for Christmas, Maude," she told the older woman. "He gave her that expensive ring. He said it was an engagement ring, just like Tippy told us. I guess he's really in love with her. So that's that. I want him to be happy."

So did Maude, but at the moment she could have strangled him. She put the groceries she was still holding on the kitchen table. "More in the car," she murmured, and went out to get them. Crissy didn't even look. She couldn't see much through her tears, anyway.

The New Year's Eve party was great. There was a set of steer horns used to mark the countdown to the new year—Calhoun Ballenger's tongue-in-cheek remark having been taken seriously by the city fathers—and most of the founding families of Jacobsville were represented at the first annual celebration at the Jacobsville Civic Center just off the town square. Janie Brewster Hart and her new husband Leo, married just before Christmas, clung to each other as an unexpected little skirl of snow drifted down over the gathering outside when the horns went down and the new year was proclaimed. Everyone smiled indulgently.

Cash bent down and kissed Crissy lightly on the mouth. She caught him around the neck and kissed him back, with a sudden enthusiasm that shook him to the soles of his feet. He returned the kiss with fervent ardor, with all his skill. She smiled under the crush of his mouth, enjoying the novelty of being in his arms. He wasn't Judd, but he was pleasant to kiss, just the same. No need to ask how experienced he really was, it showed. They were oblivious to the people around them, and to even more amused glances.

Inevitably, news of the hot kiss got back to Judd. He was now working his way through therapy and back on the job. It didn't sit well, especially since he was regretting his impulsive speech to Christabel about the divorce more with each passing day.

Jack Clark was taken up to Victoria in handcuffs to attend his brother's indigent funeral a few days after the autopsy. On the way back to Jacobsville, Jack had been so docile and polite that the kindly deputy sheriff transporting him broke protocol and left him handcuffed instead of chained. At a rest stop, because Clark said he had to use the bathroom, the kind deputy was rewarded by being knocked over the head twice with the butt of his own .38 caliber service revolver and left for dead in a driving rain in the grass next to the Victoria-Jacobsville highway. Later that day, the deputy's squad car was found deserted a few miles outside Victoria.

Unable to get down to Jacobsville that day because of his busy schedule, Judd phoned Cash Grier and told him what happened. He also had to ask the man to keep an eye on Christabel, fearing that Jack Clark had scores to settle with all of them, especially Judd and Christabel. That rankled, because he'd heard about the infamous New Year's kiss even in Victoria. One of the sheriff's deputies he shared space with was married and lived in Jacobsville and commuted back and forth to work. He'd found it amusing that cold, hard Cash Grier had been caught by such a young woman, and judging from that kiss, it was serious, too, he said carelessly.

The man didn't know that Christabel was married to Judd. Neither did any of the other men in the office, who apparently felt comfortable speculating on Christabel and Grier right in front of Judd. He couldn't bear the thought of Christabel and Cash Grier together, even while he was trying to tell himself that he wanted no part of family life.

The film crew came back for its last two weeks of shooting, including retakes, and Christabel was so subdued that she hardly noticed Tippy. She'd passed all her fall courses and signed up for the next semester.

Judd showed up early on the first Saturday morning of shooting, a cold but sunny day. Cash was already there, talking to one of his men on security duty and waiting for Christabel to get ready so that he could take her out for the day.

She hadn't expected to see Judd and she reacted uncomfortably. So did Judd. They spoke with the icy politeness of warring strangers. Christabel didn't even smile at him. Tippy saw the new tension and discomfort between the two of them and came up with an unpleasant theory about why. Gary was more amorous and predatory than he'd ever been, and she was scared to death to find herself alone with him even in company. She couldn't afford to let Judd desert her now!

So while Judd was briefly talking to the assistant director, Gary, passing the time between equipment setups, Tippy paused beside an unusually quiet Christabel, who could barely keep her eyes off Judd. He was pointedly ignoring her.

"That's what happens when you wear your heart on your sleeve, Miss Gaines," Tippy told her lightly. "You shouldn't throw yourself at men if you want to get anywhere. Sex is such a poor way to hold a man like Judd anyway. He's just too disgusted for words, can't you tell? He told me that you were embarrassing him with your behavior. All he wants is to forget it ever happened. He says you threw yourself at him and he couldn't help himself."

Christabel looked at the older woman with horror in her eyes. For an instant, Tippy felt guilty for the lie. But it had worked well, for a shot in the dark.

"Disgusted," she repeated dully, sick at her stomach. Well, that was certainly plain speaking. Judd couldn't bear the sight of her anymore. Her inexperience and headlong passion had disgusted him. He'd told Tippy all about it, that she'd thrown herself at him! He only wanted to forget what had happened. Well, was it really a surprise? Hadn't he pretty much said the same thing to her? But he hadn't been quite this brutal, even when he mentioned the divorce.

She turned away and went to get her purse. She didn't think to put on a sweater, and it was cold today. When she came back out, Judd was on the porch.

She didn't meet his eyes. She was unbearably hurt. She snagged her purse on her shoulder with jerky movements.

"Are you all right?" he asked hesitantly.

Her lips made a thin line. "I understand the sight of me disgusts you, that I embarrass you just by being here. For the time being, I can't help it, but I promise to keep as far away from you as possible when you come here. You might tell Miss Moore that she doesn't need to keep sniping at me on your account. You'll get your divorce the minute you ask for it!" Her eyes came up, wounded and furious. "How could you tell her we slept together, that I threw myself at you? How could you, Judd!"

He scowled, and started to speak, but she went out into the yard near one of the outbuildings to wait while Cash finished speaking with his man.

Judd felt his temper rising. How could Tippy have told such a lie to Christabel, after he'd already torn the heart out of her? He strode toward the model with blood in his eye, cornering her a few yards away from where Christabel was standing near the outbuilding.

"Why did you tell her she disgusted me?" he asked Tippy angrily. "Why lie to her?"

Tippy was too shocked to answer him. It hadn't occurred to her that the woman would repeat what she'd said, and so quickly. She started to speak and then a movement behind Judd caught her eye.

Christabel moved a little farther away from the painful sight of Judd standing close to Tippy Moore. She was just in time to see a thin, balding man with a leveled handgun pointed directly at Judd's back.

There was no time. Judd could react in a split second, but in the split second it would take her to call to him, he'd be dead. There was really no other decision to make, so Christabel made it.

She stepped right out into the path of the gun just as Clark fired.

Strangely, there was no real pain. She felt the impact of something hard and then it became almost impossible to breathe. She stared at the man who'd just shot her as the loud pop sounded, and with a jerky little moan, she fell to the ground face first, unconscious and bleeding.

Tippy saw it happen with utter horror. "Judd!" she squealed, her cry blanked out by the loud pop of the pistol as it fired.

With years of instinct behind him, in a single smooth motion, Judd pulled his .45 Colt automatic, turned, and fired, hitting Clark squarely in the hand. The man dropped the pistol and fell to his knees.

Judd went toward him without hesitation, noticing absently that Christabel had fainted. Cash Grier came running up, his gun out.

"I'll cuff him," Judd said. "Check Christabel. I guess she fainted." He wrestled Clark to the ground and pinned his arms behind him to clip on the handcuffs, deaf to the man's cry of pain and furious threats. "Barnes, call for an ambulance!" he yelled at the security man, who waved and began speaking into the two-way radio transmitter on the inside shoulder of his uniform.

"Judd!"

Cash's voice was oddly cracked.

The unfamiliar sound made Judd uneasy. He left Clark cuffed on his knees, retrieved the .38 caliber revolver Clark had been carrying and stuck it in his duty belt. He joined Cash near Christabel's prone body. Tippy had been frozen in place, but she moved closer, too, along with the rest of the stunned cast.

Cash's hand came out from under Christabel's chest covered with bright red blood.

Judd stopped breathing. He stopped thinking. She hadn't fainted. She lay still and unmoving. She was dead. Clark had killed her. He turned with a sharp curse and went for the hand-cuffed man with an economy of motion that was frightening.

"Judd, no! Stop him!" Cash yelled to the crew.

Three men, two of them engineers, one the assistant director, caught Judd just as he reached the shooter and wrested him away from Clark. Judd cursed roundly, his voice breaking as reality began to trickle into his numbed senses.

"Let me go, damn you!" he panted, struggling furiously with his captors.

"Judd, she's still alive!" Cash called. "She's alive, do you hear me? Get over here! I can't do this alone!"

Judd wrenched away from the men holding him as they reluctantly released their hold. He joined Cash abruptly as the other man turned her body over, gently, with hands that were visibly shaking. Judd was white in the face, breathing jerkily.

Blood was pulsing from the front of her blouse, saturating it and the ground under her. It was so cold that the warm blood made steam rise from the dead grass and dirt. She was unconscious and sucking noisily at air.

"Collapsed lung," Cash said professionally, through gritted teeth. "She's been hit somewhere in the rib cage." He looked at Judd with wild eyes. "We need blankets, something to prop her legs up with, pressure on the wound..."

Judd just sat there, horror in every line of his face as he looked at her, so white and still. For the first time in his adult life, he simply could not act. There was so much blood, he thought blankly. So much! Cash wasn't in much better shape, feeling helpless, too, at the sight of her like that.

Tippy rushed in, remembering graphically what she'd said to the other woman just minutes earlier, the lie she'd told. She hated herself. She felt sick at the sight of the blood, but she was no stranger to emergencies.

She jerked off the expensive sweater she was wearing and put it over the wound, pressing down hard to try and stop the bleeding. Grier glanced at her in surprise.

"She's going into shock," Tippy said calmly. "We need some blankets."

"Blankets!" Cash yelled.

Men started running. Maude heard the commotion and came running out of the house, only to run back in when she was told what had happened and what was needed. She ran back out carrying the bedcovers from the guest room, a big comforter and a quilt. She handed them to Cash, who covered Christabel while Tippy kept pressure on the wound. Maude rolled up another blanket and used it to elevate Christabel's legs. Tears were running down her cheeks. She sobbed as she wrung her hands and watched.

"How about that ambulance?!" Grier yelled at his man.

Even as he raged, the sound of sirens pierced the hum of hushed conversation around them. Judd had one of Christabel's small hands in his. He was holding it so hard that her knuckles were white. His eyes were dead. He didn't even seem to be aware of the people around him.

She was beginning to shiver all over, and a harsh, piteous groan split her dry lips.

The sound mobilized a frozen Judd. He brushed back her hair from her white face. "Be still, honey," he said huskily. "It's all right. I'm here. You're going to be fine. Where the hell is that damned ambulance!" he yelled hoarsely, his deep voice colored with fear.

"Right here, sir," the security man said, moving back spectators and motioning the ambulance into the throng of people. It
was followed by a Jacobsville police car, with one of Grier's officers, the watch commander, driving and another officer in the
passenger seat.

Judd still had a death grip on Christabel's hand. He managed
to stay sane long enough to send a glance at Clark, who was on
his knees in the dirt groaning from his own wound. "Get that
son of a bitch to jail," he said through his teeth, "before I kill
him!"

His eyes were testimony enough to the intent of the statement.
He'd forgotten law, duty, honor, everything, in the grip of the
worst fear he'd ever felt. If she died, he would be lawless. Nothing would matter to him in the world, ever again, except revenge.
He felt cold and sick and horrified. He'd been close to his father when he had died. He remembered holding his father's
hand just as the older man sighed out his last breath. That had
been frightening, but not like this. Nothing had ever been like
this! The cold terror had him firmly in its icy grip. He couldn't
drag his eyes away from Christabel's pain-contorted face. It
was killing him to see her like this! And still the blood ran out
of her like water out of a spigot, despite Tippy's feverish efforts
to stem the flow.

The ambulance attendants moved in, efficient and quick. Judd
wouldn't let go of her hand. They had to work around him, even
to transport her, because he climbed right into the back of the
ambulance with her, still holding her hand. He didn't even notice the other people standing outside the big vehicle as its red
lights flashed on and off.

"Don't let her die," Cash told one of the EMT's grimly. "I'm
going to see if I can get those guns away from him before you
leave," he added quietly.

He climbed into the ambulance, spoke softly to Judd, who
barely heard him, and relieved him of the two firearms, his own
Colt automatic and the wheel gun Clark had been carrying. He

came back out and the ambulance doors closed. His last glimpse of Christabel was with Judd's dark head bent over her in an agony of grief.

"Will she live?" Tippy asked Grier.

He looked down at her, belatedly realizing that she was talking to him. "I don't know," he said flatly. He was as frightened as Judd, he only hid it better.

She drew in a shaky breath. "I've never seen anybody shot."

He wasn't listening. The watch commander approached him. "Get him in leg irons and transport him to the hospital," Grier told him curtly.

"I need a doctor," Clark raged. "I'm shot. My hand's bleeding!"

Grier stared at him. "If you make a move I don't like, you'll need a mortician," he said with pure malice, and abruptly spun the Colt with a professional skill that made Clark back up a step. "Get him out of here," he added coldly. "We'll charge him with another count of aggravated assault and go from there."

"Yes, sir." The police officer wasn't inclined to argue.

"I missed this time, but I won't miss again!" Clark raged. "He killed my brother. I mean to kill him, too, and I will! I swear I will!"

Grier ignored him and handed the police officer the two weapons he'd coaxed from Judd. "The Colt is Judd Dunn's. The Smith & Wesson is the one Clark shot Christabel Gaines with. Lock them up in my office."

"We'll take care of them, sir," the second officer assured him. "I hope Miss Gaines will be all right."

"So do I," Grier said huskily, his voice as rigid as his features. It was killing him that he couldn't go in the ambulance with her. But that was Judd's right, as much as he hated admitting it.

Tippy Moore watched the ambulance drive away. She glanced at Maude, who was weeping copiously on the sidelines. She could only imagine how it affected the old woman, who was the closest thing to a mother Christabel had left. She went to the woman and put a comforting arm around her. "Come on," she said softly. "I'll walk you back to the house."

"I have to go to the hospital," Maude wailed. "But I can't drive, I'm shaking so!"

"I'll get someone to drive us," she said. "I'm going, too," she added doggedly, glancing at the assistant director, who looked ready to argue. "I'm not working any more today, in case you were going to ask. I'm going to the hospital to sit with Judd."

The assistant director threw up his hands, but at a cold glare from Grier, he just walked away without another word.

"You can ride in with me," he told the women, without looking at them. "Give me a minute to phone my office and Judd's." He whipped out his cell phone and began punching in numbers.

"You need a sweater," Tippy told Maude, herding her toward the house. "I'll need to borrow one as well. I put mine over Miss Gaines."

Maude had noticed that, even through the agony of the day. She managed a wet smile, surprised and pleased to find an ally where she'd thought she had an enemy. All her ill will toward the beautiful model vanished in a haze. "I'll find you something."

CHAPTER FOURTEEN

CHAPTER FOURTEEN

Judd was sitting in the emergency room waiting area when Cash Grier came in with Maude and Tippy. His hat was off. His dark hair was rumpled. He looked as if he'd been riding with death. There was blood on his white shirt, on his dark slacks. Christabel's blood.

He looked up as they joined him. "They've taken her into surgery," he said. "Copper Coltrain's operating."

"He's the best we have," Maude commented quietly.

"She moaned all the way in the ambulance," Judd continued, almost as if he were talking to himself. "She couldn't breathe. I wasn't sure she'd even make it here." His eyes closed on a wave of pain.

"Chest wounds are frightening," Cash told him quietly. "But hers was low on her ribcage, and not in the gut."

Judd's black eyes sought reassurance in the older man's. He relaxed, but not much. "I expect the operation's going to take time."

"They'll have to hunt the bullet," Maude groaned.

"They may not try to take the bullet out, if it's less traumatic to leave it in," Cash told her. "They'll stop the bleeding and re-inflate the lung. Then it's a matter of antibiotics and rest."

"She'd just signed up for spring semester and bought her textbooks," Maude said heavily.

"She won't be going back for several weeks," Cash returned flatly. "I'm afraid she'll sit out this part of the school year."

"Quarterly taxes are due week after next," Maude said miserably. "What a horrible thing to think about at a time like this."

"Does she do the tax work?" Cash asked her for something to say.

She nodded. "Does all the book work, except paying monthly bills." She glanced at Judd. "I never got to give you that tie tack she bought you for Christmas," she added, and tears ran down her face.

Judd got up, cut to the heart, and paced, with his hands deep in his pockets.

"He didn't get her a present." Maude explained his sudden withdrawal to the others. "I shouldn't have mentioned it, I guess. Hurt her feelings something awful, especially after he bought Miss Moore that engagement ring."

Cash glared down at the redheaded model, who was already drawing interested stares from men in the waiting room. She seemed oddly uneasy at the attention. She glanced at the ring on her finger and grimaced.

"It's not an engagement ring," she said uncomfortably.

"He told Crissy it was," Maude replied without looking at the younger woman.

Tippy's eyebrows arched. That was news. Why would he lie about such a thing? And then she remembered the whopper she'd told Crissy, trying to get rid of her rival. But she hadn't wanted this. When she looked at Judd, his anguish was almost tangible, and it hurt to think that she'd made Crissy miserable. If the woman died, she'd have to live with it. It wouldn't be easy. She was a coward. She was utterly worthless...

"How can he be engaged to you?" Cash asked curtly, scowling at Tippy. "He and Crissy are still married, aren't they?" he asked Maude.

"They're getting divorced," Maude said. "Didn't she tell you? I guess he's already started proceedings..."

"They're...married?" Tippy exclaimed, paling. "Christabel is his wife?"

"They've been married for five years," Maude confirmed miserably. "Never meant anything to him. It was just on paper, so he could take care of things when her dad went to jail."

"I had no idea," Tippy said miserably.

"Don't tell me it would have mattered," Cash said with dripping sarcasm.

She gave him an angry glance. "It would have mattered," she replied coldly. "I don't date married men. Ever."

His eyebrows went up. That was news.

A tall, redheaded surgeon in green scrubs came out of the swinging doors that led to the operating room, looking around until he spotted Judd. He walked toward him, somber and unsmiling.

"How is she?" Judd asked quickly.

Copper Coltrain shrugged. "We've stopped the bleeding. The lung's reinflated. But she's lost a lot of blood and she's not in good shape otherwise, either. She's got bronchitis. It's going to complicate her recovery."

"Bronchitis?" Judd repeated.

"I thought she sounded hoarse," Maude agreed, "but she said it was just a little cold and she wouldn't go to the doctor." She grimaced. "She said she couldn't afford to. Her insurance doesn't have an outpatient clause."

The minute the words were out, she regretted them. Judd's eyes closed and he looked tormented. Tippy looked at the hateful ring on her finger and cursed her own stupidity in talking Judd into buying her that ring. Cash Grier just sighed with misery eating at him.

"Where do we go from here?" Judd asked in a subdued tone.

"We pray," Coltrain replied flatly. "I won't give you promises I can't keep. Right now, it's a toss-up. I'm sorry. I've done the best I can do."

"I know that. Thanks," Judd said dully. "Can I see her?" he added.

"She's in recovery," he replied. "It would be better to wait until we get her into a room in intensive care..."

"I'll stay with her," Maude interrupted, just before Grier could say the same thing.

"You can't. Not in intensive care. You can see her three times a day, for no more than ten minutes each time," he added firmly. "It's too serious. She has to be kept quiet. No upsets."

Judd looked as if he'd die trying not to snap at the surgeon. But he finally just nodded defeatedly.

Coltrain put a rough hand on his shoulder. "Don't borrow trouble. Take it one hour at a time. You'll get through this."

"Think so?" Judd asked heavily.

"I know so. I'll keep a close watch on her. Try not to worry." He nodded to the others and went back down the hall.

Judd looked at the other three people with him. "I'm glad you're all here. But if anybody gets into that room, even for a minute, it's going to be me," he said shortly.

Cash looked inclined to argue, but the expression on Judd's face made him back down.

"If you want us to stay out here with you, I don't mind," Tippy said.

"Same here," Maude added.

"I'd rather you went home," Judd said. "I'm not leaving the hospital until I know something, one way or the other."

"I'll give them a ride," Cash said. "Then I'll come back."

Judd met the older man's eyes. He didn't argue. He didn't even speak. He just nodded. He didn't want to be alone, and he wouldn't have to pull his verbal punches talking about it to Cash. You just couldn't talk about gunshot wounds with civilians, most of whom had never seen one. Judd and Cash had seen their share. Judd turned and walked toward the intensive care unit.

* * *

"You took his guns away from him, didn't you?" Maude asked Cash when Cash pulled up in front of the house.

He nodded. "They're locked up in my office." His expression was somber. "But there's still a pistol and a shotgun in the house somewhere. Crissy told me. You'd better get all the ammunition and lock it up somewhere."

"The minute I get inside," Maude promised.

Tippy glanced from one of them to the other. "You aren't serious," she remarked.

Cash met her eyes. "If she were my wife, that's what Maude would be doing for me," he said flatly. "And yes, I'm serious. Maybe Judd hasn't realized it yet, but he won't have a life left if Christabel dies. It isn't logical, but it's what some men do when they're out of their minds with grief. We don't need another tragedy."

"Amen," Maude said. She dabbed at her eyes. "Well, you should go and take Miss Moore back to town," she told Cash. "Not that I'll sleep. Are you sure I shouldn't stay with Judd tonight?"

"I won't leave him," Cash assured her. "And I'll call you when I know something. I promise."

"All right, then," Maude said. She gave Tippy a gentle smile. "You keep that sweater," she told her. "I'll get yours back and wash it and press it for you."

"Thank you," Tippy said softly, and she smiled.

Cash drove her to town. He didn't speak and neither did she. In fact, she sat with her arms folded tight over her chest, looking uncomfortable.

"For a man-eater, you're surprisingly tame," he commented when he pulled up in front of her hotel.

She gave him a cool look. "I've done some stupid things. I don't like myself very much right now." She shrugged. "Did you see what she did?" she added heavily. "She stepped right in front of the gun. She saw it coming. She didn't even hesitate. She must...love him very much," she added, almost choking on the words.

"She does," he agreed, feeling the words and hating them.

She glanced at him curiously. "You're in love with her, aren't you?"

"If I am, it's nobody's business except my own," he told her flatly.

She sighed. "Now you're hostile again. Look, I have a hard time with men. A real hard time. Gary Mays, the assistant director, has been driving me up the wall trying to get me into bed. Judd pretended to be interested in me, to keep him at bay, and I took it a little too seriously. That's all it was." She glared at him again. "I wouldn't have a man for life on a bun with sauce."

His eyebrows arched and he looked at her intently. "That's just how I feel about women."

She relaxed a little. Her eyes slid over him carefully. "I trust men in uniform," she blurted out. "Cops have gotten me out of some of the worst tangles in my life."

He was beginning to get a picture of her that was disturbing. Far from the pose she affected on the job, she was shy and introverted and frightened of him when it was just the two of them, alone.

"I have to go in," she said. "I hope Christabel will be all right. Judd, too."

"Why don't you look Gary Mays right in the eye and tell him you'll have him up for sexual harassment if he doesn't back off?" he asked abruptly.

Her eyes almost popped. "It wouldn't work."

"It would. If you can stop a man, you can dominate him."

"Interesting philosophy," she said.

"Not mine. I read Juan Belmonte's autobiography. He was a famous bullfighter in the early 1900s. He said it works as well with men as it does with bulls. It does."

"You'd know," she murmured dryly.

"Yes. I would."

She got out of the truck, a little slowly. "Thanks for the ride."

He scowled and peered at her closely. "Can you see me?" he asked unexpectedly.

She was surprised by the question. She smiled. "Sort of," she replied.

"You're nearsighted and you won't wear your glasses," he guessed.

She laughed. It sounded like silver bells tinkling. "And I can't wear contacts."

He studied her. Despite the tragedy of the day, she piqued his curiosity. "You're a puzzle. I've said some things to you that I shouldn't have. You're not what I thought you were."

She was watching him with new respect. "Neither are you," she said.

"Think about what I said," he told her as he started the truck. "You don't have to take that sort of crap from an assistant director. If you can't make him stop, let me know. I'll stop him."

She shrugged and managed a smile. "I'll keep in touch with Maude."

He nodded. He didn't say another word. Seconds later, he was on his way to the hospital.

Judd sat alone in the chapel. They'd let him in for a handful of minutes to look down on Christabel's white, drawn little face. If he'd been able to get to a bar, he could have gone through a fifth of whisky afterward. It was shocking to see her like that. She was hooked up to half a dozen monitoring machines with a needle in her arm feeding her nutrients and apparently a narcotic for pain. There was a tube coming out of her side to drain her chest. Perhaps it was the same tube they'd used to reinflate the lung as well.

Not since she was sixteen had she been so badly hurt, and even then it wasn't this serious. There hadn't been the risk that she could die from her father's brutal beating. This was different. She looked fragile and helpless and so alone. Her big dark eyes were closed. There were dark circles under them. When she breathed, he heard the slow rasp of fluid in her chest. Her lips were blue. She looked as if she'd already died.

He'd touched her small hand with his big one and remembered the last thing she'd said to him before Clark showed up. Tippy had told her that he'd been disgusted with her, that he hadn't wanted her hanging on him, running after him with her heart on her sleeve. His eyes had closed with a shudder. If she didn't make it, her last memory of him would be one of pain and betrayal.

It wasn't true. He wasn't disgusted. He lay awake nights remembering the passion they'd shared. He missed her. It was like being without an arm or a leg. He'd told her he didn't want anything permanent. Now the choice might not be his anymore. He might be left alone, as he'd thought he wanted to be when he told her he was getting the divorce.

Somewhere he remembered an old adage. Be careful what you want; you might get it. He looked at Christabel's still body and saw the end of everything he loved.

A noise caught his attention. Grier was back. He sat down in the pew beside him, looking uncomfortable.

"God's ticked at me," he told Judd on an audible sigh as he looked around him. "Maybe I'm jinxing her by being in a chapel at all."

"God isn't vindictive," Judd replied heavily. "Usually He gives us a lot more leeway than we deserve."

"Your father was a minister, Crissy said," he commented.

Judd nodded.

"Shooting John Clark was harder on you than you expected," he replied quietly.

Judd glanced at him curiously. "Because my father was a minister?"

"Because you were taught to believe that killing is always wrong." Grier's eyes went to the pulpit. "I wasn't. The first thing you learn in the military is the necessity of killing, and how to do it with maximum efficiency. Men won't kill another man close up unless they're taught to do it through muscle reflex. After a few weeks of training, killing is instinctive. I was a good student," he added, his voice cold in the silence.

Judd's eyes narrowed. "It doesn't bother you?"

"It didn't. Until I got mixed up with her," he added, smiling faintly. "She was the first woman in years who didn't look at me and see a killer. She has this annoying way of making you feel important, necessary, useful. She made me feel good just by smiling at me."

Judd hated hearing that from his rival. "She's always been like that," he commented after a minute. "No matter how bad things get, she's always got a smile."

"She made me think I could fit in here, if I tried," he replied. "I've never wanted to belong anywhere in my life until now."

Judd stared at the other man with narrowed eyes. "I appreciate your company. But you'd better know that if she lives, she's never getting that divorce," he said abruptly.

Cash stared back. "You won't fool her with pity," he returned. "She'll see right through it."

Judd averted his gaze. He wasn't willing to share his deepest feelings with his only rival. "The only person I feel sorry for right now is myself. I'm the idiot who was supposed to be protecting her. How the hell did she get shot?" he asked suddenly. "I know he wasn't trying to kill her. She didn't shoot his damned brother!"

Cash hesitated, studying his hands. He couldn't tell Judd what he knew. Not yet. Not until they were sure she was going to live.

"It will all come out eventually," Cash said noncommittally.

He put his face in his hands with a long, unsteady sigh. "I'd give anything to go back and put things right," he said enigmatically.

"You, and the rest of us," Cash said philosophically.

It was a long night. The next morning a bleary-eyed Judd walked into the intensive care unit with a long face and a heavy heart. Christabel lay just as he'd seen her before. There was a new drip running, but her expression was as dead as it had been.

He leaned down, brushing the hair away from her face. He winced at just the sight of her. "I'm so sorry," he whispered. "So sorry, honey."

Her long eyelashes twitched and her dark eyes opened. Her breathing was still raspy, and she looked like death on a warming plate. But she seemed to see him.

"Christabel?" he whispered.

Her eyes fixed on his face, but she didn't react.

"Can you hear me, baby?" he asked softly.

She frowned and winced. "Hurts," she whispered hoarsely.

His big hand trembled as it smoothed her hair, her face. "Thank God you're still alive," he said, his voice breaking despite his steely control. He bent and brushed his lips over her dry mouth. "Thank God, thank God, thank God!" he groaned.

She blinked. She was barely aware of anything except the pain. "Hurts so much," she breathed and her eyes closed again.

He let go of her reluctantly and pushed the nurse's call button to tell her that Christabel was awake and in pain. Seconds later, a nurse breezed in, followed by a technician, and he was chased out with reassuring smiles. She was going to live. This was the hopeful sign they'd all been waiting for.

Coltrain nodded in passing as he went in to check her. He came back out scant minutes later smiling. "She's going to be fine," he told Judd, clapping him on the shoulder. "It's just a matter of time, now. You can stop holding your breath."

Judd thanked him and then went down the hall and leaned against the wall trying to compose himself. He'd been in hell for so long that the relief was devastating. She would live. She was going to live. He brushed away the quick moisture in his eyes.

Cash came up beside him, a question in his eyes.

"She's going to make it," Judd said huskily.

"Thank God," Cash said with heartfelt relief.

"What about Clark?" he asked suddenly, having only just remembered the man.

"Patched up and in jail, probably for the rest of his life after the trial," Cash assured him. He was watching the other man closely. "I think you should know what Tippy told me," he added, hating to reveal it even now. It meant an end to all his own hopes.

"Yes?" Judd prompted.

"She saw Clark step out and aim the gun at you. She didn't have time to react, and neither did Crissy. She said Crissy realized you wouldn't be able to save yourself, and she deliberately stepped out in front of the gun."

Judd's intake of breath was audible.

"Tippy was devastated when she saw it," he continued. "She said she felt ten kinds of a fool for the trouble she'd caused between the two of you, when she knew how much Crissy cared." He shook his head. "I wouldn't have told you if Crissy had died. But you should know. I'll go call Maude and give her the good news."

He turned and walked away. Judd stood there like a statue, absorbing the statement with a feeling of utter humility. Christabel had taken the bullet meant for him. She'd been willing to give her own life to save him. He'd never dreamed she cared so much. He was absolutely without words. Now he had to find a way to rebuild the bridges he'd burned. It wasn't going to be easy.

Christabel drifted in and out of consciousness for the first few days after her body began the slow process of recovery from the wound, which had cost her part of the lower lobe of her lung and a piece of her spleen as well. Fortunately the bullet was in the destroyed tissue which had to be removed to stop the bleeding.

She was moved into a semi-private room on the fourth day. After that, Judd never left her side. His second shooting in two weeks had landed him under administrative leave yet again, but he didn't care. It was opportune. His captain and his lieutenant had phoned twice already to check on Christabel's status. He had good co-workers. One of them from San Antonio was assigned to take his place temporarily in Victoria while Christabel recuperated from her wounds. Ranch business had to be attended to as well, even though Judd hated the time he was required to spend away from her taking care of it. He delegated as much as he could to their foreman, Nick.

Grier was also a constant visitor, but he was oddly subdued and kept well in the background. Marc Brannon and his wife, Josette, heard about the tragedy and came by to offer support. So did a lot of other prominent citizens. Tippy Moore also came by after work to check on the patient, bringing Maude with her. The actress had surprised a lot of people with her compassion, most notably Grier. He was an unintentional eavesdropper on a conversation she had on her cell phone. At first he thought she was talking to a man, because her voice was soft and full of affection. Then she mentioned tests and grades and keeping out of fights with other boys, and he realized she was speaking to a child. It turned out to be her young brother, in a military school. She confessed it with odd reserve and then walked away before Grier could question her any more.

When there were no visitors, Christabel was reserved with Judd. She didn't look him in the eye ever. She smiled when Grier and Maude came and managed to converse with them, even though she was frightfully weak. She was polite, if distant, with Tippy. But she was visibly uncomfortable with Judd.

"You should go back to work," she told him one morning when the nurse's aide got her up and into a chair while her bed was remade. "I'm only going to be in here for a few more days, the doctor says. Nick can handle things at home. I'm out of danger."

Judd, bare-headed and quiet, didn't answer her. He watched the aide change the bed and refill the ice pitcher without visible reaction. The aide finished, helped Christabel back into bed, smiled shyly at Judd, and left, closing the door behind her.

Judd still hadn't spoken. He moved to her bedside and looked down at her broodingly. Her hair needed washing. It was tangled and limp. Her weakness was evident, and she moved with difficulty because her lungs were only beginning to heal from the double peril of a bullet wound and bronchitis. She was winded just from getting up out of the chair and back into bed.

But to Judd, who'd watched her in anguish from the time she came out of the anesthetic until now, she was beautiful.

"You'll lose your job and it will be my fault," she persisted.

"I won't lose it. I have permission to be here." He lifted her left hand and rubbed his thumb over the signet ring she'd given back to him two months ago. He'd replaced it on her ring finger while she was still unconscious. "You gave us all a scare," he added solemnly.

She moved her finger experimentally, only just realizing the ring was back. "How did that get there?" she asked drowsily.

"I put it there," he replied quietly. "We're still married. I had to sign you in under your legal name."

She averted her eyes and tugged her hand away from his. "That must have shocked Miss Moore," she said very dully. "I hope she's willing to wait until we can get divorced."

He drew in a short breath and rammed his hands into his pockets. "Let's see about getting you well and back on your feet before we talk about that."

She arched an eyebrow. "Why wait?"

He turned away, frowning. Inspiration came as he studied the painting on the wall. It looked vaguely Japanese. "You're forgetting the business trip to Japan, aren't you?" he murmured. "We wouldn't want to upset the negotiations at this stage by presenting a divided front, would we?"

"It shouldn't affect the negotiations," she replied, but she didn't sound convincing.

He turned and studied her slight form under the sheet. "Let's not take chances, just the same."

She frowned, but she didn't argue. "Whatever you want to do is fine with me," she replied after a minute. "But you may have to go to Japan alone. I don't know that I'll be up to it."

"We'll cross that bridge when we come to it," he said. He moved back to the bed, his face drawn and taut with worry and lack of sleep. He reached down and touched her face lightly with his fingertips. "You're a little better today."

"It's slow," she replied.

His thumb rubbed slowly, softly, over her full mouth. It excited him to remember its ardent response on Christmas Eve. He had so many regrets. He could hardly find room for them all in his conscience.

"You don't sleep well, do you, honey?" he asked with some concern. "There are dark circles under your eyes."

She laughed without humor. "If I could get out of this bed, Jack Clark would have a few dark circles under his eyes, too, but they wouldn't be from lack of sleep!"

"He'll go away for a long time," he said curtly.

Her dark eyes sought his. "Cash said you tried to attack him."

His gaze moved to the far wall. "I didn't even realize you were shot until Cash turned you over and we saw the blood. We thought you'd fainted until then."

"I don't faint," she remarked drowsily. She sighed and closed her eyes wearily.

"You brave little idiot," he bit off, moving closer to the bed. "Why didn't you just sing out?"

"He had you right in his sights," she said involuntarily. "There wasn't time to shout a warning. By the time I spotted him, he was already pulling the trigger."

"Christabel, how do you think I'd feel if you'd died?" he asked bluntly. "Do you think I could have lived with knowing that you bought my life with your own?"

She barely heard him. She was so tired. "Couldn't...let him... kill you."

He bent with a groan and pressed his lips hard to her forehead. "Listen, there's something I need to tell you," he began.

"No, there's not," she murmured. "It was my choice. I made it. You've taken care of me for five years, Judd. It was my turn to take care of you."

He couldn't bear the pain of remembering how she'd looked just after the bullet hit her. He bent and drew his mouth tenderly over her dry lips, savoring their warmth in a tense silence.

"Don't," she moaned, putting her hand against his mouth. "Don't, please! I don't want to mess up your life any more than I already have. You don't owe me a thing."

He kissed her palm hungrily. "You don't understand."

Her eyes opened and looked up into his. "Sure I do," she whispered wearily. "You feel guilty for what you told Tippy about how I embarrassed you. Then I got shot and you're trying to sacrifice yourself to make amends. It isn't necessary. You can take this ring back. I'll give you a divorce..."

He caught her hand, preventing her from removing the ring. But coping with her suspicions was harder than he'd realized it might be. She wasn't going to listen to reason. She thought he was lying out of guilt and pity.

"You might lose her if you wait too long," she continued, her voice trailing off as she drifted in and out, on the verge of falling asleep.

"I've already waited too long," he bit off, hating the lump in his throat that he couldn't seem to lose, his eyes intent and tortured on her pale face.

But she didn't hear him. She was asleep.

Soon after they brought her home from the hospital, Christabel was struggling around the house trying to cook. Once Maude escorted her back to bed. The next day, Judd carried her there, tight-lipped and unresponsive to her protests.

"I can't just lie around here like a lump, I'll never get well," she raged when he started to put her back into bed. "Copper said I had to exercise!"

"A little at a time, and not the way you're trying to do it," he retorted curtly. He put her down against the pillows and glared down at her. She'd had a shower and washed her hair, with Maude's help, and she looked infinitely better than she had days earlier.

"All right, I'll stay put," she muttered, averting her eyes. "You should be spending time with Miss Moore. They're wrapping the film Friday and then they'll be gone."

He hadn't been able to get her to listen to a thing he'd said about his relationship with Tippy. She cut him off before he could even begin to explain it. Tippy had given him back the emerald and diamond ring, with all sorts of mumbled apologies, and he'd returned it to the jewelers for the refund of most his money. He'd wanted to tell Christabel, but she wouldn't listen. Neither would she accept the still-wrapped Christmas present he'd brought down for her, certain that it was an attempt to make up for not giving her one at the time. Maude had given him the tie tack Christabel had bought for him, and he'd kept it with him the whole time she was in the hospital. She didn't know that. He was tired of trying to make her listen.

Grier had been more visible lately, too, another source of worry, because Christabel perked up the minute he stuck his head in the door. She laughed with him as she never did with Judd anymore.

"I can't make you listen," he said in a heavy, defeated tone. "You don't want to hear me."

She glanced up at him with troubled dark eyes. "You won't listen to me, either. I said I'd give you a divorce whenever you want it. We can afford it now that we have the film company's check in the bank."

His jaw tautened. "I don't want a damned divorce!" he snapped. "I don't want to marry Tippy Moore! I never did!"

She tried to sit up and accidentally knocked over the glass of orange juice by the bed, spilling it all over herself in the process. "Now look what you made me do!" she raged.

"I never touched the damned thing!" he shot back, furious.

Tippy Moore heard the raised voices and stuck her head in. "Oh, for heaven's sake," she muttered, rushing back out again. She was back seconds later with a towel and a wet washcloth. "Out," she told Judd, holding the door.

He started to argue.

"You heard her!" Christabel seconded. "Out!"

He threw up his hands and stalked out in a black temper, slamming the door viciously behind him.

Tippy laughed. "Aren't men the living end?" she mused. She mopped up the orange juice with the towel. "Where do you keep your gowns?" she asked matter-of-factly.

Crissy told her, surprised by the woman's efficiency. She was bathed off with the washcloth, her dirty gown deftly removed and replaced by the clean one.

"Oh, I've spent years taking care of my little brother, and then a man I cared...very much for," Tippy said. "My brother's nine, now, and in military school." Her eyes were haunted. "I spent a fortune getting custody of him from my mother and her latest lover, but I wouldn't put it past them to try and kidnap him for more money. Nobody knows where he is except me."

Crissy was fascinated by this glimpse of the woman's private life. There was a haunted look about her. "You must care about him a lot."

She nodded. "He's my whole life." She picked up the towel and washcloth and gave the other woman a long, sad look. "I've made a lot of trouble for you with Judd. I want you to know that I'm sorry for all of it. I felt safe with him. He was the best man I've ever known and I got possessive. But if I'd had the slightest idea you were married, I'd never...!"

"It's all right," Crissy said, embarrassed. "You can't help how you feel about people."

Tippy sighed. "Isn't that the truth," she murmured, thinking about Cash Grier and his coldness, despite her attempts to revise his opinion of her.

Crissy, predictably, thought she meant Judd and was even more depressed.

"I gave Judd back the ring," she added firmly. "And I'm sorry about letting him buy it for me, too. I never realized how bad things were around here."

"They won't be for much longer," Crissy told her. "We're working on a new deal with an overseas market. If we can pull it off, I'll move out after we get the divorce, and he'll have everything he wants."

"Without you?" Tippy asked, astonished. "Can't you see how he feels?"

"He feels guilty," Crissy told her flatly. "That will wear off, given time." She lay back with her eyes closed. "I'm tired of being married to a man who thinks of me as an albatross. I just want out."

Tippy didn't know what to say. She stood there with remorse eating at her. Finally, she went out of the room and closed the door quietly behind her. She'd caused enough trouble for one day, with only the best of intentions.

CHAPTER FIFTEEN

CHAPTER FIFTEEN

Judd reluctantly returned to Victoria when Christabel was able to get around the ranch comfortably. He'd gone back to work the week after she'd come home, after the second shooting investigation that cleared him of any wrongdoing. But he'd commuted from Jacobsville to Victoria, to be on hand if he was needed. He and Nick had outlined new plans for the ranch, bought new materials, hired on a full-time man, and organized work schedules for maximum efficiency.

Christabel, who'd tried but failed to get so much work out of the part-time help, stood in awe of Judd when he set his mind to a problem. Nick just grinned and did what he was told, watching with amusement the way the part-timers jumped on projects and carried them through with no coaxing or argument.

The ranch was looking up, with the new infusion of money from the film project. Another film company, in fact, had targeted the ranch for a setting the following year. Christabel had groaned, but Judd had dangled promises of a new barn and improving the house even more, and she'd given in. Besides, it wouldn't happen until autumn next year. A lot could happen in that length of time, she told herself. In fact, she might not even be here then.

Meanwhile, the Japanese company had been in touch and arrangements were made for Judd and Christabel to fly over to Osaka for meetings. She'd tried to get out of going, pleading work, but Judd knew better. She couldn't even argue about not having a passport, because he'd had plenty of time to get her one. Nick was perfectly capable of overseeing what needed doing here at home, and it wasn't time for calving yet, either. She had no excuse, unless it was being reluctant to leave Cash Grier, he'd added with bitter coldness.

Cash had become her security blanket. She kept him between her and Judd, because she didn't want Judd making her any declarations out of gratitude or guilt. She knew he wanted to. She read him very well. He was still awed at the fact that she'd tried to sacrifice herself to save him. He couldn't get past that, no matter how hard he worked at it. She couldn't have made her feelings for him plainer if she'd worn a sign.

But she couldn't talk her way out of going to Japan. Even Maude jumped on the bandwagon and started insisting that she go.

"I'm still weak from being in the hospital," she argued with Judd the day before they were leaving out of the Houston airport.

He studied her with that brooding, almost painful scrutiny that had been so evident lately. "I know that," he told her gently. "But it will be a new experience for you. You need to get away from here for a while."

She gave him a long look. "Away from Cash, don't you mean?"

His jaw clenched. Just the sound of the man's name was like waving a red flag at a Texas longhorn bull. "You do live in his pocket since you came home," he pointed out.

She turned away from him, tired of the fighting. She and Cash were friends. That was all it would ever be. But it kept Judd from wallowing over the debt he owed her.

"If it had been me, in the same circumstances, you'd have

done what I did, and you know it," she said quietly, her eyes on the pasture out the window. "You're making such a big deal of this, Judd, and it isn't necessary."

She felt his warmth at her back, felt his breath stirring the hair at her temples.

"You took a bullet that was meant for me," he said curtly. "How, exactly, should I take it?"

His big hands caught her shoulders and turned her around, very gently, so that he could look down into her eyes.

"I move one step closer and you move two steps back," he said broodingly. "Are you the same woman who couldn't get close enough to me on Christmas Eve?"

She flushed. "How dare you bring that up!" she raged.

"And you hadn't even been drinking," he added with amused indulgence.

She looked everywhere except in his eyes. "It was a mistake. You said so."

"I said a lot of things," he murmured evasively.

"Yes, and now you're saying a lot more, and you shouldn't," she tried to explain, pulling away from his hands. "Listen, you want a divorce. No problem. I'm not even arguing about it. You can marry Tippy Moore and I'll go around with Cash until he decides whether or not he can live in Jacobsville for the rest of his life."

He wondered if she had any idea how much it hurt him when she made offhand remarks like that. He had no interest in Tippy Moore. But her fascination with Cash had caused him to pretend one, out of wounded pride. Cash was everything most men wanted to be. He was handsome, charming, cultured and absolutely fearless. There wasn't a peace officer in Texas who didn't recognize his name. Judd had a cursory education and some college, but he wasn't in Cash's league intellectually and he was keenly aware of it. He wasn't cultured, either, and he didn't speak half a dozen impossible foreign languages.

Worse, he knew how Cash felt about Christabel, and that,

given the least chance, he'd marry her out of hand, without a second thought.

Judd began to see how his indifference and rejection had wounded her all these long years, when he'd been so determined to keep his distance from her. He'd told himself it was for her good, so that she'd be heartwhole and innocent, so that she could pick up the threads of her life when their marriage was annulled. But it wasn't. He didn't want ties, roots, a family. He couldn't help remembering his own childhood when his mother left his father for another man. She'd been like Christabel, innocent and married in her teens, with no experience of the world or other men except her husband. It wasn't surprising to him, now, in manhood, that she would have been tempted by other men.

He'd had visions of Christabel doing as his mother had, running into some other man's arms out of curiosity after years of marriage, and it had frightened him. He'd turned away from her hungry eyes, her dreams of a life with him. Now he wanted those things back again, but she didn't. She was as remote and unresponsive as he'd ever been. With greater cause, he had to admit. He'd given her no encouragement whatsoever. Now, it seemed, it was too late. And the competition was fierce. Even he, with his massive self-confidence, felt uncertain around the threat of Cash Grier.

"I've told you until I'm blue in the face that I never intended to marry Tippy," he said through his teeth. "But you won't listen."

Because he'd said he was going to marry Tippy continually until Christabel was shot, she thought, but she was through arguing. "If I can't get out of going, I guess I'll pack," she said heavily. "Thirteen hours on an airplane. I'll be foaming at the mouth before we even get to California."

He gave her a worldly look. "We could do the initiation for the Mile High club."

It took a minute for her to realize what he was talking about.

She glared up at him. "I am not having sex with you in the wash-room of an airplane!"

"Not even if I bought you a red negligee?" he asked softly.

Maude stopped in the doorway with one foot raised. She cleared her throat, put her foot down, and almost ran for the safety of the kitchen.

Judd didn't say anything. He was laughing too hard. Christa-bel made a rough sound in her throat and beat a hasty retreat to her room as fast as she could walk.

The trip was long, and a little frightening to Christabel, who'd never been on an airplane in her life. It was noisy in the econ-omy section, but she and Judd had both refused to let the com-pany pay for business class tickets. They felt bad enough about having to take the tickets in the first place. The seats were cramped and it was difficult to relax, but just thinking about the wonder of being in a foreign country fascinated Christabel.

They were fed and soon afterward the sleepless nights caught up with Christabel and she fell asleep. It seemed like no time before Judd was kissing her awake.

The feel of his mouth on hers was electrifying, and she had to fight not to return the tender caress. "Are we there?" she whispered.

He smiled. "Look out the window, honey."

She opened the shade. She knew that, for the rest of her life, she would remember that first incredible glimpse of the Japan-ese coast. All the reading and travelogues on television hadn't prepared her for the impact of such glorious beauty. There were green mountains going up into the clouds. The coastline had sharp rocks standing right up out of the ocean. It was like look-ing at something out of a paradise fantasy. The joy of the unex-pected sight hit her right in the heart.

"Oh!" she whispered, wordless.

"That was how I felt, the first time I saw it," Judd told her qui-etly. He'd gone to Japan on a case, years before, when the Texas

Rangers were working with Interpol. "I could never manage to describe it. You have to see it."

"Yes." She sighed with pleasure. "It's so beautiful."

He was looking at her profile, drinking in the sight of her. "So beautiful," he whispered, thinking painfully that she could be dead now, so easily.

"They're going to meet us at the airport, right?" she added, worried. "I wish one of us spoke Japanese, like Cash."

He froze over. Just once, he thought, just one day he'd like to get through the whole without having her refer to the damned man.

She knew what she'd said, and she grimaced. If only he'd get over his resentment of Cash! After all, he had Tippy, a beautiful and famous woman that any man would be proud to call his own. When he came to his senses, he'd realize that Christabel was no longer part of his life. Surely he would.

The Kansai Airport was huge, a symphony in metal and glass, but difficult to make their way around. Christabel was uneasy as they went through passport control. Everything was so different.

But her worries came to nothing. They were met at customs by Mr. Kosugi himself and his business partner, Mr. Nasagi, and several colleagues.

"I trust you had a pleasant flight?" Mr. Kosugi asked, all smiles, nodding to an associate to get their bags as he joined them.

"It was wonderful. But my first sight of your beautiful country will last me all my life," Christabel said huskily, returning the smile.

"Your wife is a diplomat, Mr. Dunn," the other man laughed.

Judd slid an arm around her and tugged her close. "My right arm," he murmured, and smiled back.

The manager of the hotel and the assistant manager came out to meet the Dunns and escort them, along with Mr. Kosugi and his staff, up to their room. It was such flattering treatment that Christabel didn't know how to react.

"You make us feel so special," she told the businessman.

"As you are. It is our pleasure to welcome you to our country. We hope your room will be adequate," the hotel manager added, opening the curtains to reveal the river and bridge just below, and the city of Osaka spread out beyond it.

"How incredibly beautiful," Christabel said, aghast.

Mr. Kosugi chuckled. "We will come by for you about 6:00 p.m., if that is acceptable and you will eat at our main restaurant here in Osaka." He hesitated. "Of course, if you would prefer American cuisine..."

"But I want sushi," Christabel said at once. "And I read about freshwater eel, and I've had miso soup and I love it...!"

"Same here," Judd said with a grin. "You'll find that Japanese cuisine suits us very well!"

The surprised, and pleased, looks of their hosts said everything.

They smiled tolerantly at Christabel's struggle with the chopsticks. She didn't want them to know that Cash had tried to tutor her, but she'd failed miserably. Judd used them like a native, and took the opportunity to show Christabel how to hold them properly and get them to work.

"See?" he chided gently. "It isn't hard at all."

"Thanks."

His eyes lingered on her face while she picked up a piece of grilled eel and took it into her mouth. She was wearing a new silver dress with spaghetti straps that Judd had insisted on buying for her before they left Jacobsville. Her blond hair was down around her shoulders and she was wearing tiny white high heels with an ankle strap. She looked beautiful to Judd, who could hardly bear to take his eyes off her.

"Tomorrow we will take you to one of our branch restaurants in Kyoto," Mr. Kosugi said, "and to the farm where we raise our beef, so that you can inspect the premises. While we are there," he added, "would you like to see a castle, perhaps?"

She laid down her chopsticks. "A real samurai fort?" she exclaimed. "With 'nightingale' floors?"

It was Mr. Kosugi's turn to be surprised. "You know about 'nightingale' floors, Mrs. Judd?" he asked.

It thrilled her to be called by her married name. She grinned. "I love foreign films. I guess I've seen every samurai movie there is! I'd love to see the fort!"

He was impressed. "Then we shall go and see Nijo Castle, which dates from 1603. I will come for you after breakfast tomorrow. Shall we say 9:00 a.m.?"

"That would be perfect," she said on a sigh, and Judd nodded, smiling at her enthusiasm.

She and Judd shared the same hotel room, with its double beds, but she hardly thought about the intimacy of it. She was so tired that she barely got into her cotton gown before she was sound asleep. The next morning, Judd, already dressed, woke her and waited for her to get her casual clothes on so that they could go downstairs for breakfast.

Mr. Kosugi and his party arrived right on time to pick them up. Christabel was surprised at how much energy she had, despite the unseasonable warmth. They were going to ride the famous bullet train to Kyoto, and the station at Osaka where they got on it fascinated her. It had several levels and included the shopping mall where a scene from the Michael Douglas film *Black Rain* had been shot. She delighted in each new experience, from the warmth of the people and the joyful custom of smiling and bowing at each opportunity to the high tech tools the Japanese took so much for granted. Mr. Kosugi's wife showed her a phone which was also a music player, an Internet link, a camera, a television screen and a portable library, with a database and even a word processor. Judd was equally fascinated with it.

Their tickets were obtained by one of the staff. They had to be inserted in a slot in a long metal counter next to the turnstile, and reacquired at the end of it. The train was crowded, but they found seats and enjoyed the speed and the company.

When they arrived in Kyoto, Christabel watched Judd surreptitiously. He looked more relaxed than she'd ever seen him in her life. He strolled along among the fascinated Japanese with long, rangy strides, his boots catching as much attention as his Stetson. One cheeky teenager winked at him and said, "Howdy, partner!"

Their party walked out of the station and were picked up in a neat van which took them to the Kosugi farm, where they toured the facility and became acquainted with the very high-tech methods of beef production. Christabel and Judd liked what they saw, and said so. When they returned to the van, they were given wet white cloths rolled up in plastic to remove the sweat. They were overdressed for the unusual heat. The van driver took them to Nijo Castle, seat of the Tokugawa shogunate, and they walked around the graveled courtyard where sculptured gardens led to the castle itself, a one-level collection of rooms within sliding doors around which a long wooden walkway passed. The walkway made a sound like a bird singing when walked upon. They were shown the underside of it, where strategically placed nails and metal made contact to produce the sound. The nightingale floor as it was called, was a melodic way to ensure that enemy soldiers or ninja could never sneak up on the samurai! Christabel had a camera with her, and Mrs. Kosugi took picture after picture of Christabel and Judd together. Christabel was happy to have the shots—it might be the last she'd see of Judd after he divorced her.

There was a gift shop at the samurai fort where they could purchase soft drinks and souvenirs. Judd bought Christabel a beautiful red and black fan and postcards of the fort to carry home. Then it was back into the van, which featured white lace trim and the most courteous of drivers, and on to Mr. Kosugi's

restaurant for a late lunch. The food was delightful in Mr. Kosugi's restaurant, especially his beef, which rivaled the famed
Kobe beef that Japan was famous for. He used many of the same
techniques which produced it, including massaging the cattle.
The Dunn imported cattle would be similarly raised. They had
a beef dish with noodles that was absolutely delicious.

Christabel was becoming more expert with chopsticks since
Judd had tutored her. She hadn't been able to get the hang of it
when Cash had shown her how. She made the mistake of mentioning it while she dipped noodles expertly from a bowl into
her mouth.

Judd had been exuberant and smiling all day. But at the mention of Cash's name, he went cold. Even his appetite seemed to
suffer. He made every effort to be polite to their hosts. They
toured a temple and spoke to the Buddhist monk, who even au-
tographed the little book Christabel bought as a souvenir of the
fascinating temple, with its sprawling Zen gardens of sand, and
beautiful koi in a pond near the temple. But later, after another
train ride back to Osaka, and then a ferry ride down the river to
their hotel, Judd's pleasant manner went into eclipse. By the time
he and Christabel were alone in their hotel room, it was a different story.

"Maybe I should have stayed home and let Cash come with
you," he said with barely contained fury. "He can even speak the
language, can't he?"

She stiffened. "Yes, he can, quite fluently," she retorted, brown
eyes flashing. She pushed back her long blond hair, disheveled
from the wind. In beige slacks and a floral blouse, she looked
slender and neat and very pretty.

Judd turned, moving toward her with a suddenness that left
her heart hanging in space. He was still wearing navy blue
slacks, but he'd shed his jacket and tie and hat, and unbuttoned
the top buttons of his shirt. The thick dark hair that covered his
muscular chest was revealed blatantly, and she was remembering how it felt to be held against it in the darkness.

"But he hasn't had you," he said abruptly, towering over her. "And he won't!"

Her breath rushed out and she stared up at him with wide, perplexed eyes. "You don't want me..." she began.

His lean hands shot out and drew her to him gently, wrapping her up against the muscular length of him. "Blind, deaf, dumb and numb from the neck down, are we?" he asked with black humor as he pressed her hips into his.

She felt the irony of the statement keenly. He was completely aroused, and he'd barely touched her. She swallowed hard. Delicious little skirls of pleasure were dancing in the back of her mind. She remembered pleasure so deep it was almost pain, and sounds coming out of her throat that barely sounded human.

Her hands pushed softly at his shirt. "Don't, Judd," she said huskily. "You're just upset over all that's happened. It will wear off."

"I've been noble since they took you to the hospital," he said through his teeth. "I'm tired of it. I don't eat, I don't sleep, I can't even work. I remember your voice moaning in my ear like the cry of the damned while I was having you," he bit off, bending to her mouth. "You couldn't get enough of me. You couldn't get close enough to me. Your face when I fulfilled you...I ache every time I think about it. And you think it will wear off?"

She was losing ground. Her body was reacting predictably to having him this close, and not in any way that was going to convince him. Already her breasts were flattening against his diaphragm, her legs were carrying her closer to that magnificent arousal. She felt him all around her and she wanted him insanely.

She watched her own hands sliding inside his shirt with a feeling of horror, but she had no power to stop them. She lifted her face to his and saw the same helpless, hopeless desire reflected in his glittery black eyes.

"This time, I'm not putting out the light, Christabel," he said as he bent, lifting her clear of the floor. "And you're going to love what I do to you."

His mouth opened on her parted lips. It was like an explosion of joy inside her. To her shame, she did nothing that looked like a protest. She clung to him, answering the fierce hunger of his mouth with an insane passion, rubbing her body against his and moaning piteously.

By the time they ended up sprawled on the bed together, she was beyond words at all. Her hands were as impatient of obstacles as his, her breath jerky and quick in the utter silence of the room.

"We're having dinner...with the Kosugis," she choked as he skinned off her slacks and dragged her blouse over her head.

"In two hours," he whispered roughly, his hands going to her underwear with deadly efficiency. "With a little luck, you'll still be able to walk by then...!"

She moaned against the harsh pressure of his mouth. He found his way down her body, removing obstacles with little finesse and much urgency until they were riveted together in a nude tangle on the sheets.

"Slow down," he whispered huskily as she writhed under the brush of his lips on her breasts. "Slow down, baby. Don't hurry. There's no need. No need at all."

She sobbed, her voice loud in the stillness that was unbroken except by the soft hum of the air-conditioning. "The maids," she gasped.

"I closed the door."

She was going to mention that they had a passkey, but his lips were on the inside of her long legs and she was going crazy with pleasure. She'd never dreamed that her own desire would peak like this, explode like this, the minute he touched her.

"Maybe...I'm not normal," she choked out, clinging to him.

"Why?"

"I'm on fire," she laughed jerkily. "I'm dying for you. I'd do anything, anything...!"

"So would I. Anything to please you." He slid alongside her and cradled her head in his hands, tenderly assaulting her face. "It's been so long, honey. So long!"

His voice ended in a harsh groan as she ran her hands through the thick hair that covered him. She wondered if men felt the same as women did about intimate caresses. Driven to find out, she bent to his chest and explored him with her mouth, lingering on the flat male nipples that were the counterpoint of her own.

He arched, shuddering.

"Do you like that?" she whispered at his collarbone.

"I love it," he ground out. "Do it again."

She did, following his lead. But when her mouth reached just below his navel, he shook all over and suddenly dragged her body under his, tangling their legs together while he searched for her mouth.

His hands were in between them now, working magic on her taut body, making her writhe and moan with delicious sensations. She opened her legs to let him touch her even more intimately.

He lifted his head and looked into her eyes while his hands learned her all over again with slow, tender explorations that sent her mindless with pleasure.

"I've never wanted anyone this badly," he said in a rough tone. One long, hair-roughened leg slid in between both of hers and he moved, very gently, into complete intimacy with her. "No, don't lift your leg," he whispered. "Move this one...here, like this." He shivered. His eyes searched hers. "Now come closer. Feel me going into you. Slow and easy, honey. Slow and easy. It's good, isn't it?"

"Yes," she breathed. Her hands bit into his shoulders as she looked up at him, feeling his body slowly merge with her own. She'd expected discomfort, if not pain. But there was no barrier now, no impediment. Her eyes reflected her surprise and pleasure at the ease of his passage.

"You excite me," he bit off, watching her as he moved. "Everything about you excites me. I hated having the lights out the first time. I wanted to see your face, your eyes, while I loved you."

It was an unexpected expression. Her breath stopped in her

throat and then rasped as he shifted over her, gathering her legs in between both of his.

"Remember how it felt before, when I did this?" he asked, his voice deep and sensual as he shifted again.

"Yes," she replied. Her hands went up to touch his face, to trace his straight nose, his wide, sexy mouth, his jutting chin. She gasped as pleasure lifted her up into his body.

"There?" he whispered, and moved again, with more confidence when he saw her expression. "Yes, you like that, don't you?" His hips lifted and fell, and with each slow movement, she gasped and stiffened.

Her nails bit into his upper arms as she hung there, suddenly in a vise of building ecstasy that was as sharp as it was joyful. "Judd!" Her voice exploded with the tension and her body suddenly went rigid. She looked into his eyes with near panic. "Please...don't stop," she pleaded, her voice splintering.

"Right there?" he asked urgently, and pressed deeper, harder. His teeth clenched. His eyes closed. "Yes. Yes! Right...there!"

She was moving with him now, as if bound to him by invisible strings. She forgot the past, the future, the pain, the uncertainty. She knew only one thing, now, the desperate search for pleasure that was just barely out of her reach. She focused on it with every ounce of strength she possessed. Her breath rasped, like his. Her body trembled with each deep movement of his hips. Her eyes were blind looking straight into his as her body became demanding in its mad search for completion.

"It was never like this for me," he whispered hoarsely as his own body began to roughen on hers. He groaned and his big hands clenched the sheet on either side of her head. "I'm going to lose it...!"

"It's all right," she whispered, her voice high-pitched, urgent. "Oh, Judd...Judd...!"

His mouth bit into hers as the rhythm became chaotic and rough. "Come for me, baby," he whispered into her open mouth. "Come for me...!"

The suddenness of fulfillment caught her unawares. One instant she was reaching for some impossible height. The next, she was sobbing like a child, clinging to him, feeling her body explode with joy as it buckled and convulsed over and over and over again.

She could hardly see him in the madness that followed. Her eyes were wide-open, like her mouth, as she convulsed in one final agony of delight that seemed to throb endlessly through her body in a wave of lava-hot savagery.

His hips thrust down violently into hers and he stilled, stiffened, and cried out in the endless heat of exploding passion.

"Oh, God, oh, God...!" he choked, shaking. "Never like this... never...never!"

She held him to her, cradled him, comforted him while he shook helplessly in her arms. A long time later, he convulsed and then collapsed on her in a damp, spent tangle.

She savored the feel of his big body completely on hers, her arms holding him there in the intimacy of satiation.

Her mouth touched his shoulder, his throat. She ran her hands over his wet back, feeling the muscles ripple, feeling him shiver as each little movement of her body kindled new jolts of pleasure in the aftermath.

She felt his mouth at her ear, husky and warm as he nuzzled his face against hers.

It was the most tender interlude she could ever have imagined, after such mad, ardent lovemaking. She clung to him, trying to breathe normally, her body still intimately joined to his, their legs tangled, their bodies all but boneless with exhaustion.

He lifted his head and looked down into her eyes. He studied her as if he hadn't seen her for a very long time. His hand brushed back her damp, disheveled hair, and then traced her swollen mouth intently.

"I'm part of you," he whispered, and he sounded dazed. "I can feel you, all around me, like soft, warm silk."

She flushed and her face did an embarrassed nosedive into his damp throat.

His fingers tangled gently in her hair. He rolled over onto his side, taking her with him. His chest rose and fell heavily. "Did I hurt you?"

"Of course not."

His hand slid down her side to where the wound had been, to the slight ridge that had formed there. "Are you sure?"

"The doctor said I could resume normal, routine activities," she mused. "I guess that meant...any...activities."

He laughed huskily at her temple. "This isn't normal," he murmured, kissing her eyelids. "Or routine."

Her hands slid around his neck and she lay her head on his damp shoulder with a shaky sigh. "It's scary to feel like that."

"Yes." He didn't have to ask what she meant. He smoothed her hair down her bare back absently while his eyes found the wall beyond the bed. He scowled, thinking how close he'd come to losing her forever. He'd been a fool. But maybe, just maybe, he still had a chance.

"You haven't said any more about the divorce," she whispered, hating to even bring it up. But she felt frightfully vulnerable and uncertain of him.

"I told your friend Cash that hell would freeze over before you got one," he said quietly.

She stiffened against him slightly. "Wh...what?"

His lean hand smoothed down her back, over the faint scars, to her hips and drew her even closer. He shivered at the delicious intimate contact, and his body began to move involuntarily.

"If you're sore, you'd better tell me right now," he said in a barely controlled tone. "Before I lose it again."

She could feel his instant response to the intimacy they were sharing. It was delicious, to feel her own body opening to him, responding to him without reserve. She lifted one leg slowly to deepen his possession, and heard him catch his breath.

"I wouldn't tell you even if I was sore," she whispered huskily. "I want it again. I want you again. I want...to be...part of you."

He made an odd noise, deep in his throat. Seconds later, his mouth bit into hers and his body moved helplessly against her, pressing her hungrily down into the mattress. He'd never known that it was possible for a man and woman to share a body, but they were certainly doing it. And that was the last sane thought he was able to snatch before he went down into the flames again.

He drew her into the shower with him, somber and quiet, bathing her as naturally as if he'd done it all their lives.

She was shell-shocked by the sudden intimacy of their relationship. They'd barely touched each other since Christmas, and now they were lovers. Really lovers.

He kissed her tenderly in between soaping and rinsing her smooth body. He traced her breasts with breathless appreciation and kissed them before he gave her the washcloth and coaxed her into using it.

They were like children, exploring each other in a silence throbbing with joy.

He dried her, wrapped her in a towel, and did the same for himself. Then he led her to the built-in hair dryer and used it on her long hair.

It was as if time had stopped still for them. She couldn't remember ever feeling so close to another human being in her whole life. Her eyes searched his hungrily, hoping for something more than the exquisite pleasure she'd seen in them earlier.

"What are you looking for, Christabel?" he asked gently.

She averted her gaze with a quick smile. "Nothing."

He put the hair dryer down and tilted her chin upward. His scrutiny was intent, and his black eyes were solemn. "There's no tomorrow. Only now. We live one day at a time, until we go home. Okay?"

She swallowed, meeting his eyes. "Okay, Judd," she whispered.

He bent, brushing his mouth slowly over hers. Then he led her back into the bedroom and dressed her himself, with a new tenderness that made her heart ache.

After that, there was no going back. They held hands going places. Judd smiled at Christabel as if he'd never looked at another woman. He held doors open for her, walked on the street side of her, pulled out chairs for her. He presented her with the sexiest red negligee set she'd ever seen and coaxed her into modeling it for him. The result was predictable. Every night, she slept close in his arms, loved to sleep with a tender passion that grew more exciting with each passing day. She dreaded the very thought of going home. But of course, the trip ended. They boarded a plane for Dallas, and fears of losing what she had with Judd kept her silent and remote the whole way home.

Judd noticed, and his conclusion was that she was having second thoughts about continuing their relationship. He backed off, to give her space. And that, of course, led her to the certainty that he had regrets of his own and she was just now seeing them.

CHAPTER SIXTEEN

Not too long after they returned from Japan, Crissy started losing her breakfast. The first time it happened, Maude wasn't home. The second, she pretended to have forgotten something in her room and barely made it to the bathroom in time. She slipped into town, bought a home pregnancy test, and waited until Maude was away at her sister's on the weekend to use it.

She was staggered by the results. It was all her fault. She'd let Judd believe she was on the Pill, and then he'd continued to believe it when they were intimate in Japan. Now she was pregnant and he was avoiding her. He denied it, but she knew he was going to marry Tippy. The film company was back for a reshoot and he was always around to drive the model back and forth to her hotel. He couldn't apparently bear to look at Christabel since they'd come back from Japan, and after so many exquisite, wonderful nights in his arms. But what if he found out about the baby? He'd feel obliged to stay married, of course he would. She'd ruin his life, Tippy's life, her own life...

She sat down hard on the edge of the bathtub and wished she could go back to Christmas Eve and tell the truth. It was weeks too late now. Besides that, there was no privacy with the film company around, even if it was just for a few days, to reshoot one scene that someone had accidentally destroyed.

Maude found out, of course. It was impossible to hide anything from her. When Crissy lost her breakfast the following week and had to lie down, Maude confessed that she knew. She didn't confess that she'd confided her fears to Cash.

She glared at Crissy with her arms crossed. "He's down at the barn with the film crew," she said. "You march right down there and tell him, or I will."

"You will not!" Crissy said furiously, wiping her face with a wet cloth. "I have decisions to make."

"So does he," came the blunt reply. "It's his baby as well. He'll want it."

Crissy wasn't sure what Judd would want. He'd avoided her since the trip to Japan. In fact, he only came around now when the acting company was here. When he did, he was around Tippy coming and going. He still drove her to and from the hotel. He made sure that Crissy knew it, which hurt even more. It never occurred to her that Cash was hanging around, too, and Judd might be jealous.

"He spends most of his time with Tippy," she said heavily. "Besides, he'll file for divorce any day. It's not fair to rob him of the little chance of happiness he has."

"Little is right," Maude scoffed. "I don't have anything against Tippy, she's been kind to both of us. But she'll ruin his life. He could never fit in her world. Any more than you could fit in Cash's," she added pointedly.

"That's Judd's decision, not mine."

Maude sighed. "I can't argue with you, can I?"

"It doesn't do much good." Crissy had to agree. She smiled gently. "But I suppose you're right. It isn't something I can hide from him."

"You got that right." She glanced out the window. "He's standing outside the barn with Gary and Tippy. You can catch him before he leaves."

"I'd have better luck catching a cold," Crissy muttered. "Okay, okay, I'm going!" She got off the bed and followed Maude down the hall.

Maude opened the back door for her with a wicked twinkle in her eyes.

"Don't get your hopes up too high," Crissy said as she passed onto the back stoop. "Judd told me that he doesn't ever see himself as a family man."

"You wait until he holds that baby and tell me that again."

Crissy hoped she was right. But she had a bad feeling about the whole situation, and it got worse the closer she went to the barn. What if he thought she was lying? Worse, what if he thought it was Grier's child? He'd seen her birth control pills at Christmas, he'd even remarked that he wouldn't have touched her if he hadn't known about them. But he still didn't know that they were old and unused.

Nevertheless, she wasn't going to be able to hide a pregnancy in Jacobsville, Texas, where everybody knew her and Judd. She might as well get it over with. After all, there wasn't much he could do...

Her mind stopped dead at the sight that met her eyes when she rounded the corner. Gary, the assistant director, was back-talking to his camera- and soundmen. He glared toward the barn and turned away in disgust. Crissy wondered why until she could see inside. The barn was deserted except for two people. Judd was leaning against one of the high stalls, and Tippy was leaning against him, her beautiful body almost part of his in the posture as they kissed with something akin to desperation.

Crissy felt sick to her stomach. There was no way she could march in there and tell Judd he couldn't divorce her because she was pregnant—not when it was patently obvious now that he was physically involved with Tippy. It was impossible to shrug off a kiss like that one. He'd told her he didn't want Tippy!

She turned and went back the way she'd come without making a sound. Tears almost blinded her as she walked numbly to her old truck and got in behind the wheel. She pulled out the spare key she kept under the mat and started the engine. She drove away with no thought for her license or her insurance card, or even her purse.

Slowly, feeling returned. The pain was overwhelming. She saw that hungry kiss over and over again. It wasn't Tippy kissing him, either. It was mutual. Apparently, he was so certain of the divorce that he was already making plans with the supermodel. It was difficult to see Tippy trying to live on a Texas Ranger's salary, even with the dividends the ranch paid Judd as well as Crissy. The woman was beautiful and much in demand. She traveled the world to appear in fashion shows with the most famous designers. She must really love Judd if she was willing to give up all that money and fame. It shouldn't have been surprising. Judd was a handsome, sexy, very masculine man. Tippy wouldn't be the first woman who'd found him irresistible.

There wasn't much traffic on the roads. It was too late for lunch and too early for the school buses to run. School. Her hands tightened on the steering wheel. She would have a child in school in just a few years. Judd would have to know. There wasn't any way she could keep it secret from him. The baby he didn't want would ruin his life, his hopes for the future. He would hate it, and Crissy.

She turned off the main road toward the high banks of the river on a narrow dirt road. Her mind was whirling. She couldn't decide what to do. She could go away. But he'd find out, someday. It wasn't as if she could go to a clinic; she couldn't live with that, no matter what the cost. Blindly, she pressed down hard on the accelerator. She could see Judd kissing Tippy, she could feel the agony the sight had caused, like a fresh wound. Judd loved Tippy. He loved Tippy...!

She moaned out loud. She couldn't tell him. She couldn't! It was all her fault. She hadn't been careful. She hadn't taken precautions. The responsibility was hers. She should have to pay the consequences, not Judd.

She clenched her teeth and closed her eyes as she saw that kiss again. She wasn't paying attention to the road. There was a narrow little bridge over the river—it didn't even have guardrails. The river wasn't so deep, but the bank was easily ten feet above it. When she opened her eyes, she was out of the ruts and headed straight for the bank...!

She gasped and jerked the wheel. Her foot hit the brake, hard, within inches of certain death. The truck slid to a stop with its front tires barely a foot from the edge of the embankment.

She leaned her head onto the steering wheel, shaking with relief. She felt hot tears wash over her hands at the close call she'd had. So much for driving when you were upset, which Judd had always told her not to do. If she hadn't opened her eyes at that exact instant, she'd have gone right into the river. She might have been killed, to say nothing of her baby. Her hand went protectively to her slightly rounded stomach.

She fumbled her way out of the cab and went to the dented front bumper, propping against the side of the headlights while she looked down into the fast current of the river. She pulled a paper towel from her pocket, one she'd used to blot her lipstick that morning, and wiped her sweaty face. Her hands were shaking. She'd never had such a close call. Well, she wasn't getting back into that truck until she was calm enough to drive safely.

The sound of a car going by on the state road that paralleled this dirt one caught her attention. It was a police car. It slowed just for a few seconds before it shot ahead. The policeman probably wondered what she was doing out here all alone with the front end of her truck hanging over a bank. Well, he could just wonder. She wasn't going home, not yet. She'd give Judd plenty of time to get away first. She couldn't bear to see him again right now, with the memory of that kiss eating her alive.

Judd was walking back to his SUV when he saw Maude standing on the back stoop, looking concerned.

He turned and went within earshot, smiling gently. "Some-thing wrong?" he asked.

"Did Crissy tell you?" she asked abruptly.

He scowled. "Tell me what?"

Maude hesitated. "Have you seen her?"

"No. Should I have?" he demanded impatiently.

"She was on her way to talk to you," Maude amended. "I don't see her truck."

He felt his body tense. If Christabel had come to the barn, she must have seen him with Tippy. He'd kissed her to keep the as-sistant director, Gary, from trying to put the make on her again. The man was becoming a pest. It had been completely innocent, a stage kiss. But if Christabel had seen them...

"What was she going to talk to me about?" he asked, think-ing about how often he tripped over Grier when he came here. It had gotten to the point that he hardly spoke to Christabel. He was so jealous he couldn't even hide it anymore.

Maude cleared her throat. "I don't know, she didn't say," she hedged. She drew in a long breath. "I suppose she went to get the mail or something. Never mind."

Maude went back into the house. Judd hesitated. Maude was acting strangely. He wondered why Christabel hadn't made her presence known. It wasn't like her to ignore what she'd think of as betrayal. The old Christabel would have raised hell and he and Tippy would have had a royal battle on their hands. It bothered him that Christabel had walked away without saying anything.

He got into his truck and decided to run into town and see if she was at the post office. But even as he put it in gear, he heard a call on the police band.

"Is Cash around?" a young man asked.

"He's in conference with Chief Blake and the city manager. Why?"

"When he comes out, tell him that his lady is standing on the banks of the river next to her truck out on J. Davis Road, would you?"

"Why does he need to know?" the dispatcher queried.

"Because the front wheels of the truck are barely on the bank, and so is she," the young man replied. "If I were him, I'd get out there quick."

"I'll tell him the minute he comes out. It shouldn't be long."

"Thanks." The young man gave his vehicle's call sign and left the air.

Judd burned rubber getting out onto the road.

Christabel heard the approach of a vehicle and she tensed. It was a lonely place, and she could find herself in trouble. Maybe it was just that policeman who'd gone by earlier, wondering why she was here. She hoped it wasn't someone looking for trouble.

The big black SUV came into view and her body tensed. The last person on earth she wanted to see right now was Judd Dunn. Her dark eyes glared daggers as he stopped behind her truck and got out with an economy of motion.

She was wearing her sneakers, which robbed her of height. He looked very big in his leather boots and cream-colored Stetson, with that big .45 caliber Colt automatic in its hand-tooled leather holster on his hip. The silver Ranger badge glittered in the sun, like his black eyes as he approached her.

"You're too close to the bank," he said without preamble.

She folded her arms tight over her chest and averted her gaze back to the current. "I'm not," she argued.

He stopped just behind her, waiting for her to speak, to accuse him, to explain. But she didn't.

"What are you doing out here alone?" he persisted.

"I had some things to work out," she said in a strange tone.

He hesitated. He didn't know how to ask if she'd seen him with Tippy in the barn.

"What things?" he asked instead.

She drew in a steadying breath and turned. Her eyes were just faintly red, but she was calm and resolute. "I want you to buy me out."

It was the last thing he'd have expected her to say. He was bereft of speech for several long seconds. "What?"

"I've decided that I don't want to spend the rest of my life trying to raise beef, despite the Japanese deal," she said calmly. "I've got a little money saved. I don't want to go back to the vocational school. I want to go to college."

"All right," he said. "I'll talk to Murchison at the bank. You can live at the ranch while you commute..."

"You misunderstand me," she interrupted. "I'm going to school in San Antonio, not here."

She was going to leave. He wouldn't see her again. The ranch that had been their primary link would be his alone. She would live in another town, work in another town. She wouldn't be here when he came to look at the books, check the livestock, pick out the culls. He wouldn't see her at all, even with Grier. The thought paralyzed him.

"I'd like to leave at the end of the month," she added. "If you can't tie things up by then, it doesn't matter. Arrange it however you like. I'll sign any sort of papers."

He scowled ferociously. Something was very wrong. She loved the ranch. It had been in her family for three generations. She'd hated even sharing it with him, at first. Now she wanted to leave it for good. Why?

"Maude said you had something to tell me," he said. "Was this it?"

"Yes," she said, grateful that Maude hadn't been more forthcoming with him. San Antonio wasn't far enough, but it was a good jumping off point. She'd go there and then find someplace else to escape to, before she started showing.

"Christabel," he began.

Before he could organize his thoughts, he heard a siren and a very loud, racing engine. They both turned in time to see a Jacobsville police car come roaring down the dirt road, leaving a huge wake of dust. Grier, damn him!

Grier slammed to a stop and barely took time to cut off the

siren and the lights before he got out and strode quickly toward Christabel.

"You okay?" he asked abruptly, ignoring Judd altogether.

She felt a wave of relief. Now Judd couldn't pump her for information. "I'm okay," she said. "I just needed a quiet place to think."

Grier wasn't buying it. His eyes narrowed and he stared at her doggedly. "I'll follow you back to the ranch," he said.

Christabel let out an angry sigh. "I don't need a keeper!"

"The hell you don't," Grier ground out. "Look where you've parked!"

"I'm a good foot off the bank!" she argued.

Grier held out his hand. She glared at him, but she gave him her truck key.

"I'll move it back. What are you doing out here?" he asked Judd belatedly.

"Talking to my wife," he returned with mocking arrogance.

"I'm not your wife," Christabel choked. "I'm just the hired help."

Grier wisely left them alone and went to move her car.

"What the hell does that mean?" Judd demanded.

She wouldn't look at him. She wrapped her arms tight around her chest. "I'm cold."

He glanced at her bare arms and his voice softened. "No wonder. You aren't even wearing a sweater."

She ignored him, watching Grier whip the truck around with easy expertise.

Judd's sigh was audible. "We need to sit down and talk..."

She met his eyes evenly. "I have nothing to talk to you about ever again," she said solemnly. "Talk is just words. They don't mean anything."

His jaw tautened. "You saw me with Tippy," he said gruffly. "I can explain."

"What do you care what I think?" she asked evenly. "I'm not part of your life. I never was."

He winced. "Christabel..."

"Crissy! Let's go! You'll catch cold standing out here!" Grier said shortly.

She forced a smile for him. "Look who else isn't wearing a jacket," she accused gently.

Grier looked as if he'd die keeping his mouth shut, but he did.

She shrugged. "Okay. I'm coming."

Judd's big fists were clenched at his sides. "Wait a minute."

She looked up at him. "Your life is your own business now. I won't interfere. I'll expect the same courtesy from you."

"Damn it!"

"You saved the ranch, Judd," she said quietly. "You saved me, too. You've sacrificed five years of your life just keeping me solvent. I'll never forget what I owe you. But I don't expect you to go on making sacrifices for me," she added huskily. "If anyone ever deserved a little happiness, it's you. I'm...glad you have Tippy, waiting for you. I won't stand in your way."

She moved back from him, like a shadow merging with the forest, and her attention went to Grier, who was holding the driver's door open for her. He handed her the truck key.

"Okay, I'm going home," she told Cash, making a face at him and laughing.

He smiled back. "Don't speed."

"I never speed."

"Ha!"

She got into the truck and drove off. She didn't look at Judd as she passed him.

Judd stalked over to Grier, who was getting back into his patrol car. "She isn't divorced yet," he said in a blatant challenge.

Grier gave him a cold look. "She might as well be, for all the notice you take of her lately."

"How could I take notice of her when I can't come to my own ranch without tripping over you! Besides, my relationship with Christabel isn't your business."

Grier only smiled. "We'll see about that." He started the police car.

"What do you know that I don't?" Judd asked abruptly.

Grier hesitated uncharacteristically. "Ask her. Better yet, ask Maude. That's how I found out."

Before Judd could persist, Grier drove away.

But Judd wasn't giving up. He knew something was going on, and he had a sinking feeling that he was involved. He followed Grier to town and right into the police station.

The Jacobsville Police Department shared a building with the fire department. The men were almost interchangeable. Many started out as firemen and trained as policemen later, and vice versa. It was a good group of kindhearted men. Most were family men. Some were loners. A lot were ex-military.

Even among the loners, Grier stood out. At first he made the men uncomfortable. Later, he made surface friendships, especially after the other officers learned that they could always depend on him in a pinch. It didn't take very long for his past to catch up with him, in whispers that stopped whenever he entered a room. He raised eyebrows wherever he went, especially when some of his wilder escapades were embroidered even more. So very soon, he resumed his old role as a permanent outsider.

He didn't really mind so much. He had the glamour of danger to attract women when he was interested—which wasn't often these days—and that same aura kept most men from trying him in fights. There was always the exception.

In fact, one was just walking in the door, mad as hell and determined to get to the bottom of a mystery he didn't like.

Grier knew he couldn't save the situation with words. Dunn was too much like him. The two men had backgrounds that should have made them fast friends. Instead, they were always in competition.

Judd closed the door behind him and pulled down the shade that the former assistant police chief had used to shield himself from prying eyes while he did his exercises on his lunch hour.

Grier used the shade rarely. Judd was obviously putting it in place to keep the curious men from getting involved in a personal conflict.

With a sigh of resignation, Grier stood up and started unbuttoning his uniform shirt and loosening his tie.

"Can't you fight dressed?" Judd asked sarcastically.

Grier lifted a corner of his mouth and kept working buttons. "I haven't got a clean replacement for this. I don't want to get blood on it."

"Mine, or yours?" the other man asked.

"Either. You're wearing a white shirt," Grier pointed out.

Judd didn't reply this time. He took off his gunbelt, weapon and all, and laid it on the desk, dropped easily into a balanced stance and waited.

"We don't have to do this," Grier tried one more time.

"No, we don't," Judd agreed in a deceptively pleasant tone. "Tell me what she's hiding and I'll go back to my office."

"Can't do that," Grier replied. "I gave my word."

Judd shrugged his broad shoulders. "Then, it's my way or the highway," he said, and as he spoke, he stepped forward and threw a lightning punch at the other man.

Grier's reputation wasn't based on exaggeration. He ducked, whirled, and caught Judd with a spinning heel kick worthy of Chuck Norris.

Judd went down, but he was like a cat on his feet. He popped up again, wiped blood from the corner of his mouth, and smiled. That smile was all too well-known in Ranger circles. Grier had one just like it.

Grier almost ducked in time, but a roundhouse kick caught him in the stomach, followed by a back roundhouse that sent him over a chair.

The loud noises, even during lunch, drew attention. Grier's door opened just as the assistant chief made a dive at Judd and carried him over the desk and onto the floor.

Somebody yelled "Fight!" and there were suddenly blue uni-

forms everywhere, getting a ringside seat. Grier was certain he
heard somebody taking odds, but his ears were ringing from
Judd's latest punch. Damn, the man hit hard!

He matched Judd's next swing with a jump kick that threw
him into the wall. While he was trying to recover, Grier spun
and caught him in the side of the head with a graceful high kick
that was pure poetry to watch.

Judd landed with equal grace and bounded back onto his feet.
The two men, well matched in size and skill, eyed each other as
they moved toward each other. Hand blows were dodged or
blocked, kicks were avoided or blocked. Thuds of contact were
sharp and harsh. Both men were getting bruised, and both were
bleeding.

Grier got in another unexpected kick by feinting with a punch.
Judd took the blow, but spun and backhanded Grier into his own
desk.

The crowd was getting louder, and apparently, larger.

Grier glanced toward their audience with narrowed dark eyes
almost as black as Judd's. "You're going to get me fired," he
growled at Judd.

"Fat chance, Chet's your second cousin." Judd shot a lightning heel kick that unbalanced Grier so that he fell beside the
desk. "Get up!" he muttered when the other man hesitated.

Grier did, but with a blurring sweep of his powerful leg that
almost unbalanced Judd. But Judd recovered quickly, swung the
other man up by one arm and gave him a hip toss that landed
him squarely across the one comfortable chair in the office in a
winded sprawl.

It was going to be a draw, no matter how it came out, Grier
surmised. He and Judd were too evenly matched for one to put
the other down. Worse, Grier himself had taught Dunn quite a
few of those lightning moves. He stayed put in the chair, rubbing his jaw.

"Don't stop now," Judd said in a soft, angry tone, his black
eyes glittering. "Get up and let's finish it."

"Not me," Grier told him amusedly. He chuckled, shaking his head. "I know when to quit."

"Get up!"

Grier's eyebrows rose. "Better reconsider that. If I get up, I'll arrest you for assault on a police officer. You'll be handcuffed, fingerprinted, booked and locked up, and I'll call the newspaper myself to give them the scoop. Think how that will look to your captain, much less the brass in Austin!" he added with twinkling dark eyes.

Judd was furious. He didn't want to give up this easily. He hadn't learned anything. "She says she wants to sell me her half of the ranch and move to San Antonio. I'm not leaving here until you tell me what's wrong with her," Judd persisted stubbornly. "One way or another," he added darkly.

Grier knew that if he didn't tell him, Judd would go back to the ranch and start on Crissy. That could be dangerous. She was already obviously very upset. Knowing her as he did, he could imagine that she was making all sorts of wild plans to escape Jacobsville by now. She could easily lose herself in San Antonio. That wouldn't do, not in her condition.

"All right," Grier said finally, with a heavy sigh. "I'll talk. But not in front of witnesses," he added, glaring at their audience. "Out, or you'll all be pulling double shifts at the grammar school crossing!"

They left vapor trails exiting the door and the windows. Grier got to his feet slowly, feeling bruises rising all over him. Judd Dunn's face looked like a relief map of west Texas. Along with the cuts, it was turning interesting shades of purple. Grier could imagine that he didn't look much better. His jaw hurt.

"Now, why couldn't you just have told me in the first place?" Judd asked brusquely.

"I thought you might feel sorry for me and go away."

Judd laughed coolly. "Dream on."

Grier shrugged as he shouldered into his uniform shirt, buttoned and tucked it in, and put his tie back on. "I imagine that

Christabel wants to go to San Antonio because it's big and she can get a bus or a train out of there to anywhere without much risk of discovery until it's too late."

Judd scowled as he put his gunbelt back on. "She said she wanted to go back to college."

Grier perched his tall frame on the corner of his desk and gave Judd a patient look. "She thinks you want Tippy," he replied. "She's going away so that she won't get in the way of your happiness."

"I never said I wanted to marry Tippy," he said defensively.

"It's none of my business, of course. But I'd be happy to see you marry her and get out of Crissy's life. I'll marry Crissy and spoil her rotten."

Judd's pride was choking him. He couldn't bear to think of Christabel with this man, not in even the most innocent way. "She's my wife," he ground out. "Until that changes, she's mine."

"I understood her to say that you'd started divorce proceedings."

"Not yet," Judd gritted.

"It's just a matter of time, surely? You're the one who's pushed it from the beginning."

That was true, and it hurt. Judd had made so many stupid mistakes. It was incredible that a man of his experience couldn't manage to sort out his own feelings for a little slip of a girl whom he'd known most of her life.

"We're getting off the subject," Judd said evasively. "Why does she want to run away?"

Grier sighed. "You can't guess, of course."

"It can't be because of you," he said mockingly. "Or she'd be fighting to keep her half of the ranch."

"No," Grier agreed quietly. "She's a wonderful young woman. I'd give a lot to be the man in her life, but that hasn't happened. I'm not even in the running."

For one, long, horrified moment, Judd wondered if there was

some other man. But then he realized it was impossible. Then if it wasn't Grier, and she was running...

"You can't count, can you?" Grier drawled. "You've been back from Japan for about two months. She came home starry-eyed and hopeful, and then she lapsed into depression that hasn't lifted since, because you've avoided her like the plague. Now, suddenly, she's avoiding you."

"I noticed," Judd said. "You're not telling me anything I don't already know!"

"I am, if you'd listen," Grier returned, folding his arms across his chest. "Think. Why does she want to run away? Why is it important that she gets someplace where you can't *see* her?"

It should have been clear much sooner than this. It hit him between the eyes like a baseball bat. She was trying to hide because her body was changing. Because she was...

"She's...pregnant?" Judd almost choked on the words.

Grier just nodded. "That's what Maude says. She's had morning sickness for two weeks and none of her clothes fit anymore."

The other man's face went white. She hadn't been taking birth control pills. She felt guilty because of it. She'd avoided him. She'd seen him with Tippy in the barn. But Christabel didn't know that it had only been a stage kiss and now she was determined not to get in the way of his happiness, not to ruin his chances with a child he didn't even know about. Maybe she thought he wouldn't want it, either.

He dropped onto the sofa and sat there, quiet, brooding, shell-shocked.

"Babies are nice," Grier said. "I'm just at the age where I think about them a lot. I can live anywhere. If you want Crissy to go, I'll tag along. Maybe she'll give in one day and marry me. I'll adopt the child and love him as if he were my own."

Doors were closing. Somewhere along the way, Judd had lost Christabel and the baby in a bleak, sad future.

He looked up at Grier with nightmares in his eyes. He'd worshipped freedom. The thought of spending his life with a woman, having a family, had been utterly terrifying to him. He was uncertain. He'd lived alone, worked alone, been alone, most of his adult life. He hadn't want ties, responsibilities. He'd hated the thought of living in a cage. But then she got shot, taking a bullet meant for him, and his whole attitude had changed. He'd done everything in his power to show her how much he cared, but she'd gone cold on him and started clinging to Grier. It had hurt. Couldn't Christabel see that? How could she believe he preferred Tippy to her?

What sort of life would he have if he let Christabel leave town, and Grier went with her?

"If I were you—and thank God I'm not—I'd go home and think about this real hard," Grier told him with faint amusement. "You haven't got a lot of time."

Judd didn't snap back. He looked at Grier as if he really didn't see him at all. He got to his feet, vaguely aware of bruised places that were uncomfortable and cuts on his face that felt wet.

"A few small adhesive bandages wouldn't come amiss," Grier prompted.

"Look in a mirror, Grier," Judd told him.

"I can't stand to. If I look half as bad as you do, I'm wearing a paper sack to work tomorrow."

"That's cute," Judd growled as he strode toward the office door. "You'll be lucky if you have a job tomorrow, when Chet Blake sees this office."

"Oh, I'll tell him you did it all," Grier assured the younger man with a grin.

"Try it."

"The first thing you need to do something about is your sense of humor," Grier pointed out. "To say nothing of your poor skills in diplomacy."

"Your idea of diplomacy is a cocked pistol," Judd pointed out.

"Only with hardheads like you."

Judd had his hand on the doorknob when he paused and

glanced back at the other man. "Don't tell her I know about the pregnancy."

"Don't worry. People still don't know what I really did in Iraq."

Judd frowned. "I didn't know you were ever in Iraq!"

Grier grinned. "See?"

Judd opened the door.

"One more thing," Grier called.

"What?"

"Next time you do that reverse roundhouse kick, keep your axis stable. You'll lose your balance every time if you tilt your upper body when you swing."

Judd looked at the ceiling and shook his head as he walked out. He noticed that the men on the desk were suddenly very industrious as he went toward the front door.

CHAPTER SEVENTEEN

CHAPTER SEVENTEEN

Cristabel was doing the laundry when a vehicle drove up outside. She was still too shaken by her near-accident to be very aware of her surroundings. Besides, the loud hum of the old washing machine drowned out anything more than a room away.

But Maude was in the kitchen, finishing her bread, when Judd walked in. She stopped with her hands full of dough and just stared at him. His handsome face was covered with cuts and bruises, and blood was pooled at the corner of his mouth. His once-spotless white shirt was dotted with blood.

"Grier looks worse," he told her with a shrug. "Where's Christabel?"

"Doing laundry," she managed to say. He was shocking to look at. She hadn't seen him in a fight since the day Crissy's father had beaten her. That was a long time ago.

He turned and went to find Christabel. She had her back to him. He paused in the doorway of the laundry room to study her, his eyes shuttered, his mind working like crazy.

She sensed eyes on her. Abruptly her head jerked around. She stood up slowly, facing him, and her jaw dropped.

"What in the world happened to you?" she exclaimed.

"Grier doesn't volunteer information without a little coaxing," he said grimly. He moved closer, his face unreadable. He looked at her with an expression that she couldn't understand.

"What kind of information were you after?" she asked blankly. She knew it couldn't be about the baby. Cash didn't know she was pregnant.

"Never mind," he muttered. "It took a lot of bruises not to find out anything," he assured her. His black eyes narrowed. "I don't like him hanging around here, and I told him so. Now I'm telling you, too. You're married."

She glared at him over a towel that she'd dragged out of the aging dryer. Absently, she wondered if they'd ever be able to replace the machine. Not that it didn't work, but it was fifteen years old. She folded the towel. "You kissed Tippy Moore!"

"Yes, I kissed her," he bit off. "The assistant director's doing his damned best to seduce her and she's afraid of him! It was a stage kiss."

"Oh, pull the other one," she shot back. "Tippy Moore, international model, afraid of a piss-ant little assistant director! I'd like to see the man she's afraid of!"

He moved closer, taking the towel away from her. He tossed it onto the dryer. "She has a history I can't tell you about," he said bluntly. "It's enough to tell you that she's genuinely afraid of men. *That's* why she's been hanging on me. I've never touched her, and that's the draw. She feels safe with cops—with any law enforcement people in uniform."

Christabel was gaping at him. She'd been envious of Tippy, hated her for that exquisite beauty that made Judd and other men so covetous. Now she felt both sad and sorry for the other woman. Pieces of a puzzle fell into place. It must have been something terrible, she guessed, to have made the lovely woman like that.

"I can't come here without tripping over damned Grier," he persisted, black eyes blazing down at her. "If you want the truth, I was getting even!"

Her lips fell apart. Whatever she'd expected him to tell her, that wasn't it. He was jealous...of her? She could feel her heart beating like a wild thing in her chest.

He calmed a little when he saw her expression. She looked fascinated. Apparently, she wasn't eager to rub it in, either. He relaxed even more.

"I...only went around with Cash because it hurt me to see you with Tippy all the time," she confessed without raising her eyes.

His heart jumped up into his throat. So many misunderstandings, all for want of a little honesty. It wasn't Cash after all. He started smiling and couldn't stop.

She lifted her face to his and was trapped by the look on it. He laughed, deep in his throat.

"Tippy's got a case on Cash, but you can't tell him," he murmured. His fingers went to brush back her long, soft blond hair.

"Why?"

He shrugged. "He thinks she's the happy hooker. She said a man like that knew more about most women than they knew themselves."

Her eyes searched his. "You really haven't slept with her?" she asked doggedly.

He sighed. "I'm married, Christabel," he mused, linking his hands behind her waist.

"So?" she asked, flushing.

He bent his head. "I don't sleep with other women, baby. Only with you. And just lately," he groaned against her soft mouth, "my bed has been very empty."

She let him kiss her. A few seconds into it, she forgot what she was doing altogether and lifted herself against his powerful body with a sob.

"Wait. Wait a minute," he said urgently. He moved away from her long enough to close and throw the bolt on the door. Thank God it had one, he was thinking, while he could still think.

He backed her up into the dryer and kissed her again, hungrily. She was probably wearing a dress, he mused, because none of her jeans would button and he'd notice. He smiled against her mouth as he reached under her dress and slipped off her underwear.

"Judd, no, we can't!" she whispered.

He nibbled her upper lip while he peeled off his gunbelt and put it aside and reached for his belt buckle. "It's okay, baby. We can do it without the red negligee," he teased huskily. "Besides, we're married. I'll show you the license again." He lifted her up to him and his mouth covered hers as his lean hands brought her over him. "We'll go look for it...later," he groaned as he went into her.

She stopped protesting, thinking, breathing. She clung to him, moaning into his devouring mouth as he drove into her with the noisy washing machine concealing the noises they were making. She hoped it wasn't near the end of its cycle. She was so hungry for him that she sobbed with every quick, hard motion of his hips. She wanted to drag his clothes off, push him down on the floor, ravish him...

She didn't realize she was saying it until they wound up in a tangle of limbs on the linoleum, with his body heavy on hers as they clung to each other in a raging fever of desire.

She'd never experienced such instant passion. In the last lucid instant, he lifted his head and watched her face as he drove her right over the edge into ecstasy. She shuddered and shuddered, her cries almost inhuman as her nails bit into his hips. Seconds later, his body corded and arched. He made a hoarse, harsh cry and his face contorted. She watched him, so excited that her whole body felt on fire with the overwhelming heat of fulfillment. Even in Japan, it hadn't been so intense. She couldn't stop shivering. Tears ran down her cheeks while he moved helplessly against her in the pulsing aftermath.

Just as he collapsed on her, the washing machine stopped abruptly between cycles. She felt his body shake. It wasn't until he lifted his head and she saw his dancing black eyes that she realized why. He was laughing.

"What a relief! That damned soundman can hear an ant walk across a sponge at fifteen feet, and he likes to record people when they don't know he's listening," he murmured breathlessly. "If that washer had stopped a few seconds sooner..."

She laughed, too, trying to imagine the embarrassment. The washer started up again, noisily, and he moved against her, his mouth tracing her lips, her cheeks, her ear. He nibbled her earlobe. She kissed his cheek and he groaned.

"Sorry," she murmured, noting that she'd kissed a cut. She touched his bruised face gingerly. "Does your jaw hurt?"

He nodded. "Grier hits hard."

"What did you want him to tell you?" she persisted.

"That he'd keep his distance from you," he invented. He pursed his lips and moved deliberately, so that she could feel the slow, delicious burgeoning of his body. "But I don't think that's going to be a problem now. Do you?" He moved again.

She gasped. She was still sensitive, and those tiny motions were so sweet that she started moving with him. "Maude..."

"The cycle lasts fifteen more minutes," he reminded her, bending. "But I doubt if I will..."

"Let's see," she whispered rakishly, and pulled him down to her.

They were standing again, when the washer wound down for the second time. She'd just pulled her underwear back up and he'd refastened his jeans. But he glanced down at his shirt and sighed. "Grier took off his shirt first. I should have done the same. Have I got a clean one? I can't go back to work like this."

She smiled radiantly and nodded, going to the clothes rack. She pulled out a clean, ironed white shirt and handed it to him.

He took off the one he was wearing, baring an undershirt also liberally splattered with specks of blood. "Damn," he muttered.

"You've got a clean undershirt, too," she said, turning to pull one out of the clothes basket where she'd been folding laundry. "Here."

He stripped off the undershirt, aware that she was eating him with her eyes.

He tossed the undershirt and the white shirt into the laundry hamper and moved closer, bringing her hands to his hair-roughened chest. "I didn't even have the presence of mind to undress first, I wanted you so badly," he mused with a smile. "I'm going to commute to Victoria from now on. I'll spend my nights here, where I belong, and we won't be sleeping in separate beds."

"You're going to sleep with me?" she asked, fascinated.

"Of course." He traced around her soft mouth. "Unless you'd rather I stayed in my old room? That might be interesting. You could put on the red negligee and come seduce me in the night."

She hit him gently and laughed. "I'll sleep with you and do my seducing in comfort. You're my husband," she whispered, feeling every word.

"You're my wife." He bent and kissed her gently, drawing her hands back and forth over his chest. "I'm sorry you wouldn't open your Christmas present."

"Why?" she asked absently.

"It was pearls. Pink pearls, your favorites. But there were two presents. Tippy gave me back the ring. She'd teased me into buying it, which I did to save my pride. When I returned it," he added gently, "I bought a set of rings—one for you, one for me. Wedding bands. So you get two presents, not one."

She just looked at him.

He shrugged. "I never wanted a divorce," he confessed. "Not really. My mother was young, like you, and maybe she wasn't ready for marriage. I saw my father die inside after she left him. He never got over the divorce, and he mourned her until he died. I didn't want to end up like him. I was afraid of commitment. I knew you cared about me, but I was afraid it was just a crush," he confessed.

"Some crush," she said with a smile. "It lasted five years."

"I knew that when you took a bullet for me," he said quietly. "That was when I knew you felt something powerful for me. But

Grier was always around and better men than me have felt inferior to him."

"Cash is a sad and lonely sort of person," she replied. "I felt sorry for him. I know things about him that you don't, Judd. He was married just briefly, and there was going to be a child. I don't know what happened, but they divorced bitterly. He was just a friend."

He grimaced. "I didn't know that. I was crazy with jealousy. I finally realized that you weren't going to wait forever while I sorted out what I felt for you. That was when I knew that I was going to fight to keep you."

She gazed at him, encouraging him to continue.

"You know, my parents were exact opposites. He was in love, but she married him without really loving him. She did fall in love, with another man, and she couldn't help what she did. I never understood that before, because I'd never been in love." His voice turned husky. "But I understand her actions better now, even if I still don't approve of them. Love takes away your choices. You and I think alike and I believe deep down I knew all along that we have enough in common to make a good marriage. But I just couldn't let go of the past—of the fact that you and Cash seemed so close. I couldn't be certain what you felt for him. He gave me some bad moments, especially after we came back form Japan."

She smiled slowly. "Tippy gave me some. She's beautiful and sophisticated."

"Sophisticated, like Grier." He traced her ear, pressing her soft hair behind it. "They can console each other," he said with a wicked grin. "But they're both out of the running."

She hesitated. "Are you sure?"

His dark eyebrows lifted. "Just how many women do you think I've ever ravished on the floor of a laundry room?"

Her eyes narrowed. "It had better only be one," she returned with mock anger.

He chuckled. "Now you sound more like yourself." He

reached for the clean undershirt. Her hands fluttered against the thick hair on his chest as she reluctantly moved away. He smelled of aftershave and soap. She liked the masculine scents, far too much. "I've got to get back to work. I'm tying up loose ends in the Clark cases." He glanced at her. "I never told you. Guess who was doing the poisonings down here?"

"Not Jack Clark," she guessed.

"No. His brother John was poisoning the cattle, and he killed old Hob. He got a friend and co-worker—the same man who loaned him the pickup truck—to give him an alibi for the time of old Hob's death by making him think a jealous girlfriend was checking up on him. Jack Clark killed the young woman for testifying against him and sending him to prison for six years. Jack was our prime suspect for the poisonings because he lived in Jacobsville, and he knew it."

"Don't leave anything out!" she demanded.

"The councilwoman who was showing Jack the properties in Victoria had no idea that he was establishing an alibi, while his brother was down here poisoning bulls. They poisoned Brewster's bull because it was one of the progeny of Handley's Salers bull. They poisoned ours because they were both getting even with us for firing Jack. But if it hadn't been for you, I might never have solved the murder case in Victoria."

"Me?"

He pulled his shirt on, fastened it, and stuck the star back on the pocket. "You mentioned how the fence was cut," he said. "We had a cut fence at the scene of the last homicide. I checked it against the picture you had Nick take of our cut fence. It was a perfect match. Our fence—that you had sense enough to save—has become prime evidence. Not to mention that black pickup truck that belonged to John Clark's friend, Gould, in Victoria. Then, those colored fibers I mentioned that were found at the crime scene matched a swatch from a flannel shirt you remembered Clark wearing when he confronted you on the ranch. It was with a box of his belongings that John Clark took to Victoria with him. There's one other crucial bit of evidence we latched on to, also."

"Don't keep me in suspense," she said excitedly.

"Besides a hair found on the shirt at the crime scene, the evidence technician noted teeth marks on the woman's breast. She hadn't been dead long, and her body was half-covered by the shirt when she was recovered. The technician said her body was still warm when they found it. He played a hunch—he put sterile water on a swab and went over the woman's breast. She got DNA evidence that links the murder directly to Jack Clark. And that hair on the shirt the woman was wearing matched one of Clark's exactly. That evidence is all admissible in court."

"I didn't know you could do that!" she exclaimed.

He chuckled. "I'll have to clue you in more about forensic evidence."

"But why did he kill her, do you know?" she asked.

"She was the young girl who testified against him for sexual assault and battery and vanished. He spent six years in prison on her testimony. After he was released he and John went to work for Handley, who had the purebred Salers bulls. Handley was her husband's best friend. Handley fired them about the time Jack recognized the young woman and decided to get even. John Clark poisoned his bulls, Jack raped and killed the woman."

"Good Lord. And what about poor old Hob?" she continued.

"When we told Jack Clark about the concrete forensic evidence against him, he gave in and confessed everything with the public defender sitting right beside him. He said his brother went to Hob just to threaten him, to keep him quiet. Hob refused to be threatened. He was going to call the police and tell them the Clark boys cut the fence. John hit him in the throat with a fire poker. He didn't mind bulls, but he couldn't live with killing a human. He told Jack he was going to rob a bank and if he got killed he didn't care."

"Poor old Hob," she said sadly. "What a sad way to die."

"So Jack's going away for a long time. It's a good thing, because the behavioral psychologist who evaluated him said he might have killed again. Clark still hates me, of course, for what happened to his brother and for helping put together the evidence that's going to convict him for murder." He grinned at her. "Like I care."

She hugged him, hard, secure for the first time in her marriage.

"And you didn't believe me about the cattle or the fence at first."

He drew her close. "No, to my cost, I didn't. That could have had fatal consequences if Clark had been a little more confident. I'm sorry, too. But those days are over. You tell me black is white, baby, and I'll believe you now." Lifting his head, he searched her drowsy, happy eyes and smiled. "Kiss me. I have to go back to work."

She looped her arms around his neck and kissed him hungrily. "Take me with you," she whispered.

"I'd never get a thing done," he teased. He put her away reluctantly and buckled on his gunbelt. "I'll be home by six."

She felt as if her whole life had changed in a space of hours. She couldn't stop smiling. "Okay. I'll lay out my red negligee."

He chuckled delightedly. "That's a date."

He unlocked the door and they walked hand in hand to the front door. He looked down at her and wished that he could tell her what he knew. She was carrying his child. He'd never felt closer to her. He'd never loved her so much. But he had to wait, to bide his time. If she found out that he knew, she might think he was staying with her for all the wrong reasons. He didn't dare let on. He kissed her goodbye and drove off, making a mental note to phone Grier and warn him again not to spill the beans. Maude didn't say a word, but she couldn't stop smiling, either.

The next morning, the crew was working again. But this time, it was different, because everyone could see what was happening between Judd and his young wife. Tippy felt as if it had become open season on her. After one particularly difficult scene in the barn, Gary Mays called "cut" and moved into the set with his back to the barn door to slide a very familiar arm around Tippy's shoulders, deliberately forcing her against his body. Gary had become Tippy's worst nightmare all over again.

"Now, listen, doll," Gary coaxed, "just do the scene the way it's written, and don't try to do any real acting, got it? All I want is for you to look pretty and swing those sexy hips for me." He smoothed his hand lingeringly over her bottom with a leer worthy of a paroled convict.

Seconds later, his hand was in midair, facing backward, with a very cold-eyed Cash Grier on the end of it.

"I don't think you meant to do that, did you, Gary?" Cash asked pleasantly, and flexed his hand a fraction—just enough to make Gary flinch. "Sexual harassment is such a nasty term. Think what the press would make of it, in our politically correct society. You do see my point?" he added softly, and that hold tightened again.

"I see it...perfectly!" Gary gasped, turning into the hold, to keep from having his hand wrenched off.

"And even though I can't arrest you for it, since it's out of my jurisdiction, I can call one of my buddies who works for the sheriff's department, and he can arrest you. So you won't touch her like that again. Will you, Gary?" Cash persisted, smiling.

That smile sent cold chills down Tippy's spine.

"Not ever in my life, I swear!" Gary gasped.

Cash let go of his hand, still smiling. "I think you might like to call a ten-minute break," he added. "I'd like a word with Miss Moore."

"Go right ahead," Gary gritted. He gave Tippy a look of pure loathing. "Ten minutes, everyone!" he called, and then got out of Cash's vicinity as quickly as he could manage, holding his wrist in his other hand.

Cash motioned to Tippy with his head. She went to him like a lamb, without a single protest, and stood looking up at him with wide, perplexed green eyes.

"Why do you let him handle you like that?" he asked quietly.

She was shaken. She wrapped her arms around herself. "I'm twenty-six years old," she said. "I have a nine-year-old brother to support. Modeling doors are already closing for me. I have to make it in film or I won't have a source of income."

"And you think money is worth letting that second cousin to a tarantula climb over your body like a fungus?" he persisted. "What did I tell you at the hospital when Crissy was shot, about looking him in the eye and saying 'no'?"

She looked up at him with pain in her eyes. "That's easier to say than do."

His chin lifted slowly. His black eyes were steady and narrow on her face.

"But you're going to try it. Aren't you?"

She nodded, because he had that sort of effect on people. "You could have hurt him," she said hesitantly.

His eyes pinned hers and traces of his past made cold shadows in his eyes. "I could have broken his hand as easily as I bruised it. A few years ago, I wouldn't even have hesitated." He was thinking. His mind was adding up facts and producing conclusions. "You're sex on a half shell until a man comes within two feet of you. Then you ice over. But under the ice, there's fear. You're afraid of him," he murmured, pointing toward the man with his chin. "But not," he added softly, "as afraid of him as you are of me."

She swallowed. She hated being so transparent, but Gary's boldness had unnerved her.

He noted her posture, her defensive stance. "You weren't afraid of Judd at all," he recalled, with narrowing eyes. "But he never touched you, did he?"

Her face gave him the answer at once.

He nodded slowly. "So that was it."

Her eyes lifted to his, full of surprised curiosity.

He moved a step closer, torn by conflicting emotions as he watched the pain crawl across her beautiful face.

She looked like a startled doe, but she didn't move away. He fascinated her. She couldn't remember since childhood a man who stood up for her, as he'd stood up to Gary, except for Judd. Policemen had been kind to her, long ago. Cash was wearing a uniform.

He stepped closer deliberately, towering over her. She could see the black freckles scattered over the bridge of his straight nose, the thickness of the mustache over his sensuous mouth, the tiny triangular goatee under his lower lip. She could see the faint wave in his thick black hair where it was pulled back into a ponytail. He smelled clean and masculine. She liked being close to him. That was a shock, and it filtered into her gaze. But being so close to him made her nervous, and she took a quick step backward.

Her behavior puzzled him. It was common gossip in the tabloids that she'd lived with a man for six years, a motion picture star twice her age who had an almost obscene reputation for his blatant love affairs with women. She had a reputation in the industry for being sexually aggressive. But how could she be experienced and make a habit of backing away from any man who came too close? She might have been pretending nervousness. But he could tell that she wasn't. None of this made sense to him.

His dark eyes narrowed as they searched hers. "He's not going to bother you again, because you're not going to let him. Right?"

She swallowed. Gary made her skin crawl, but she'd never stood up to him. Usually she just made a dead set at men and made them uncomfortable, deliberately making them feel that they could never measure up to her ideal. But Gary was a frog, and he reminded her too much of that man in her past. She couldn't use her wiles on him. She was afraid of him.

"Right?" he prompted.

She nodded, as if a string was attached to her chin.

"Tippy," he repeated her name, scowling. "What's it a nickname for?"

"Tristina," she said bitterly. She brushed her hair out of her eyes. "It's supposed to mean 'sadness.' My mother felt that way when she had me, or so the story goes," she added. "She didn't like having kids, but she did love to sleep with men. The more the merrier." She hesitated. "She said she wasn't sure who my father was."

He didn't look as if it mattered to him. He studied her quietly. "He must have been a good-looking man" was all he said.

She grimaced. "My mother is a knockout, even now. She has red hair and green eyes, like me, and a figure that even years of alcohol abuse hasn't fractured. She's not stupid, either. I had a hard time getting Rory away from her, but money does talk. I have sole custody now, and I'm not giving it up."

"Rory?"

"My brother."

He reached out a big hand and moved a strand of red-gold hair out of her mouth. "Why do you have custody?"

"Because her new live-in boyfriend hated him, and beat him up, bad enough to put him in the hospital, when he was four. A policeman I know called and told me."

"What the hell was your mother doing all that time?" he exclaimed.

She swallowed. Hard. "Holding him down."

His sigh was audible. Looking at her, he began to get disturbing images, almost as if they were passing from her mind directly to his. His dark eyes narrowed. He added up her defensive posture, her fear of men, and disregarded the licentious reputation of the man she'd lived with. The solution he got was very disturbing.

"She's not getting him back," she said coldly. "No matter what it costs me."

"Including putting up with lizard lips over there?" he said, jerking his head toward Gary.

She looked up, surprised, and a tinkle of laughter escaped her.

"Gary can nurse his hand all day and think of me," he said with narrowed dark eyes. "Come on."

He went with her back to the set, at a comfortable distance so that he didn't make her uneasy. He even smiled at Gary.

Tippy walked right up to the man, feeling unusually confident. "He says that if you put your hands on me ever again, Gary, I can have you arrested and sue you for harassment." She smiled prettily. "You do carry insurance, don't you, darling?"

Gary went pale. He glanced at Cash and cleared his throat. "All right, people, we've wasted enough time. Let's get back to work!"

Tippy gave Cash a quick glance and a shy, odd little smile before she went back to work.

Judd's resolve not to let Christabel suspect he knew about her pregnancy lasted exactly four more days, until he came home from work early and found Christabel on the back of a flatbed with Nick, tossing bales of hay off to the cattle in one of the pastures.

To say that he raised hell was an understatement. He lifted her off the truck, carried her to his SUV, put her in the seat, and drove her, tight-lipped, straight to Dr. Jebediah Coltrain's office. He went with her to the desk and told the receptionist that she had to be seen immediately. The waiting room was empty.

"Copper's not here," the girl stammered, "and Lou is just about to leave, too..."

"Not yet, she's not."

He drew Christabel with him through the door into the hall-way. "Lou!" he called.

Dr. Lou Coltrain came out, first startled and then amused, when she looked at her visitors.

"Can I help you?" Lou asked Judd.

His lips made a thin line. "I want a pregnancy test, right now."

"OOOOOkay," Lou replied, trying not to giggle. "When was your last period?"

"Not me, her!" he ground out, glaring down at an astonished Christabel. "She was tossing bales of hay off a truck, for God's sake!"

Lou's smile faded. "That's not wise, if you're pregnant, Crissy," she said gently.

Christabel started crying. "You can't know!" she cried at her husband. "How do you know?!"

"I'm not blind, am I?" he muttered. "You can't fasten your slacks and you can't eat breakfast, either!" He hated himself for not telling the truth.

"Maude told you!" she accused.

"Maude didn't tell me anything," he defended himself.

"Let's take a blood sample, Crissy," Lou said, intervening. "When was your last period?"

She had to say, with a smug Judd listening to every word. Lou got Betty and they did the test. It was positive. Lou arranged for an appointment for Christabel to see an ob-gyn specialist in Victoria who also worked at Jacobsville General. Then she prescribed vitamins.

"No more lifting," she cautioned. "And eat properly."

Christabel agreed meekly. She was relieved at the way Judd was taking the news of impending fatherhood. He wasn't even upset. It relaxed her.

Back in the SUV, he couldn't stop grinning. He reached for her hand and linked her fingers with his.

"So much for Grier," he said smugly.

She studied him intently, watching for signs of unrest. There weren't any.

"You aren't angry?"

"I'm delighted. I'm also relieved," he countered. "Now I can sleep nights without worrying that you'll leave me to run away with Grier."

"He likes babies," she retorted.

"He can find another woman and make some of his own. This one is mine." He sighed heavily. "What a Christmas present I'm going to get this year!"

In fact, the baby would be due just before then. She was fascinated by the play of emotions on his dark, lean face. He couldn't have pretended so much pleasure. She wondered if a woman could faint of pure happiness. She'd never felt so safe, so secure, so cared for in all her life. He was fond of her, of course, and he wanted the baby. Maybe, in time, he might even come to love her. She had so much to look forward to. So much!

The film company said goodbye and left for the airport. Tippy made a wholesale apology to Christabel and Judd about the problems she'd caused and said they'd both be invited to the premiere of the movie in New York when it came out in about seven months. That would be in November, and the baby would be due that month.

Cash Grier went to the airport just as she finished checking in and started toward the metal detectors.

"Wait a minute," he said quietly, pulling her aside. He handed her a business card with his name and phone number on it. "Just in case you have any more trouble over your little brother," he added. "There's a private number written on back. If you ever need help, use it."

She gasped. "Why would you do that for me?" she asked, all at sea. "You hate me!"

His dark eyes met her green ones evenly. "Hell, I don't know! Do you have to question everything?"

She reached out hesitantly and touched his sleeve, although her hand dropped almost as soon as it made contact. He was wearing his uniform. He looked very neat and clean. "Thank you, for what you did about Gary. For what you made me do. I was so afraid of losing the only job I had." She smiled shyly. "I've had some problems getting work lately. But you were right. Nobody should have to take that, just to keep working."

"See that you remember it," he replied coolly.

She studied his face, so far above hers, with real interest. "You can come with Judd and Crissy to the premiere of the movie, if you like. I'll send a ticket anyway."

He cocked his head and studied her. "I'll come," he said unexpectedly.

She flushed. Her eyes brightened. She laughed inanely. Around her, men were staring, women were staring, at her startling beauty. She seemed totally unaware of the attention. She had eyes only for the man in front of her.

"I'd like that," she said huskily. "Thanks, Mr. Grier."

"I'm no more than twelve years your senior," he pointed out. "You can call me Cash."

Her smile lingered. "What's it short for?"

He sighed. "Cassius."

"Really!"

He nodded. "My mother was fond of the classics."

Her eyes went to his black hair in its neat ponytail, to his mustache and the tiny triangle of hair just below his sensuous mouth. "You loved her."

He nodded. "Very much."

She sighed and bitter memories pressed the smile from her full lips. "It must be nice." She glanced toward the metal detector, where the crew was slowly passing through. "I'd better go." She put the card in her pocket. "Thanks again."

He shrugged. "I like movie stars," he murmured blithely, and grinned at her.

That grin hit her right in the heart. She smiled again. "I like cops." Her eyes glanced off his, and she turned and went quickly toward the metal detector. Just before she followed her suitcase and purse into the secure area, she looked back at him. She'd never felt so alone in her life. He was still watching her, too.

He watched until she was out of sight, for reasons he couldn't begin to understand.

As for Christabel, she discovered new things about her own husband in the months that followed. He loved to make things. He had a workshop out in the utility shed, but it had been idle for a long time. Now, he bought some new equipment and lumber and started making baby furniture.

But just before the baby was due, the tickets came for the New York premiere of Tippy Moore's movie. Christabel knew that

Judd would go, and she was suddenly insecure and frightened of the future. He'd never made any confession of love to Christabel, who had a sneaking suspicion that he'd known about the baby before she ever told him. So what if he went to New York and discovered that he really loved Tippy after all?

CHAPTER EIGHTEEN

Surprisingly, Cash Grier decided to go along with Judd to New York. Christabel and Maude saw Judd off from the front porch. It was so far along in her pregnancy that he didn't want her to risk the trip, or even to go to the airport with him. She didn't want him to go without her, but she was out of excuses.

"I'll be back day after tomorrow," he whispered, bending to kiss her tenderly. "Don't have the baby until I get back," he added with outrageous, tender humor.

"I'll do my best. Don't you get...entangled with Tippy again," she blurted out, and then flushed.

He scowled. Didn't she know how he felt?

"You're going to miss the plane," Maude said worriedly. "Don't speed to get to the airport."

"Yes, Mama," he murmured on a sigh. He gave Christabel one last kiss and jumped into the SUV, speeding up the driveway.

"He never listens," Maude muttered.

"He won't speed," she said comfortingly. She smiled. "Come on. Let's have some nice warm milk and talk about labor."

"All right, darlin', if we must," Maude said gently.

* * *

The premiere was a gala event. Tippy Moore lived up to her publicity, dazzling in a black velvet dress with diamonds dripping from her ears and throat. She went into the theater on the arm of her leading man, Rance Wayne, with the director, Joel, and his wife right with them.

Cash and Judd had seats near the front, and they watched the movie with real interest and helpless humor as the story came alive on the screen. Laughter echoed along the rows as Tippy and the cowboy bounced dry lines off each other and ended up embracing wildly in a puddle of mud as they discovered their two worlds could meet and merge at last.

There was a standing ovation. Tippy had tears in her eyes. Her new career was almost a sure thing.

She met Judd and Cash as they came out of the theater, hugging Judd warmly, but acted reticent and nervous with Cash.

"You were great," Judd told her with a grin. "It's going to be a blockbuster."

"Do you really think so?" she asked hopefully.

"Is your brother here?" Cash asked suddenly.

"Why...yes," she faltered. She turned and motioned to a nice-looking young boy with dark hair wearing a neat suit. He had a very conventional haircut and he looked like the product of a military school until he got closer and they could see the twinkle in his dark green eyes.

"You were pretty good, sis," he mused, bumping against her playfully. "Didn't fluff a single line!"

"Watch your mouth, buster," she chided, laughing genuinely as she hugged him. "Rory, this is Judd Dunn. He's a Texas Ranger, and a friend of mine. He and his wife are expecting their first child any day," she added, to make sure he understood the relationship.

"Glad to meet you," Rory said, shaking hands. "I've read a lot about the Texas Rangers since Tippy told me about you," he added excitedly. "There's even several Web sites about the Rangers, past and present, on the Internet!"

"They're educational, all right," Judd chuckled. "Nice to meet you, too."

"This is, uh, Cash Grier," Tippy said, nodding toward the older man. "He's assistant police chief in Jacobsville, Texas, where the movie was filmed."

Rory looked at the man in the ponytail for a long moment. He seemed subdued. "Tippy told me a lot about you. I, uh, mentioned you to our commanding officer. He knows you. He said you were in Iraq together." He caught his breath. "He said he never knew anybody as brave as you were. He said, uh, he said they caught you and tortured you..."

"Rory!" Tippy exclaimed, horrified.

Cash's face had hardened. His eyes were glittering like black diamonds.

"I'm sorry," Rory said. He moved closer, uneasy again. "You're sort of a hero of mine. I'm messing everything up because I can't talk the way I want to. I think you're great, sir. A soldier's soldier."

Cash took a sharp breath and averted his eyes. He didn't like remembering his tour of duty in the middle east, or what he'd done and what had been done to him there. The boy was walking on broken bones and didn't even realize it.

"Rory, why don't you go on to the restaurant with Joel and his wife, and I'll be right along," Tippy said quickly, trying to smooth things over.

"Yes, ma'am," Rory said, wounded and ashamed.

But as he turned away, a big, strong hand came down on his shoulder and stayed the movement.

"Honesty is an underrated virtue," he told the boy. "You say exactly what you think. I don't pull my punches, either. I don't like remembering Desert Storm," he added quietly. "I survived. The other seven men who went in with me didn't. They were good men, too."

Rory's breath caught. "I'm glad you aren't angry, sir."

"Cash," the tall man corrected, and he managed a smile for the boy. "I'm glad we got to talk."

"Me, too!" Rory grinned, all boy again, and flushed a little as he glanced at Judd and his sister and took off toward Joel Hunter.

"He's all mouth sometimes," Tippy murmured, worried at the look she'd seen on Cash's face. "I hope he didn't offend you."

He shrugged. "Everybody offends me, as a rule, but I like a boy with grit. He'll do," he added quietly.

She forced a smile. "Thanks."

His chin came up and the look in his eyes was different suddenly. "So you talked about me to him, did you?"

She went scarlet. It was such an odd reaction for an international model and a newly emerging film star that Judd's eyebrows met his hairline. Cash's eyes began to twinkle. He actually laughed.

Tippy made an impatient sound in her throat and glanced after her brother. "There's a cast party at a restaurant close by, but you could stay and come home with us, if you like," she added, talking deliberately to Judd.

"Well," he began, at the same time as Grier's cell phone vibrated madly in his pocket.

He frowned and pulled it out, opening it. He seemed to have trouble hearing whoever was on the other end. He turned away, with a hand over the ear that wasn't on the phone. "All right, calm down," he said gently. "Now tell me what happened!"

He nodded, glanced at Judd, grimaced, and murmured something into the phone. "It's Maude," he said. "She's been trying to reach you on your cell phone but your battery must be dead. So she phoned me instead. Crissy had a fall. They've taken her to the hospital..."

He was talking to thin air. Judd was at the curb, hailing a taxi. He glanced at Tippy. "Sorry, we have to go," he said apologetically. "Rain check, on the visit?" he added to her surprise.

Her face became radiant. "Y-yes! Anytime," she blurted out.

He smiled, genuinely. "Then I'll see you. Tell Rory goodbye."

She nodded. He ran to Judd, who was motioning wildly and jumped into the cab with him seconds before it took off. Judd was too preoccupied to even wave goodbye to Tippy. His heart was clenched inside his chest. He was terrified. Christabel was hurt.

"What about the baby?" he asked.

"Maude said they didn't know anything yet," Cash told him, and he was worried, too. "We'll go straight to the hospital. Listen, babies are surrounded by embryonic fluid," he added gently. "It takes a lot to hurt them."

"What do you know about babies?" Judd asked angrily.

Cash averted his face. "I almost had one of my own, once," he said through his teeth. "Don't bother asking any more," he added when Judd opened his mouth to speak. "I don't talk about it. Not to anyone."

Judd didn't know what to say, so he said nothing. But he did wonder about the odd statement.

It took forever to get back. But when they drove up together at the hospital, Judd in his SUV and Cash in his pickup truck, they left the vehicles sitting and ran together into the emergency room.

"Christabel Gaines...Dunn," Judd faltered at the desk, his face set, his eyes wild. "She was brought in after a fall. She's pregnant. I'm her husband."

"Oh...Mr. Dunn." The clerk stared at him dumbly and he held his breath, terrified. Then she smiled. "She's already in a room. Just a second..." She pressed in numbers and spoke to someone. "Room 211," she added. "It's down that way...congratulations!"

The last word didn't even register through the fear. They were both running, in blatant defiance of hospital rules, until they reached the room, pushed open the door in unison, and stopped dead at the sight that met their eyes.

Christabel was lying there with a tiny bundle in her arms, breast-feeding. She looked at Judd with her heart in her eyes. "Darling!" she exclaimed.

He could barely see her through the mist in his eyes. He went forward, shell-shocked, oblivious to Maude and one of the Hart brothers and a woman he didn't recognize and a nurse puttering around the room. He touched the tiny face pressed so close to Christabel's soft skin and then he looked down into her wide, soft dark eyes. He touched her face with a hand that was just a little unsteady.

"All we knew was that you'd had a fall," he whispered. "I was so afraid..."

"I'm fine. The baby's fine..."

He was kissing her, hard, hungrily, a broken groan going into her mouth just before he managed to lift his head. "I love you," he whispered roughly. "If anything had happened to you...!"

"But it didn't," she whispered, overwhelmed at the look in his eyes, at what he'd said. "You never said you loved me before," she murmured.

"I always meant to," he replied, calming. He smiled with wonder as he searched her eyes. "You okay?"

She grinned. "It wasn't much of a fall. I was putting up curtains in the baby's room. Twisted my back. I thought I'd killed myself, and it turned out to be labor!" She indicated the tiny thing in her arms. "Would you like to meet your son?"

His breath caught. "A boy."

She nodded.

"*And* a girl," came a deep drawl from across the room at the window, where Cash was bending over the bassinet and playing with a tiny finger, an ear-to-ear smile on his face.

"W-what?" Judd stammered.

Christabel pursed her lips and looked mischievous. "You were so worried about me all the time that I was afraid to tell you it was twins," she confessed, smiling up at him. "I was saving it for a surprise." She grinned. "Surprise!"

"Twins. A boy and a girl. Two of them." He seemed bereft of words. His eyes clouded and he had to dash away moisture before anyone saw it.

Cash had the little girl up in his big arms and he was making really un-Cash Grier sounds as he spoke to her.

"Hey, give me back my daughter," Judd told him with a mock scowl.

Cash looked crushed. "Can't I have this one?" he asked. "I don't have any of my own, and you've got two. How is that fair?"

Judd burst out laughing, and so did Christabel, at the expression on Cash's face. He moved forward, handing the child gently to Judd, his eyes soft and tender on her face.

"She looks like her mama," he told Judd, and for an instant, there was a flash of sadness over his hard features as he looked at Christabel, which he quickly erased.

"Yes, she does," Judd said huskily, bending to kiss the tiny forehead. "Two of them! She looked like a VW in front, and I never connected it...!"

Christabel was laughing with pure delight as she watched the big, strong men fuss over the little tiny girl. No need to wonder if she was going to be spoiled rotten. And they said men only wanted sons. Ha!

"Names?" came a deep voice from the back of the room. It was big, handsome Leo Hart, with his wife Janie beside him, both grinning. "Have you picked any out yet?"

"Jessamina for a girl," Christabel said proudly. "We'll call her Jessie. And..."

"And Jared for our son," Judd interrupted gently. "For my great-great-grandfather, Jared Dunn, who was a gunman and a Texas Ranger, and then a famous trial lawyer in San Antonio back at the turn of the twentieth century," he added.

"Well, congratulations, again. We'd better be off," Leo said. "We have to get down the hall and see Rey and Meredith. They have a brand-new daughter, Celina, born about the same time your brood was."

"Tell her we said congratulations," Christabel called to them.

They nodded, grinned and walked out together.

Cash was still watching the tiny girl in Judd's arms hungrily. Judd made a face and handed her back to him. "You can hold her, I guess," Judd said with a sigh. "Just remember who she belongs to."

Cash grinned at him. "She can live with you, but I'm going to be her godfather," he said, making faces at the tiny little thing in his arms. "Daddy Cash is going to teach her how to fight hand-to-hand and use flash bangs in SWAT assaults!"

Maude let out a wail of pure horror.

Christabel burst out laughing. "He's joking, Maude!"

"No, he isn't," Judd murmured dryly.

Cash ignored both of them, wrapped up in the glow of new godfatherhood.

When they were finally alone, Judd sat beside the bed and held Christabel's hand tight in his. "Two babies," he said, still shell shocked. "I can't believe it. You didn't breathe a word. Maude didn't breathe a word!"

"I swore her and the obstetrician to secrecy," she said with a weary smile. "You had so much on your mind, darling, with the Clark trial and the changes in our lives. Besides, I was in perfect health and there was no danger. I'd have told you if there was, really."

The Clark case had made national headlines, especially after Clark was convicted and sent to prison for life, without hope of parole, for murder. Judd and Christabel and Cash had all testified against him.

He squeezed her fingers in his. "Okay."

"How was the film premiere?"

He chuckled. "The premiere wasn't quite as interesting as what happened afterward," he mused. "Tippy and Cash raised eyebrows."

Her last secret fear of losing him to the model floated away like a loosened balloon. "They did?" she asked happily.

"It seems she told her little brother quite a lot more about him than she did about me, and the boy said so." He grinned. "Cash was almost strutting when Maude phoned and interrupted us."

"Wow."

The amusement faded. "Apparently the boy's commandant at

military school was with Cash in Iraq. He told the boy that Cash was captured and tortured, and every other member of his unit was killed."

She winced. "I don't imagine that's the only secret he's carrying about his past."

He nodded. He turned her hand in his and looked at it. "Crissy," he said, using her nickname for the first time in their lives, "he was really crazy over you."

Her fingers curled into his. "It wouldn't have mattered, because I've been in love with you almost all my life."

His cheeks went ruddy. He studied her face hungrily. "I've been in love with you since we married. But you were so young, honey, and you knew nothing of men or the world outside the ranch. I was afraid..."

She squeezed his hand. "You were afraid it would be like your father and mother. But, sweetheart, your mother liked adventure and parties and excitement," she reminded him. "I love cattle and ranching. Nothing the world could offer me would match what I already have with you. And now our babies. The Japanese deal has put us into a six-figure income bracket, the ranch is prospering, we're branching out into raising purebred Salers bulls, Nick is taking over as ranch manager and improving our equipment and facilities...and you've been offered promotion to Lieutenant again! How's that for a year?"

He grinned. "It's great, I guess. But I don't want to have to work out of San Antonio," he added quietly. He gave her a long look. "What do you think?"

She smiled at him. "I think you should do what you want to."

He frowned thoughtfully. "Even if it means staying a sergeant?"

"Even if it means staying a sergeant," she replied softly.

He pursed his lips. "There's another alternative."

She stilled. "Yes?"

"Chet Blake was offered a job over in El Paso. He has family there and he really wants to take it." He lifted his eyes. "Cash would bump up to police chief of Jacobsville, which would leave his job open."

Her breath caught. "You're thinking of taking it!"

He nodded. "It's a little less demanding than Ranger work, although I love what I do. But I'd like to be home all the time, with you and the babies. I know most of the guys on the force." He shrugged. "Cash is going to be our babies' godfather, and I'm not jealous of him anymore. Well, not very jealous," he amended. "What do you think?" he added.

Her eyes softened. "I'd give anything to have you close by all the time," she whispered. "But I would never have asked you...!"

He got up, bent and kissed her hungrily, loving the fierce clasp of her arms around his neck. She kissed him back, just as hungrily, tears running down her cheeks. It was like a dream come true. Jacobsville was a great place to be a policeman. It wasn't like being a Ranger and having to go all over the state, all over the country, all over the world on cases. He'd still have the challenge of law enforcement work, but he'd be a little safer. That mattered now, that they had children, and his job would be largely administrative.

The loud clearing of a throat interrupted the fierce kiss. They lifted their heads at the same time and looked toward the door.

A nurse was standing there with two little bundles. "Sorry, Mr. Dunn, but you're blocking the babies' supper, and they're hungry."

He chuckled, standing up. "God forbid!" he said dryly, standing aside. "Bring them along."

"Pity you can't help do it," Christabel teased as she sat up against the pillows and unfastened the hospital gown.

"I'm too flat-chested to be of any help," he pointed out with a grin.

The nurse laughed as she handed Jessamina to Crissy and Jared to Judd. He cradled his son while Christabel fed their daughter. The nurse left them alone with their family, smiling wistfully as she went out and closed the door.

"Twins, on the first try. I wonder," Judd said thoughtfully after a minute, frowning as he studied his young wife.

"Wonder what, sweetheart?" she asked, smiling.

"If it was the red negligee," he replied wickedly.

She laughed huskily. She wasn't wearing it on Christmas Eve, but she'd gotten pregnant in Japan, and she *had* been wearing it then. "Maybe it was green tea," she countered playfully.

He looked down at his son with quiet, tender eyes. "Whatever it was, thank God," he breathed, touching the little boy's cheek with a long finger.

She seconded that silently, watching the expression that washed over his hard features with almost painful delight. She'd never thought of Judd as a father. Suddenly, it was impossible to see him as anything else. He took to it like a duck to water.

She was thinking back over her life, from the horrible beating that had brought their marriage about, through the long years of hopeless longing, the danger of the Clark brothers, the wonder of Judd's ardor at Christmas, the anguish of the months that followed, the gunshot that almost ended her life, the Japanese trip, the jealousy and, finally, the melting together of their lives. The pain had been almost unbearable at times. But as she looked from her children to her husband and back again, it occurred to her that happiness came at a price. For those who were courageous enough to pay it, the rewards were great.

"You look thoughtful," he murmured, smiling at her expression.

She met his eyes with quiet wonder and sighed happily. "Yes. I was remembering something I read once, about people who live quietly in the shallows and never really savor life because they're afraid to risk the depths. Or something like that. I was thinking that we pay for what we get in life, one way or another. And that the greatest pleasure comes only after the greatest pain."

He nodded slowly. "I understand."

Her dark eyes smiled into his. "I was thinking," she added, "that everything I've ever been through in my life, was worth it."

His black eyes burned as they looked deep into hers. "Yes. We're rich in a way that has nothing to do with money, aren't we, baby?"

She grinned. The baby at her breast smoothed its tiny hand over the soft skin and she looked down and touched its tiny head lovingly. "Richer than pirates."

He burst out laughing. His son made a sound and he brought the tiny little boy up to his hard lips, kissing him tenderly.

Christabel laid her cheek against her daughter's head and closed her eyes. The joy she felt was too great for any words to express. Any words at all.